SHERRY

A DAY OR TWO MORE OF THE SIMPLE LIFE
IN THE WOODS AND HE WOULD BE
FIT AS A FIDDLE

Page 50

SHERRY

BY

GEORGE BARR McCUTCHEON
Author of "Graustark," "The City of Masks," etc.

FRONTISPIECE BY
C. ALLAN GILBERT

NEW YORK
DODD, MEAD AND COMPANY
1919

CONTENTS

CONTENTS

SHERRY

SHERRY

CHAPTER I

"THAT'S my last dime," said young Redpath, as he deposited the coin with elaborate precision upon the shiny surface of the bar. As the bartender slid the glass and the bottle in front of him, he added, unsteadily: "And this is my last drink."

The dispenser of drinks did not smile. He had heard that sort of proclamation before. He tenderly polished the surface of the bar with his towel, squinted at it, and removed a recently deposited splotch of water, the result of his patron's unsteadiness of hand in pushing aside the "chaser."

"Good!" said he, squinting again. "You mean the last for today," he added, turning to the cash register. His customer watched him ring up the amount, starting slightly as the bell gave forth its peremptory clang.

"The last *ever*," said the patron, and dashed off the brimming glass of bourbon. His throat contracted with the spasm customary to him who drinks his liquor "neat": and then, thinking better of his habits, he reached out and lifted the small glass of water to his lips. It had been his vainglorious boast that he always took his whisky straight. Somehow this "last

1

drink " seemed to burn a little more fiercely than usual. He looked into the empty glass wonderingly.

"What's the matter with it?" demanded the barkeeper sharply. "Ain't it all right?"

"Sure," said Redpath. "I was just wondering why a fellow's last drink should go down harder than the first one. I don't remember that my first drink took the skin off like that one did. Maybe it's just as well that it did burn. Something to remember all the rest of my unpickled days."

The barkeeper now eyed him with interest. "Going to cut it out for good, eh?" he said derisively.

"Ab-so-lute-ly," said the other, meeting the look with one that was strangely direct, considering his condition.

"Good work. Stick to that, Sherry, and you'll be somebody in spite of yourself. You been boozin' pretty steady for a feller of your age and —"

His customer, still reflecting, expounded his reflections aloud. "You see, it's really the first time I ever took my last drink. My insides simply can't understand it. They don't believe that such a thing exists as a last drink, Patsy."

"They'll feel different in the morning," said Patsy. "They'll be asking for another last drink, and they'll keep on askin', they like it so well. But, say, kid, you're young enough to cut it out. Taper off gradual-like —"

"But I'm never going to take another," said Redpath, in some surprise. "Didn't you hear what I said? I've quit, Patsy,— quit for good. And, say, I hope you notice that I'm quitting with a little edge on,

too. Anybody can swear off when he's sober or getting over a bun, but it isn't every one who can stop
right in the middle of one. Well, that's what I'm
doing, Patsy. I'm doing something nobody else on
earth ever did. I've turned decent and respectable
and industrious right in the middle of a jag, that's
what I've done. It isn't human nature to do that,
now is it? I leave it to you, Patsy."

"Well," said Patsy, "I've seen 'em turn religious
and sing psalms right at the very top of a jag, and I
know one feller that always says his prayers when he's
full. I'd call that being decent and respectable,
wouldn't you?"

"Say, I believe you're trying to kid me," growled
Redpath, straightening up suddenly. He laid his fist
gently upon the bar. "You don't believe I'm in earnest. You don't think I can do it. Well, let me tell
you something right now, Patsy. That was my last
drink. I'll never take another one as long as I'm conscious. I said a long and permanent farewell to booze
when I swallowed that last ten cents' worth. I've noticed that you never touch a drop, Patsy. Why is
that?"

"I couldn't hold my job if I touched that stuff," said
Patsy, promptly, almost severely. "I haven't had a
drink in — let's see, this is 1910 — seven years. You
never see any souses behind the bar, my boy."

"Well, speaking of jobs, I'm going out to look for
one myself," said Redpath firmly. "And I'm going to
begin by being as good as any bartender on earth. If
a bartender can be good, so can I."

"You'll never get a job in this burg. They know

you too well. You never did a lick of work in your
life, and these people in this town won't let you begin,
no matter how virtuous you — virtuous ain't the word
I want, but it will do in a pinch. No matter what you
do, they'll pan you to a finish. Get out of this town
as quick as you can and — say, ever think of going
farther West? "

"I refuse to go West. I'm going to stay right
in this town. Good Lord, who'd want to go any farther West than this? "

"I mean some place like Seattle or California," explained Patsy. "You can brace up and be something if you get away from these blood-suckers around
here." He lowered his voice. Two men seated at a
table in the corner were watching them with interest.
With an almost imperceptible jerk of his head, he indicated the pair. "Couple of 'em setting' over there.
Between 'em they've got a small fortune out o' you."

Redpath bestowed a lofty stare upon the couple,
checking the barkeeper's speech with an upraised
hand. "They can't get anything more out of me,
Patsy, because I haven't got anything more for them
to get. Not a red. I'm strapped. That was my last
dime. What do you suppose Joe Stetson would say
if I walked over right now and tried to borrow five
dollars of him? He'd say I was drunk, and that he'd
let me have it in a minute if I was sober. I'm through
with that gang."

"Gosh," said Patsy, sorrowfully, "what a chance
you had — and what a mess you made of it! There
never was a boy in this town that had the —"

"Never mind, never mind," interrupted the other,

frowning. "That's all dead and gone. I buried the last of it when I took that drink. I started out with a couple of hundred thousand dollars, and see where I am now? Well, I'm going to see if I can do any better by starting without a red cent. Everything to gain and nothing to lose. See what I mean? I'm going to see how it feels to make money. I certainly know how it feels to spend it."

"I always said your dad made a mistake sending you East to college," said Patsy. "Never catch me sending a son of mine to college. Why, I used to work in a —"

"My dear sir," broke in Redpath, with extreme gravity, "you will be interested to hear that I never touched a drop of liquor durin'— during the three years I was in college. Not a drop."

"Come off!"

"It's the honest truth. Ask anybody. Ask the faculty. I —"

"Well,— be that as it may," said Patsy, with the air of one admitting nothing. "What was you fired for?"

"Who said I was fired?"

"Don't it take four years to go through a college?"

"It depends entirely on whether you start in the fress — freshman or the soph'more class," said his customer, loftily.

"Wasn't you ever a freshman?" demanded Patsy, amazed.

"Never!" said Redpath, profoundly. "Never in my life."

Patsy was thoughtful as he wiped a tall glass after

breathing on it carefully. " Maybe that explains why you never took a drink in college."

" Not at all. I promised some one I wouldn't drink until I was through college."

" Some girl, eh? "

" No," said the young man, lowering his eyes suddenly. " Some one better than any girl, Patsy." He went no farther, but Patsy understood and nodded his head.

" It's a pity," the bartender began and then stopped, an innate sense of delicacy reminding him that a public bar is not the place in which to allude to one's mother. It had been on the tip of his tongue to say that it was a pity she hadn't lived to look out for her boy after he came out of college.

" 'Gad," began Redpath, a quizzical grin on his handsome, flushed face, " you wouldn't think to look at me now that I'm not a drinkin' man, would you? "

" No, I wouldn't," said Patsy. " I'd say you indulged once in awhile," he added sarcastically. " About once every twelve or thirteen minutes."

" Well, that's what makes it all seem so queer to me. Here I am half-full and yet I am not a drinkin' man. I don't drink a drop, Patsy,— not a drop. I used to drink,— Lord, you know that, don't you? — but I don't drink now. Funny, isn't it? "

It was four o'clock in the afternoon of an August day. Trade was always slack at that hour, Patsy Burke explained; in fact, he was in the habit of dozing comfortably over the *Police Gazette*. The soda-founts and ice-cream parlours on Main Street took his customers away from him at that time o' day. Later on,

of course,— about six or half-past, say,— things
would pick up. The same fellows who went into the
drugstores for phosphates and sundaes would drop in
at his place,— not always for the purpose of getting
something stronger to drink but to see who was there,
— and they would stay on till supper-time. (Patsy
did not know that some of his more advanced customers called it dinner-time.)

The saloon was quiet, and dark, and delightfully cool
from the refrigerators that preserved the "draft
beer." There was chipped ice beneath the bar, and the
tiled floor was in a constant state of being washed with
cold water by a sleepy negro who paused in his mopping every now and then to restore his failing energies
at the proprietor's expense. The glare of the hot sun
failed to penetrate to the interior of this cool retreat;
two huge ceiling fans stirred the damp, sluggish air
with gentle persistence; the glassware ranged along
in front of the vast mirror glistened pleasantly and reflected cleanliness; bottles of many hues lent cheer and
gaiety to the almost cloister-like retreat; ecclesiastical
somnolence prevailed!

, Except for the sticky fly paper at the opposite ends
of the bar, somewhat ostentatiously protected from
human elbows by plates of free-lunch,— which con-
sisted of crackers, cheese, dried herring, ham-sausage
and pickles,— the place was as immaculate as a chapel.
An artistic manipulator of castile soap had placarded
the borders of the long mirror with such legends as
these: "We won't go home till morning," "One good
turn deserves another," "All others cash," while directly above the elaborately carved stretch of mahog-

any Patsy,— a true wag,— had hung this motto, done
in green and yellow worsteds: "God Bless Our
Home."

Three large and flourishing palms, set in tubs, established the boundary line between bar and billiard
room. There were four tables,— two for pool in the
foreground and two for billiards at the back; — all of
them were now neatly swathed in their black oilcloth
shrouds, awaiting the reviving influence of electric
lights later on in the evening. Racks of cues and tri-
angles of pool balls were solemnly at rest in the dark-
ened area beyond the palms, for this was their sleep-
time.

Outside the palms were two small tables, each offi-
cered by a tiny but business-like call-bell, while in the
corner nooks on either side of the street-door stood
similar objects. At one of the latter, two men were
seated,— sporty looking chaps who conversed in con-
fidential tones, as is their wont.

This was the fashionable saloon of the town. The
best men in the place did their shopping there. Even
the travelling salesmen who, in all reason, should have
patronized the bars connected with the Tremont House
and the New Savoy, where they were registered and
where they were on speaking terms with all of the wait-
resses,— (both hostelries had tried coloured waiters
and found them wanting) — even the "drummers" affected the Sunbeam, which happened, through rare
good luck or because of a stupid miscalculation on the
part of the owners of the two hotels, to be so advan-
tageously situated that if you missed either of the
hotels you couldn't help finding yourself in front of

the Sunbeam. In other words, it was two doors west
of the Tremont and three doors east of the New Savoy,
and just across the street from the Grand Opera
House.

It had its regular clientele. Selecting any one of a
certain number of men and hitting upon the exact minute,— say, eight-thirty-five in the evening, or half-
past eleven in the morning, or a quarter before twelve
at night,— you would only have to dodge into the
Sunbeam and there he would be,— unless, of course,
the unforeseen had transpired unbeknownst to you,
such as his sudden death or a necessary visit to Chicago.

Upstairs there was a commodious smoking-room
where the window-shades were always down. Round
tables covered with green felt, surrounded by leather-
bottomed chairs, stood on a carpeted floor, so thickly
padded that the footstep of the heaviest individual
gave forth no sound. Except for a few gaudy prints
of a sporting nature, there were no other articles of
furniture or decoration in this room. Men addicted
to prolonged fits of smoking frequently sat around
these tables all night long, and some of them went
home at daybreak with hundreds of dollars in their
pockets while others went forth with barely the price
of a breakfast in theirs.

Poker was the only game played, and you couldn't
get into the " smoking-room " without being carefully
scrutinized and properly introduced. The frequenters
of this room were very particular about who got into
their midst, and at the slightest suspicious sound from
without chips and cards disappeared into nowhere

with the most amazing celerity and completeness. Policemen had visited this room somewhat abruptly on
more than one occasion, and they had always found
the occupants smoking placidly, and engaged in innocent, even desultory conversations. Roulette and faro
lay-outs never had found their way into the " smoking-room." They were self-convicting contrivances
and as such had no place in a respectable and orderly
establishment, such as the Sunbeam professed to be
even in the face of ill-timed and likewise ill-fated cru-
sades on the part of certain church-going individuals
who insinuated a great deal to the contrary. A " gentleman's game " was the only one tolerated in the room
above the saloon; you were no gentleman if you complained about your losses or boasted of your winnings.

The population of Farragut was not a matter of
doubt, notwithstanding the vast statistical gulf that
lay between the figures of a malignant census-bureau
and those supplied by reliable and loyal citizens. It
was absolutely impossible to doubt the statements of
the latter without inviting trouble,. and, as the census-
bureau was a homeless and indifferent institution born
to be execrated by every intelligent man, woman and
child in the United States of America, no one could
possibly get into trouble by denouncing its functionar-
ies as liars, thieves, malefactors and even idiots. Not
a person in Farragut doubted for an instant. There
were 27,332 inhabitants, exclusive of cemeteries,— just
10,201 more than reported by the census-takers.

The *Morning Dispatch* took a census of its own.
The *Dispatch* had a " bona-fide " circulation of 4,627.

It owed a fair and just count of noses to its subscrib-
ers; it announced editorially that it couldn't sleep
until it had rectified the mischief done by the United
States government; it would set Farragut right in the
eyes of the world. And when the result of its count
was announced and Farragut was found indisputably
to be all that it claimed to have been, not only in the
matter of noses but in mouths as well, the things that
were said about the miscreants who granted the city
a paltry 17,131 souls must have been heard in heaven,
for at the very next election the Republicans were
turned out of office and the whole country went Democratic. Oddly, however, the vote in Farragut was 412
short of that cast in the election of 1908,— a circumstance that puzzled even the most sanguine of "boost-
ers," for it was generally believed that every eligible
citizen had done his duty at the polls. As a matter
of fact, not a few of them got into rather serious trouble by doing it twice.

Farragut is about one hundred miles from Chicago.
It was its proudest boast that it had been a thriving
little city when Chicago was a mere trading post at
the foot of Lake Michigan — or was it Lake Superior?
There once was a time when travelling theatrical and
minstrel troupes "played" Farragut and never even
thought of going to Chicago. The oldest inhabitant
— and a number of citizens competed for the distinction if not the honour — would tell you that he could
remember the time when he had to pause and ponder
before recalling the name of the measly little village
on the Lake.

One of the most interesting features of Farragut

was the evergreen memory of its ancients. The older
they got, the better their memory seemed to become.
Judge Emmons, who was eighty-six, remembered things
in his eighty-fifth year that he couldn't possibly have
remembered when he was seventy. He had reached the
safe old age when no one in Farragut could dispute a
thing he said. The death of Col. Jilson, at ninety-two,
cleared his memory to a wonderful extent. As long as
Col. Jilson remained alive and in possession of his faculties, Judge Emmons had to be exceedingly sparing
with his reminiscences. Occasionally they got to Col.
Jilson's ears and his comments were such that people
experienced considerable difficulty in deciding which of
the two old gentlemen it was safest to believe.

One of the oldest and most firmly established families in Farragut was that to which Sheridan Redpath
belonged. Belonged is hardly the proper word in this
case, however; the family had disowned him. Two
uncles and an aunt, with at least a dozen first cousins
and no end of seconds and thirds, pronounced him a
disgrace to the family, and looked blank when his
name was mentioned, as if to say: "Who is this fellow that bears our name?"

His forebears came to Farragut early in the nine-
teenth century, when the town was a civilization out-
post, and for more than one hundred years the name
of Redpath had been associated with its life and des-
tinies. Only one other bearer of the name had been
a disgrace to the family, and that was so long before
the Civil War that the present-day Redpaths could
hardly be called snobbish for failing to remember his

existence, much less the fact that he had been shot as a horse-thief.

Sheridan's father was the eldest of his generation. He died when the boy was eighteen and in his sophomore year at college. His estate was small. For reasons best known to himself he had, soon after his marriage, deeded to his wife practically all of the real estate of which he was possessed. Subsequent litigation proved the wisdom of this course, for creditors who descended upon him after his failure in business, — he owned and conducted several big grain elevators, — found themselves unable to collect on judgments and were obliged to sit back and see their debtor live in plenty if not luxury on the fruits of his foresightedness. His wife, quite well-off in her own right, received the rents and paid the taxes on the one-time property of her husband, and creditors could do no more than " grin and bear it." It is worthy of record that Redpath, Senior, acting as her agent, made the collections himself and deposited the money to her account in the banks; also that he devoted six days in each week to living up to a reputation for business sagacity, and the seventh to living it down.

He was a deacon in the church.

CHAPTER II

IT was not until after Sheridan Redpath left college with his hard-earned degree, and an enviable record at both guard and tackle on the unhallowed scrub eleven, that he fell into evil ways.

Strict adherence to a promise not to drink did not deprive him of the right to indulge in other dissipation. Well-supplied with money, he went through college without learning the first thing about its value. He acquired a great deal of utterly useless knowledge about the things that made of him a Bachelor of Arts, and failed significantly to learn how to make anything else of himself. A native brightness aided him in getting through without a great deal of study. Only at examination periods was it necessary for him to labour seriously; the remainder of the time he took life easily and found it agreeable. He acquired no grasp on self-dependence, no initiative aside from that which had to do with pleasure, no symptom of a real purpose in life. He overlooked the fact that he possessed one of the rarest traits in human character: — determination. The fact that he had no thought, no inclination to break his promise to his mother produced no effect whatsoever upon his own estimate of himself. He knew dozens of fellows in his classes who had made similar vows to their parents, and who broke them without compunction. It did not occur to him to feel that he was made of stronger stuff than they.

14

Self-indulgence, made possible by a too lavish gen-
erosity and an unconscionable stupidity on the part
of his adoring mother, led him, with amiable disregard
for consequences, into the wildest forms of pleasure.
He spent money freely, recklessly. It signified nothing to him except through its power to meet the chal-
lenges of folly. His frequent and surreptitious trips
to New York were never-to-be-forgotten whirlwinds of
joy. He raked Broadway fore and aft; the popular
bars and restaurants and dance-halls knew him well,
and the denizens thereof marvelled not a little over
the joy he got out of life without the aid of liquor.

New York will never understand how a total ab-
stainer can have any fun in life. This youngster was
a mystery; he was incredible. His tremendous vitality,
cradled and developed by the strong and mighty West,
carried him along at top speed all of the time. He
set a pace that but few of his fellows even attempted
to follow, and those who did so fell swiftly behind.

Being a Western boy, he assumed that the only way
to make a place for himself in an Eastern college was
to equal if not to excel in pernicious activities. He
met the arrogance of the East with a ruthlessness that
swept it aside and gave him a fair, clear field. An un-
sound popularity was his reward. His unfailing good
nature, his buoyant spirits, his sporting integrity, his
more or less old-fashioned repugnance for foul language, his utter independence, a quaint sort of modesty, and, above all, his incomprehensible scorn for the
cup that cheers, gained for him a certain distinction,
but it was not the kind of distinction that endures.

Except for his misapplied energies he would have

earned for himself a lasting and enviable place among the heroes of that particular college.

He was in college a full year before he realized that profligacy is not the surest way to the hearts of the level-headed. He was conscious at first of a bitter disappointment over the penury of certain rich men's sons; later on he came to recognize this feeling as nothing less than disillusionment. The really worthwhile fellows with millionaire fathers, he discovered to his amazement and disgust, got along on one-third the allowance he demanded, and were seldom hard-up. In time he began to contrast these poverty-stricken millionaires with the vulgar, showy, new-rich fellows whose funds were unlimited, and in his wild, shamed young heart he despaired. He was not the " real stuff "; he was one of the money-spending muckers. The thought of it hurt him more than he cared to admit, even to himself.

Believing himself doomed to a place among the muckers, he cast restraint to the wind and increased his excesses. He despised the profligates as deeply and as utterly as any one else in college; there was a grain of comfort for him in the belief that if he refrained from drinking as they drank he would not be put in a class with them. It was his rather pitiful boast that he didn't " trail " *that* crowd, and yet he knew that it was with them that he really belonged.

He had the instincts of the true gambler. His methods were daring yet cautious. In his senior year he was regarded as the shrewdest card-player in college. Fair-minded, wild-hearted lad that he was, he never rejoiced in winning from his friends. To them he preferred to lose. It went against the grain to "clean out" the fellows he liked, and who, as he knew, in most cases could ill-afford to lose.

Once and only once did he sit in a game of poker with the "vulgar rich," as he called the little coterie of outsiders. The news went around next day, following an all-night session in the Babylonian apartment of a spoilt young New Yorker, that Sherry Redpath had "trimmed" them in a most historic manner. Stories of his "winnings" varied. The lowest figures breathed by sophisticated seniors put them at two thousand dollars, while one freshman wrote to a friend in Harvard that Sherry had won a trifle over one hundred thousand. The whole student-body rejoiced, not over his winning but because the others had lost. Deceived by the universal glee, he took upon himself a great deal of glory; he found comfort and happiness in the belief that his fellows were grateful to him for having "massacred" the Philistines.

For many a day he lived in an atmosphere of supreme self-exaltation, only to come smashing to earth with the sickening discovery that he was not wanted in the exclusive senior society for which his name had been proposed. He was, in a sense, blackballed. He never got over the sting of that humiliating and, to him, astonishing slap in the face. It meant, in plain words, that he wasn't desirable.

He left college hating the years he had spent there, despising himself for his mistakes, scoffing at the degree he carried home to his mother, and cursing the ill-fated loyalty that ordered him to sacrifice his strength and good-nature for three successive sea-

sons to the development of the 'varsity foot-ball eleven
when, as viewed in retrospect, he was certainly entitled
to a place in the first squad instead of among the
drudging, buffeted scrubs. It never occurred to him,
in his sullen fury, that abstinence from alcohol is not
the only requirement exacted by the trainers and
coaches.

His mother, still believing him to be impeccable,
pursued her course of folly; she sent him off on a lux-
urious and extended trip around the world.

He was in upper India when she died, quite suddenly.
Many days went by before word of her death reached
him in Bombay.

Since leaving college,— and with her tacit consent,
if not actual approval,— he had abandoned his stand
in regard to strong drink,— (it was *her* stand, not his,
he was wont to argue),— taking to the mild indulgence
that is supposed to establish manhood on the estate
once occupied by adolescence. His mother had cried
a little over him, though she managed also to smile,
when he came home a bit tipsy for the first time.

He was careful after that, and drank sparingly.
He did not like the tipple he was taking in order to
become a man. During the two or three months of
idleness at home prior to the long trip around the
world, his behaviour was quite exemplary. Despite the
raw edges left by his disappointments at college and
the consequent grudge against fate, he managed to
conduct himself so admirably, that he was in danger
of being referred to as a " molly-coddle." It was
not until he was far off in the Orient that he found
pleasure and stimulation in drink. He fell in with

brandy-drinking Englishmen and expatriated Amer-
icans in Japan and China, where drink is food, and,
still disliking the stuff, drank steadily and heavily because it was his nature to excel,— if such is the word,
— in any contest with his fellow-man.

The death of his mother, whom he loved with all
his wild, hungry heart, was the final, desolating trag-
edy. The winds from that day on took care of his
development. He sowed with the wind and he reaped
with it as well.

A fortune of three hundred thousand dollars came
to him as recompense for the loss of the one person
whom he loved and who, he believed, was the only one
to love him. He despised the money. He could look
upon it only as something substituted for that of
which he had been robbed, something in the shape of
palliation, something he ought to be thankful for because it is the beloved of all mankind.

It is not necessary to go into the history of the next
five years. Young Redpath went the pace that kills.
Money ran through his fingers like water through a
sieve. He drank and gambled and squandered with
such amazing recklessness and perseverance that even
to him the end was soon in sight. He did not have to
be told by the wise men of the town that he was going
to the devil. He knew it quite as well as they, and he
did not resent their well-meant advice. In fact, he
rather enjoyed having them preach to him, for it gave
him many a laugh that otherwise he might have missed!

Paris, London, Monte Carlo, Rome,— all of them,—
took tribute from him. His trips to New York and
Chicago were referred to as " classic " by envious

would-be sports in Farragut, but they were looked upon as something else by the fathers and mothers of these same young men. His name was the synonym of all the vices known to man. He was pitied and feared and scorned by every soul in Farragut. Small children were told that they would grow up to be like Sherry Redpath if " they didn't behave."

Strange as it may appear, his degradation was not in any sense accelerated by the central figure in the well-known trinity: wine, women and song. A singular, almost unnatural wisdom preserved him from the wiles of the women who despoil. He was uncanny in his ability to avoid the gravest of all co-operatives in the career of the squanderer. He had no respect for man, but he succeeded in keeping his respect for woman. Evil in woman was repulsive to him. He refused to look upon the bad woman, and the good woman was not allowed to look upon him. Of this state of affairs he was acutely sensible. So he avoided both the good and the bad, and owed nothing to either.

And then came the day when he had to pause and take stock of himself and his affairs. He estimated himself on a piece of hotel notepaper. His hand was unsteady, his eye wavering, but his brain was strangely clear. Piled in front of him were a score of bills, long overdue,— his tailor and hatter and all the rest of them. His check-book revealed the extent of his balance in bank,— all that was left of the handsome fortune handed down by his mother. He had had no drink that day. For half an hour he wrote checks, a grim smile at the corners of his mouth, a frown in his eyes. His extreme gravity in purchasing fifty cents'

worth of stamps at the news-stand so impressed the
young lady behind the counter that she assisted him in
licking and putting them on the hotel envelopes.   Then
he went to the desk and paid for the stationery, much
to the clerk's surprise, and also demanded, with considerable *impressement*, his bill for the past six weeks.
It amounted to ninety-seven dollars and thirty-five
cents.   This called for further calculations on the surface of a blotting pad, together with countless attempts
to subtract something from something else on the last
stub in his check-book.   Finally he gave forth a deep
sigh of relief — and triumph — and asked for the loan
of a fountain-pen.   He had conquered his balance
completely.   Handing over the check to the clerk, he
said:

"Give me the rest in cash, Harry,— two dollars and
ninety-three cents."

Receiving the cash and the receipted bill, he made
his way down the sweltering street to the stand of
Nicky the bootblack.

"Polish 'em up, Nicky," he said, taking his seat in
the chair.   "How much do I owe you?" he inquired,
later on, squinting at the highly polished shoes.   "I
mean all-told."

Nicky consulted his vest-pocket ledger, a look of resignation in his eyes.   Was he about to have ten cents
added to the account?

"One dollar sixty-five, Mr. Redpath," said he,
gloomily.

"Take it out of this," said Sherry magnificently,
thrusting a two-dollar bill into the little Italian's hand.

He jingled the change in his pocket as he sauntered

away, leaving Nicky in such a state of excitement that he ran after him for fifteen or twenty paces, trying to wipe invisible specks of dust from the far from stationary extremities of his late customer and debtor.

The spendthrift dropped in at the little flower shop near the corner, where he bought a gay boutonnière. The young lady pinned it on the lapel of his crumpled blue serge coat.

" Sprucing up a bit today, old sport," said she, with fine disregard for conventionality. " What's the matter? Goin' to a masquerade? "

" How much? " said he, ignoring the flippancy.

" Fifteen centuaries," said she. " Two for a kovort. Better take two. Then you'll be *sure* you're seein' two instead of one."

" Hush, Minnie," said he gently, and strolled away.

Presently he entered the Sunbeam. He was square with the world and still had ten cents in his pocket. He did not owe a penny to anybody.

An hour later the owner of the saloon came into the place. He was likewise the owner of the biggest brewery in the town. Redpath was sound asleep in a chair under one of the boundary palms.

" Throw him out o' here, Burke," growled the owner, glaring at the flushed, perspiring face of the sleeper. " This ain't a drunkards' home. He's nothing but a bum now, and you'll have him sneakin' in here every day for just that sort of thing if you don't nip him at the start. Throw him out. It don't look pretty havin' a loafer like that —"

" He's left a good many thousands o' dollars on this bar, Herman," said Patsy absently.

"Well, he got his money's worth, didn't he?"

"I'll wake him up," said the barkeeper.

"Tell him to get out and stay out."

"I won't have to do that. He beat me to it. He ain't coming back any more. He's reformed."

Herman Schwick stared. "Refor — well, for the love o'—"

Patsy was shaking Redpath gently by the shoulder.

"Wake up, Sherry. You'll ketch cold settin' out here in the woods."

CHAPTER III

THE proprietor's heart smote him. He knew how it felt to wake up with a head. "Say, Sherry, have a drink on the house. It will do you good. Patsy, fix him a Tom Collins."

Redpath straightened up, and met Schwick's eye. "Nothing doing, Herman. Not even a pick-me-up. I've cut it out."

"You need a bracer to —"

"No, thank you."

Schwick looked troubled. "Men don't break off sudden like this, Sherry. It's bad. Taper off gradually."

Redpath moved toward the door. He was quite steady on his legs, but his head was going round.

"Guess I'll slip out before the regulars ooze in. I can't buy drinks for 'em any more, Herman, so I'll not use up valuable space waiting for some one else to thaw. So long, Patsy. Good-bye, little Sunbeam!" His hand described a sweeping farewell to the four corners of the bar-room; a whimsical smile spread over his face. "I may drop in again all togged out in a Salvation Army suit, passing my little tin box around for spare change, or I may come in as the iceman, but otherwise, — never again! So fare-thee-well, merry Sunbeam. Good-bye, palm trees and free-lunch,— and *good-bye, booze!*"

Patsy followed him to the door. Except for Her-

24

man Schwick, in his crisp linen suit, the bar was empty.
The court-house clock was banging the hour of six.
The sidewalk was almost deserted. Pedestrians were
using the opposite side of the street, keeping to the
shade.

"Where are you going, Sherry? Still got your
room in the Tremont?"

"No. I've got two suit-cases and a hat box in the
check-room over there, but — I say, Patsy, have you
any use for a silk hat?"

"I never go to funerals," said Patsy, without a
smile. "See here, what are you going to do for grub
and a place to —"

"Patsy," said Redpath, with extreme gravity,
"I'm going to be a squirrel and live on nuts. I've
taken lodgings up in Compton's Woods,— a large, airy
room trimmed with oak and elm and with a nice green
carpet that stretches as far as the eye can see.
There's where I'm going to sleep while the weather lasts.
I'll get plenty of fresh air on these hot nights, and
there's running water with fish in it right at my elbow.
All I'll have to do is to roll into Burton's Creek and
roll right out again. Beats drawing a bath all to
smash. Don't worry about me, Patsy. I'm young
and I used to be strong. I'm going to sleep almost as
long as Rip Van Winkle did, and when I get up you
won't know me for the whiskers. Nobody will know
me. That's how I'm going to deceive my prospective
employer. He won't know until it's too late that I'm
me and not old Santa Claus. Excuse me if I run along
and —"

"Say, boy, I'm worried about you," said the barkeeper, looking over his shoulder anxiously. "You ought to be 'round where you can have attention if you —"

"Oh, I'm not that far gone. I'll not get the dee-tees."

"But you can't stop short with your hide full of the stuff, you know. You'll get sick or —"

"If I do I'll call in old Doc' Nature," said the young man, affecting airiness.

Patsy laid a hand on his shoulder. "I like you, Redpath," he said, seriously. "You've played hell with your life, and I've watched you doin' it, and couldn't say a word. Now, I believe you got it in you to buck up and be a credit to yourself and this here town. The only way to do it, though, is to get started right. You got to get braced up and all set for the start. I've got a closed-in porch up at my house on Ellum Street and a swingin' hammick in it. All you've got to do is to drop in late of evenin's, after the kiddies are in bed, and the Missus and me will —"

"That's — that's awfully good of you, Patsy," interrupted Sherry, his face turning a darker red. He looked away suddenly. "I couldn't think of bothering your wife and —"

"No bother at all. Nothing to it!"

"Thanks,— but I think I'll stick to Compton's Woods."

"Anyhow, in case it rains you can hike down to my house and turn in on the porch. And I'll fix you up with coffee and —"

"You're awfully good," repeated the young man, his voice husky. "Awfully." Then, after a moment, he squared his shoulders and smiled. " But I shan't need help. I'm going to fight it out alone. Never mind about me. As soon as I get pulled together a bit, I'll get out after a job. I don't care what it is, I'll take it. I'll sweep streets or curry horses, or anything. So long. I think I'll sneak up to Compton's Woods now and pick out a nice mossy bed and — turn in. I need just forty-eight hours' sleep."

He started away. Patsy called out after him: " Keep out o' the sun, kid. It's ninety-two right now. And don't forget about the hammick."

" I won't," said Sherry, without looking back.

He slept under the moon and stars that hot, stifling night. Below him lay the town, its sweltering thousands gasping for a breath of refreshing air. Not a leaf stirred in the trees above his grassy bed. Before he dropped off to sleep, his mind flew back to the days when, as a child, he had looked upon the dark, forbidding vastnesses of Compton's Woods on the lofty hill as the abode of bandits, imps and all the foul creatures with which nursemaids threaten the noisy and sleepless when they have made sure that no one else is listening. He grinned sleepily as he looked, blear-eyed and stupid, into the still, peaceful clouds of foliage overhead, and pictured himself at the tender age of six howling his lungs out in terror at the very thought of being alone at night in Compton's Woods. There had been nightmares, peopled by the most horrific bogimen; the mere mention of Compton's Woods chastened him as no reprimand could have done. And what a quiet, harmless, dull place it was, after all!

The barking of a dog put an end to his reflections.

He was suddenly conscious of a glare in his eyes, but many minutes passed before he realized that it was broad daylight and that he was staring up through an aperture in the tree-tops at a fiercely white sky. The barking of the dog continued,— sharp, staccato, very business-like barks.

He rolled over on his side, blinking, and discovered an audience of two hard-by: a barefoot boy of ten and a bristling fox terrier. They were not ten feet away and both were eyeing him with an equally vast interest, not to say alarm. With his abrupt, convulsive movement the dog retreated a few paces, but the boy, perhaps through sheer inability to stir his stumps, remained motionless.

"What do you want?" demanded Redpath, more gruffly than he knew.

The boy began slowly to edge away.

"What time is it?" he went on, more gently, rubbing his hot, smarting eyes.

"Gee," gasped the boy, "you *are* alive, ain't you?"

"Alive? Well, I should hope so. Is it rumoured that I am dead?"

"I never saw a dead man. You looked like you might be one. But I guess I'll be going. Huh, Sport!" With more haste than seemed really necessary the youngster scooted for the fence that paralleled the distant roadway, preceded with even more unseemly haste by Sport.

After a moment, Sherry sat up and laughed,— not a hearty, joyous effort; on the contrary, it was a painful one.

"I'd run too," he commented, aloud. "Well, it's to-

morrow," he reflected, a puzzled scowl on his brow.
"When did it arrive? Where did it come from so
sud —" He fumbled for his watch, and gazed dizzily at
its bronze face. It was nearly one o'clock. "Holy
Smoke! One o'clock,— and it must be afternoon.
Get up, Rip! You've slept long enough. It may be
next week for all you know. No, it's only tomorrow,"
he decided shrewdly. "Watch would have stopped —
Oh, what a thirst!"

He was lying on a mossy bank at the edge of Burton's Creek,— a clear, cool, swift little stream that
gurgled appealingly. Crawling down to the edge he
plunged his hot face into the water. He well knew it
would be cold, for there were springs in the hill above
that fed the stream. Drinking his fill, he sank back
refreshed.

"Too late to take my tub," he mused, regretfully.
"Must get up earlier after this, if I'm to have a bath."
Leaning back against the huge trunk of a tree, he rum-
inated lazily, hazily.

He craved something, but it was not food. His
throat was parched, his skin felt tight and drawn, his
eyes ached. It occurred to him that he ought to be
hungry,— very hungry,— and then came the whimsical
notion that if he could fall asleep again it wouldn't
in the least matter whether he was hungry or not.

"It's cheaper to sleep than it is to eat," he reflected,
and rolled over into the shade.

When next he opened his eyes he was in absolute
darkness.

A hoarse voice assailed his ears. He had just been
dreaming of a thunder-storm.

"Wake up; ye've had sleep enough for a lifetime."

"Who the — who is it?" cried Sherry, sitting up, blinking his eyes. He could distinguish nothing except the bulky, indistinct trunks of trees, nothing — Ah, one of them was moving! And it was from this mobile tree-trunk that the voice issued!

"The Czar of Roosia," announced the bulk in a rich Irish brogue. A brilliant light flashed suddenly upon the rotund, smiling face of an old friend and supporter: Officer Barney Doyle, as genial a "cop" as ever lived, and a good one too.

"Hello, Barney," mumbled Sherry. "Wha — what am I wanted for?"

"Bless me soul," cried Barney Doyle, running the light of his dark lantern over the recumbent figure, "ye're wanted for supper. Have ye an idee what time it is? Bedad, it's a quarter av twelve. Ye must be starved."

"Supper? I'm not hung — yes, I am! By George, I certainly am hungry! I never was so hungry in my life. Queer how suddenly it struck me —"

"Well, I've got a bountiful repast fer ye, as they say in the newspapers. D'ye mind Patsy Burke at the Sunbeam? Well, he drops in at roll-call this evenin' and says he to me, 'Barney, who's workin' the upper half av the Sixt' Ward nights?' 'No wan but meself,' says I to him. 'Well,' says he, 'would ye know Sherry Redpath if ye were to see him?' 'I would,' says I, 'if it were in the jungles av Africa.' 'Thin,' says he, 'will ye do me a favour? He's up there in Compton's Woods sleepin' off a five-year bun, and I'd like ye to take a stroll through the woods this night

and see if ye can lo-*cate* him.' 'Compton's Woods?'
says I. 'Sure,' says he, and started in to tell me
where it is, a refliction on me ability as a policeman,
bad luck to him. 'It is not on me beat,' says I; 'and
besides it's a dom big woods,' says I. 'It'd be like
lookin' fer a needle in a haystack.' 'Thin ye won't do
me the favour?' says he, and called me a lot o' names
I wouldn't take from another soul but Patsy Burke.
'I'd do anything fer ye, Patsy,' says I, 'but I can't
spind the night in Compton's Woods lookin' fer anything short av an assassin. I haven't been in the dom
woods since I was a boy.' 'Well,' says he, ' ye pass it
by a half dozen times every night av your life, don't
ye? Couldn't ye stroll in and take a look? Ye may
be the means av savin' a man's life. Ye wouldn't want
a fellow crature to freeze to death all alone up there
in the woods, would ye?' 'Wid the temperature at
the roastin' point,' I says, 'no, I wouldn't; and I'll
take a walk t'rough the woods fer ye, Patsy,' says I.
'Whin ye find him,' says he, ' give him this box of grub;
and tell him there's a small lookin' glass and a razor
and soap and brush in the bottom av the box. He's
goin' to look for a job, and I don't want him sawin'
wood in people's back-yards like a long whiskered bum,'
says he. So here's the grub and, bedad, on me own
hook I've added a toot' brush I bought fer ye. Knowin'
ye as I do, I felt certain ye wouldn't be carryin' wan in
yer vest pocket."

Redpath listened attentively to the voluble copper.
He was as hungry as a bear, but he wouldn't have interrupted Barney's discourse for anything in the
world.

"It was mighty fine of you, Barney, to come so far out of your way to —"

"God love ye, lad, I enjoy the change. Now niver mind thankin' me. Get to work on the grub. I'll tell Patsy I seen ye, and that ye are as well as could be expicted." He flashed his light in all directions and then, lowering his voice, inquired: "Would ye be feelin' the need av a drop av somethin' to pull ye together? Say the word. I have it in me hip pocket."

"No, thank you, Barney. I'm drinking nothing but Burton's Creek now," said Sherry, with a grin. "If you should notice that the creek is running dry, don't be alarmed. I've drunk barrels of it. Have you ever tasted water, Barney?"

Barney appeared to reflect. "I have," he said. "It was once when I fell in the river below the bridge and swallied a couple o' buckets of it before they pulled me out. As I remimber it now, I didn't like the stuff. Well, I'll be movin' on. So long, lad. Save a bite o' that fer the breakfast. Ye might stop on the way downtown in the morning and get a cup av coffee at my house. I live at 1433 Hooper Street, just below here a bit. I'll tell the old lady to — Here, what's the matter wid ye? There's nothin' to be blubberin' about, lad. Have I said a word to hurt yer feelin's?"

Sherry had buried his face in his arm, and convulsive sobs shook his long frame. It was some time before he could speak, chokingly, to the burly policeman who stood over him and marvelled.

"I'm just foolish, that's all, Barney. You — you are awfully kind. I've never realized what it meant to have any one kind to me, because I've never felt that

I needed it. I'll not forget you and Patsy. You're both fine."

"Oh, hell!" said Barney, resorting to what he thought was tactfulness. "Don't mention it. We'd do as much fer a dog. Bedad, I — I wouldn't mind sleepin' out here in the woods meself, nights like this," he went on heartily. "It's a dom sight better than — Well, so long, Sherry. Will ye, by any chance, be roostin' here tomorrow night?"

"I suppose so. I'll not show my face in town until I'm in shape to convince people that I'm actually sober. Good night, Barney."

"Sleep tight," said Barney, from the shadows. The sound of his footsteps died away.

The young man ate his midnight repast with a relish. He had had countless suppers at midnight but not one had been as delectable as this simple feast of sandwiches, hard-boiled eggs, cold chicken, bottled milk and doughnuts. With a sort of grim frugality he denied himself all that his new-born appetite demanded. He reflected that a day or two ago he would have eaten all that he wanted and thrown the rest away. But he was no longer a prodigal. He was careful to preserve in the pasteboard box every scrap that was left over, tucking it away as tenderly as the miser puts away his gold.

This new sensation of thrift amused him. Sitting with his back to a tree, the box once more tied up with its good stout string, he allowed his thoughts to range with some clarity over a career of wastefulness. Long afterward he realized that he was holding the lunch-box tightly against his breast, and that he was

gripping it with a strength that meant he would defend
it as he would defend his life.

It has already been stated that he was, despite his
waywardness, a clean-minded fellow. He was quite as
honest with himself as he was with the world to which
he revealed his sporting integrity. He blamed no one
but himself for his present condition; he had no ax to
grind, no grudge to feed. He believed in his soul that
he could be and would be a nobler man without money
than he could possibly be with it, unless it was obtained by no uncertain sacrifices on his part.

There was not the remotest doubt in his mind, as he
sat there in the black depth of Compton's Woods, that
he would be able to fight his own way out of the slough
into which he had deliberately and foolishly immersed
himself. Indeed, he was looking forward with pleasur-
able interest and a surprising zest to the struggle that
lay ahead of him. His was an adventuresome nature;
he liked to think of himself as opposed by difficulties
which only courage and prowess could overcome. In
a sense, he was a moral braggart, but in no sense a
physical one. If pinned down to an analysis of this
peculiar condition, he would no doubt have tranquilly
contended that his life was his own and he could take
care of it better than any one else,— and this notwithstanding the sickening muddle he had made of it.

The night was dark; a starless sky hung over the
black wood, and the world he had known seemed a million miles away. He could scarcely believe it had ever
existed for him.

He was alone; it seemed to him that he was alone for
the first time in his life. Slowly he became conscious

that an odd sort of dread was stealing over him.   He
knew there was nothing to fear, and yet he shivered
occasionally and caught himself listening for ominous
sounds in the darkness, just as he had listened when a
tiny boy in the great big bed-chamber where he slept
alone.   In those nights of childish terror he had called
out shrilly and his mother had come to him.   How long
ago was that?   He counted the years.   They represented ages now as he looked back to them.   His
mother had come to him, always she had come and
quickly, and she had driven away the fear of night that
caused his little heart to thump so violently.

His mother!   She was sleeping alone over there in
Greenvale Cemetery,— ah, but not alone!   There were
countless dead and ugly things lying beside her in —
He sprang to his feet, a cold sweat on his brow.   She
was alone over there!   Alone at night in that dreadful
place.

Hardly knowing what he did, he rushed headlong
through the darkness, his eyes fixed on the faraway,
straggling lights of the street that formed the lower
line of Compton's Woods.   He avoided the fallen and
the upright trees, the boulders, the underbrush and
the tiny ravines as though guided by Providence, and
came at last to the broad clearing at the base of the
hill.   Gasping for breath,— for he was no longer the
trained athlete,— he staggered weakly to the fence,
and almost fell from the top of it upon the gravel sidewalk beyond.

CHAPTER IV

A QUARTER of an hour later he was passing the long, low stone wall that formed the State Street front of Greenvale Cemetery. There were few houses in this part of the town, and street lamps were widely separated. He was a lonely pedestrian in this sparsely settled region. The bark of a dog would have been a welcome, cheery sound in his ears, which now were filled with the noise of his own thick, heavy breathing and the pounding of his feet on the firm macadam roadway. But the night itself was as still as death, as still as the place he was coming to.

Vaulting over the wall at a spot far below the big iron gates where stood the sexton's house, he made his way stealthily through the winding avenues and across the green sward to the place where his mother slept. It was a well-remembered spot; he had been there many a time before. Time and again, between his drinking bouts, he had visited her grave, always carrying flowers to lay upon the mound. He never forgot her, and he never went near her grave except when he was completely sober.

It was not maudlin sentiment that inspired the words he muttered as he lay face downward upon the lonely mound. They were tender, consoling words, bidding her to be not afraid; he was there; she was not alone in the night; he would not leave until the darkness was gone.

And when the first faint glow of sunrise stole in among the evergreens and ever-whites, he arose and stood looking down upon the place where he had lain.

"The day is here," he said to her. "If I could, I would come to you every night. I cannot bear the thought of you being here all alone in the dead of night, with — Ah, but Lord! How well off you are! You are not here to see your son as he is today. You went away while I was still worthy of the hope and trust you had in me. You loved me then, and you'd love me now in spite of everything. You would never have ceased loving me. That's the rotten part of it. You would be loving me now just as much as ever, and you would have come to me up there in Compton's Woods tonight without a word, just as you came when I was a kid. Just because you were — Mother."

He brushed his hand across his eyes and turned away. A cock crowed in the distance. Lifting his head, he stood for many minutes watching the pink and grey light steal up into the blue-black dome. A soft breeze was blowing through the trees. Birds began to chirp sleepily, and then with sudden vehemence burst into shrill and stormy acclaim. The sparrow, the pewee, the wren and the sweet-voiced thrush opened up their little throats and gave glad welcome to the new day, utterly unimpressed by the fact that they were in the city of the dead.

He stood there amid the ghostly grave-stones, bewildered by the sudden revelry, so sacrilegious and out-of-place. He opened his lips to hiss a shocked, reproving, "Sh!", and then was conscious of a strange, amazing revival of his own spirits,— so strange that he wondered what had come over him.

A curious light-heartedness affected him; an inexplicable sensation of energy, of exhilaration surged through him. He flung up his head and gazed about in the lessening gloom; the breeze struck his face with a gentle, kindly touch; his brain seemed in that instant to have been released from the trap that held it fast; his whole being shed something that was heavy and clumsy and pressing; he felt himself expand.

In absolute wonder, he cried out aloud: "I — I never felt like this before. I — I guess I must be — sober at last."

Seized by an impulse that could not be resisted, he dropped to his knees beside his mother's grave and, with ineffable tenderness, patted the thick grass with his open hands, lovingly, caressingly. Then he leaped to his feet and strode briskly away. Vaulting into the roadway, he retraced his steps toward Compton's Woods.

Cocks were now crowing everywhere; raucous voiced cocks and shrill, treble voiced fellows; faraway cocks and cocks nearby; and all of them proud and happy cocks.

"Gad!" he cried exultantly, as he swung along.

Houses and barns and poles and fences were taking shape in the growing daylight, desolate objects that soon would stand out clear and sightly in the mellow dawn.

"Gad!" he repeated. "I'm hungry again."

Soon he was wending his way among the sturdy oaks

and elms of Compton's Woods, pointed like a hunter
for the forgotten lunch-box. He essayed a joyous
whistle, but his "wind" was not what it used to be.
Rapid walking had told upon him. He panted, much
to his disgust.

As he drew near the spot where he had slept the
early part of the night, he was greeted by an appari-
tion that caused him to pause in no little surprise and
considerable dismay. A burly, ragged, unkempt individual was examining the contents of the box with obvious interest and glee.

"Hey!" shouted Sherry, starting forward again.
"Drop that! Put it down, damn you!" Every drop
of blood in his body leaped to fighting heat.

The stranger looked up quickly and was about to
take to his heels with the treasure. A second glance
at the gaunt, disheveled person who uttered the command, encouraged him to stand his ground. The scowl
deepened on his already unprepossessing face.

"Come and get it, you shrimp," he roared, with a
prodigious oath inserted for full measure of contempt.

Sherry halted a few yards away. He was clear-
headed now and sensible enough to take stock of his
man before venturing into combat. Courage was by
no means lacking.

"It belongs to me," he said levelly.

"The hell you say," sneered the tramp. "G'wan
away now, you, or I'll beat the face off'n you. Skip!"
His manner was most alarming.

Sherry had sized him up. He was a big, flabby, but
powerful looking fellow, filthy with the dust and sweat
of travel.

"I'll give you a minute and a half to put that box where you found it," said Sherry, cold with determination.

"You will, eh? Oh, you will? Why, you —"

"Put it down!"

"Say, I don't want to hurt you, young feller. You look sick an'—"

"Put it down!"

"How do I know it's yours? And even if it was, it's mine now. Don't try any rough stuff or —"

"If you were half way decent, I'd share it with you," said the other. "You may be as hungry as I —"

"That's got nothin' to do with it. Beat it!"

Sherry hesitated. He was suddenly curious. "Say, answer this question before I fix you so that you won't be able to talk at all. Where did you spring from?"

The tramp glared at him. "Come to think of it," he said, ominously, "I *will* put it down. I'll put it down just long enough to bump that purty face of yours so that your mother, damn her, won't know it."

He hurled the box to the ground and advanced swiftly upon the young man.

Sherry quickly placed a tree between himself and the approaching foe.

"I t'ought so!" roared the tramp. "Come out o' that till I —"

At that instant Sherry came "out o' that," divested of his coat. The light of battle was in his eye, the joy of a righteous cause in his soul. He sailed into his adversary like a whirlwind.

"I'll show you!" he shouted gleefully. He knew that he would have to make short work of the fellow. No one knew better than he the price that excesses such as he had practised exact of the strongest constitution. The vast strength of his old football days was still in his body but it was not to be depended upon in case of a prolonged encounter.

The onslaught was so swift, so vicious, that the tramp, over-confident in his burliness, sustained the shock of his life. He was fairly smothered by the blows that rained upon his face and body. Almost before he knew that the fight had begun, he was defending himself with fear in his soul. He tried to cover up, but the savage blows beat down his guard. It was too late to run away, much as he wished to do so. Never had he been so deceived as this! What was he up against? How could he possibly have dreamed that this pale-faced, hollow-eyed stranger was a prize fighter out for a morning sprint — And just then he saw a million stars. The back of his head struck the ground first. He remembered that much very clearly for half a second or so, and then he felt suddenly cold and wet. Somehow he was having great difficulty in getting his breath,— and no wonder, for he was floundering face downward in a far from shallow place in Burton's Creek.

When he did get his breath,— it was more of a spray than a breath,— he scrambled to his feet and dashed for the bank. With singular foresight,— all the more remarkable because he couldn't see,— he chose the bank farthest removed from the one he so lately had occupied. He slipped backward twice on the muddy ledge, but he persevered without so much as a glance behind. All the while he was sputtering something which might have been recognized, by stretching the imagination, as " for God's sake! "

Once out of the water, he shot a swift, scared look over his shoulder, but he did not pause. That glance revealed to him a tall, white-shirted figure standing very erect on the opposite bank, his chin high and his arms, — what mighty arms they were! — folded across his chest, for all the world like a picture he had once seen of an actor,— he couldn't at the moment remember who,— representing somebody in one of Shakespeare's plays,— he couldn't for the life of him remember which one it was. He was having a hard time of it remembering anything. There was one thing he had forgotten more completely than anything else: the appetite that had got him into the trouble. But he never forgot that heroic, defiant figure on the opposite bank, nor the look of exaltation that transfigured the face of his conqueror.

A hundred feet away, he slowed down to a walk, and turned to hurl anathemas — and also a fair-sized stone — at the motionless — But the amazing creature suddenly came to life and leaped forward in pursuit! He did not see,— for obvious reasons,— but he distinctly heard the splashing of water and the hoarse shout of victory as the pursuer crossed the creek.

With head thrown back and eyes lighted by the fire of a superlative ambition, the vagabond resumed his onward progress, this time with a purpose and intensity that left no room to doubt that he was in a great and vital hurry. Never in all his life had he tried to run so fast, and never had he seemed so distressingly stationary. As a matter of fact, a deerhound couldn't have caught him.

When Redpath stopped to lean against a tree and laugh, his late adversary had picked up a lead of at least a hundred yards and was still running for dear life, crashing through obstructing underbrush and hurdling fallen logs with all the vanity of a scornful rhinoceros.

Sherry watched him until he disappeared over the brow of a small hill, and then walked slowly back to the scene of battle. He was wet and exhausted, but he was very happy.

"Gee," he said to himself, his hand pressed tight against his side, "I'm glad he didn't let me catch him. He would have made mince-meat out of me. I'm all in."

Crossing the stream on the exposed boulders, he threw himself upon the ground and panted for breath.

"But wasn't it great?" he mused blissfully.

For an hour he lay there, gazing up into the cool green foliage, a queer little smile on his lips, reminiscent of triumph, and, as the painful thumping of his heart subsided, a peacefulness stole over him, for he knew that he had made a good start up the long hill.

He shaved with cold water and was philosophical about it. Then, glowing warmly, after a plunge into the stream, he set himself down to a most unusual breakfast. Never before had he partaken of lettuce sandwiches for breakfast, and never had he dreamed it possible for a sane person to relish pickles at that ungodly hour in the morning. He contrasted his cus-

tomary breakfast of a piece of dry toast and a cup of
coffee with this feast of sandwiches, eggs, pickles and
— Yes, fruit cake,— and chuckled. Certainly he was
entertaining a strange man at breakfast. This
couldn't be Sheridan W. Redpath who scraped up every
crumb and devoured it so eagerly. Here was parsi-
mony unequalled!

His thoughts ran down the hill to the home of Officer
Barney Doyle, and they were of hot coffee. The mere
thought of a brimming cup of coffee with thick cream
— well, the most exquisite longing engaged his vitals.
Had the amount been in his pocket at that instant,
he cheerfully would have given a hundred dollars for
a cup of coffee. If only he had that last ten cents
back in his fingers again! What a glorious treat he
could give himself down at the junction lunch-room!

He ate with a vast pride and no little self-esteem.
Had he not battled for and preserved his breakfast?
There was a tremendous satisfaction in feeling that he
owed his present state of contentment to a superior,—
though sadly battered,— pair of fists, and a stout
heart.

Strange as it may seem, he had not the slightest
craving for an alcoholic stimulant. The thought did
not enter his head that he actually *needed* such a thing.
He wanted coffee and nothing else.

All that day he kept to the woods. By nightfall
he was ravenously hungry. From time to time during the day he inspected himself in the little mirror,
and always he shook his head resolutely. His eyes
were inflamed and his hand shook as he held it up for
inspection.

" No," he said ruefully, " you won't do yet, Sherry.
You're just one notch removed from a hang-over, and
everybody on earth hates a hang-over.   You're not all
here yet,— not by any means.   I certainly can't afford
to be seen on the streets with you in your present condition.   People wouldn't have a particle of confidence
in me if they saw me associating with you.   They'd
say I was in very bad company."   He looked himself
over.   His linen was far from immaculate, his blue
serge suit needed pressing badly.   He sighed.   " Pretty
seedy, old top, pretty seedy.   I shudder when I look
at you.   I'd hate to meet you in a lonely spot on a
dark night."   He sighed again.   " I see that I'll have
to take a run into the city tonight, when all the good
people are asleep, and reclaim your wardrobe."   His
fingers encountered the round brass hotel check in his
trousers pocket.   " It gives me an awful shock when
I come in contact with that infernal check.   It feels
like a half dollar, and for a second or two I think I'm
rich again."

From his sequestered hiding-places in the depths of
Compton's Woods he could see the roadway below.
As the day wore on, he became aware of an increasing
interest on the part of the people who passed along this
more or less unfrequented street in the outskirts of
the town.   Even from a great distance he could see
that pedestrians were gazing intently into the wooded
region above.   Drivers of delivery wagons leaned forward and searched the forest with unmistakable curiosity.   People in automobiles pointed their fingers in
a vaguely general direction and put their heads together as if living up to the theory that two heads

are better than one when in doubt. Moreover, he noticed, as the afternoon progressed, that the number of
passing automobiles increased. Most of them moved
with funereal slowness and some of them actually
stopped at points of special vantage.

He was not long in grasping what it all meant. A
bitter smile came to his lips and a look of dismay to
his eyes.

"The whole darned town knows I'm up here," he
reflected, clenching his sore hands. "They're probably saying I'm completely surrounded by whisky bottles, loaded to the guards, guzzling and sleeping and
guzzling again. Lordy, what are they *not* saying!
Probably saying that women are not safe as long as
I'm at large, that children mustn't come within a mile
of Compton's Woods, that I ought to be locked up and
then run out of town! The newspapers are describing
me as a wild man of the woods, and all the old fogies
in town are saying 'I told you so.' That scamp of a
Sherry Redpath is up there drinking himself to death,
thank the Lord,— that's what they're saying,— and
'What a God's blessing it is that his poor mother is
in her grave and can't see her son now.' Rubber, you
infernal idiots! You can't see me from the road, and
there isn't one of you that's got nerve enough or charity enough to come in here to see what's become of me.
I might die of starvation for all you care. Enjoy
yourselves!"

He leaned forward to devote his undivided attention
to a certain object.

"Well, can you beat *that?* As I'm alive, it's Uncle
Henry and Aunt Phoebe taking in the sights! Show-

ing me their new car, too. Now that's nice of them.
What a beautiful new Ford they've got! They want
me to see it before they have it washed. What kind,
thoughtful people they are! Cheering me up always.
Couldn't bear to think of me dying up here without
having something pretty to look at before I croak.
Returning good for evil, too. Showing me they've
forgiven me for punching Cousin Ben's nose last spring
when he called me down for saying hello to him on
Main Street."

When nightfall came he eagerly made his way down
to the lower end of the woods. Barney Doyle would
be along soon, traversing the lonely street on his first
round of the night. With gleeful anticipation, he
waited at the point where Hooper Street intersected
Compton's Road. Here he would intercept the kindly
policeman and —

His soul turned sick with the possibility of disappointment. Barney would surely come, but would he
bring another box from the wonderful Patsy?

And Barney came and was startled almost out of his
helmet when the half-famished, eager young fellow
sprang over the fence, squarely in his path, and cheerily ordered him to throw up his hands!

This time there was a thermos bottle filled with hot
coffee, besides an even larger box than the one of the
night before.

" Me old lady sends ye the coffee with her kindest re-
gards," said Barney, " and I'll run ye in if ye don't
return that bottle by six in the mornin'.""

" You tell her I'll kiss her if I ever meet her," cried
Sherry, happier than he had ever been in his life.

"See that ye do," said Barney, magnanimously.
"She hasn't had a young felly kiss her in twenty-five
years, and, bedad, I think she'd enjoy it."

The cheery policeman stopped for half an hour,
chatting with the young man while he ate of the good
things the barkeeper had sent up to him.

"There's a bum in jail this minute who says they's
a crazy man up in Compton's Woods," said Barney.
"And by the looks av him I'd say he was an uncommonly vicious lunatic. I never saw such a pair av
eyes as the poor divil's got."

He left a couple of Chicago newspapers with Redpath, and went his way with an ill-timed prayer for
rain. The country was parched from the effects of a
six weeks' drought. A thunder-storm was the only
thing that would cool off the air, and a three days'
rain was needed. Or, at least, so said Barney Doyle.

Far back in the wood, Sherry built a little fire that
night, and lying close beside it, read the papers. He
had not failed to observe that Barney tactfully neglected to leave either of the local dailies.

CHAPTER V

H IS third day in the woods brought a beautiful
adventure. He awoke bright and early and
hungry. His first act was to take account of
himself in the looking-glass, and his spirits went up
with a bound. The bleary droop was gone from his
eyes; they looked back at him with something of their
old brightness and vivacity. Despite a certain blood-
shot condition, which he knew time alone could erad-
icate, they were most agreeably clear and direct.
The old smile was in them and they no longer blinked
uncertainly when he tried to focus them on any definite object.

He sang as he splashed in the cold waters of Burton's
Creek, and whistled as he shaved. And glory be! the
coffee was still hot in the thermos bottle. His spirits
soared higher and higher.

Late the night before he had stolen down the back
streets and, long after twelve o'clock, presented himself at the check-room in the Tremont. From one of
his suitcases he brought forth a supply of clean linen,
his hair-brushes and a long-despised bottle of lilac
toilet-water. The pipe he had smoked in college was
also forthcoming, and a tin of smoking tobacco that
he had forgotten he possessed. Rolling these articles
up in a newspaper he tramped back to his lodgings in
the wood, but not until the night watchman, who was
also the hotel valet, had pressed his blue serge suit.

A day or two more of the simple life in the woods and he would be as fit as a fiddle. He remarked, however, as he grew stronger and his brain cleared, that it was impossible to rest comfortably on the hard bed that Mother Earth provided for him. This, he argued, was most encouraging. Only a night or two before he wouldn't have cared whether his bed was hard or soft. A greensward is all very well when you are drunk, but it is a cruelly unresponsive thing when you are sober. His mind took frequent excursions to the hammock in Patsy Burke's porch; it would swing very nicely between two stout saplings and — He sighed deeply. Alas, he had a thousand saplings at his command but not a single hammock.

Shortly after breakfast he started off on a long walk through the woods, his pipe going busily. He had cut for himself a stout walking-stick and in the band of his panama hat he had jabbed the gaudy wing-feather of a blue-jay. With all the cunning of a forest-dweller, he made safe the remnants of his breakfast by hiding it among the thick branches of a stately oak. His discarded linen, clumsily washed in the stream, hung out to dry on a less imposing tree!

Right jauntily he swung along through the shady *bois*,— he employed the French because his mood was gay,— twirling his stick and whistling an inconstant air.

"Bedad," he said, abandoning the French for Barney Doyle, "if I felt any better I'd die."

Compton's Woods spread out over a huge tract of land, running back from the city to a point nearly three miles from Hooper Street, its northern boundary.

Topographically it represented a succession of hills
and vales covered by an apparently endless sweep of
timber.

For many years this expanse of forest-land had been
in litigation. As far back as one could well remember,— excepting the oldest inhabitant, of course,—
Compton's Woods had been in the courts, the battle-
ground of countless lawsuits, apparent compromises
and renewed wrangles. Combative heirs could not be
induced to agree upon a partition of the property; so
bitter was the animosity governing the conflict that
neither side would give an inch. Through a sort of
hereditary spite on the part of the contestants the
forest remained as God created it, and no man's hand
had been allowed to improve upon His handiwork.
Narrow, serpentinous dirt roads transversed the tract
by virtue of a necessity which disregarded property
rights, and on these roads certain unrestrained farmers and gardeners found a " short cut " to the lower
end of the city. In the main, however, the roads were
unfrequented. They were not inviting to motorists,
and, in these days of rapid transit, even the most
lowly of agriculturists prefers the long road to the
short one if only to keep his place in the procession
along the broad highway, where he may see and be seen,
a product of advancing civilization.

South, east and west ranged the broad grain-fields,
the level savannas, and the stock-farms of the ever-com-
plaining but independent agriculturists. Compton's
Woods stood like a green oasis in the midst of a sheer
desert of yellow wheat-fields at the time of which I
write. The harvesters were at work in the fields; the

threshers would soon be grinding away in their place.

On one side of the tract ran the huge farms of the Compton family; on the other those of their bitter enemies, the Burtons. In all that part of the State there were no wealthier, no more powerful landed interests than those represented by the holdings of the Comptons and the Burtons. For fifty years they had fought each other vindictively because a common grandfather had grievously erred in the matter of a title to the stretch of timberland that lay between them. In the old days, when the sword was mightier than a pen in the hands of any lawyer, they had fought with sanguinary effect in the recesses of the wood, and many a Compton had nursed a battered countenance as the result of such encounters, for, be it said, the Burton branch of the family was the sturdier and more primeval in its habits. The Comptons were confessedly " quality," while the Burtons were as " common as dirt."

That was in the old days. In these new days, the Burtons regarded themselves as simon-pure county aristocrats, while the Comptons no longer were a significant power in the community. Singular as it may appear, there were now no male Comptons, while the Burtons were fairly alive with masculinity. The male of the Compton species was apparently extinct; the ranks were beginning to be decimated as far back as the early nineties, and at the outset of the twentieth century there remained but one masculine member of the family, and he was venerable, if not venerated.

His wife now survived him with her five daughters. There were aunts and female cousins in abundance, but

no uncles except by marriage. The stock was thin-
ning out. In place of Comptons there grew up an
assortment of Browns, and Coles, and Binghams. On
the other hand, Burtons were multiplying. There
were sons and uncles and nephews without end; visibly
the Burtons were bipeds. The petticoats of the family were acquired by means of the ancient and sacred
rites of matrimony.

And so it came to pass that there were a dozen heads
to the Burton family, and but one for the clan of
Compton: a sharp, autocratic little old lady who had
mothered five daughters and despised herself even
more than she pitied her husband. If she could only
have brought one promoting Compton into the world!
If she could only have had grandchildren named Compton instead of Brown, Bingham, Cole, Stevens and
O'Brien! (The youngest of the five had run away
with and married a farm-hand whose christian name
was Patrick.)

Mrs. Compton reigned alone in the midst of her
acres. As far as the eye could reach in the southwest-
ern part of the county the fields and pastures were
hers. Her sons-in-law, with the exception of Patrick,
went to the city to live to bring up their children.

Patrick did not go to the city. He was still trying
to obtain forgiveness for himself and his wife,— after
five years of unsuccessful effort,— when a horse kicked
him in the pit of the stomach and he died. Mrs. Compton forthwith forgave her daughter.

The Compton homestead,— one might be justified in
saying the Compton headquarters,— was situated at
the top of a long, sloping hill, not more than a quar-

ter of a mile from the southern boundary of the woods.
Visible to the eye for miles from at least three points
of the compass, it was a singularly bleak and cheerless
looking house of a quasi-colonial type: high and
square and flanked by unimposing though practical
wings which rambled off at various angles in the direction of the huge barns, granaries and silos. A Vir-
ginian forefather had built the house long before the
Civil War; each succeeding generation felt called upon
to add something to it, the result being seen in the off-
shooting wings with their shingled roofs, their brisk
chimney tiles and their less severe façades. The old
part of the house was roofed with slate, escalloped in
dual colours. The whole structure was of brick, each
cube carefully outlined by a narrow, geometrically pre-
cise strip of white. The four lofty columns protecting
the porch and gallery that fronted the house were
snowy white and sometimes glistened in the sun.

It was here that the family conclaves were held, and
the Christmas and Thanksgiving dinners, and, not in-
frequently, dances to which young people from town
were brought in bob-sleds or automobiles by the enterprising grandchildren of the mistress of the house.

Sherry Redpath, having traversed the length of
Compton's Woods in his joyous stroll, sat down in the
shade of the most southern oak and gazed passively at
the not distant birthplace of all the Comptons.

A wide macadam highway skirted the lower end of
the woods. By travelling directly westward for four
miles one would come to the homes of the Burtons. The
sons and daughters of this family had stood by the
soil. They were content to remain farmers or farm-

ers' wives. Their homes were modern and substantial, and there were half-a-dozen of them scattered over the family possessions. There was something arrogant, even Teutonic, in the smugness of these carefully placed houses, like so many fortresses guarding exposed territory.

Young Redpath knew but little of the history of the two families. The grave disputes were of another generation; today, the survivors merely sat quiescent in the midst of their belongings and refrained from open conflict. Sherry's interests were of the city, not of the country. A farm was, to him, no more than a succession of fields, populated by cattle, and sheep, and horses, and conducted for the sole purpose of supplying city people with the necessities of life. He knew two or three of the younger Burtons, and, in a remote way, several of the granddaughters of old Mrs. Compton. They were little girls in the grade-schools when he was in the high-school. When he came home from college he found them in long frocks and easily diverted by the attentions of young gentlemen. They were all, at this time, somewhat vague to his memory.

The riches of the old lady on the hill meant nothing to him, for he too had been rich in his day. He did not envy her the possession of all these acres. There was no rancour in his heart. He had no grudge against the well-to-do and prosperous. His only thought of Mrs. Compton as he gazed upon her habitation was one of pity because she was old and her course so nearly run. He pitied her because he was so young and had so much ahead of him to live for.

Suddenly his gaze fell upon a solitary figure that ap-

peared as if by magic in the avenue leading up to the
house on the crest of the hill. It was some time before
he realized that the figure had emerged from the thick
hedge that lined the avenue, evidently employing a short
cut to the big gate at the bottom of the hill. There
was a swiftness in the approach of the pedestrian that
signified more than an ordinary effect of haste, and a
purposefulness in the hunched attitude that soon explained itself in the laboured effort to manage two
heavy suitcases, pendant at the extremities of a pair of
rigid arms. He observed the costume of the person
who struggled so manfully with the two bags and yet
was as far from being manly as any creature he had
ever seen. It was tan coloured, surmounted by a
smart, somewhat rakish panama hat from which flut-
tered the ends of a green veil.

Arriving at the bottom of the lane, the young person
dropped the two bags and, before opening the gate,
stretched her lithe, slender figure in very evident relief
and relaxation after a strenuous, back-breaking quarter of a mile.

Then she opened the long, white gate, and, with positive dismay, took up her double burden again. The
unseen watcher at the edge of the wood was sharply
aware of a suspicion concerning this toiling young
woman. He glanced at his watch, and found that it
was a few minutes after seven o'clock. His conclusion
was instant and startling. The young person in the
tan dress was making way with the Compton family
plate! She was an early bird!

A thrill of excitement swept over him. Here was a
pretty kettle of fish. What was he to do? Stop her

and turn her over to the police or — Just then she
sat down upon a huge boulder at the roadside and
patted her brow with a small white handkerchief. The
bags reposed at her feet. Ah! He knew what was
coming! An accomplice in an automobile would dash
up in a minute or two and whisk her off with the booty,
— And what an uncommonly pretty girl she was, too!
He couldn't recall having seen a prettier one.

From time to time she looked anxiously down the
road, and once or twice sent an apprehensive glance
toward the house at the top of the hill. Her shoulders
sagged a little. He was close enough to see that she
breathed deeply and rapidly as if from exhaustion.

Presently her eyes fell upon him. He was not more
than fifty feet away, and there was unmistakable interest in the gaze with which he favoured her. Her
body stiffened, her breathing seemed to stop altogether.
She appeared to be extremely ill-at-ease, not to say
dismayed.

He found himself wishing that the automobile would
hurry along and relieve her anxiety. It wasn't any of
his business if she got away with the Compton silver
and jewels. He certainly wouldn't interfere. If old
Lady Compton left her plate and jewels lying loose
about the house, she ought to expect to have them
" lifted." In any event, he wouldn't pounce upon a
creature so helpless and so tired and so pretty as this
one, and drag her back to the scene of her crime,— not
for anything in the world. He was not such a brute
as all that. Besides, the old lady probably did not
know how to treat a servant,— especially a pretty one,
— no doubt underpaid and overworked her.

He stared with renewed interest when she nervously pulled down the top of a long glove and glanced at the watch on her wrist. Rather a smart, unusual sort of servant, he thought. The longer he looked, the more he was convinced that she was decidedly unusual, even in these days when it is so difficult to distinguish between mistress and maid unless you know the name of the dressmaker. She had quite an air about her,— quite a definite air.

She was frowning now and tapping the ground impatiently with a small, neatly shod foot. He began to feel ashamed of himself. Certainly it was not very gentlemanly to be lounging across the way and staring her out of countenance. In some embarrassment, he came to his feet and stretched himself with poorly assumed indifference. To his surprise, she also sprang up, and grasped the handles of the heavy bags. She lifted them with an effort, and, without so much as a glance in his direction, started off down the road in the direction of town.

He watched her progress for some minutes, and was not surprised when she set the bags down to rest her weary arms. Really, thought he, she ought not to be carrying those stupendous — Why, she was such a slim, dainty little thing,— and yet how manfully and resolutely she took up her burden again! Once more she was off, the bags banging against her knees, her head bent to the toiling.

He came to an abrupt decision. The confounded automobile wasn't coming after all. Something had gone wrong with her plans. But that was no reason why he, a big, strong lout, should allow her to carry those bags, no matter what they contained. He was not long in overtaking her. The fence was still between him and the road along which she trudged so arduously.

"I beg your pardon," came an eager, masculine voice to her ears. She stopped short and dropped the bags. He distinctly heard her murmur, "Oh, dear me!" and then she faced him defiantly. His hands were on the top rail of the fence, but her manner had a strangely subduing effect on his ardour.

"I am not going back," she began, with decision in her eyes if not in her voice, which suffered sadly from lack of breath.

"Not a bit of it," he exclaimed promptly. "I should say *not*. I don't want you to go back. Allow me to suggest that —"

"Nothing,— nothing in the world will induce me to go back," she went on, her voice gaining strength and a deeper, more natural note. He thought it a very lovely voice. "I don't care who you are, or what you intend to do, I —"

"Please don't be alarmed," he made haste to reassure her. "I'm not a detective. I only want to help you with those bags. You needn't be afraid of me. If you'll let me carry them for you, I'll be as happy as a — well, as anything."

She drew herself up. "Thank you, but I think I can manage them."

"They're awfully heavy," he reminded her. "I'm really an uncommonly strong chap, and if you'd —"

"What are you doing out here in the woods at this hour of the morning?" she demanded sharply.

"Enjoying a constitutional," he explained. "You see, I'm taking a rest cure. May I enquire if it is your intention to walk all the way to town, carrying these bags?"

"Unless I can catch a ride," she replied, melting a little. "I should think some one would be coming along in a car or wagon before — Are you sure you are not employed to watch — I should say, didn't my grandmother ask headquarters to send some one up to —"

"Your grandmother?"

"Yes. Don't you know who I am?"

"I regret to say that I —"

"Well, I'm glad of that," she said, composedly. "Thank you,— and good day."

She stooped to take up the bags again.

"You will not pick up a ride at this time o' day," he declared, noting with satisfaction that she strained a little at the lifting. "Too early, you see, for motorists, and the rubes don't go to town until after they've done a half-day's work. Besides, it's Thursday. Saturday's their day. A quarter-past seven. It's a good three miles to the nearest street-car line, and — by the way, it looks like rain. See those clouds?"

She walked slowly,— very slowly,— her feet set straight ahead but her ear turned toward the tempter. "We need rain badly," she said.

"What have you got in those bags?" he demanded suddenly, a marked change in his voice.

CHAPTER VI

SHE stopped and faced him, but did not relinquish her grip on the handles.

"None of your business," she said, flushing. "Please do not annoy me any —"

"What did you mean by 'headquarters' a moment ago? Why should police headquarters be sending a man out here to watch Mrs. Compton's house? And what are *you* doing out here at this time of the morning? Looks like a getaway to me."

"Getaway? What do you mean?"

"You know what I mean."

She paled slightly. "If you — if you mean that I am — stealing anything from — How dare you!"

"Well, if you haven't anything but your own property in those bags you'll let me carry 'em for you," he expounded.

She surprised him by smiling,— radiantly. "Oh, dear me! It does look as though I was making off with the family plate, doesn't it? How thrilling! And how shocking!"

"Thank heaven, you're innocent!" he cried.

"How do you know I am innocent? I may have the jewels —"

He was climbing over the fence. She stood her ground, unafraid. He looked honest, and a gentleman.

"I am looking for work," he said, stopping in front

of her. "I'm not a tramp, but just a poor wretch who hasn't a penny to his name, no place to sleep except in the woods, and nothing to eat —"

"My goodness!" she broke in, staring hard at his good-looking, eager face. "Why,— why, is it possible that you are the Redpath person that every one is talking about? The wild man of the woods?"

"That's just who I am. Don't run away! I'm not dangerous, you know."

"But — but you are such a terrible — so terribly dissipated. You —"

"Not a bit of it," he cried. "I don't drink a drop. I'm as sober as a judge — 'Gad, a good deal soberer than some of them I happen to know. So you've heard of me, eh?"

"Everybody has," she confessed. "You are as famous as Zip the What-is-it or the Siamese Twins in Barnum's Circus. Now I understand. You haven't a penny. The whole county knows you haven't a penny. You poor thing!"

"No sympathy expected," he said, unoffended. "I'm stony broke and I'm happy." He hesitated a moment. "It just occurred to me that I might start out earning my daily bread by acting as porter for you this morning. I'll carry your bags to the car-line for twenty-five cents. That, I'm sure, will put us on the proper footing. You — you've got twenty-five cents, haven't you?" His expression was one of concern.

"Indeed I have," said she, a dubious shadow in her eyes. "But I have me doubts about you," she went on, affecting an Irish brogue. "It's a subterfuge

you're attempting. Why should you want to carry
my luggage three miles for twenty —"

"I need the money," he said engagingly. "Surely
you will not deny me the opportunity to earn an honest
quarter,— the first penny I've ever attempted to earn,
mind you. You may be the means of starting me off
on a brilliant, successful career. What I need, you
see, is encouragement. I had planned to go down town
today to look for a job. I'm going to —"

"They say you are utterly worthless, that you'll
end up in the gutter or the — Oh, I'm sorry! I
didn't mean to hurt your feelings."

"You couldn't hurt 'em if you tried," he assured her
cheerfully. "Don't look so distressed. Just give me
the job, that's all I ask."

"What will you do with the quarter if I give it to
you?" she demanded. "Buy drink with it?"

"I shall keep it for ever as a lucky coin. Didn't
you hear me say a moment ago that I don't drink?"

"I have as much right to question your integrity as
you have to question mine. You thought I was a
thief."

"Well, supposing you are," said he, "what difference should it make to a fellow who wants to earn a
penny honestly? I don't know who you are, but I do
know that you're in a tremendous hurry to get away
from that house on the hill before any one catches you.
I ask no questions, however. I offer my services at a
price. You couldn't get any one else to carry them for
you for less than a dollar, and there's not much chance
for a lift at this ungodly hour."

"I'll give you fifty cents," she said, after a moment,

with a rueful glance at the bags. "You see, what makes them so heavy is this: I've got all of my toilet silver and photograph frames and — don't laugh! — shoes, and my own private library, and some jars of strawberry preserve,— do you like strawberry preserve? — besides as much of a wardrobe as I could stuff into —"

"Well, we'd better be on our way," he interrupted, with a sharp look up the hill. "Yes, I do like strawberry preserve. Here, let me have those bags. Fifty cents on delivery." He took up the bags. "As light as feathers," he said.

She did not stir. "You ought to know about me before it's too late," she said, nervously. "I don't want to involve you in any —"

"Come along!" he urged impatiently. "Talk as we walk."

She took her place beside him, and together they moved off briskly toward the city. He was surprised to find she was taller than he had at first thought. Indeed, now that she was relieved of the burden that dragged her down, she was quite well above the medium height for women. She was five feet seven or eight and as straight as an arrow.

"You may get into all kinds of trouble, helping me in this way," she went on uneasily. "What with your reputation and my transgressions, we can't hope for much in the shape of amnesty if we are caught red-handed like this, so to speak. You see, I'm running away from home."

He slowed up suddenly. "Running away? You — you don't mean that you are — eloping?"

"How could I be eloping?" she cried. "Who would I be eloping with? Do you see a man anywhere in the vicinity? You can't elope without having some one to elope with, can you? I said I was running away from home."

"Is that your home up there? Old Mrs. Compton's?"

"It has been my home for fifteen years, but it isn't any longer. I'm leaving it for ever. She is my grandmother, you know."

"Oh! I remember you mentioned a grandmother." He looked back over his shoulder. "By George, I believe I'd run away from that place myself if I thought I had to live there for ever. It doesn't look especially cheerful. Why doesn't she set out a few trees around the house? It looks as cold and barren as a Siberian —"

"She had them all cut down when I was a little girl," explained the young lady. "They were black walnut, you see. Do you know what black walnut is?"

"It's wood," he replied.

"It's worth a lot of money in these days. You buy it by the ounce, it's so rare. The walnut that used to grow up there is now trimming the insides of a millionaire's house in Fifth Avenue."

"May I enquire why you are running away from home?"

"Surely. It's because I want to."

"Where are you going?"

"I engaged you to carry my luggage, Mr. Redpath," she said pointedly.

"I beg your pardon." For as many as three minutes, neither spoke. "You have relatives in town, I believe. I suppose you'll go to one of them —"

"I'm running away from them too," she was quick to inform him. Indeed, she was rather glad he did not regard her rebuff as a permanent obstacle to confidences. "I intend to make my own way in the world. Oh, don't look so sceptical. I can do it, never fear."

"Sure you can," said he warmly. "You won't have the least bit of trouble getting married. That's the way most women get along in the world."

"The world is full of competent, capable, independent women who —" she was saying indignantly.

"Are you a suffragette?" he broke in.

"— Who never even think of marrying," she concluded. "It's the men who want to marry, sir. If they didn't, they wouldn't be asking us all the time. Walk a little faster, please. That's better. I am trying to catch the nine-twenty train for Chicago."

"Chicago? It's a wicked city."

"It isn't as wicked as Paris, and I lived there for six years. It's dirtier, that's all."

"You didn't answer my question a while ago. Why are you skipping out like this?"

"I did answer it, but I'll go a little further now. I feel as though I ought to talk to some one about it. I just can't get along with grandmother, if you must know. She is dreadfully set in her ways."

"And you are not, I take it."

She flushed warmly. "At any rate my ways are not stupid and old-fashioned."

"I've always heard Mrs. Compton spoken of as a fine, high-minded old lady," said he.

"She is that!" exclaimed the girl, with decision.
"I'll not have a word spoken against my grandmother.
She is wonderful. But, of course, that doesn't mean
she cannot be wrong once in a while. No one is perfect. Isn't that so?" She seemed to be appealing to
him for support.

"I don't know," said he, non-committally. "Let's
hear your side of the controversy first."

"Meaning that I may be perfect? Well, I'm not.
I'm quite as much at fault as she. No doubt she considers me an ungrateful — yes, Mr. Redpath, she must
look upon me as a snide."

She appeared to fall into moody reflection. Some
time passed before she sighed and resumed her comments. "The whole trouble with grandmother is that
she doesn't realize that I am nearly twenty-one years
old, or, if you care to look at it the other way,
that she is nearly seventy-one. It's quite natural
that we shouldn't see things in the same light, isn't
it?"

"For instance?" said he adroitly.

"Well, for instance," she began, frowning, and then
thought better of the impulse. "Really, you don't
think I'm such a goose as to tell you of my private,
personal affairs, do you?"

"We're on a public highway," he said.

"I haven't asked anything about your affairs, have
I?"

"It isn't necessary. Everybody knows about me.
I'm common property."

"I think, if you don't mind my saying so, that you
deserve a great deal of credit for swearing off drink

and — I do hope you'll stick to your resolution, Mr. Redpath. They say it's very difficult to stop suddenly. Quite dangerous, sometimes, I believe. My uncle, Henry Bingham,— know him? — says that your — that is, a man's system demands —"

"Henry Bingham never took a man-sized drink in his life," said Sherry scornfully. "What does he know about it? Forgive me for speaking disrespectfully of your uncle, but he is the darnedest old sissy in Farragut."

Her eyes sparkled. "Good! I'm glad to hear you say it. I wish grandmother could hear you. That's just what I've been trying to tell her."

He stopped. "Well, if it will assist you in smoothing things over with her, I'll go back with you right now and tell her exactly what I think of her son-in-law. If *that's* all,—" He paused eloquently.

"No," she said thoughtfully, "it would be fatal. She has a very poor opinion of you. You wouldn't be any help, I'm sorry to say. Come, let's be moving along." She looked at her watch. "It's half-past seven. I'm afraid I'll miss my train, Mr. Redpath. Would an extra half-dollar spur you on any? "

"Not at all. If I started in to run with these things, with you tagging along behind, some farmer would have a shot at me with a gun, taking me for a highwayman,— Well, what's the matter now? "

"Didn't you hear the honk of an automobile? Let's stop here and wait. Better to ride than to walk, especially —"

"Maybe it's your grandmother in pursuit. Did you think of that? "

"She will not pursue me," said the girl, with conviction. "I told her last night that I'd be leaving the first thing in the morning, and she said I could do as I pleased about it. You don't know my grandmother. She'll *never* beg me to come back."

"It's a big red car," said he, looking back over the road.

"We'll wait," said she, with relief. "She despises red."

The motor approached rapidly. When it was barely a quarter of a mile away, she started violently, a look of dismay in her lovely eyes.

"Come! I know that car. I wouldn't get into it if my legs were dropping off. That's a Burton car."

"Burton? I never heard of the make. Something new —"

"I mean it belongs to a Burton. Step to one side, quick — The brute wouldn't hesitate to run over me. Don't you know about the Burtons?"

"I know Jimmy Burton, and Aleck —"

"I mean about the Burtons and — us. We're enemies."

"Sure. I remember now. Well, there he goes."

The big red car shot past, throwing a cloud of dust over them. The driver, a dark-faced young man, gave them a look of interest as he passed, and turned later on to favour them with another.

"I hope he looks back again and runs off the road while he's doing it," she said vindictively. "I trust he is no friend of yours, Mr. Redpath," she went on, with an ominous cloud in her eyes.

"Not at all," he assured her. "You forget who I

am. By the way, if I threw off ten cents, would you tell me your name? It seems —"

"You may have it free, for nothing. My name is O'Brien, Morna O'Brien. They called me Mickey at school. Me fayther was Patsy O'Brien." She made delicious use of the brogue. "I am not allowed to be Irish, however. My grandmother hates the Irish. She insists that I'm all Compton, and that's one of the reasons I'm leaving her. My father was the very worst divvel that ever lived, in her estimation. I daresay he was not all that a man should be,— my mother sometimes said as much,— but some of his blood is in my veins and I love a ruction. Whenever I am especially irritating to Grandma Compton she says it's the beastly Irish in me,— and last night I said it was nothing of the kind. I said it was the unspeakable Compton in me. The result was awful. She said she was going to town today to see her lawyer and change her will, cutting me off with a penny. I told her that it wouldn't be necessary to hurry so much as all that, she could do it any time this week. I wouldn't touch a penny of her money even if she died before the will could be changed. She has been bully-ragging me about the Compton money all these years, and I'm tired of it. Money isn't everything, is it, Mr. Redpath?"

She was in a fine state of indignation now. Her dark eyes were snapping and her breast was heaving with something that was not the result of exercise.

"Well," said he judicially, "it isn't so much to a strong, able-bodied man, but I should say it would come in very handy for a frail, inexperienced girl —"

"Do I look frail?" she demanded. "Don't I look

as though I could earn my living anywhere in the world? Thousands of girls —"

" I take it all back," he cried hastily. " I only meant to suggest that — well, that it isn't to be sneezed at, Miss O'Brien. Better think twice before you give up your share of the Compton fortune. Better —"

" I'll carry my bags, if you please, sir," she said loftily. " Here is your half-dollar,— or was it a dollar? I shan't need your services any —"

" See here," he said, stopping abruptly to confront her, a serious note in his voice, and an even more serious expression in his eyes, " are you sure you know what you are doing? Aren't you likely to regret all this? Wait! I'm speaking for your own good, Miss O'Brien. This is a pretty serious step you are taking. It's no use glaring at me like that, either. I'd be a fine sort of a man, wouldn't I, if I let you go on without trying to show you what you've got ahead of you. You have a little row with a nice old lady, fly off the handle, slam a few doors, get madder and madder —"

" That's just what I'm doing now," she cried in exasperation: " getting madder and madder. In the first place, you don't know anything about it, and in the second place you're as fresh as paint. Has anybody asked you for advice? When I want that, I'll write to Laura Jean Libbey or some other newspaper. I —"

" I expect old Mrs. Compton will cry a little in the solitude of her room when she finds you have skipped out. And she'll cry a little every day, too. She'll miss you, and she'll grieve —"

" I wish you wouldn't talk like that," she cried out irritably.

"She has been good to you, hasn't she? Didn't she take you to Paris and educate you and — oh, well, do a whole lot of things for you? Hasn't she made a real bang-up city girl of you instead of bringing you up like a country jake? And hasn't she saved you from being an ordinary little Mick? Answer me —"

"Mr. Redpath! How dare you!"

"Well," said he resignedly, "I'll let up if you're going to get sore about it. Thank the Lord, I've given you something to think about though. I can see the tears back there in your eyes now."

They walked on in silence for many minutes. Finally she turned to him. Her eyes were soft and dark and sweet, and there was a shy smile at the corners of her mouth.

"I'm sorry I spoke as I did to you. You'll forgive me, won't you?"

"I've been thinking for the past five minutes that I ought to ask your forgiveness. I —"

"Well," she said quaintly, "if you'll forgive me I'll forgive you."

"Done!"

"But, mind you, I'm not going back," she declared resolutely. "I'm going to be free, and I'm never going to touch a cent of her money."

"Just as you like," said he magnanimously. "That reminds me. You're starting out in the world on your own. How much capital have you? How much money have you got in your pocket?"

She hesitated. "I guess it's perfectly safe to tell you," she said. "It's broad daylight. I have thirty-seven dollars and fifty cents cash and my Savings Bank pass-book. I have nearly a thousand dollars in the bank. Now are you satisfied? "

He gave a sigh of relief. " Well, that alters things considerably. I sha'n't reproach myself for having helped you to run away. And, by the way," with an uneasy glance overhead, " I'd suggest that we do a bit of actual running. It will be raining in thirty seconds, and unless we can make that bridge ahead there, you'll be drenched to the skin. Come along! "

She had paid but little heed to the darkening skies; her mind was too completely occupied by the enterprise that confronted her. But he had watched the gathering clouds with concern. From afar off he had sighted the concrete culvert that spanned the dry run through which, in the wet spring months, flood waters from the hillside fields rushed down to swell the torrent in Burton's Creek. He saw no other shelter. They would have to scramble down the embankment and establish themselves under the protecting arch of the bridge.

Morna O'Brien outraced him. She was strong, fleet footed and free in her stride.

" Hurry! " she called out over her shoulder, a thrill of exultation in her voice. She plunged recklessly down the side of the road and scuttled like a rabbit into the shelter of the bridge. A second later her bags and her porter came clattering after her,— and then the deluge.

" Gosh! " he gasped, leaning weakly against the concrete wall. " They must be filled with pig-iron! "

CHAPTER VII

NEVER had he known it to rain so hard. The water came straight down in sheets, with a roar that was almost deafening, and so thick was the curtain it produced that Compton's Woods to the left and the yellow wheat-fields to the right were completely obscured. There was thunder and lightning too,— venomous crashes and flashes.

Miss O'Brien shrank against the wall, her hands pressed to her ears. Her eyes were tightly closed. She was panting from the wild dash she had made for shelter.

"It will soon be over," he shouted, his lips close to an obstructing hand.

"What?" she gasped, opening her eyes slightly.

"Just a little thunder shower," he bawled.

"An hour? Oh, dear me, I —"

Gently but firmly he removed the hand nearest him, and repeated his observation, adding: "Lay the dust nicely too. Cool the air off wonderfully."

She stared into the veil of water. "Cats and dogs," she remarked,—" and pitchforks. Goodness, what a torrent! I'm glad we got here ahead of it, aren't you?"

"I never knew before why the county builds concrete culverts," he said, breathing heavily. "Retreats for tramps. Hello, we're going to have a raging river zipping through here if it doesn't let up pretty soon."

The dry bed of the run was already hidden by a rapidly increasing stream of water. He took off his coat and spread it on the base ledge of the abutment.

"Hop up," he said, "you'll get your feet wet if you — that's the way! High and dry." He placed the suit-cases on the ledge and then sat down beside her. Their heels were well above the still puny stream. "We can watch it grow into a regular rivulet," he explained. "I've never seen a rivulet grow, have you?"

"Thank you *so* much for running the way you did with those silly bags," she said irrelevantly. "I never could have managed them myself. Oh, goodness! I'll bet *that* struck somewhere near!" The most appalling crash splintered the air. Even Redpath cringed. "I — Oh, I do hope it didn't strike grandma's house. She's mortally afraid of lightning. Would you mind peeping out to see if — But, how stupid of me. You'd get soaked,— and I can't ask you to do that for fifty cents. Come back! You'll be struck and killed. Oh, dear me!"

He came back, but not before peering intently if fruitlessly down the road. "I beg to report that the house is still standing."

"You're wet. How silly."

"Would the old lady be in a closet or under the bed? What are her habits in time of —"

"I'll thank you not to speak disrespectfully of my grandmother," she broke in, stiffly.

"That's right," he agreed. "I don't seem to know my place. You see, it's my first job."

She was not listening to him. Her brow was furrowed, a troubled light in her eyes. "She always has me come in and get into bed with her when it storms, and in the daytime she closes all the windows and pulls down the shades. I — I wonder what she's doing now. I wonder if she has been calling to me — Oh, dear! Say something cheerful, Mr. Redpath. I don't like to think of the poor old dear creeping out of bed to look for me and —"

"Only to find that you've vanished," he supplied as she paused. He spoke softly, but she heard him.

"Do you really think it will soon be over?" she asked, twisting her fingers nervously.

"No telling," he replied grimly. "That's a fearfully exposed place for a house too." He waited a few moments. "I suppose she'll be terribly worried if she thinks you're wandering about in this storm,— By the way, I hope her heart is good. Old people sometimes go just like that." He snapped his fingers. "Seems awful that she should be all alone up there — But, of course, she isn't alone. Your brother is undoubtedly —"

"I have no brother," she said miserably. "She is all alone. The servants sleep in the west wing,— Oh, I wish I'd waited till this afternoon."

"I'm glad you didn't," said he. "I'd be out of a job if you had, you know. And what's more, I'd probably be out there in the woods with lightning striking the trees on all sides of me. Gee! That was a ripper, wasn't it? That hit something big, sure as you're alive."

She had her hands over her ears again, but her eyes were wide open.

" Poor old granny! She has been awfully good to
me, Mr. Redpath. Awfully. And I was a terrible pest
when I was little. I *was* like my father, I suppose.
Oh, dear, will it never stop? " She turned on him re-
proachfully. " You said it was only a summer shower!
Look at it! Listen to it! No! Don't try to explain.
Any fool can see that it isn't a shower. It's the wrath
of God! It wouldn't have happened if I'd stayed at
home. The sky was as clear as a crystal when I
started out. Then, suddenly, everything got black
and —"

" I think it's beginning to let up a bit," he broke in
soothingly.

" Is it truly? " she cried. " The thunder does seem
to be a little farther away, doesn't it? "

He was silent, thinking hard, trying to decide a very
serious question that had been troubling him for a
quarter of an hour.

Finally she sighed, somewhat contentedly. " Granny
will be perfectly delighted with all this rain. She has
been praying for it for days. All of our harvesting is
done, you see."

" Umph," was his only response. He was staring
thoughtfully at the new little brook.

She gave him a look of annoyance.

" Of course, it's pretty hard on the farmers who
haven't got their wheat cut and — Is there anything
the matter with you? " she demanded querulously.

He had reached a conclusion. The proper course
revealed itself quite plainly and he would follow it up.
It was a part of his strategy to look gloomy and distrait.

" I beg pardon? "

" Do you think you've caught cold? " There was a
small note of concern in her voice. " I have some asperin in my bag,— I don't know which one,— and if
you'll take ten grains —"

" I'm all right, thanks," he said, the sadness deepening in his eyes. He rather liked her for thinking of
the asperin. He knew her kind. She was one of those
gentle-hearted girls who are always trying to " mother " a fellow.

" Cheer up," she cried. " See how light it's getting,
— and the rain is stopping." He was unresponsive.
She studied him for a long time in utter perplexity.
What had come over him? He had been so gay and
— impulsively she laid a little hand on his arm.
" Have I said anything to hurt your feelings? I'm
sorry if —"

" Lord love you, no," he interrupted. " I know it
will make you very angry, but I can't get my thoughts
off that frightened old lady — But there! Never
mind; I'll try to forget her. She's nothing to me, of
course, so why should I care what happens to her?
Still I —" and he fell to brooding again without completing the sentence.

" Oh," she said, and looked away suddenly. Presently she began to beat a soft tattoo with her dangling
heels.

" I know it's silly of me," he resumed, " but I'm such
a soft idiot that I just can't bear the thought of —
well, especially old people being miserable and unhappy,— and afraid. You see, it's so much worse
when old people are afraid of things. Young people

don't matter so much. But old people get to thinking about death and —"

" I wish you wouldn't talk like this," she cried.

" Well, they do, you know," he persisted. " It's only natural. They know they haven't many years left and — Oh, what's the good of getting all worked up like this over nothing? I daresay your grandmother is good for ten or fifteen years more,— and besides she may not have heard the storm at all. Lots of people sleep right through the most horrible —"

" She never does," cried Miss O'Brien unhappily. " And she hasn't been very well lately, either. I — I wish I knew how she —" She broke off to look at him with eyes in which trouble lurked and spoke volumes.

A marvellously pretty girl, thought he.

" Of course," he reflected aloud, " it isn't likely that anything could have happened to her this — Oh, by the way, she was all right when you left, wasn't she? "

She looked startled. " I — I suppose so. I went out the back way, Mr. Redpath. She sleeps till eight."

" Sometimes they never wake up," he began sententiously, " and then, on the other hand," he made haste to qualify, noting the distress in her eyes, " she may not have slept at all last night, worrying over the way she abused you,— her unspeakable cruelty and arrogance, and all that. It wouldn't surprise me in the least to hear that she's had a stroke. Is there any one about the place with sense enough to telephone for the doc —" He broke off suddenly as if dismayed by his lack of consideration for her feelings. " Oh, I'm sorry if I've alarmed you with —"

" She's not a termagent," said Miss O'Brien, paling,

but managing with considerable effectiveness to maintain her dignity. "If I conveyed such an impression, I must correct it at once. Mrs. Compton is not harsh or cruel or overbearing. She is one of the best women in the world."

"Well, I'm sorry to hear that," he said.

"Sorry? And why?" she demanded.

"I wanted to hate her for your sake, but — by George, it's hard to hate her, if she's all you now say she is, left alone up there to grieve and droop and, as I said before, blame herself for having made you so unhappy you couldn't endure the thought of living in the same house with —"

"Mr. Redpath, if you don't stop talking like this," said she, "I shall have to ask you to not speak to me at all. I employed you as a porter and not as a — a what-do-you-call it? — a wet blanket. Goodness knows I'm not happy, running off like this, and to have you,— Why, you positively make me feel like a criminal. I thought you might cheer me up a bit as we went along, but, good heavens, you're the worst gloom I've ever seen."

"We'll talk of something else, then," he said, soberly. "Heaven is my witness, I don't want to think of that poor old lady up there, eating her heart out because — No, sirree, I prefer to think of something cheerful. Naturally, I'm an optimist. I'm never blue or lugubrious. It's nothing to my discredit, however, that I happen to be tender-hearted, and when I come up against a situation like this, I just feel as though I can't resist the impulse to go back there and do what I can to console and comfort —"

"There you go again!" she exclaimed, and her lip trembled.

"Here you are, young and strong, with the world ahead of you, going forth to conquer, and there she is, old and — didn't you say she was not feeling up to the mark lately? — and frail — Yes, yes, it's much better not to think about it, Miss O'Brien. You are quite right. We'll be cheerful. I think the rain has stopped altogether. We'd better be on our way. Nearly eight o'clock. We'll have to sprint some if we are to catch that train."

He heard her sigh as he took up the bags and picked his way along the edge of the little stream toward the opening. The storm was over. The sun was trying to sift its way through the dispersing clouds. The world looked bright and clean and sweet and the air was laden with the scent of wet soil.

He looked back. She was still perched upon the ledge, and her chin was lowered. Subduing a desire to grin all over, he began the laborious ascent of the muddy, slippery embankment.

Some little time passed before she appeared at the bottom of the cut. He went half way down to give her a hand in ascending. Clutching her skirts with one hand, she gave him the other, and was whisked up the bank.

"Wait," she said, as he took up the bags. Her eyes were very dark and wistful as they gazed past him in the direction from which they had come. Then they searched the clearing sky with speculative severity. "I don't believe the storm is over," she said. "See those dreadful clouds?"

He looked. "The tag end of catastrophe," said he, reassuringly. "We're safe enough now, Miss O'Brien."

There was a far-away, faint flicker of lightning in the north, whence the storm had swept.

"See!" she cried triumphantly. "Did you see that terrible flash? It's coming back."

He appeared gravely alarmed. "I hope not. They're always more violent when they come back over a partially devastated territory. Seems as though they want to finish up the job —"

"Mr. Redpath," she began, with decision in her voice, "I have been thinking over what you said a few minutes ago. If you'll carry the bags as far as the gate I'll be ever so much obliged; I will carry them the rest of the way myself."

He could hardly conceal his satisfaction. "You mean you are going back home?" He tried to look incredulous.

"I shall catch the afternoon train," she said, with some asperity. "It leaves Farragut at four o'clock."

"I see," said he. "I think it's a very good idea. Allow me to suggest, however, that I go on to town now with the bags, and deliver them to you at the station. It will save carrying them —"

She faced him squarely. "I may as well confess, Mr. Redpath, that I've changed my mind. I'm not going away. Don't ask questions, please. I sha'n't answer them."

"I don't have to ask 'em," he said readily, "because they're already answered."

They trudged along in silence. He had difficulty in

keeping pace with her. She did not attempt to avoid
the puddles in the road, but forged ahead eagerly, her
eyes fixed on the house at the top of the hill.

" She has been a mother to me," said Miss O'Brien,
after many minutes, addressing her remark to the hori-
zon.

" If we hurry we may get there before she finds out
that you've left," said he, with singular penetration.

" Do you think we could? " she cried, her eyes shining.

" I'll tell you what," said he enthusiastically: " you
run on ahead and let me follow as fast as I can. You
may be able to get in,— the back way,— before
she —"

" How clever you are! I would never have thought
of that. Oh, I'd give my very soul if I could —"

" Well, beat it! " he cried. " Don't worry about
the evidence. I'll hide 'em in the hedge if you think
best. She may never know."

" No," she said, compressing her lips. " I sha'n't
deceive her. I've never deceived her in my life, Mr.
Redpath, and I sha'n't begin now. I'm going to tell
her everything. I *want* her to see the suit-cases and I
want her to see me carrying them home. Maybe she'll
forgive me sooner if she sees me — Do hurry, please!
She has been complaining of a pain in her left side,
and — Look! There's a car coming down our drive.
I — I wonder —"

" It's the chase," said he, thrilled by a new excitement. " And they're coming fast too. I say, did you
leave a note for her? "

" Yes," she said, " I did. I pinned it to my pillow.

Just a good-bye note, telling her — Oh, dear, I wish I hadn't said what I did in that note."

"Snippy?"

"I said I'd never darken her doors again. I — I hope they're not going for the doctor — good heavens, I'm trembling like a —"

"There's a woman in the back seat,— a woman with a black bonnet," he broke in, gazing intently.

"That's Granny!" she cried joyously. "Don't look at me, please!"

An unmistakable sniffle came to his ears. He could control his eyes, but not his ears; nor could he control the twitching sensation that troubled his lips. He was having great difficulty in keeping a smile from expanding into a grin that would have been most offensive if she had caught him at it.

The big automobile had whirled into the highway and was coming toward them at a furious rate. Miss O'Brien began waving her handkerchief frantically.

Sherry deposited the bags at the roadside and wiped his forehead. His whilom employer sped onward, forgetting him completely. Quite well pleased with himself, he up-ended a suit-case and sat down upon it to await developments, overlooking the fact that mud, while not as penetrating as water, is by no means as clean and sparkling.

A hundred feet away the machine came to a stop. Sharp, treble-voiced cries sounded above the purr of the engine. A black-crowned head popped over the side of the car and black arms gathered in the tan-coloured figure that had scrambled onto the running board. Sherry studiously inspected the forest.

Presently a coarse, unlovely masculine voice disturbed his pleasant reflections. Diverting his gaze, he looked with some annoyance upon the individual who shouted. The driver of the car,— a red-faced fellow in his shirt-sleeves,— was beckoning him to approach.

"Hey! Bring them valises here, will you?"

He took up his burden once more and advanced. Miss O'Brien's head was resting on the shoulder of the little old lady, and neither observed his approach.

"Put 'em up here in front, young feller," ordered the driver, eyeing him with unmistakable animosity.

"All right," said Sherry cheerily. He succeeded, with well-managed clumsiness, in putting one of them rather earnestly against the exposed knee of the driver, who said something under his breath, and threw in the clutch viciously. Sherry sprang aside as the car leaped ahead, preparatory to making the complete turn for home. He had the impression a moment later that the fellow was trying to back the machine over him as he stood there, hat in hand, beaming upon the unheeding occupants of the tonneau.

Then the car shot off homeward, leaving him standing with bared head, the smile dying in his eyes long before it disappeared from his lips.

"Well," he mused, as the driver turned in at the distant gate, "my first job wasn't a lucrative one." He fingered the brass check in his pocket. "Anyhow, I'm glad she's happy enough to forget everything else in the world. It was a good day's work, even though I didn't get a cent for it. It was worth fifty dollars just to hear her sniffle."

CHAPTER VIII

HIS sigh was a long one, as of pleasant fatigue. He was far from being vexed. As a matter of fact, it would have been most embarrassing for him when the time came for her to produce the coin that was to settle their account. A fifty cent piece was such a small thing! The more he thought of it, the more relieved he was that she had gone off without paying. He was spared a most unsentimental moment,— and so was she, no doubt. His cogitations, as he climbed the fence and set off briskly through the woods, included pictures of her confusion in passing the coin to the notorious spendthrift, Sheridan Redpath,— and there were other thoughts that bespoke a certain jauntiness in his physical as well as his mental reconstruction.

Deep in the woods he suddenly realized that he was repeating over and over again the melodious, plaintive word "Morna." Morna! What a world of tenderness there was in those two syllables. One couldn't utter them harshly if he tried — and he did try. He drew the first syllable out in a long, soft whisper, and, letting it die away in the second, was conscious of a queer delight in the tunefulness of it. He cut the syllables off then in quick, staccato, business-like jerks and still there was a gentle caress in them. The name was one he had never heard before. Then and there

he decided that if he ever had a daughter he would call
her Morna. Meadow-larks were calling to each other
in the distant wheat-fields. He loved the lilt of the
meadow-lark. Two songs now were running through
his brain,— and both were of the fresh, new morning.
An impulse to be nearer the blithe caroller in the wheat-
fields came over him; an aimless sense of wandering
gave way to definite purpose; he turned and walked
slowly back over the ground just traversed.

Several hundred yards from the highway, he stopped
to cut for himself another walking stick. He was conscious of a sudden sheepishness. The cutting of the
" shoot " from the base of the haw-tree provided an
occupation, ·and, to some extent, a definite reason for
his return to that particular part of the woods. He
recalled, in pleased self-apology, that he had remarked to himself as he passed this very tree earlier in
the morning that never had he seen sprouts so admirably shaped for walking-sticks as these.

He leaned against a tree and vigorously whittled
away on his new cane, stripping the twigs with especial
regard for nobbiness, and with a laudable desire to improve upon the one he had cast aside when he took up
the burdens of Miss Morna O'Brien. Now and then
he directed a somewhat intensified gaze upon the house
of the Widow Compton, plainly visible from a singularly
well-chosen position among the trees. At such times
his knife, fortunately, was idle.

A pensive, far-away look settled in his eyes. How
long it remained there he never knew; having the means
but not the inclination to calculate time, he was content
to dawdle. And, curiously enough, the meadow-larks,

singing louder than ever before, poured their melody upon deaf ears. He was day-dreaming,— an unpardonable offence in a man who sleeps well at night.

Suddenly he started, his eyes lost their dreamy expression, his body its indolent attitude. An automobile stole out of the barnyard gate on the hilltop, and a moment later shot into the hedge-lined avenue; then it came racing down to the main highway.

A delighted grin spread over his face. No spy-glass was needed to tell him who was driving the car at such break-neck speed. There was no other occupant. She came alone and the gay panama hat was missing.

With the perversity of a woman, he deliberately hid himself behind the tree against which he had been leaning, and, from the obscurity of shadow and distance, spied warily upon the actions of Morna O'Brien.

Coming to the highway, she brought the car to an abrupt stop. Then she stood up and peered cityward along the road. He was too far away to make out the expression of her face, but her attitude bespoke intense concern. After a moment, she flopped back into the seat and began to ply the Klaxon horn. Never had he heard a more appalling din than she made for the next two or three minutes. Failing to resurrect him from any comfortable nearby resting-place, she threw in the clutch and drove rapidly toward town, but not before she had indulged in a long and intense scrutiny of the thick woodland.

He laughed aloud in his elation. "She's remembered the fifty cents, bless her heart," he said to himself. "Well, that's all I ask, just that she should remember it and try to do the right thing. Good-bye,

Morna O'Brien! You gave me a little sunshine and a mighty nice job to boot. I may never see you again, so I thank you for the first happy hour I've had in years. I'll never have another just like the one you gave me,— you and your excess baggage. God love you for trying to find me,— and forgive me for hiding!"

Happy once more, and strangely exalted, he fled into the depths of the wood again. Somehow he did not relish the prospect of witnessing her return after the fruitless search for her creditor. Afterwards it occurred to him that he might have spared her many a twinge of conscience if he had stepped forth to collect his wage.

In time he came once more to his " camp." Devastation met his gaze. The rain had played havoc with the paste-board box in the forks of the tree. It was a sorry spectacle. He climbed up and recovered the one object that retained its customary shape: Mrs. Doyle's thermos bottle. Cleansing it in the stream and drying it carefully with his handkerchief, he stuffed it into his pocket, and, after collecting his " laundry " from the mud into which it had been blown by the wind, he set out for town. His cherished luncheon was gone, soaked out of all recognition by the storm, but he was not down-hearted,— not even dismayed. He would earn his next meal, or go hungry, said he to himself as he strode down the slope toward Hooper Street. The time for loafing and rehabilitation was over. His eye was clear, his brain was awake, and his limbs were strong and steady.

The awakening of a long passive gallantry impelled

him to deviate widely from his course to visit a thick clump of wild rose bushes. There he made up a huge bouquet of fresh red roses, and, with these in his hand, sauntered gaily down the street to the home of Officer Barney Doyle, oblivious to the stares and grins of unsentimental passersby.

If Mrs. Doyle, a comely woman of forty-five, was surprised by the delicate tribute of this tall young man she was also immensely pleased. So pleased indeed was she that she aroused Barney from his early morning slumber and ordered him forthwith to appear in the little parlour. Nor was Barney irritated when he came sleepily downstairs, half-clad, to greet the disturber.

Sherry declined their hospitable invitation to partake of a specially prepared breakfast.

"No more hand-outs for me," said he resolutely. "I'm an able-bodied labourer from now on, Mrs. Doyle. I shall work for my breakfast, my dinner and my supper,— and I'll sleep when the good Lord lets me." He gave her his whimsical smile. "You don't happen to have any wood that needs chopping, or a lawn that requires shaving, or —"

"God bless me soul," said Barney Doyle. "Will ye listen to that!"

"And you a college graduate," said his wife, aghast. "The son of Robert Redpath doin' the work of a dago — Why, Mr. Redpath, your poor father would turn completely over in his grave, God rest his soul."

"Well," said Sherry, "I have reason to suspect he has had to do it a good many times, if he has kept tab on the actions of his only son and heir."

Barney's shrewd little eyes were studying him speculatively. "Bedad," said he at last, "ye might do worse than mow a lawn or two."

"For the love of Mike!" exclaimed Mrs. Doyle, witheringly. "Go back to bed."

Her husband ignored the command.

"Hard work hurts no man," said he, "and sometimes it makes a fella forget his troubles, likewise his sins. Come here to the windy. Look! D'ye see that break in the stone wall around Mr. Gilman's garden-patch? The storm washed out the dirt foundation this morning. He was over here before eight o'clock askin' for me wife's brother,— just over from Ireland, — at present an odd-job man, being "— (this he interpolated behind his hand) —" too short a while in the country to get a place on the force,— to see if he could hire him to help in the patchin' up av the wall. The work's too heavy for the old gentleman himself, or he'd be at it this minute. Bedad, he's up there now mixing the mortar,— and him worth a million or more. If ye think —"

Sherry sprang to his feet. "I'll tackle him at once."

"Don't be too much in the sun," cautioned Mrs. Doyle, as their visitor ran down the front steps.

"He will pay two dollars a day," advised Barney. "Me wife's brother went to work for the gas company yesterday or he'd be —"

"Mind you come back here for your dinner, Mr. Redpath," called out the wife. "We have it at half-past twelve."

Mr. Gilman was not favourably impressed with the applicant. On the contrary, he was suspicious,— and quite naturally so. This fellow had none of the ear-

marks of a day-labourer and many of those that identify the confidence man — such as clean linen, well-kept
hands, a platinum watch-chain and silk socks,— to say
nothing of a stout, formidable looking cudgel fashioned
ostensibly for walking purposes but no doubt intended
for the more sinister business of suppressing pedestrian-
ism in other people.

It was not until Officer Doyle walked over and put in
a word for the young man that old Mr. Gilman,—
who was on the point of sending for Barney anyhow,
— consented to give Sherry a trial.

"Understand, young man," he said testily, "I'm
only taking you on trial. This is no soft snap. Have
you a pair of overalls?"

"No, sir," said Sherry. "I never thought of that."

"Well, you'll find something of the sort in the car-
riage house. I knew your father. I also know a whole
lot about you, and it isn't good. You don't get your
pay until the job is finished. I'm not going to have
you sailing off tonight and getting drunk and leaving
me in the lurch tomorrow. Understand that, young
man?"

"I don't drink, Mr. Gilman," said he good-humour-
edly.

"You don't?" exclaimed Mr. Gilman, blinking his
eyes.

"Not a drop, sir. Ask Barney."

"Not a drop, sir," repeated Barney Doyle, without
being asked.

"Then all these stories I've heard about Bob Redpath's son going to the devil are —" Mr. Gilman hesitated.

"Damn lies," said Officer Doyle. "He's simply goin' to work, sir."

"For my bread and butter," added Sherry, truthfully. "Nothing altruistic about it at all, Mr. Gilman."

"Not a bit av it," vouchsafed Barney Doyle, unstaggered.

All the rest of that broiling day the young man laboured cheerfully, lifting and setting the heavy boulders in the mortar laid down by his indefatigable employer. When the time came to knock off for the day he was so tired he could hardly straighten his broad back. His arms and shoulders ached and his hands were so sore that he winced when he tried to close them; they were sadly scratched and bleeding.

Contrary to his announcement, Mr. Gilman paid him for the day's work. Although he had worked but little more than half the day, the old gentleman gave him a crisp two-dollar bill.

"I can't change it, Mr. Gilman," said Sherry, flushing.

"Never mind," said his employer. "We'll call it an honest day's work. The first you've ever done, I take it."

"Yes, sir," replied the young man frankly, "the very first. And I am much obliged to you. I'll be here at eight in the morning."

He slept in Compton's Woods that night, and the next, so dog-tired that he missed the usual serenade of the frogs and katydids. He had his meals at Barney Doyle's, insisting on paying for them in advance, much to the disgust of Barney's wife, in whose warm Celtic heart lingered the thrill that his bouquet of roses had produced. She would take no more than a quarter for each meal. He did not make the mistake of bringing roses to her on the succeeding mornings; nothing so banal as that entered his head; she was not to feel that the delicate attention could be made cheap by repetition.

Toward the close of the third day the last stones were being set in place; the repairs to the wall neared completion, and he would soon be out of a job. In some pride he stood off with old Mr. Gilman and surveyed the reconstructed wall. There still remained the task of filling in with dirt and gravel the gap behind the wall. That would require shovelling from the big pile of earth that had been dumped at the edge of the hole earlier in the day by a teamster, and a certain amount of tamping.

"Pretty good job, young man," said Mr. Gilman, eyeing the work critically and not without pride.

"Ripping," said Sherry, wiping his brow with his bare forearm. "The Egyptians couldn't have done better."

The old gentleman looked at his watch. "It is now half-past three. I don't believe you can move all that dirt by five o'clock. Could you finish the job by seven?"

"I could," said Sherry promptly. "Don't you worry about it, Mr. Gilman. You're tired. Go up to the house, sir, and leave all this to me. I don't belong to a union. I have no regular hours."

Right cheerfully he shovelled and as cheerfully he tamped. Automobiles passed by in Hooper Street, un-

seen and unheard by the one-time owner of high-speed
runabouts and racers. He had no time to think of automobiles — but, yes, he did think occasionally of a
big touring car with a hatless girl at the wheel.

Indeed he was thinking of that very combination
when the violent shrieking of a Klaxon horn caused
him to whirl suddenly as if to leap out of danger, so
close at hand was the machine. Not thirty feet away,
standing perfectly still in the street, was a big green
touring car. The girl at the wheel was not hatless
now, nor was she alone. A little old lady in black sat
beside her, speechless but eloquent.

" Come here! " called the young lady peremptorially.

" My dear," said the old lady, visibly annoyed.

" I can't," said the young man, grinning with delight. " My boss is watching." Nevertheless, he
hopped over the wall and did as she commanded.

" You went away without waiting for your pay,"
said Miss O'Brien severely, when he stood before
her.

" I went away? " with emphasis on the pronoun.

" Morna, is this the young man who —"

" This, Grandma, is the wild gentleman of the woods.
I owe him fifty cents — or is it seventy-five? "

Mrs. Compton's sharp little face lighted up. " And
I owe him a great deal more than that," she said.
" You transformed a vile, stubborn, unreasonable
hussy into a meek and sensible darling, sir, and sent
her home —"

" Now, Granny, we'll quarrel again if you are not
careful. And the next time I won't blubber and run
home as I did the last time."

Mrs. Compton was appraising the young man with her shrewd grey eyes. "So you are the much-talked of Sheridan Redpath. If I were a bright, precocious child I might be excused for saying that you don't look at all like an example. You —"

"We are keeping Mr. Redpath from his work, Granny," broke in Miss O'Brien curtly.

For three days she had been displeased with herself for having forgotten to pay the labourer his hire, and at the same time irritated with him for not presenting himself with a demand for the money. His aloofness indicated something more than resignation on his part: it savoured unpleasantly of disdain — and by no process of argumentation could she convince herself that it was the money he disdained. She was humiliated. She did not like being humiliated.

"You may keep the change." With a loftiness that should have shrivelled him, she thrust a silver dollar into his hand,— or, strictly speaking, *at* his hand, for it was not extended.

But he did not shrivel. Instead, he expanded. "Thanks. I think I can make change today. Fifty cents, Miss O'Brien. Here's your —"

"Keep it," she said, compressing her lips. "Don't you always expect a tip?"

He was not offended. "Tip? And what is a tip, if I may ask?"

She bit her lip. "It happens to be fifty cents in this instance. Oh, take it," she cried in exasperation.

For answer he placed his own half-dollar carefully on the spare tire, and addressed himself to Mrs. Compton, affecting grave solicitude. "I trust Miss O'Brien

is a careful driver. Otherwise it may be jostled off
and lost for ever."

Mrs. Compton permitted a faint smile to steal into
her eyes. " Offering a tip to you, Mr. Redpath, is
like carrying coals to Newcastle, I should say. You,
I am told, are the source from which more blessings
in the shape of tips have sprung than —"

" Granny, dear," interrupted Miss O'Brien firmly,
" we did not stop to pay compliments but to pay wages.
Good day, Mr. Redpath. I am sorry to have been so
long in paying you — in paying —"

" I'll crank it, Miss O'Brien," said he, obligingly.
" This year's models have a self-starting contraption
that — Don't get out! I'll do it."

He had cranked a great many cars in his day, but
never had he encountered one so unresponsive as this
one. He jerked and pulled and hauled until he
thought his neck would burst.

" Let me do it," said a calm voice at his side. He
turned, red-faced and exasperated, to look into her
tantalizing blue eyes. She actually elbowed him aside,
and gripped the crank with her little gauntleted hand.
A quick jerk or two and — the engine was throbbing!

" Simple twist of the wrist," she said sweetly, and
went back to the wheel.

" I see," said he, jumping to one side to avoid being
run down. " It's a trained car. Performs only for
its tamer."

" Thank you just the same, and — good-bye."

The car leaped forward so suddenly that Mrs. Compton clutched her bonnet and suspended utterance.
She too had started to say " good-bye."

He went back to his shovelling, and did not whistle his merry tune. A perplexed frown appeared on his brow. From time to time he shook his head and sighed. He couldn't, for the life of him, solve the problem. She was inexplicable.

"Treated me like a dog," he mused. "Quit your dreaming, old boy. You're awake now. She hasn't any more use for you than —" A tender light came into his eyes and he rested on his shovel to look up the street in the wake of the vanished car. "But you've got the gentlest, softest, prettiest name in the world, I'll say that for you," he pronounced, by way of contrast.

CHAPTER IX

A SURPRISING thing happened when he reported to Mr. Gilman a few minutes before seven o'clock. He was invited to supper.

"I'd like to have a good, sound talk with you, young man," said his late employer. Noting the younger man's change of expression, subtle though it was, he added, with a sly twinkle in his eye: "I promise not to lecture or advise you, or anything like that, so you need not be alarmed. Mrs. Gilman hasn't been downstairs to a meal in seven years. I like a bit of companionship once in a while, my lad, and somehow, of late, I've taken a fancy for the company of the young and strong. I hope you'll stay. It is barely possible that I may not bore you, even though two whole generations separate us."

"I'll be happy to stay, sir, if you'll allow me the time to run over and tell Mrs. Doyle not to expect me."

"That's one thing I admire in you," said the older man. "Your consideration for others. Supper will be ready at half-past seven. Bring your appetite."

"No fear. My appetite will bring me."

After supper the two men,— one old and gaunt and crusty, the other young and vibrant,— sat on the broad veranda and smoked. Redpath, still a little dazed and bewildered by the unexpected affability of his host, was further surprised by the excellence of the cigar he held in his fingers. All his life he had heard

Mr. Gilman spoken of as a skinflint and miser. He was looked upon as the stingiest man in town,— and nothing worse than that could be said of any individual, for Farragut, according to Sherry's estimate, was full of stingy people. And here he was now, smoking his second thirty-cent Corona-Corona, taken from a box that was passed to him without the slightest indication of reserve or reluctance. Their supper had been excellent. At the home of any one of the social leaders in town it would have been regarded as a " bang-up " dinner. Mr. Gilman, however, apologized for it. He lived very simply, he said.

During their association as wall-builders, Sherry had found the old man silent and unapproachable. He seldom spoke. When he did it was to give a terse order, or, on occasion, to express criticism. His helper soon came to regard him as a sour, grumpy old party, and abandoned all efforts to be agreeable. The invitation to supper came as a distinct surprise, and but for the strange wistfulness in the old man's eyes would have been declined. As it was, he accepted because he had no ready excuse for declining, and now he was glad that he had done so.

Andrew Gilman,— he was known over town as Andy Gee,— exposed an amazing side to his character, hitherto unsuspected by the young man. He was chatty, agreeable, and at times witty. Before Sherry had been in the house ten minutes he found himself absurdly free from the constraint so natural in the young and well-bred when in the presence of their seniors. Convinced at the outset that he would be bored and uncomfortable and eager for the hour of departure to come, he had entered the house with misgivings, and, to a certain extent, prepared for unpleasant though no doubt well-meant references to his own past and future.

But Mr. Gilman talked of himself and not of his guest. More than that, he talked unreservedly and with a twinkle in his sharp little eyes. The truths he uttered had to do with the successful career of Andrew Gilman and not the unsuccessful career of Sheridan Redpath.

With the rest of the population of Farragut, young Redpath had looked upon Andy Gee as a soulless, hard-fisted money-grabber in whom neither charity nor humour had an abiding place. As a small boy he had stood in actual awe of the old man. In common with his kind and generation, he had made faces at the miser from behind fences and other redoubts; he had hurled derisive but humorous shouts after him as he passed along the street, and had scooted for dear life when the object of scorn turned a mephitic eye upon him.

And here he was now, sitting in the ogre's house, enjoying himself! That he should be there laughing at the quaint remarks of Andrew Gilman was almost beyond comprehension. Why, the man was no ogre at all! He was a kindly, unctious old chap that you couldn't help liking.

Sherry knew little about books, saving the lightest sort of fiction,— (you might say daily fiction),— but he was not so ignorant that he failed to grasp the significance and importance of the library in which he had his coffee with Mr. Gilman. There were thousands of volumes in the great cases that lined the room from floor to ceiling, and it was not necessary for him to be

told that his host admitted no light fiction to those exalted shelves. There were etchings and engravings in
the hall and living-room; an atmosphere of quiet ele-
gance, of rare good taste, pervaded the house. He
found himself wondering what sort of woman Mrs. Gilman must have been in her day to have wrung all this
splendour out of the soul of a miser. Later on he was
to know that the old man himself was responsible for
everything.

"Few people, aside from the tax collectors, know
that this library exists," said Mr. Gilman, as they left
the room to seek the coolness of the porch. "We
rarely have visitors here. The doctor sits with me here
once in a while, and occasionally the minister comes up
to see me,—although I am beginning to fear that he no
longer considers it worth his while. I give a certain
amount to the church each year, and so much extra
for home missions. The fund for the construction of
the proposed new church lacks my contribution. The
old church is quite good enough for me. It is large
enough for its congregation and it still resembles a
place of worship, which is more than can be said for
some of them. But, as I was saying, our visitors are
few and their visits far between. I suppose you are
aware of the fact, young man, that I am a very cordially despised person. Have you ever heard a good
word said for me?" He put the question with a smile.
There was no bitterness in his voice.

"Yes," admitted Sherry; "I've heard it said that
you are a splendid judge of real estate." He spoke
lightly and without fear, and the old gentleman
chuckled,— just as he was expected to do.

"Well, that's something," he said, drily.

"And you are good pay," added Sherry.

The old man stared out over the shrubbery on the lawn. An electric lamp, suspended in the street below, seemed to afford attraction for his gaze. Presently he spoke.

"I can count on one hand all the friends I have in this city, Redpath. A few years ago it would have been necessary to employ the digits of both hands, but even good friends can't go on living for ever, you know. You may think that I am a lonely as well as a despised old man. I am seldom lonely, for I am always busy. A busy man is never lonely, remember that always, my young friend. Five years ago I retired from active business, but that does not mean that I retired from active life. I want to live to be a very old man. That may be accomplished only by keeping mind and body active. Don't give the mind a chance to grow dull with introspection, and don't let the body go to seed. I lost my only son a good many years ago. He never could see any sense in my getting down to business at seven o'clock in the morning, usually ahead of any of my employés. I always walked to and from the store. People said I was stingy. I claim that I was merely sensible. Nowadays I ride about in an automobile, and I drive my own span of thoroughbreds. I do the one because I must keep up with the procession, the other because I can afford to stay behind it and enjoy myself if I prefer."

"That's the right way to live," said Sherry. "I guess I kept pretty well ahead of the procession," he added ruefully. "I too, sir, have retired from active business. My business was to get rid of money, while yours was to acquire it. That's just the difference between us, Mr. Gilman."

"You are mistaken. The difference between us is, I should say, a matter of fifty years. With me it is what I *have* done, with you it is what you are still to do. I am through. You are just beginning. When I was twenty-five I did not have more than ten dollars to my name. How old are you? Twenty-seven? And you have six dollars in your pocket,—"

"Four and a quarter," corrected Sherry. "I paid my board bill at Barney's."

"Well, you have the youth and the stamina that I once enjoyed and you know more about money than I've known in all my years. I should say that you have a decided advantage over me as I was at twenty-seven. You are not lazy. A lazy man couldn't have gone through with all the money you possessed in so short a time without working pretty hard to do it. But I promised not to talk of your affairs,— at least, not of the past. I should like, however, to discuss the future with you. What are your plans, my lad?"

"I have no definite plan, Mr. Gilman," said Sherry. "I shall work until something better turns up," he added quaintly.

"Have you — er — a position in prospect?"

"No, sir. I like the idea of earning money, however. Next month I shall look for a permanent job."

"Next month? Do you expect to subsist for a month on the four dollars and a quarter?"

"I shall do odd jobs for the next couple of weeks," said the young man, serious despite his words. "I

have thought the whole thing out, sir. The three days
I spent with you on that wall convinced me that I am
not yet in a condition to settle down to steady employment. Young as I am and strong, I don't mind confessing to you that there were times when I thought
I'd keel over from weakness. The only thing that kept
me going was your example. I couldn't give up as
long as you were going strong, you see. So I stuck
it out. I need a few weeks of hard work in the open air
to put me in any sort of form. If I can earn no more
than my daily bread, I'll be doing myself a good turn.
You see, sir, I have lived a rather abnormal life. I
owe it to my regular employer,— if I get one,— to be
normal in every particular. So I intend to split rails
or break stones or — well, you see what I mean, don't
you? "

Mr. Gilman, watching him through half-closed eyes,
nodded his head slowly. " Replenish the fires, eh? I
see. It seems a pity that so fine a specimen of young
manhood as you appear to be should have abused —
ah, well, we'll say no more about it." He was thoughtful for a few moments. Redpath's meditations appeared to be centred in the coils of smoke he was blowing into the soft, still air. The old man cleared his
throat. " We've had a very agreeable evening —
don't get up, please. I don't mean that it is over and
time for you to leave, my boy. What I meant to con-
vey is that we have been rather good company for each
other. You haven't found me as terrifying or as ugly
as you thought. In fact, you are disappointed in me.
Permit me to observe that I have been studying you for
a couple of days. You are not bad, you are not even

half-bad, despite your evil reputation. Your eye is clear and straight, and your right hand appears to know what the left is doing. This brings me to the point. How would you like to enter my employ?"

Sherry started. "Are you in earnest, Mr. Gilman?"

"Certainly. I rarely jest."

"But I understood you to say you have retired from active business, sir."

"Quite so. I sold out my business five years ago. The wholesale grocery concern of Andrew Gilman & Co. exists only on the letter-heads of the house; there is no Andrew Gilman in the business. I not only sold out the stock and good will, but my name as well. That, I submit without conceit, is an asset, no matter how bitterly hated I may have been."

"You have taken me by surprise, sir. I — I don't know just what to say."

"Well, if I were in your place, I'd ask what sort of employment is intended,— whether it is nefarious or honourable, in fact,— and I'd discuss the question of hours, wages and the prospects of advancement," suggested Andy Gee, smiling.

"The prospect of advancement is the only thing I should care to discuss at present. Hours and wages are adjustable, you might say. I don't want to take steady employment unless I see a chance to go ahead. What would be required of me, Mr. Gilman?"

The old gentleman hesitated. When he spoke it was in lowered tones.

"Ostensibly you would be my secretary and agent. You would collect the rents from my tenants, and —

Well, there is a good deal more that I could find for you to do. You —"

" But, I have had no experience, sir. How could you entrust important matters to —"

" You profess to be honest, don't you? "

" Certainly."

" No one has ever intimated that you are crooked; your worst enemy would call you no more than a fool."

" My best friends call me that, sir."

" And with reason," said Andy Gee. " On the other hand, no one has ever called me a fool. They have called me a great many other things, but they have spared me that. I would be a fool, however, to employ you in any capacity,— save as a day labourer,— if I were not thoroughly satisfied that you are the man for the place. You are honest, sober,— I believe you will remain so, too,— dead broke, and you have seen better — or worse days, take them as you will. Above all other recommendations, you are strong of body and quick of mind. I require the services of a brave, lusty young fellow, who could have no other object than to be loyal to my interests."

" Meaning," said Sherry boldly, " that the collecting of rents is a job for the strong and courageous."

" Not necessarily," said Andy Gee, frowning. " I collect them with reasonable thoroughness."

" So I have heard." There was a hard light in the young man's eyes.

" No doubt," said the other quietly.

" I have also heard, Mr. Gilman, that certain of your tenants in the lower part of town have threatened your life. You have had several men put under bond to keep the peace, if I remember correctly.   I suppose it would be my duty to collect the rents down there; and if they didn't pay promptly to use my highly spoken-of strength to throw them out in the street."

" Not at all.   I shall continue to collect the rents of those people in person.   They are afraid of me, old as I am, and they would never be afraid of you as a rent collector."

" Is it true that last January you evicted a family in Endsley Street, and that the wife and little daughter froze to death? "

" No," said Mr. Gilman.   " You have the right to ask the question, however, and I am not offended. Jim Moore was not evicted.   He claims that he was, but only to save his own face.   The truth about that case is this: he had been drinking hard and as he is a brute when sober you may well imagine what he is when intoxicated.   He threw his wife and children into the street, hurled the furniture into the alley, and — well, I was blamed for all of that, my boy.   As a matter of fact, his wife had paid the rent.   She took in washing. He resented her paying me when he had other uses for the money she had earned.   She did freeze to death, and the little girl too.   He declared that I had put them out of the house.   People said some unkind things about me, you may remember.   I own twenty-two small houses in that part of town.   Not one of my tenants has a good word to say for me.   They hate me because I am their landlord.   Some of them have threatened my life.   Will you be good enough to explain why these able-bodied men should not pay their rent? They all have jobs, and are well-paid as things. go.

Most of them work in the railroad yards and round-house. In the past year ten families have moved out of my cottages down there, and all of them have said they were evicted. They are now living in other houses and they will move out of them, just as they did out of mine, and they will never have paid a cent of rent during their occupancy. I did not put them out. They went of their own accord, owing me the rent from the day they moved in. They belong to the class that never pays. And yet, the whole lower end of town heaped maledictions upon me when these people moved their pitiable belongings out of my houses and sought other landlords. The neighbours said: 'Old Andy Gee is at it again, curse him for a dog.' You must not be deceived into the belief that these vagabonds are the ones who threaten my life, nor that anything serious will result from the blusterings of drunken Jim Moore. They will not harm me. It is not a part of their scheme of existence. But there are others, my boy,—and they are to be feared."

"You mean, sir, that you actually fear that some one will try to — get you?" He leaned forward in his chair and peered through the darkness at the face of his companion. A deep, solemn note in the older man's voice sent a sort of chill through his veins. He suddenly regretted the harshness of an earlier remark.

"I cannot discuss the matter until I know that you are willing to accept the position I am prepared to offer."

"And I am not willing to accept until I know what is in the wind, sir."

"I will be quite frank with you. I want you to act, after a fashion, as a personal body-guard."

"Body-guard?" gasped Sherry, startled.

"After a fashion, I remarked. Ostensibly as my secretary. Don't misunderstand me. You will have secretarial duties that will keep you fairly busy. I am too old to attend to all of the private business that accumulates from day to day. Such of it as I care to trust to the hands of another you would be required to look after,— and no more. My lawyers are quite capable, I believe, of handling the more important matters." He was now speaking in a slightly satirical manner. "I may add that I feel myself still capable of handling my lawyers. You suggested a while ago that you would take no regular employment that did not offer an opportunity for advancement. Well, I cannot promise you that. I can only say that your salary will be a liberal one to begin with, and that I shall increase it as your value expands."

"Well, I'm still considerably in the dark, Mr. Gilman."

"I want simply to engage your strength, your youth, your loyalty, and not especially your ambition. I want to have near me all the time a young man who can't be bought. Do you understand? Who can't be bought. You are unique in your way, my lad. Money does not mean as much to you as it does to the average man. You have had it, and you have thrown it away. You are starting out to acquire fortune and honour, after having had both of them in your brief career. Your money is gone; your honour remains. You have no greed in your soul. You have enjoyed affluence, and, having done so, are singularly well fortified against the evils that often inspire him who yearns for it and the power it gives. I could hire a robust, husky truck-driver who would serve admirably as a so-called body-guard, but he would never be more than that, and he would afford me no mental relaxation or security. You have mentality, spirit, education and good-breed-ing. Your companionship will mean a great deal to me. I am seventy-seven years of age. My time may be short. I have thought of a way to make this job attractive to you, a sort of gambling chance. Every year for the first three years your salary would be in-creased one hundred per cent. Your first year it would be twenty-four hundred dollars. Your living would cost you nothing for your home would be with me. The second year you will have forty-eight hundred dol-lars, the third ninety-six hundred. After that the in-crease will be but ten per cent. annually. Assuming that I live ten years longer, a little computation will prove to you that you would be getting a rather hand-some salary when you are thirty-seven. You would be drawing a salary of — er — something over eight-een thousand a year, besides the income from the in-vestments of previous years. Not to be sneezed at, eh? Don't look so startled. I am not insane, nor am I at present afflicted with paresis or softening of the brain," said the old man, smiling.

"Just the same, it's a crazy idea," cried Sherry.

"Not at all. I may die inside of two years, or even less. I am not likely to live more than ten, you will agree."

"And what will happen to me if you live ten years

longer and your heirs discover that you have been paying me as high as eighteen thousand dollars a year as
secretary and — Why, they'd put me in jail for life.
It couldn't be explained. Undue influence, they'd call
it, and what could I say in —"

"Quite a reasonable conjecture. That's what I
like about you. You think. You reason. But all of
that can be avoided if we enter into a bona-fide contract, with all the terms set forth. For example: I,
Andrew Gilman, being of sound mind, and so forth, do
hereby agree, and so forth, to pay Sheridan Redpath
a certain salary, plainly stipulated,— and so forth,—
in return for which said Redpath agrees to perform
certain services for me. No one can go behind that,
you know. I have known you for three days, and no
one can say that you have unduly influenced me in so
short a time. Moreover, the proposition is mine, not
yours. I think you need have no fear of consequences."

"Sign a contract, eh? That would mean that I'd
have to stick to you to the end, whether I wanted to do
so or not."

"You may end the agreement by giving me a year's
notice. That would be fair to you and fair to me. I
should reserve the same privilege."

"Supposing I wanted to get married and have a
home of my own. Such things happen to the young
and strong, you know."

"Your marriage would immediately cancel the contract," said Mr. Gilman promptly. "I would even
prefer to have you refrain from falling in love, but I
daresay neither you nor I can regulate that."

"I may be permitted to fall in love, eh?" said Sherry musingly.

Mr. Gilman started. "You are not already in love, I hope."

"No," said the other, and sighed. "Not a bit of it."

"Then you may contrive to stay out of it," suggested the other hopefully.

Sherry fingered the sequestered silver dollar in his left hand pocket, and smiled tenderly. "I think I'd like it, however," he said.

"Well, you mustn't," snapped the old man. "There is nothing on earth so useless, so valueless as a young man in love. He isn't worth his salt. I know, because I've had dozens of them in my employ. Their minds were on a perpetual vacation,— and drawing full pay all the time."

"But the minds of the married men must have made up the shortage. They never get a vacation."

"We're talking nonsense now. Let us go back to the text. Does my proposition appeal to you?"

"It interests me," said Sherry coolly. "The question of wages being settled, how about the hours? Is it to be a twenty-four hour job, like a nurse's, or do I work in shifts?"

"Virtually a twenty-four hour job, for you will sleep in a room connected with my own."

"Any vacations? Physical, I mean."

"No. Your days will not be irksome, however. You may have considerable freedom when it comes to the hours between seven A. M. and seven P. M., except when winter shortens the days. Your nights must be spent in this house, except when I see fit to grant a brief leave of absence."

"The question of hours appears to be settled," said Sherry, sighing again. "Everything seems clear now except the principal feature of my job, if I take it. Who or what is it that I am to guard you against?"

"It is not necessary that you should know," said the old man, a queer hoarseness in his voice. "The only requirement I shall impose upon you, aside from your duties as my secretary, is that you be near at hand and ready at all hours of the night. Your integrity will not be violated, your work will be honest. More than that, it is not necessary for me to speak."

Redpath drew a deep breath and was silent for a long time. The situation was extremely interesting. His curiosity was aroused. What did it all mean? What was behind that grim old man's proposal? What was ahead of him if he accepted the place? The thrill that goes with the mysterious and unexplained crept into his blood. Why shouldn't he take the job? There certainly was something dark and sinister behind it all, else this sound, intelligent old man would not be seeking a protector,— and all the more sinister would it appear to be in view of his determination to keep the prospective guardian absolutely in the dark concerning the object of his fears. It was most uncanny: guarding a person against the unknown!

"Give me a day or two to think it over, Mr. Gilman," said he at last, and there was a quiver of excitement in his voice.

"Very well. Give me your answer on Saturday. I

need not remind you that all this is in strict confidence. I trust to your honour and discretion."

" Not a word, sir, to any one.   Before I can consent to take the place, sir, I shall have to ask two questions which must be answered."

" Ask them now, my boy."

" Is your life in peril? "

" I don't know.   That is why I feel the need of a body-guard.   If I knew, I would not need you."

" I see.   Now for the other one.   Would I be called upon to take the life of some one else in order to preserve yours? "

There was a long silence.

" No," said Andy Gee; " you wouldn't."

CHAPTER X

MORNA O'BRIEN was lonely.

This simple, presignifying condition, and nothing else, was responsible for her amazing and ill-considered flight on a recent early morning. There was no getting around the fact: she was lonely to the point of desperation. She longed for the broad companionship of strife, the blandishments of adventure, the joys of uncertainty. Anything was better than the placid, uneventful existence she led amidst the rural comforts of a home in which the days were all alike and the nights even worse. The only breaks in the monotony of life as it moved in the ancestral abode of the Comptons came with the regular if somewhat perfunctory Sunday visits of uncles and aunts and cousins from the city. She did not know which she despised the most: the visits or the visitors.

Thinking it over, in solitary depression, she decided that it ought to be the visitors, since they alone were the cause of the visits.

Her girl cousins were snippy, bazaar-loving creatures, and her boy cousins were singularly unfunny despite an enterprising determination to be otherwise at all times and on all occasions. All of them were conscious of a certain superiority over Morna, notwithstanding her envied residence in Paris, a year in New York, and the knowledge that she was the favourite of a common grandmother. They could not permit them-

selves to overlook the fact that her father had been an
Irish farm-hand, and that her mother had married far
beneath her station. It rather hurt their pride to
have a cousin named O'Brien. They also were annoyed
by the occasional trips she made to Chicago with her
grandmother.

Moreover, it was distinctly irritating to the girls to
hear their young men friends exclaim: "That cousin
of yours is the prettiest girl I've ever seen."

A hum-drum life was not the life for Morna. She
was devoted to her grandmother, and she was loyal, but
down in her gay, warm heart dwelt the yearning for the
things that belong to the young. She longed to be out
in the world with the inhabitants thereof, and not to be
mooning her youth away in the solitudes. She had
tasted the sweets of life and she liked them. They
were to be found among the multitudes and not in the
pastoral sanctity of a good home!

Thousands of girls make their own way in the world,
and get a good deal out of life. Why shouldn't she
do the same? Thousands of girls forsake the comforts
of good homes and fare forth into a world of stern ex-
actions, there to bloom in full view of all observers.
Morna did not want to bloom unseen. True, she worshipped the comforts of life; there were times when she
doubted her ability to get along without them, as con-
ceivably she might have to do if she undertook to make
her own way in the world. Sometimes she shuddered
over the possibility of privations, but never did it occur to her to be troubled by doubts concerning the
morality of the world into which her young beauty
was to venture unattended.

She was seven years old when Mrs. Compton made
her first and only trip across the Atlantic.   The child's
father had been dead two years.   While every one else
seemed to consider his widow a very lucky person in
being so satisfactorily bereaved, the lady herself was
not able to reason along the same lines.   She had
loved her good-looking, light-hearted Irishman, and he
had loved her.   Relatives, near and remote, were
agreed that it ought to be a tremendous relief, and told
her so in what they considered a very warm and sympathetic manner.   Certainly, they argued, it was not
an affliction to be restored to the family fireside after
five years of poverty and Catholicism.   God, they said,
had snatched her from the Roman Catholic church, and
they could not understand why she refused to thank
Him for the profound benefaction!   She could now
come back into the church of her forebears and —

But one day she turned on them with eyes that blazed
and a voice that trembled with fury.

" I am a Catholic and I shall remain one as long as
I live — and afterward, too.   I loved my husband and
I love his church.   I shall strive to bring my little girl
up to be a good Catholic.   If she chooses to forsake our
church when she is older, I shall not oppose her.   She
has as much right to be a Protestant as I had up to the
time I was married, and, if she sees fit, she may again
become one of you, for she has the divine right to
change her mind.   She may,"— and here she smiled in
a way they did not like, because they could not com-
prehend —" she may even marry a good Protestant.
There are such things, you know."

Only Mrs. Compton spoke in reply to this.   That

shrewd, far-seeing lady held up her hand, checking the angry retort of an outraged son-in-law.

" Just because Patrick O'Brien had cause to believe there are no good Protestants," she said, " is no reason why his child should grow up believing the same. Let us try to convince her as we go along that there *are* good Protestants. I don't believe in arguing politics oɪ religion. We cannot get into heaven any easier by arguing, but we sometimes get there a little bit quicker, depending on the temper of the person whose religion we abuse. I daresay we shall meet a number of Catholics in heaven, and they will probably be as dumbfounded to see us there as we are to see them. Let the mother alone, I say, and let the child alone. They still belong to Patsy O'Brien, dead though he may be, and we can't do anything about it. Time mends everything. I only hope it may soon mend Harriet's heart. Her soul will take care of itself. I will be overjoyed if she sees her way clear to renouncing this new religion of hers, but if she doesn't — well, there sha'n't be anything more said about it. So let her alone, all of you."

But so inexorable was the resentment of her sisters and her brothers-in-law that Harriet O'Brien, after enduring for two years the polite tolerance of these worthy Christians, declared to her mother that she could stand it no longer. Thereupon Mrs. Compton, to the utter dismay of all the relatives, packed herself and Harriet off to Europe, and spent a most enlightening year in travel. She came home alone. For ten years Harriet and her daughter remained in Paris, where the child was given every advantage that love and money could obtain for her. Harriet O'Brien did not return to Farragut until they brought her back from New York City to lay her in the Catholic cemetery alongside the grave of her unforgotten and always-beloved Patsy. Morna was nineteen when her mother died. On the day of the funeral,— which many Protestants attended, by the way,— she took up her abode with Mrs. Compton in the house on the hill, and there she remained, cut off from the world she loved, but happy in being permitted to repay in some measure the great debt of kindness she owed to the mother of her mother.

She was a tonic for the old lady. Her vitality, her engaging smartness, her cosmopolitan airiness, and above all, her warm, affectionate nature, brought more to the lonely old woman than is possible to relate in words. Mrs. Compton, the formidable, became acutely dependent upon her exhilarating granddaughter; she fell into new ways without abandoning old habits, and, instead of shrivelling under the age that had come upon her, throve in spite of it. A time there was when the head of the Compton family considered it a vain extravagance, not in money but in time, to attend the theatre. Now she went frequently and, to her secret amazement, enjoyed herself.

One of her sons-in-law took it upon himself on a memorable Sunday afternoon to drop a few hints concerning the dignity of old age, and received a shock. She told him to mind his own business.

Morna knew but few young men in Farragut. She had occasional " callers " at the house on the hill, usually circumspect individuals who because of their affiliation with Mrs. Compton's church assumed a brisk

familiarity that did not long endure. They did not
represent Morna's idea of true manhood although it
must be said for them that they neither drank nor
smoked nor ventured beyond a perfect " pshaw " in the
matter of blasphemy.

The " live " young men of Farragut were frowned
upon by Mrs. Compton; she had no use for the dancing
crowd whose names one always encountered in the social columns of her newspapers. The few dances
Morna attended after her period of mourning was over
afforded some lively studies in contrasts. She discovered the " drinking set," and was disgusted, if not
shocked, by the broad unconventionality of these
young men toward the women of their acquaintance;
and a painful lack of resentment on the part of the
women, married or single, who belonged to the so-called
smart set. Morna was not ignorant; she had learned
many things in the girls' schools; but her stock of wisdom was put to the test before she had been more than
thirty minutes in the company of one particular group
of young men and women in a home that stood for the
highest ideals. She heard things said in the presence
of young girls at this big supper table that should have
called forth instant rebuke from certain matrons,—
and were received instead with hilarious laughter by
every one present.

Morna was clean-hearted. The shrieking attempts
at *double entendre*, the broad play on words, the smart
though veiled obscenities, were not funny to her. She
did not laugh. She went home disgusted with the
whole lot of them, and was astonished to learn that her
cousins thought these bold young men amazingly bright

and clever.   She did not like the sanctimonious nin-
compoops who came to see her; she could not endure
the brazen worldlings; and, as there appeared to be no
young gentlemen of intermediate qualifications handy,
she concluded in her own mind that a very forlorn
time lay ahead of her.

Being lonely, she did the thing that all lonely and
romantic-minded young people do at one time or another in the transitory stages: she began to write a
novel.   All lonely people try to write novels.   Writing
is the solace of the socially unemployed.   Six chapters
of a very dreadful love story were completed before
Morna realized how unutterably bad they were.   Her
Irish impulsiveness was quick to take advantage of a
momentarily weakened state of Compton doggedness.
It was responsible for the sudden destruction by fire of
two hundred pages of foolscap paper.   Shortly after
this lamentable literary calamity, she quarrelled with
her grandmother — and ran away from home.

As we already know, she got as far as the concrete
bridge, and then went back again.   Since that memorable morn,— now five days past,— she had been con-
sciously keeping alive a new grievance against circumstance.   Try as she would, she could not extract comfort from any argument in defence of her oversight
on the morning of the flight.   She had neglected to
pay the man his wage, and he had added to the misery
of the situation by disappearing in a most significant
manner before she had a chance to recall the obligation.
He should have awaited her pleasure and convenience.
She would have got around to it in time.   In any event,
a person is expected to at least put in a claim for his

pay. Who ever has heard of a menial failing to demand his due? But this young man had calmly
walked away, leaving her in a most unenviable position.

She obtained but little solace in paying him at Mr.
Gilman's garden wall a couple of days later. The ep-
isode was not quite all that she had intended it to be.
He was not in the least crushed or humiliated by her
top-loftiness. Indeed, he had rather the better of the
situation. She had made a complete muddle of the
whole business. That is why she sat up nights wishing him all sorts of misfortune.

Who was he anyhow? A ne'er-do-well, a drunkard,
a wastrel, a pariah — (she had made use of these words
in the construction of her uncompleted novel because
they had a sound literary flavor) — a disgrace to his
family and a — But there always intervened an alle-
viating recollection of his good looks, his good-hu-
moured gallantry, and, above all, the singular effect he
had on her emotions that morning. She may have forgotten to pay him for carrying her bags but she would
never forget that she owed him an incalculable debt for
the change of heart he had brought about in her.
Still, she was very sure that she did not like him. He
had behaved most abominably.

Occasionally she wondered what he was doing.

After night-fall the black depths of Compton's
Woods had an extraordinary fascination for her.
Sometimes she shivered as she looked down upon their
sombre solitudes; nothing in all the world could have
hired *her* to sleep out there!

On the night that Sherry dined with Mr. Gilman and

listened to his staggering proposition, Morna and Mrs.
Compton attended the theatre in town.   There was but
one first-class play-house, the Grand, and, as Morna
kept herself well posted in matters theatrical, very few
of the worthwhile " attractions " appeared there without finding the two women in the audience.   On this
particular August night a brand new " musical com-
edy " was having its " try-out " preparatory to an
opening in Chicago two weeks later.   While it was, as
a matter of fact, experiencing its real " opening night,"
any one of the performers sarcastically would have reminded you that it was being " tried on the dog," and
that the only safe place to do such a thing as that is
in a " tank town."   The press agent did not, however,
speak of Farragut as a tank town; in his advance notices he called it an enterprising, discriminating city,
accustomed to and entitled to the very best of everything.   He would " no more think of sending a No. 2
company to Farragut, than he would think of putting
a Sunday school choir in the Metropolitan Opera
House."   He paid Farragut a compliment by uttering
in small caps that Chicago's opinion of the show would
be moulded largely after what Farragut had to say
about it.   If, said he, a play " got over " before such
a discerning, intelligent audience as Farragut was able
to produce, it was a " pipe " that it would " go " anywhere in the world,— even in " little old New York,"—
and the newspapers printed it without " quotes."

Be that as it may, the hour of midnight arrived before the fall of the final curtain, and lucky it was for
Farragut that its inhabitants were not permitted to
hear what was said by the manager and the stage di-

rector to the unfortunate cast and chorus behind that
protecting screen.

Among other things: "If you can't make these
damned boobs laugh, how do you expect to get a smile
out of real people? Why, they'll laugh at anything in
a burg like this, and you ought to have had 'em cacklin'
so hard, with all the stuff this piece has got, that
they'd be chokin' themselves to death on the peanuts
and popcorn they brought with them."

It was nearly one o'clock when the green touring
car slowed down for the sharp turn into Mrs. Compton's driveway. The headlights swung full upon a tall,
solitary figure standing just outside the big gate,
which had been left open for the return. The driver
put on his brakes.

"What are you doing here?" he demanded as the
car came to a stop and he leaned over the wheel to peer
at the man, who was now in darkness once more.

"What is it, August?" cried Mrs. Compton querulously, coming out of a pleasant doze.

Morna bent forward, staring, a flutter of alarm in
her breast.

"Don't be alarmed," came from the indistinct figure
at the roadside. His voice was quiet and reassuring,
although a suppressed note of excitement would have
been detected by a close observer. "It's all right,
Mrs. Compton. Nothing at all to be alarmed about."

"What are you doing here?" queried Morna, a
quick little catch in her voice. She did not realize that
she was repeating the words August had uttered; they
were the same, but the question had a totally different
meaning. She emphasized the pronoun.

"Who is it, Morna? What does this mean, sir? Who —"

"Keep still, Granny. It is Mr. Redpath. He won't bite us. Now what *has* happened?"

"Nothing,— really. It didn't happen, you see,— though it might, just as easily as not." He chuckled.

"Drive on, August," commanded Miss O'Brien sharply. Her heart sank. He had been drinking, she was sure of it.

"Better let me jump out and chase him —" began the burly August.

"Drive on!" cried Morna. "Don't stop to —"

"What business have you here at this hour of night, young man? How dare you —"

Redpath stepped forward into the light of the lamps and held up an object for their inspection. It was unmistakably a sack made of bed-ticking and it was quite full of something that jangled.

"See this sack? In reality it is a pillow case, and it contains, I fancy, most if not all of the Compton silver, with perhaps a soupçon of diadems, crown jewels —"

"What!" shrieked the two women. August half arose from his seat behind the wheel. "Thieves?" added Mrs. Compton shrilly. "My silver?"

"Here! Hand that stuff over!" barked August, finding his voice. He had at no time lost his courage.

"Don't you want to hear about it?" inquired Sherry, almost plaintively. "It's a corking good story. I've waited nearly an hour to tell you the —"

Morna took the matter into her own hands. "Get into the car, Mr. Redpath," she cried, her voice quiv-

ering with excitement. " Come up to the house with
us. If — if there has been a robbery, I — we wouldn't
dare go in without a man to lead the way. Goodness,
Granny, isn't it thrilling? "

" There may be a mistake," mumbled Mrs. Compton,
still bewildered. " I don't recognize the pillow case.
It —"

" I can search the house, Miss Morna," interposed
August loudly. " We don't need any help."

" Perfectly safe thing to do, August," said Sherry.
" One of the thieves is locked up in the stable now,
guarded by a couple of Swedes, and the other is lying
in the fence corner just behind me, securely bound in
leathern thongs,— a belt, Mrs. Compton,— and a
very stout necktie, the absence of which I would de-
plore were I standing before you in broad daylight.
However, I shall be delighted to go up to the house
with you, provided August remains here to stand guard
over our captive. I —"

" We must telephone to town for the police at once,"
began Mrs. Compton briskly. " Morna, get up in
front and drive. August, you may stay here and —
Dear me, where is the fellow, Mr. Redpath? You say
he is securely tied? Let me see him if —"

" He is tied but not gagged, Mrs. Compton. He is
in a blasphemous frame of mind, so I'd advise you to
forego the pleasure of viewing what remains of him.
You see, being bound, he can't very well remove the
stains of battle from his face, and he isn't a pretty
thing at best."

" Is he — injured? " cried Morna.

" Merely damaged. I overtook him here at the

gates. It was so dark he couldn't see the rock I fired at him, so he didn't dodge. He's all right, however. For the last half-hour he has been telling me what he's going to do to me when he gets out, so I'm sure he is not permanently hors-de-combat. Incidentally, the police have been notified. They ought to be here before long."

" Has he got a gun? " demanded August, now on the ground and staring at a black, indistinct object alongside the fence.

" Not now, August. Here it is. Perhaps you'd better take it. There are three shots left in it, I think."

" Only three? Then — why, by gum, there must 'ha' been some shootin' ! ' "

" Desultory firing," remarked Sherry, from the tonneau, where he had deposited the sack of silver and was seating himself beside Mrs. Compton.

Morna whirled in the driver's seat. Her voice was filled with alarm. " Did — did he shoot at you? "

" I don't know. He didn't hit me, if that's what you mean. You see it was so dark the poor wretch couldn't get a perfect aim at anything. He says he didn't shoot at me. Says the thing went off without his knowing it,— just as revolvers always do. He has the nerve to tell me that he didn't know it was loaded."

A few minutes later the three of them were in the dining-room, going over the contents of the sack. The cook and the maid-of-all-work were separating the small and flat silver into piles, all the while interrupting Redpath's story with sharp, excited promptings of their

own. Even the emphatic Mrs. Compton could not
restrain them. There were *some* things about the
robbery that Mr. Redpath didn't know and they did,
so why shouldn't —

"One of these 'ere teaspoons is missin', Mrs. Compton," broke in the cook triumphantly.

"Never mind; we'll find it, Lizzie. Go on, Mr. Redpath, and, Kate, please count under your breath. It
isn't necessary to bawl out like that."

"Well, all the jewels is safe anyhow," said Lizzie.
"Not a thing missin'. Here's that little turkey pin
that I give you for Christmas back in —"

"How many o' these forks ought there to be, Mrs.
Compton?" inquired Kate, holding up a sample.

"One dozen," groaned their exasperated mistress.

"That's right. There's just a dozen."

"Funny what a robber would want of a silver thim-
ble," commented Lizzie. "As I was sayin', the screen
in the south winder at the back of the —"

"*You* were saying, Mr. Redpath," broke in Mrs.
Compton, after staring Lizzie into utter silence, "that
you followed the men up to the house. Now go on,
please. Where did you first encounter them?"

"It's really quite a short story, Mrs. Compton, and
everything was so simple that you'd hardly believe it.
You see, I've been sleeping in Compton's Woods these
sultry nights. Miss O'Brien may have told you so."

"Yes, yes, I've heard about that," impatiently.

"Tonight I dined out and, being a bit exercised
over some news I'd had during the evening, I — but
I think I've already mentioned this —"

"Yes, you have. Pray get on. The police may be

here any minute, and I want to see the fellow in the stable before they take him away. Lizzie, ask Matson and 'Ole to fetch him into the kitchen at once. I may be able to identify him. Proceed, Mr. Redpath."

"Well, I concluded to take a long walk,— just to quiet my nerves, don't you know. Somehow or other I meandered clear down to this end of the woods. It was about half-past ten o'clock. My bedtime, I may say. Inasmuch as I've been making my bed wherever it is dry and convenient, I didn't see any sense in tramping clear back to the other end of my bedchamber when the turf is just as good at this end, so I concluded to turn in for the night just a little way above your gates. There is a fine bit of turf about a hundred yards back in the woods,— much superior, in fact, to anything I'm accustomed to,— and I was stretching my bones out very pleasantly when I heard some one speak on the opposite side of the clump of hazel brush to my right."

"Oh, dear!" murmured Morna, breathless with excitement. "Weren't you lucky they happened to come up on *that* side?"

"Rather. And you were lucky, too, that they stopped there for consultation. Otherwise I wouldn't have known what was in the air. I don't want to be classed as an eavesdropper, so I was on the point of coughing just to warn him that some one was listening,— you see, Mrs. Compton, when a fellow sleeps out in the woods as I've been doing, he hears and sees things that no one is expected to see or hear — just to warn him to be careful what he said, when his companion spoke, and I discovered, to my surprise, that he was also a man. It isn't such bad form to listen to

what two men have to say to each other, so I thought
better of it and didn't cough. To shorten the story,
I distinctly heard these two fellows arranging their
plans for the burglarizing of your house. It seems
they knew you were in town at the theatre,— which
was news to me, of course,— and that the two hired
men sleep above the stable. The plan was to get into
the house through the west wing,— your side, I gathered, and therefore quite unoccupied at the time.
The servants were supposed to be asleep at the far end
of the other wing. They —"

"That's where they got fooled," broke in Kate.
" We was in bed but not asleep. I —"

" They appeared to know a good deal about the interior of the house, where the silver is kept, and the
jewels, and all that sort of thing. They also knew
that you are afraid of dogs in August, Mrs. Compton,
since a setter went mad a good many years ago and
bit a lot of cattle."

"Goodness! Just fancy that?" cried Mrs. Compton. " Local talent, Mr. Redpath, you may be sure."

" So they didn't have to worry about dogs. That
seemed to please them immensely. I'd hate to tell you
what they said about people living in the country without plenty of dogs about."

" You needn't. I can surmise."

" Now you'll get the Airedale I've been —"

" Never mind, Morna. Let Mr. Redpath finish his
story."

" They had it all figured out that you wouldn't get
home before midnight. Ample time to do the job and
make their getaway. Then they sneaked out of the
woods and started for the house. It was very dark,

but I thought it best not to risk following too close behind, so I gave them a few minutes' start. There
isn't much more to tell. It was all very simple. One
of them stayed outside the window while the other went
in. I managed in some way to surprise the outside
man and he succumbed,— without a word, you might
say. But it was quite another thing to tackle the inside fellow. The situation called for reflection. He
would have a gun and he would have the advantage if
I went in after him. While I was trying to figure it
out, the most unearthly yell went up from somewhere
in the house. I've never heard anything so blood-
curdling. Then I heard some one running on the inside. The screeches continued. That was reassuring.
Then I heard a shout from the stable. Like a flash
the peril of my own position dawned upon me. Those
men of yours would come piling out and, not knowing
me for a friend, would begin blazing away at me with
shotguns or something. I'd have the burglar shooting me from one side and they from the other. It
wasn't a nice idea, was it, Miss O'Brien?"

"I — should — say — not!"   gulped   Morna.
"Only granny refuses to let anybody have a gun on the
place. But, of course, you didn't know that, Mr.
Redpath."

"It was Lizzie that let out them screams," said
Kate, defensively. "I never opened my mouth. I —"

"Discretion being better than anything else I had
in stock, I scooted around the corner of the house, and
waited for events. Out of the window came something that jingled when it hit the ground; then there
was some subdued blasphemy, and after that a solid

thud on the gravel walk. Two seconds later, a man
shot past me on the dead run. He was carrying the
thing that rattled and jingled. I knew what it was.
Loot! I lit out after him, and, by Jove! What do
you think happened then? He mistook me for his pal
and called back to me to beat it for myself, not to
mind him,— separate, go our own ways,— do you see?
We went down the lane at a wonderful clip. I was a
runner at college, Mrs. Compton, besides being the
prize scholar. Down there at the gate I overtook him.
He had tumbled to me some time before, however. I
wasn't playing the game. I wasn't separating. He
knew I was a pursuer. Just as we got to the gate his
revolver went off. He says it was an accident, but I
didn't know that, of course. So I stopped up very
suddenly and began looking for the same kind of am-
munition that David used on Goliath. I was also a
base-ball player at college, Miss O'Brien. Just as his
revolver went off the second time, I let fly at him with a
fair-sized boulder,— we call them dornicks sometimes,
Mrs. Compton. I don't know how it happened, but it
got him full in the face. He went down like a log and
— but, I'll omit the rest, if you don't mind. I tied him
up before he came to. Down the road came one of
your men. He stopped at my command, and after a
little while I got him to understand the situation. He
ran back to telephone for the police. He said he had
left Matson sitting on the other thief, while a couple
of very brave and faithful young women tied him hand
and foot with clothes-line. That's the whole story —
except that I waited for over an hour down there at the
gate. I thought you would never come. What was
the play, Miss O'Brien? "

CHAPTER XI

M RS. COMPTON was scrutinizing the surly, half-dazed "outside man" when a lieutenant of police arrived with a squad of men, among whom was Barney Doyle, bringing with them from the lower gates the sorry looking victim of Sherry's expertness.

The "outside man" was a poor specimen of humanity. He was a bony, weak-faced, fishy-eyed young fellow whose aspen-like fingers, cigarette stained and bloodless, were constantly employed in wiping his mouth or rummaging inside his loose, filthy looking collar. He was not one's idea of a real burglar. He expressed nothing sinister or terrifying. Mrs. Compton sniffed at him.

"Do you call *this* a burglar, Mr. Redpath?" she inquired ironically. The fellow glowered back as best he could at the glistening nose-glasses through which she scrutinized him. He squirmed a little as Ole's big hand tightened on his arm.

"No," said Sherry dubiously. "I can't say that I do. I think I should call him a caterpillar, Mrs. Compton. Have you ever seen him before?"

"Never. What is your name, young man?"

"You go to hell," said the young man, indistinctly. Immediately afterward he said "ouch!" with great distinctness.

134

"Don't hurt him, Ole. I wouldn't have believed he had the spunk to say that, even to a woman. He has more character than I suspected, Mr. Redpath."

Sherry grinned. He was beginning to like Mrs. Compton.

"You should have heard his partner, Mrs. Compton. He — Hello, there's an automobile. The police, I suppose."

"Late, as usual. Kate, tell them to come around to the back door." Then she added drily: "I am receiving here tonight."

The second burglar was as formidable as his companion was insignificant. He was big and powerful-looking, and he was a sight to behold. One eye was completely closed and his face was caked with blood. From the other eye he glared balefully.

"Wash his face, Doyle," said the lieutenant of police.

"Never mind," growled the man.

Officer Doyle was staring in amazement at Sherry Redpath.

"Wash it," said Mrs. Compton firmly. "Lizzie, get some soap and hot water. Morna, don't be silly. If you can't stand the sight of blood, go into —"

"Castile soap," said the burglar, resignedly. "None of your kitchen-sink soap. I know what's what, all right." His eye rested upon his shrinking partner. "You little — oh, what's the use! There isn't a word in the language that will fit you."

"He got me with a rap on the bean," began the "outside man" whiningly. "Say, honest to God, I never knowed what hit me. I swear to —"

"Shut up!" snarled the big man, and the little one began to cry.

Sherry Redpath slipped his arm through Morna's and pressed it encouragingly. She looked up into his face, surprised but not resentful. Indeed, she was immensely grateful for the support of his strong arm. He had noticed the pallor in her cheek and the tightly closed fingers.

"Don't keel over," he whispered. "Your grandmother is a marvel, isn't she?"

Morna nodded her head and tried to smile.

"Better not look at him until after Barney gets through washing his face," he advised gently. "I get a little squeamish myself sometimes when I see the open cuts. Chicken-hearted, you know."

"*You* chicken-hearted?" she murmured, turning away at his bidding. He squeezed her arm again.

From time to time Barney Doyle looked up from his job at the kitchen sink, and always his gaze sought out Sherry Redpath, perplexity deepening in his eyes with each successive glance. He was rapidly reducing the big burglar's sanguinary countenance to a recognizable condition.

Mrs. Compton observed the handcuffs on the fellow's wrists.

"They are quite strong and safe, I hope?" she said, with a jerk of her head which the lieutenant interpreted.

"Sure," he replied. "The very latest," he added with convincing pride.

"That's good," said Mrs. Compton, relieved.

At that moment Barney put the final touches on his

subject's face and wheeled him about to confront the waiting audience. Two policemen tramped into the kitchen. Saluting the lieutenant, one of them reported that no further clues had been found.

" Clues? " cried the mistress of the house. " Aren't the men themselves clues enough? "

" He means evidence, ma'am," explained the lieutenant. " Now, let's have a look at this guy. Look up, you! "

The big burglar lifted his head. His eyes transfixed Mrs. Compton. One standing close to her might have heard the sharp intake of her breath. Redpath, after a brief glance at his victim's livid face, turned his eyes upon Mrs. Compton, who stood straight and unafraid in front of the man. His gaze remained fixed by the curiously rigid, tense look in her eyes.

" Strange mug to me," advanced the lieutenant. " Ever see him before? " He addressed the three bluecoats. They shook their heads.

" Chicago," said Barney Doyle, and they all nodded their heads, apparently satisfied.

" This is the one that described the house and grounds, Mrs. Compton," said Redpath, still watching her closely. " He appeared to know the place quite well."

" Aha, is that so? " said the lieutenant, scowling upon the burglar. " Knowed the lay o' the land, did he? Well, that's important. Have you ever seen him before, Mrs. Compton? Ever work on your place? "

She did not reply at once. When she spoke, a moment later, Sherry was absolutely certain that she answered but one of the two questions: the last.

" Never," she said slowly, her gaze still meeting the glittering eye of the captive.

" Some of these servants of yours may recollect him," said the officer, applying her response to both of his questions. While he was examining the servants, Mrs. Compton looked at each of them in turn, and there was something more than inquiry in her eyes. There was uneasiness, apprehension. Redpath realized that something unusual, something mysterious was transpiring before his eyes; there was not the slightest doubt in his mind that Mrs. Compton had seen the man before.

Morna was breathing jerky, shuddery comments on the vicious appearance of the big burglar. From her remarks, he was convinced that she did not share the secret, if there was one; it rested with her grandmother and the thief.

He was conscious of a curiously warm, exquisite glow that spread through his body from head to foot. The air that he breathed was full of tender, delicious shocks, and there was a fragrance that — So impelling was the emotion of delight that he looked down wonderingly into her face, and for the moment forgot Mrs. Compton and her burglar. He therefore missed the almost imperceptible shake of the head delivered by the latter over the shoulder of Barney Doyle, and the sharp contraction of the eyes of the only person who witnessed the movement.

A few minutes later, the captives were bundled out of the kitchen by the police. From the door the big one glanced back at Mrs. Compton. Redpath, coming up from behind, was sure that he saw her shoulders lift in a slight convulsive shudder.

"A good night's work, Mrs. Compton," the lieutenant of police was saying. "We have nabbed a couple of bad ones. It's a habit we're getting into. Mighty few of them get away, ma'am. Good night to you."

"Any room for me in the car, lieutenant?" inquired Sherry. "I'll ride up to town if you —"

"Not a bit o' room," said the officer, eyeing him coldly. He knew nothing good of Sherry Redpath. What the dickens did he mean by asking for a ride up to town in the police department's private automobile? "And now that I think of it, what are *you* doing out here? I guess I'll just take you along in anyhow, and put a few questions to you after we get to headquar — Say, what's the joke? Come on, now! You won't think it's so funny —"

"It happens to have been Mr. Redpath, officer, who nabbed your men for you," said Morna indignantly. "He took both of them, single-handed."

"Well, what the —" began the officer, his eyes bulging.

Barney Doyle stuck his head in at the door. He was grinning from ear to ear.

"I say, Sherry, bedad, you're the joy av me heart! The big guy just swore he'd get ye some day, an' then out came the story. Ye nailed both av them, did ye? Well, bedad,— beggin' your pardon, ma'am, for swearin'—"

"You did it?" gasped the lieutenant, passing his hand over his brow.

"Who do you think did it? These ladies?" inquired Sherry, good-naturedly.

The lieutenant stuck out his hand. "I take off my hat to you, Redpath. I hear you're lookin' for a job. Well, the force is lookin' for just such material as you —"

"Thanks, Charlie. I've got a job. But I'll take the lift to town if you'll give it to me."

"I will have August take you up to town, Mr. Redpath," said Mrs. Compton. "Allow me to do that much at least for you. I would like a few words with you before you go, however, if you don't mind waiting."

When the house was quiet once more,— and it was no easy matter to obtain quiet with Lizzie and Kate still willing to talk,— Sherry accompanied the two ladies to the parlour. (The parlour, still extant in certain sections of this broad land, is a room that by any other name would smell as musty.) Morna switched on the electric lights. Everything about the room represented primness, preciseness, immobility. Not an article had been moved in years from its hallowed position. Each and every piece of furniture and bric-a-brac, dusted once a week, had been set back upon the exact spot from which it was shifted. Morna could have told you that the big arm chair in the corner had not moved an inch from the spot on which it stood when she first looked into the room as a tiny child, sixteen years before. The same fresh-looking prodigiously flowered brussels carpet covered the floor and the identical wall paper was on the walls. It was, in fact, a real and unmistakable parlour that Sherry was ushered into at two o'clock that morning.

"Mr. Redpath," said Mrs. Compton, after Morna had closed the door at her silent bidding, "you spoke of sleeping in the woods tonight. May I not induce you to sleep in this house, instead? I am not a timid woman,— at least, I have never considered myself to be one,— but I am unnerved tonight. I will confess that I am more shaken than I have ever been in my life. I feel the need of a strong, responsible man in the house. Will you not do me a great kindness and remain here? We can make you comfortable and —"

"My dear Mrs. Compton," interrupted he, "there isn't a thing in the world to be uneasy about. There were only two of them —"

"Quite true. I am not afraid of burglars. On the other hand, you must remember that I am a woman. Women are never afraid until after the crisis is past. Perhaps you do not know that to be one of our characteristics, but it is a fact. We face things with amazing fortitude and go through with them with even more composure than men, but as soon as they are behind us we collapse. We are not cowards before the fact, but after it,— as the lawyers might put it if they had sense enough."

"I will gladly stay," said he, with a quick glance at Morna, who was watching her grandmother with puzzled, incredulous eyes. He too had noted the ashen cheeks and the sudden haggardness in the elder woman's face. It was as if she had aged ten years in a single hour. Her hand shook as she put it out for the

support of the centre-table. " A real bed will be a
novelty, I assure you. But," he went on seriously,
" there is no further cause for alarm. You are as safe
as a bug in a rug. No one will —"

" Thank you," she broke in, her face lighting. " It
is very good of you to stay. I know you will pardon
an old woman's whimsey. I am your debtor twice
over, sir. Tonight you performed the lesser of two
deeds by which I am the gainer. I might, perhaps,
reward you for restoring my silver to me, but not for
what you did the other day. You are not only a brave
man but a good one. Young men in this day and age
of the world are not given to persuasion of the sort
you exercised the other morning. Usually, I believe it
is the other way about. You are making a fresh start
in life, and you will need friends. You have at least
one firm, sustaining friend upon whom you may call
at any time; you will not find her wanting. I forgave
Morna the other day. I hope you will do the same."

" Forgive?" cried he, amazed. " What have I to
forgive in —"

" I will tell you, Mr. Redpath," broke in Morna
rapidly. " I was very rude that day in front of Mr.
Gilman's. I —"

His hearty laugh brought a quick flush to her
cheeks. " Oh, I understood *perfectly*, Miss O'Brien,"
he said. " You were peeved. I knew you'd be sorry,
so I wasn't offended,— not in the least. Listen!
Hear that? Your silver dollar is making all that
noise. I'm never going to spend it, you know. It is
my lucky piece. The corner-stone of the new house
of Redpath. If that's all I have to forgive, we'll —"

"I wasn't peeved," she objected. "I hate the word. There isn't any such word to begin with, and — No, I was simply horrid and insulting, because it's my nature to be that way, and I hope you will not think any the worse of Granny because she puts up with me."

"My dear, my dear," began Mrs. Compton, trying to smile. She failed, and her chin quivered despite the resolute compression of her thin lips.

"I shall sleep on the couch in your room, Granny," said Morna quickly.

"Not on my account, my child," said the mistress of the house. "If you are afraid to sleep in your own room you may come to mine, not otherwise."

"But if you say you are unnerved, apprehensive —"

"I shall not be, my dear, with Mr. Redpath in the house. Now let us be off to bed. I will conduct you to your room, Mr. Redpath. We breakfast at eight. Say good night, Morna." She spoke to her granddaughter in the manner and tone of one addressing a small child. The habit was one she had never outgrown, even with her own middle-aged children.

Morna favoured Sherry with a sly grimace and curtseyed quaintly. "Good night, sir," she murmured.

In the narrow hallway upstairs, Mrs. Compton drew close to the side of her tall companion. She spoke in low and guarded tones.

"My friend, the police did not ask you whether you ever had seen either of those burglars before. I suppose they took it for granted that you had not. I ask you now."

He shook his head, watching her covertly all the

time. Something told him that his answer was to
mean a great deal to her.

"No, Mrs. Compton, I have never seen either of
them before."

He fancied he heard her draw a long breath. "Evidently they are not what you would call local talent,
— or the police would have known them."

"Undoubtedly. The police in this town are quite
up-to-date. They would know them if they belonged
here." He tried craftiness. "I was impressed, however, by the big fellow's reluctance to have his face
washed. It struck me that he feared some one present
might be able to recognize him. No one recognized
him, however, as you know."

"This is your room," she said, stopping before a
door. "Mine is just beyond and Morna's is across the
hall." She pushed an electric light button. "You
are very good to stay. I shall never forget all that
you have done for me. Good night."

"Good night, Mrs. Compton."

"Good night," she repeated absently.

Standing before the mirror on the square old ma-
hogany bureau a few minutes later, divested of a portion of his rumpled apparel, he looked himself straight
in the eye and said, half-aloud:

"You've got more to live down than you thought,
old top. Wanted to question you at headquarters,
did they? That *was* an eye-opener. You're looked
upon as a suspicious character, Sherry; no getting
around it. I wonder how I kept from sinking through
the floor."

Presently he sat down on the edge of the bed, his

head cocked at an angle of meditation, his eyes dreamily elevated. After a long time he sighed profoundly. A tender smile lurked about his lips as he laid himself down to sleep. It had been a great night.

He was aroused at eight o'clock by a sharp rapping on the bedroom door. Just at that instant he was in the thick of a dream in which countless adversaries were shooting at him from all conceivable points. He awoke to the certainty that they were using gatling guns, and it was some time before he could convince himself that a friendly and not a hostile hand was behind the fusillade.

" All right ! " he sang out.

" Get up," came back in Morna's voice. " It's eight o'clock."

" I'll be down in ten minutes."

Five minutes later he stepped out of his bath and said to himself : " Except in the middle of winter, Burton's Creek beats a porcelain tub all to smash."

Before descending, he carefully restored to its original position on the bed the linen sheet in which he had wrapped his long body in lieu of the customary and time-honoured garment that all proper gentlemen slept in up to the introduction of pajamas into the Occident.

Morna met him at the foot of the stairs.

" Granny's out in the garden," she said as they shook hands. " She has been up since six o'clock. Do you mind having breakfast alone with me? "

He pinched himself. " Will you be good enough to kick me, Miss O'Brien? That's what we always did at college when we couldn't get a fellow up any other way. I must be still asleep. I'm dreaming."

"Consider yourself kicked. Now, answer my question."

"I don't in the least mind having breakfast alone with you," he said.

"You don't appear to be any the worse for wear," she said, as they walked down the hall together. She was studying his face closely and in the most matter-of-fact way.

"I'm as fresh as a new-born daisy," he announced, "but as hungry as a bear."

"Granny didn't get a wink of sleep," said she, her brow clouding. "I left my door open, so that I could hear her if she called. When I went to sleep,— I really couldn't help it in spite of the excitement,— her light was burning, and when I awoke at four o'clock,— I thought I heard a noise on the back porch — did you happen to hear it? — When I awoke her light was still going, so I pounced out of bed and rapped on her door. She told me to go back to bed. And now she's out there fussing around the garden. She says she will not go to the police court this morning. I've never seen her so nervous and upset."

"Pretty strenuous night for one as old as she is, Miss O'Brien," said he. They were seated opposite each other at the table in the long, low dining-room. "In any event, I don't see why she should go in for the hearing of those fellows. It isn't necessary. The police judge simply binds them over to the Circuit Court. I can do all the testifying that's required. As a matter-of-fact I'm the only eye-witness."

She was silent for a moment or two, her eyes bent

thoughtfully upon the plate in front of her. His rapt gaze was not employed in a similar occupation.

" Do you know," she said slowly, looking up at him with troubled eyes, " I had the queerest feeling out in the kitchen last night, when the police and those men were there? "

" You did? " He leaned forward.

" Yes. It was absurd, but I — I —" she lowered her voice and glanced toward the door,—" I couldn't help feeling that my grandmother recognized one of those men. Of course, she couldn't have known him, but I — well, I —"

" Miss O'Brien," he said, as she hesitated in some distress, " I am confident that she recognized the larger of the two men." He was very serious. " I don't understand what it all means, but there isn't the remotest doubt that the man knows her and that she knows him."

" I lay awake thinking about — Sh! She is coming. Don't for anything in the world let her suspect that we —"

Mrs. Compton entered the room at that instant. Sherry sprang to his feet and went forward to meet her. His face was bright and cheery.

" Good morning," he exclaimed. " I hear you've been up for hours, a reproach to lazy-bones."

She was quite calm and serene. He looked for reflections of inward perturbation in her sharp old eyes, and found none. No doubt, thought he, her face was always as grey as it was this morning.

" I did not sleep well," she replied. " Pray sit down,

Mr. Redpath. I will sit here with you. Has Morna told you about the telephone message from the police? "

"Yes," he said, drawing out a chair for her. "I shall be happy to shoulder all the responsibility this morning, Mrs. Compton. You will not have to appear."

"So I told them," she said coolly. "They have asked that you appear against the men, however. I am loath to impose upon you —"

"It will give me great pleasure to testify against any man who points a revolver that is not supposed to be loaded. Such a person ought to be kept in jail for life on general principles," said he. "I daresay they will both plead guilty," seeking to comfort her. "Caught red-handed, you know. You will never see either of them again, Mrs. Compton."

She regarded him searchingly. "I may have to appear against them at the final trial."

"I don't believe so."

"I dislike being in court," she explained briefly. He realized that he would get nothing more out of her. "There is something else I want to speak to you about, Mr. Redpath. You said last night that you have taken a position. Was that the truth, or merely a remark for the benefit of the police officer? "

"Neither. I have had a position offered me, Mrs. Compton."

"I can cheerfully recommend you," said Morna, smiling, "as a lusty, obliging porter. Don't fail to call upon me if you need a reference."

"Thanks. I'm getting on in the world, however.

Yesterday I was a day labourer. Now I am offered a place as private secretary."

‚ "You would also make a lusty secretary," said Mrs. Compton, eyeing him strangely. It seemed to him that she was reading his mind. "You have not yet concluded to accept the place, I gather."

"I told the gentleman who offered it to me that I would give the matter consideration and let him know in a day or two. I shall decide today."

"You will take it?"

"Nothing better is likely to turn up, Mrs. Compton."

"And what will be your real duties as secretary to Andrew Gilman?"

He started. "How did you guess it was Mr. Gilman?"

"He is the only man in Farragut, so far as I know, who would have the shrewdness and the foresight to employ a black sheep for night work."

"'Pon my soul, Mrs. Compton! You—"

"I know Andrew Gilman. He does not require the services of a secretary or a business agent. If he lives to be one hundred, he will still manage to handle his own private affairs and look carefully after his dollars and cents. He wants you to live in the house with him, does he not?"

"Yes, that is one of the requirements. By Jove, you are wonderful."

"That is what I meant by night work. I am sorry if I offended you by using the term 'black sheep.' I did not mean to offend. You may be sure that Andrew Gilman would not take you into his house unless he had every confidence in your integrity. It is quite

a compliment, coming from him." There was palpable
irony in her voice. " He believes in you,— as I do.
I have heard no good word of you, nor has he, I daresay. You have turned over a new leaf. Andrew Gilman has read you through and through. He never
makes a mistake. He feels absolutely safe in your
hands. You will not rob him, nor abuse his trust in
you, nor resume your prodigal habits, nor — well, he
knows he has found a man whom money cannot buy nor
vice reclaim. You have had all that you want of both.
He knows you are bound to make a man of yourself.
Not another man in town would have considered you
worth the powder to blow you up, but Andrew Gilman
is smarter than all of them put together. I shall not
ask you to tell me what your duties are to be, nor what
he offers to pay you in the way of salary. Those are
matters between you and him. I can only say that I
believe you will find the position a difficult one. Do
not allow yourself to fall into his ways. Do not become hard and grasping. He has no friends. If you
do his bidding in all particulars, you will lose the few
you already have. I am not trying to discourage you.
You are young and you may still have a few illusions.
Mr. Gilman is old and never had an illusion in his life.
He may try to dominate you. In that he will fail, I
am more or less convinced. Pray pardon this gratuitous lecture, Mr. Redpath. I am an old woman and,
like old Andy Gee, have no illusions."

"You have paid me the highest sort of a compliment, Mrs. Compton, by speaking so frankly and so unreservedly about my humble affairs. I never really

knew Mr. Gilman until last night. I dined with him. He was charming, friendly —"

"Did Mrs. Gilman dine with you?" she broke in.

"No. I understand she is an invalid. She hasn't been downstairs to a meal in a great many years."

"A great many years," repeated Mrs. Compton, almost inaudibly. A faint purplish hue appeared on her brow and temples. "So Andy Gee was charming, was he?" she went on, recovering herself. "Well, he knows how to be. I knew him fifty years ago. He used to come to my father's house long before I was married. He came to see my sister. It may interest you to hear, Mr. Redpath, that the invalid who never comes down to her meals is my eldest sister."

There was a moment of utter silence in the room. Morna was gazing blankly at her grandmother.

"I didn't know, of course, Mrs. Compton," said Sherry. There was no reason for him to be surprised by this statement of hers, and yet he experienced an unaccountable shock.

"Your sister, Granny?" cried Morna, still staring. "Old Mr. Gilman's wife? Why, I never knew,— you have never mentioned —"

"You never knew, my dear, because the subject is one that has not come up in this family during your lifetime." Something in her manner checked the question that flew to Morna's lips. "I fear, Mr. Redpath," went on Mrs. Compton, glancing at the tall old clock in the corner, "that you will have to be off shortly. The car will take you to town." She arose from the table. "You have fifteen or twenty minutes to spare, however," smilingly, " so pray do not gulp your coffee."

She turned at the door and said, almost shyly: " And please remember that it will not be necessary for you to sleep in the woods again. My house is open to you from this day on. Come to us tonight in case you do not find a better place to lodge."

CHAPTER XII

O N the morning of the third day after the robbery at Mrs. Compton's, Sheridan Redpath entered the First National Bank and walked up to the receiving teller's cage. He deposited, in checks and currency, nearly four thousand dollars to the credit of Andrew Gilman. The teller, who knew him by sight and reputation, blinked his eyes a little more rapidly than was his wont,— he had a habit of "batting" them with great frequency because of the nervous dread that he might some day be taken in by a counterfeit bill. What on earth did *this* mean? Had old Andy Gee gone stark, staring crazy? A member of the board of directors he was, too!

"Morning, Mr. Cole," greeted Sherry cheerily. "My name is Redpath. I used to be a member of your Sunday school class. You may remember seeing me occasionally, just about Christmas time, a good many years ago."

"Ahem! Quite so. You were much smaller, if I am not mistaken. Ahem! Er — pleasant day, isn't it?"

"Very. Thank you. Good morning," and out strode the cause of the first shock that Mr. Cole's smug serenity had sustained since the historic raise in salary twelve years before.

Over in the lobby of the Tremont, old Judge Emmons fanned himself with a broad palmetto leaf, and

dwelt profoundly upon a bit of news that had reached
his ears that very morning while he was at breakfast.
He had as an audience four gentlemen of Farragut,
not one of whom could hold a candle to him in the
matter of antiquity, and yet the youngest of them
boasted of feeling fine at seventy-two.

It is worthy of mention that none of these chair-
warmers was a paying patron of the Tremont. They
merely occupied chairs there. The lobby of the Tremont was a cool spot in hot weather, and a warm retreat in the dead of winter. Years ago, before the ac-
cursed cuspidors took the place of sand-boxes, these
same gentlemen of Farragut had formed the habit of
making themselves at home in the most conspicuous
corner of the hotel office, and they had been at it ever
since. Latterly, however, they were obliged to confess
that they couldn't feel as much at home there as in the
good old days, because of a silly rule about not spit-
ting on the floor. Indeed, they maintained, the Tremont was rapidly losing the atmosphere that had made
it one of the most noted hostelries in the Middle West.
It was degenerating into what the ignorant were
pleased to call a first class house. Ever since the new
management ripped up the historic oak floor and put
down this confounded crazy-quilt tile, the place, according to the oldest citizen, was deprived of its real
flavour. It was no longer a haven of comfort and con-
geniality.

These new-fangled, New York ideas were running
the good old Tremont into the ground. The anti-
quated plush settees and chairs,— good enough for the
men who had made the town what it was,— were a long

sight more attractive to the eye and infinitely more
fitting to the flesh than the slippery, high-armed con-
traptions now in use. A man couldn't throw his leg
over the arm of one of these chairs to save his life.
As a result, gentlemen who always had looked comfortably at home in the lobby of the Tremont, now appeared to be about as much at ease as a person waiting in a railway station for a train to come along and
take him away. "Might just as well be a woman," declared Judge Emmons, putting the concrete estimate
upon the practicability of the new chairs in the Tremont.

The judge's news was forty-eight hours old, but, as
he was nearly ninety years older than the topic, it is
not surprising that he was a bit slack in getting
around to it.

"And what's more," he was saying, shrilly, "Andy
Gilman ain't as rich as people think he is anyhow.
He ain't John D. Rockefeller, not by a long shot! He
ain't even Andrew Carn*eegy*. Men as rich as they are
can afford to take chances on losing a million or two.
But *he* can't. Now you take this young feller we've
been talking about. He —"

"Nobody's been talkin' about him but you, Judge,"
broke in old Mr. Meggs. "Don't drag me into it."

The judge affected deafness at such times as this.
"He ain't seen a sober day since — since when, Ben?
Never mind. It don't make any difference. Now you
put a feller like that in a position where he can lay his
hands on a lot of money and — Well, all I've got to
say is, it's risky. This town is full of upright, self-
respecting young men, just achin' for a chance to get

ahead in the world, and what does old Andy Gilman do? What does he do? Well, sir, he ignores 'em, turns his back on 'em, and hires this good-for-nothin' scamp of a Redpath. For instance, take my grandson, George Belknap's boy,— the one that's been working in Fisher's insurance office,— now, there's as fine a lad as there is in the whole United States of America. You could trust him with a million dollars in gold, right in his pockets, and, begad, you could count it every night and you wouldn't find a nickel of it missing from one year's end to the other. Teaches a Sunday school class and acts out Santa Claus every Christmas Eve. They say there ain't been a better Santa Claus in a coon's age. Deportment first-class, honest as the day is long, high-school education,— thank God, he was spared from college! — and wanting to get married the worst way and can't because the insurance business is so derned bad he can't more than make his own salt. Just the boy for Andy Gilman. I hope to God this feller he's hired gets away with some of Andy's money. Serve him right. He —"

"They say he's been layin' around drunk up in Compton's Woods for nearly a week," said Mr. Meggs, unable to hold in any longer. "Rip snortin' drunk."

"Who? Andy Gilman?" snapped Judge Emmons. "He don't drink, sir, and you know it."

"Too stingy," observed Col. Barker sententiously.

"Livin' like a hog," went on Mr. Meggs. "I haven't anything against drink in moderation, and I never say a word against a man who once in a while gets a leetle too much aboard, but this thing of soakin' up all the liquor in —"

"As I was saying," put in Judge Emmons, "Andy Gilman has done enough harm to this town without insultin' it to boot. Look at it any way you want to, it's an insult to the decent, law-abidin', ambitious young men of this town to give a job to —"

"What does he pay this Redpath boy?" demanded Col. Barker, ever practical.

"Pay him?" snorted Mr. Meggs. "He never paid decent wages to anybody. A decent, self-respecting man wouldn't work for the wages he pays. That's why he hires this rum-soaked loafer. In some ways it's an outrage to impose on a feller like that. Too tight to know what he's doin', so old Andy Gee takes advantage of him."

"What's this I see in the paper yesterday about him capturing a couple of burglars out in the country the other night?" inquired Amos P. Adams, after missing the cuspidor.

"Probably in cahoots with them," responded Mr. Meggs, promptly. "Betrayed 'em at the last minute for the reward. Beats the devil what a man will do for money when his system craves liquor like that. Betray his own mother, and never bat an eye."

"Papers spoke pretty highly of him, however. Didn't look to me like a put up job."

"You don't suppose he'd allow it to *look* like a put up job, do you? All done for effect on Andy Gilman. He —"

"Gentlemen," interrupted a brisk, persuasive voice, "if you will step into the bar and have a drink with me, the porters will clean up here a bit during your absence, and — be careful, Judge! Don't try to be too spry. Let me help you. First door to your left, gentlemen."

The speaker was the manager of the hotel. He always approached the group at this hour of the day, and always his interruption took the form of a polite, even obsequious invitation. A rare sense of delicacy ordered him, on all occasions, to signify the "first door to your left," notwithstanding the fact that any one of the old men could have closed his eyes and *backed* into the bar-room without even so much as touching the door-jamb with the sleeve of his coat.

Even the hard-headed, progressive new management of the Tremont hesitated about improving the lobby of the hotel by anything so drastic as the complete eradication of this coterie of ancient loafers. They represented tradition, and so they were coddled and tolerated at the expense of convenience.

The second day after the attempted robbery, and but one after the preliminary hearing of the two burglars, Andrew Gilman sent an "item" to the newspapers. It was brief and to the effect that Sheridan Redpath, son of the late Robert W. Redpath, had accepted a position as private secretary with Mr. Andrew Gilman and would enter upon his duties at once. The city gave a convulsive gasp. No two characters within its gates were more widely known than Andy Gee and Sherry Redpath; they personified the infinite in extremes: the miser and prodigal.

The grandfathers in the lobby of the Tremont voiced the sentiments of every intelligent man, woman and child in Farragut when they put the blame for this social earthquake upon the head of Andrew Gilman.

From one end of the town to the other extended a
pleased, if stealthy grin, and back of that grin reposed the joyous conviction that when the wastrel got
through with the miser " there wouldn't be enough left
of him to justify the bother of digging a grave for him
in the potter's field." No one blamed Sherry Redpath for taking the job. Indeed, there was a subtle
wave of sympathy for him, which grew apace as the
full significance of the situation developed under discussion.

Soon it was being said that old Andy Gee ought to
be tarred and feathered for putting temptation in the
poor wretch's way!

People began to look far ahead, and as they looked
their hatred of Andrew Gilman increased. It would
be just like the old man to prosecute the boy after
virtually inviting him to become a thief. One citizen
went so far as to prophesy, in the Sunbeam, that they
never could " get a jury in God's world " that would
convict Sherry Redpath under the circumstances!
The whole city, it must be assumed, took it for granted
that Andrew Gilman was at last about to get what was
coming to him; no one, in the general excitement,
stopped to consider that young Redpath, despite his
other faults, was absolutely honest!

It is not necessary to turn back to events that followed close upon the capture of the burglars. Redpath appeared against the two house-breakers at the
preliminary hearing. On his evidence alone they were
bound over to the grand jury, both waiving examination. As he sat in the police court-room, waiting for
the appearance of the judge, he studied the face of the

larger of the two men, searching for something in his
features that might throw light upon the strange behaviour of Mrs. Compton. A close, careful scrutiny
might refresh his own memory; it was not altogether
improbable that he too had seen the man before, back
in childhood days.

From time to time the fellow turned a cold, unwav-
ering eye upon him, and he almost fancied that there
was mockery in the glance.   One side of the prisoner's
head was bandaged, and he was unshaven. His gar-
ments, rough and of the cheapest quality, were ill-fit-
ting, yet he had the air of a man who was accustomed
to good clothes.   The contrast between him and the
smaller thief was remarkable.   The latter was plainly,
unmistakably a " crook " of the commonest type, morally and intellectually.

They listened to Redpath's brief account of the adventure without emotion.   The big man did not take
his eye from the face of the witness; the little one sat
with his chin on his breast, afraid to look up, They
gave their names as George Smith and John Brown,
and as such they were docketed.

George Smith was a man of forty-five. His hair
was slightly touched with white, and his face was
deeply lined: a hard, immobile face that denoted force,
reserve, and incalculable cunning. Redpath had never
looked upon a more impassive countenance, and yet he
was tremendously impressed by its power; understanding and intelligence lurked beneath this sinister mask.
Save for the occasional mocking,— even confident! —
glance that he bestowed upon the witness, his face was
as cold and imperturbable as that of the Sphinx.

Sherry finally awoke to the fact,— strangely unpleasant it was too,— that a deep significance marked
the attitude of George Smith toward him. He discovered that he alone was favoured with these singular
glances. The police, the prosecutor and even the
judge came in for the cold, fixed stare of one who hates
and does not fear. There was something disturbingly
personal in all this. The fellow had made the threat
the night before that he would " get him." There was
nothing in his manner today to indicate venom or a desire for reprisal.. On the contrary, he appeared to be
making a confidant of his accuser! To him alone was
conveyed, in that mocking glance, the message that
nothing,— absolutely nothing,— could come of all this
pother! And all this despite the very damaging, un-
impeachable testimony that the young man gave
against him.

It was most extraordinary. The man seemed to be
saying to him: " You and I know they'll never get
me for this, so let them go on deluding themselves. It's
a pleasure to watch the dam' fools, isn't it? "

They were bound over in the sum of two thousand
dollars each to await trial at the September term of the
Circuit Court. Redpath left the court-house in a decidedly uneasy frame of mind. He was conscious of a
strange depression. The conduct of George Smith not
only puzzled, it alarmed him. What was back of it
all?

Erect, bright-eyed, confident in his physical and
mental elevation, the erstwhile town disgrace strode
up Main Street, boldly headed for the Tremont. The
morning newspaper had " double-leaded " portions of

the story of his adventure with the two burglars, under scare head-lines, and by this time the city was awake to the new sensation.

Men and women who formerly had avoided him in the streets, or at best looked the other way when they encountered him, now frankly stared — and were rewarded by what they saw. They could hardly believe their eyes. Could such a miraculous transformation have taken place over night, so to speak? It seemed but yesterday that he was a blear-eyed, shuffling figure, dodging in and out of questionable places, headed hellward as fast as the devil could drive him, a night-farer who had no love for the light of day that shamed him. No wonder they stared and then discredited their eyes. Without exception, every head was turned for a second glance over the shoulder, and not a few were the collisions that resulted.

(Particularly unhappy was the head-on bumping of Mrs. Dr. Blake and the wife of the Methodist minister. Under ordinary conditions it was extremely difficult — some said impossible — for these two women to see each other; when by chance they happened to come into contact at " social functions " a stony silence fell upon two otherwise loquacious ladies. For five years they had kept their skirts clear of each other. Now they came together with shocking force. The silence of five years was rent and splintered as by a bolt of lightning. They gave vent to a great many utterances that had been accumulating, — many of them in unison, — and then, having set their hats aright, went their separate ways, sniffing the soft August air with

an eagerness that suggested the hope that distance
would fumigate it considerably.)

Redpath entered the Tremont. He waved a genial
greeting to the clerk behind the desk, smiled sweetly
upon the young lady at the news-stand,— (causing
her to tremble delightedly, he was such a good-looking
fellow, you know),— and strode briskly into the barber shop.

Six barbers looked up from their recumbent victims.
A barber invariably looks up when a newcomer enters
the shop, no matter where his razor may be engaged.
On this occasion the combined stare of six shavers remained fixed until the customer, after handing his hat
to the brush-boy, dropped into a carefully selected seat
under the revolving fan. Then six barbers leaned over
and whispered, whereupon the occupants of six chairs,
converting themselves into cortortionists, managed to
obtain a somewhat unsatisfactory view of the astonishing Mr. Redpath.

Three of them called out " halloa," as if they were
glad to see him, even under exasperating circumstances,
and one other added: " Some little old Sherlock,
eh? "

Then ensued a race in which six barbers frantically
strove to " finish his man " ahead of the rest, so that
he could call " next " to the most interesting citizen
of Farragut. Growls from the present occupants of
chairs met with scant consideration. The head barber
finished his man in triumph, elevating him to a sitting
posture with such decision that a sharp, explosive
grunt followed the jolt.

"What the —" began the angry customer.

"Next!" called out the head barber, thrusting a celluloid check into his late customer's hand, and bowing graciously to his successor.

"Shave, Mr. Redpath?" he inquired, fondly.

"Once over," was the brief response.

"Nice day," volunteered the latherer, feelingly.

"Umph," said Sherry.

Later on: "Hair-cut, Mr. Redpath?"

"Take a little off, Otto."

"Need rain badly, though."

"Badly." This was disheartening. Otto seemed to have grave difficulty in getting his customary conversational impetus.

"Sea-foam, Mr. Redpath?" he inquired, later on, clearly beaten.

"Dry shampoo, Otto," said Mr. Redpath, luxuriously.

"I hear you got a job," ventured Otto resolutely, but as if he doubted it.

"That's so? Where?"

"Haven't you been doin' some work for old man Gilman?"

"Oh, yes. It was so long ago I'd forgotten it. Masonic work."

"Pay well?"

"Fairly. I can afford a shampoo if that's what you mean. Go ahead, Otto."

Presently: "I see your name in the paper this morning."

"Yes?"

"Yes."

Ordinarily Otto was a most persevering conversationalist. His tongue seemed to be tied this morning, however. He wanted to say a thousand things and couldn't, for the life of him, understand his own backwardness. He made another effort, conscious that the whole shop was listening.

"If we could just get a little rain it would make a lot of difference," he said.

"Cool things off," agreed Sherry.

"Certainly would. Neck shaved?"

"You know I don't have my neck shaved."

"That's right." After long reflection: "Yes, a little rain certainly would do a lot of good."

"Cool things off," said Sherry, absently. He was thinking of a recent early-morning thunder-shower.

"Certainly would," said Otto, helplessly.

Out in the hotel lobby, Sherry found several men waiting for him. They surrounded him, slapped him on the back and jointly and severally invited him to have a drink.

"No, thanks," he protested, smilingly. "I'm not drinking."

"Aw, come off! What are you givin' us? We —"

"I've cut it all out, gentlemen. Never again."

"Just have a little one, Sherry," insisted a man who had declared a hundred times in the past that any one who bought a drink for Sherry Redpath ought to be run out of town. "A little one won't hurt you. I'm old enough to be your father. I wouldn't ask you to have a drink if I thought it would —"

"If it's just the same to you, Mr. Simons," said Sherry coldly, "I think I'll stick to my resolution."

"A glass of beer, Sherry, on a hot day like this," began another.

"We got to do something to show you how proud we are about that little fracas of yours last night," said a third, grasping the young man's arm. "You are the man of the hour. We all —"

"Sorry, gentlemen," said Redpath, stiffening. "You will have to excuse me. Good day." He walked away, leaving them staring after him somewhat indignantly.

"He won't stick to it a week, the poor nut," said the youngest man in the group.

"A week?" snorted Mr. Simons. "Why, he's been drinking this morning. That wasn't bay rum you smelt on him, Billy. It was booze. He'll be soaked to the gills before twelve o'clock."

CHAPTER XIII

THESE men were representative, self-respecting citizens of Farragut. As a matter of principle, they would not have suggested a drink to him a fortnight ago for anything in the world.

As he was leaving the hotel, Sherry encountered an old friend, no other than Patsy Burke, the barkeeper at the Sunbeam.

"I heard you was in here," said Patsy, eyeing the young man critically, "so I thought I'd skip over and say hello. You look fine. Fresh as a daisy. I been tellin' 'em you meant it. No one believed you could do it. Lord, man, I'm glad to see the white of yer eyes. For a few days I worried meself sick over you. I kept sayin' to the old lady if you could only stave it off for a week you'd be as safe as a man in the penitentiary for life. Would you believe it, my old lady puts in a word for you in her prayers every blessed day. She's a dam' fine woman, if I do say it as shouldn't,— seein' as she's a bartender's wife and all that,— and she has a heart of gold. 'Twas she that sent the grub up by Barney Doyle. I only did her biddin'."

Passersby, seeing the two in close, earnest conversation of the most intimate nature, and being denied the privilege of hearing what they had to say to each other, at once leaped to a natural and obvious conclusion. What else could they be talking about?

Mrs. Compton's automobile was standing at the curb just beyond the entrance to the hotel. After shaking hands again with the beaming Patsy, Redpath,— to the utter amazement of the occupants of various shop-windows as well as certain pedestrians who had paused with apparent unconcern in close proximity to the two men, stepped into the tonneau of the car and was whisked swiftly out of sight.

Before noon a report gained wide circulation that young Redpath had rented a second-hand Packard, 1908 model, and was starting out to " tear the town wide open " on the money borrowed from hero-worshipping citizens in the lobby of the Tremont.

The reporter for the *Evening News*, in describing the trial and the incidents leading up to it, spoke of " our completely rejuvenated young fellow-townsman, Sheridan Redpath," and had a sorry session with the managing editor, who advised him to look in the dictionary for the definition of the two words: rejuvenate and regenerate.

The object of all this interest, instead of tearing the town wide open, travelled swiftly and as directly as the old turnpike would permit to the scene of the late adventure. He had promised Mrs. Compton,— at the earnest solicitation of Miss O'Brien,— to return with a full account of the hearing. He found the latter very deeply interested in the proceedings; the former was singularly indifferent, even distrait. After the midday dinner, he announced his intention to spend the afternoon in Compton's Woods, where he could reflect seriously upon the proposition of Mr. Andrew Gilman.

" I have been thinking it over, Mr. Redpath," said

Mrs. Compton, as the three of them stood on the porch. "I do not like my brother-in-law, but I believe you will do well to accept the place he offers. It will go far toward re-establishing you in the eyes of the doubters. My antipathy is personal. If you serve him well and faithfully, he will repay you with interest. I will say that much for Andrew Gilman."

Morna walked with him down the hedge-lined lane to the big gate. His heart was light, and there were moments,— as when she looked straight into his eyes, — when he was absolutely certain that his head was light as well. It pleased him vastly to feel that she had, in a sense, taken him under her wing, and that she was disposed to order his immediate future in a somewhat direct and arbitrary manner. She was very cool and confident about it, and he was surprisingly meek and acquiescent.

For example, she made it quite impossible for him to ever touch another drop of alcoholic liquor by declaring that she would never speak to him again if he did, and she said she liked men who smoked cigars or a pipe because, really, cigarettes were only fit for women. (She enjoyed one herself on the sly, she admitted — having gone to school in Paris.) And she had a great deal to say about the danger of sleeping out in the damp, miasmic woods,— the dew was likely to be very heavy; there were poisonous spiders, typhoidish mosquitoes and bats, to say nothing of crawly things.

He shivered inwardly, but not with dread; it was a shiver of pure delight. All the while he watched her sprightly, adorable face and marvelled. Could this be he, Sherry Redpath, ne'er-do-well, shunned by all the

decent people in Farragut,— could this be he indeed?
If it were he in truth, then life was certainly worth
living, and living right. If being decent and respectable and clean of mind and body brought this sort of
thing into a fellow's life, then nothing on earth could
induce him to be anything else from this day forth.
He shuddered at the thought of all that he might have
missed if he had not spent his last dime and taken his
last drink on that day in the now glorified Sunbeam.
And now he understood why he had never really cared
for girls! He had never seen one before! Now that
his eyes were full of one, he couldn't see anything else.
It was all quite wonderful,— provided, of course, this
really was he.

There was a fly in the ointment, however. Morna,
— (he kept on caressing the name),— Morna was
much too cool and matter-of-fact. Her manner gave
him no hint that she too was indulging in delightful inward shivers. On the contrary, it was quite evident
that she was interested in him only because her grandmother had taken a fancy to him.

Her deep, violet eyes regarded him with the most im-
personal, yet serious interest. (How had he failed to
grasp the full effect of their loveliness on that first engaging day?) They peered up into his from the shadows of a cavern-like sun-bonnet. He always had
thought of sun-bonnets as abominations affected by
rural old maids who cherished the notion that they still
had complexions. Henceforth he would have no such
illusions; they exemplified absolute perfection in head-
gear.

They passed through the gate and lazily sought the

shade of a gnarled old apple tree whose branches over-
hung the snake-fence bordering the main highway.
She sat down upon a great, moss-covered boulder. He
gave a huge sigh of satisfaction. This was more than
he had expected or even hoped for. Fearing that she
might change her mind if he hesitated, he promptly
deposited his long frame on the ground beside her.

She was speaking of her grandmother and Andrew
Gilman.

"The surprising part is that no one, not even my
aunts, has ever dropped the slightest hint that Mrs.
Gilman is Granny's sister. You could have knocked
me over with a feather. As I was saying, she brought
the subject up herself after you left this morning. I
was dying to ask her all about it, but I didn't dare.
Granny's queer about a good many things, you see."

"So she hasn't spoken to her sister in thirty years?
That's a long time to hold a grudge."

"She hasn't even seen her in twenty years. I don't
know whose fault it was in the beginning, but I do
know that Granny has always hated Andrew Gilman.
She hates him even more than she does the Burtons,
and that's saying a good deal. Mrs. Gilman is two
years older than Granny. That would make her sev-
enty-three. She has been confined to her room,— so
the report goes,— for over ten years, an invalid.
Grandmother does not know the nature of her ailment,
but she as much as said to me this morning that she believes her mind is gone and that Andrew Gilman keeps
her locked up."

"By Jove, I wonder if that's what I'm likely to be
up against if I go to work for him," he said anxiously.

"Did he say anything to you about his wife?"

"Very little. Merely explained her absence from the table by saying she hadn't been downstairs to dine with him in years."

"Have you seen any one about the place who looked like a nurse or attendant?"

"I didn't notice. Of course, I wasn't rubbering."

"I hate that word."

"Well, then, snooping."

"I got this much out of Granny," she went on earnestly. "Soon after Mr. Gilman married my grandmother's sister,— that was a dreadfully long time ago, — he bought up at tax sale, or something, a lot of real estate in Farragut on which the Blair family,— that was my grandmother's maiden name,— had failed to pay taxes. The family thought they could redeem it any time they felt it convenient to do so,— times were very hard I believe she said,— and didn't worry about it. Well, things went on for about ten years and then the family got a chance to sell the property to some one for a very good price. When they got ready to sign the papers, or something, Andrew Gilman stepped in and spoiled the whole thing. It seems that he had had the property put into his own name, or something, and they were completely out of everything. The rest of the family accused him of being a snake in the grass, and he came back at them by volunteering to deed the property over to his wife, or something, and she could do what she pleased with it. Well, that's what he did, and then what do you think? His wife snapped her fingers at her poor old father and her brothers and her only sister,— who by that time had

married Grandfather Compton and didn't need any
money,— and refused point blank to restore their land
to them, even when they offered to pay the old taxes
and interest, or whatever it was. Of course, they all
understood why she acted in that way. Andrew Gilman forced her to do it. She —"

"I don't see how they figured it out in that way.
Why did he deed the property over to her —"

"That's just it," she cried. "He did it because he
was so frightfully mean that he wanted to make it appear that his wife was meaner than he was. Of course,
as Granny says, her brothers had been very careless
about letting the thing run along as it did,— they were
not good business men, she said,— and they seemed to
think it was all right for Mr. Gilman to hold the bag
until they got ready to relieve him of it. But he
wasn't that kind of a man. Well, an awful quarrel resulted. From that day to this not one of the family
has spoken to either of the Gilmans, and vice versa.
Granny is the only one left now. Her three brothers
are dead. I used to see one of them occasionally when
I was a little girl. He was a terrible old man, drunk
half the time and absolutely no good. Granny used
to give him money. He had a son, too, who was also
worthless. Her other brothers were fine men. So,
you see, just Granny and Mrs. Gilman are left, and
they are not friendly. It seems too bad, doesn't it?"

Sherry did not respond to this direct question. A
strange thought had flashed into his brain.

"Did your grandmother say what had become of
this son you spoke of,— her brother's son, the worthless one?"

"She didn't mention him at all. I have heard my cousins speak of him. He went away from Farragut a good many years ago."

"I see," he said, deeming it wise to keep his thoughts to himself. A rueful expression fell upon his face. "I certainly hope Mrs. Gilman isn't — er — non-compos mentis."

"Whatever that is," said she, her gaze fixed on a far-away cloud of dust on the highway. "You intend to take the job?"

"I still have a little calculating to do," he replied, thinking of the cumulative salary that Mr. Gilman had offered the night before.

A red runabout came swiftly down the road. The two watched its rapid approach in silence. A good-looking, sunny-faced young man was at the wheel, and he was alone in the car. As he flashed by he bowed and smiled cheerily upon Morna O'Brien, who bowed stiffly and unsmilingly in return.

"One of the Burton boys, wasn't it?" Sherry inquired.

"The one they call Jimmy," said she briefly.

"I thought the Comptons and Burtons never deigned to —"

"It isn't my fault, is it, Mr. Redpath," she said sharply, "if one of them chooses to speak to me?"

"At the risk of a snub," he added and took occasion to glance at her face. To his surprise her cheeks were rosy. It required but half an intelligence to see that she was blushing. "Or *did* you snub him?"

"I am quite sure I should like him tremendously if he were not one of those detestable Burtons," she said musingly. "He is extremely good-looking, isn't he? And he *is* nice, Mr. Redpath. Even Granny admits that. We just barely nod to each other, however,— nothing more. I haven't spoken to him since — well, it was over a year ago. Oh, dear," she sighed, "why is it that the men one could really like are the ones that can't be liked at all?"

"That sounds Irish.

"Just because he is a Burton I am obliged to despise him. I —"

"And, by the same reasoning, he is forced to hate you."

"I don't believe he hates me," she protested. "Didn't you see his smile? Did that look as though he hated me? Did —"

"It certainly did not," he said emphatically.

"Last summer Granny and I went to the circus in town. It was the evening performance and while the show was going on a big wind storm came up. Jimmy Burton,— the fellow who just went by grinning like an ape,— was sitting in a section of the reserved seats a good way off from us. The —"

"You could see him, however, in spite of the distance?"

"Certainly. I knew who he was," she went on calmly. "Well, the tent began to wabble in the wind. Everybody was nervous and excited. It got worse. People began to rush for the doors. Then, all of a sudden, a fearful gust of wind got under the edges of the tent and — woof! down it came! There was a dreadful panic. Women —"

"I know," he interrupted. "I was there."

"Really? Wasn't it frightful? Did *you* go to the rescue of any fair lady in distress?"

"I went to the rescue of the bareback rider who was in the ring at the time, if that is sufficient proof of my chivalry. She was thrown from her horse and fell just in front of the section in which I was sitting."

"Oh," she said doubtfully. "I remember now. She was quite pretty. Did you get her out safely?"

"I believe so. I am a little hazy about what happened. You see, that was before I had turned over my new leaf."

"Well," she resumed, dismissing his exploit abruptly, "Granny and I were caught in the crush. The canvas was flopping all about us, and the little quarter-poles,— that is what Jimmy Burton called them and he seems to know a lot about circuses,— well, they were banging around, and I didn't know what was to become of us when suddenly some one grabbed me by the arm and shouted out to keep cool. How on earth he ever got over there so quickly from where he was sitting just the minute before I can't conceive. In no time he lowered both of us over the tops of the seats and then jumped down after us. We were out in the rain in twenty seconds, safe as anything. He didn't leave us until we were in the automobile and off for home."

"That was bully of him," exclaimed he. "And I don't blame your grandmother for liking him too."

"Oh," she said quickly, "Granny doesn't know to this day that it was one of the Burtons who rescued us."

CHAPTER XIV

R EDPATH'S first month in the service of Andrew Gilman ended on the 28th of September. On that day his employer handed him ten crisp twenty dollar bills. If Mr. Gilman knew that his new secretary had gone through the last two weeks of that month without so much as a penny in his pockets, aside from the cherished silver dollar, he gave no sign; in any event he made not the slightest move toward relieving a most distressing condition. Perhaps he knew and considered it an excellent way to test the young man's character. If such was the case, he could not have been other than gratified by the absence of a petition on Sherry's part for a small advance against the month's pay. The former spendthrift suffered more from mortification than from actual need, however. There were times when a twenty-five cent piece would have saved him from humiliation,— as, for example, when he encountered Morna O'Brien on a very hot morning directly in front of Gibson's ice-cream soda "parlours" and was forced to ignore the inevitable appeal in her tender blue eyes,— and another and even more depressing occasion when he walked down the street with her until they came to Gibson's, where she deliberately stopped and cried:

"Oh, for a chocolate sundae, or even a cherry phosphate! I must have something to — come on in. Are you so busy these days, Mr. Redpath, that you can't spare a little time for light refreshment?"

He turned very red in the face, stammered something about being in a terrible rush,— although his progress had been leisurely up to that instant,— and, lifting his hat awkwardly, said good-bye to her. What would she think of him? His ears burned as he strode swiftly, angrily down the street. Lord! What *could* she think of him?

But Morna was a discerning young woman. She understood, and for hours afterwards she harangued herself for putting him in such an embarrassing position. She even changed her mind about the soda-water after climbing nimbly upon one of the high stools in front of the marble counter. The bold, arrogant inquiry of the pimply dispenser of soft drinks: "Well, what you going to have?" afforded her the excuse for hopping down from the stool and withering him with a look that he never forgot. "Nothing," she said icily, and walked out of the place. Young Mr. Redpath had disappeared.

It may be advisable to record here at least one or two of the significant incidents that marked young Redpath's apparently successful effort to rehabilitate himself. Inside of a week after taking up his new work, the word went around town that he was handling considerable sums of money belonging to Andrew Gilman. This was important news to a certain clique that infested the very heart of the city. A dozen professional gamblers took heart at once. Money in the pockets of Sherry Redpath was a most encouraging sign; things would soon be looking up.

One day the proprietor of the most important gambling place in town came upon his former patron in

a tobacconist's shop.   His pleasure at seeing the young
man was profound, and undoubtedly genuine.   He
seemed happy in forgetting the fact that he had barred
the doors of his place against him not many weeks
before and threatened to have him thrown down-stairs
if he came " nosing around " again.

All of this was amiably forgotten by Mr. William
Colgate, better known as " the Widdy," but it had not
slipped the mind of his one-time associate.

" And say, boy," the Widdy was saying in a confi-
dential undertone, " if you're temporarily embarrassed,
all you got to do is to mention it.   For old times' sake
I'll lend you anything up to five hundred.   You was a
good sport and I'm glad you've pulled yourself together.   There ain't nobody in this town that's as
pleased as I am over the way you've come up after
practically being down the third time.   If I had half
your grit I'd cut out this rotten business I'm in and —
What say? "

Redpath had interrupted him, smilingly and without
malice.   " I am hard-up, Bill, all right enough, but
I've been getting used to it for a long time.   As for
that ' old time ' stuff, don't fool yourself.   You are
not fooling me, you know.   You did me a better turn
when you ordered me out of your place than you'd be
doing if you lent me five hundred, so we'll let it stand
at that."

" Oh, say, now, Sherry," protested the Widdy, in
a hurt voice, " you mustn't forget I was tryin' to save
a little of the old mazoom for you when I advised you
to stay away from the joint for awhile,— till you got
a chance to sober up anyhow.   Them tin-horns were

skinnin' you alive, and I couldn't stand around and see
'em —"

"All right," broke in Sherry cheerily. "No hard
feelings on my part. It's no use, however, Bill. You
are wasting your time and breath. I'm going to work
for my money after this, not play for it. You needn't
expect me up at the rooms. If you've got an idea in
your head that I'm crooked, you can get it out at once.
Mr. Gilman's money is quite safe with me. So long,
Bill."

"Oh, I say, now, kid, this is a hell of a way —"

"See here," said the other, turning on him hotly,
"would you offer to lend me five hundred dollars,— for
old times' sake,— if I came to you, sober and straight
as I am now but without a job, and asked you for it?"

"Certainly," said the Widdy with great dignity.
"Of course I would. That's the kind of a man I —" -

"Yes, you would!" sneered the other. "You'd
laugh in my face. As I said before,— so long!"

The Widdy watched him through narrowed, evil eyes
as he crossed the street and entered the bank. A mean
smile played about his lips. "It seems that the idea
ain't original with me," he was saying to himself.
"He's been thinkin' of it himself. Well, we'll see."

The same afternoon Sherry was hailed from behind
by a loud, joyous voice, and as he turned to see who
had called, two heavy-breathing pedestrians in very
loud clothes drew up beside him and stuck out their
hands.

"Well, by Jiminy, if it isn't our little old Sherry
boy as big as life and twice as —" began one of them,
a sallow-faced individual with a thin, drooping mous-

tache and a perpetually drooping pair of greenish
eyes.

"I said it was you, kid, the minute I saw you," put
in the other, an elderly person with watery eyes and a
bulbous nose. "Put her there, Redpath, my boy."

Sherry kept his hands in his pockets. "It's no use,"
he said, shaking his head slowly; "not a bit of use,
boys. I've quit."

"Quit?"

"Quit what?"

"Talking with my hands," said Sherry, and to them
it was a perfectly intelligent remark.

"Just as you like," said the sallow one, lifting his
gaze for a singularly keen and searching examination
of the young man's face. Without another word, he
turned and walked away.

"I was just going to suggest a drink, Sherry,"
mumbled the older sport, and then, suddenly aware of
his companion's defection, called out: "Wait a second, Ike!" and was off in his wake without so much as
a word of explanation or farewell to the unresponsive
Redpath.

These and similar experiences provided unwhole-
some food for thought. It was clear to the young
man that his old-time associates of the bar-room and
den anticipated a return to the habits that had
wrecked him and were alive to the importance of being
prepared for the new harvest.

His duties were not many, but they were onerous.
He was not surprised to find that his employer attended to practically all of his correspondence, and
kept his own day-book and ledger. Later on, ex-

plained Mr. Gilman, this work would fall to him, but
not until experience along other lines had developed
a capacity for details and thoroughness. The rents
of selected tenants were to be collected by him, and
he was to accompany the old man when he went into
the lower and rougher parts of town to collect from
others. There was a definite understanding as to his
hours. It struck him as significant that he was to
have one free night a week,— that is to say, one night
for enterprises of a social character,— and that on
such occasions Mr. Gilman would remain up until his
return to the house, no matter what the hour.

When he undertook to assure his employer that such
a course was unnecessary, the old man cut him off
shortly with the remark that under no condition would
he retire until the house was closed for the night.

It was required of him, moreover, that he should
specify the night on which he wished to be out and to
obtain the consent of his employer before making an
engagement for that night. Aside from this rather
rigid provision, the requirements of his position were
not out of the ordinary. Mr. Gilman promised to
keep him busy. A signed contract covered all of the
essentials.

The young man was not deceived as to the nature
of his position in the house. During his profound calculations in the woods that sunny afternoon, when he
scribbled for an hour or more on the backs of envelopes in proving to himself the astounding growth of
his progressive salary, he did not fail to take into consideration the possibility of the old man's death long
before his pay reached its stupendous ultimate, and

with that thought came the conviction that his principal office would be the prolongation of Andrew Gilman's life.

In other words, Mr. Gilman's proposition had a very definite .purpose behind it. The longer he lived the greater would be the profit to the " party of the second part," otherwise Sheridan Redpath. There was not the slightest doubt in the young man's mind that Andrew Gilman lived in dread of some sinister force, that he lived in fear of something that would come only in the dead of night, and strike not with the hand of God but the hand of an assassin!

" Well," said the party of the second part to himself, as he thrilled under the excitement and uncertainty of what lay before him if he accepted the post, " I don't know what's in the wind,— and I guess it's just as well that I shouldn't know,— but it looks as though I'm expected to sleep with one eye open for the next few years."

He was given a room on the second floor of the sombre, silent old house,— a large, airy room with doors opening into other rooms on either side. Mr. Gilman explained that his own bed-room was to the right, while to the left was a sitting-room used by his wife when she was able to be up and about,— which was at rare intervals. Mrs. Gilman's bed-chamber was beyond this sitting-room. Across the narrow hall and directly opposite, was the room occupied by a female attendant who had taken care of Mrs. Gilman since the beginning of her illness.

" One of the reasons why I expect you to be in bed, or at least in your room before I retire," explained Mr.

Gilman, " is that I always enter my own room through this one. I do not use the door opening from my room into the hall. That door, I may add, is locked and barred. It is never opened. It is only fair to you, my lad, to explain that Mrs. Gilman's affliction is of a nervous character. Not mental, as you may conclude, but of an extremely unhappy nature, just the same. She cannot bear the idea of having the doors to her own room locked. Indeed, the mere thought of it induces the most excruciating suffering. She wants to be alone at night, but she does not want to be locked in her room. This door, therefore, which opens into her sitting-room, is never locked, nor is her bed-room door beyond. As you may readily see, I can pass from my own room to hers, at the far end of the house, without going into the hall. Her hall door is always closed but never locked. Miss Corse, her nurse, is required to keep her own bed-room door unlocked. It will not be necessary for you to lock your hall door. You will observe that there are no means of locking the doors between your room and those on either side of you. The locks have been removed, — at the request of Mrs. Gilman, I may say. Her comfort and pleasure come first with every one connected with this household, Sheridan. She keeps close to her room. No one intrudes upon her privacy. You will see but little of her, my boy. It is not necessary, of course, for me to remind you that this privacy is not to be disturbed."

"Certainly not, sir. I am sorry that Mrs. Gilman is —"

"These two windows face the street," interrupted

Mr. Gilman abruptly. "The roof of the veranda, as
you may have observed, runs the full length of the
house. I must ask you not to step from your window
upon that roof. The fact that some one was outside
her windows would be very disturbing to my wife, as
you may well imagine. She is very sensitive to noises,
and even to the remote presence of strangers."

Redpath moved his few belongings into the house and
prepared to make the best of a rather uninviting prospect. His first night was a sleepless one. He could
not divert his thoughts from the room at the extreme
end of the hall. What of its occupant? Was she,
after all, a mad woman? Young and strong and fear-
less as he was, he experienced an occasional creepiness
of the flesh; his ears were alert for sounds; his eyes,
closed tight, were ready to pop open at the slightest
noise. Try as he would, he could not go to sleep. All
the grewsome sensations that he had felt in the dead of
night when he was a small and lonely boy came rushing
up out of the past to confront him once more. He
could not laugh them away. They persisted, and he
was a foolish boy again.

His bedstood stood almost directly in front of the
door leading to Mr. Gilman's room. The door was
closed. It could not be opened without coming in contact with his bed, and because of the obstruction could
not be thrown completely ajar. He was lying, therefore, so close to the thin barrier that he could hear the
heavy, stertorous breathing of the old man in the next
room. Save for that, there was not a sound in the
house from midnight till dawn. There was something
eerie about the silence that enveloped him.

After a few nights this sense of oppressiveness wore off, and, while he awoke at the slightest sound, his slumbering was sweet and natural. The queer feeling of dread left him. Nothing had happened and apparently nothing was going to happen.

Aside from the odd circumstance of the old woman who was never seen nor heard, day or night, the household was as commonplace as any other he had known. There were two women-servants, both old in the service of the Gilmans: a cook and a general housemaid. The chauffeur, who also acted as gardener and outside-man, did not sleep on the place. Miss Corse, the nurse, attended to all of the wants of Mrs. Gilman. She carried her tray to and from the kitchen, prepared her food, took care of her rooms and actually stood as a barrier between her charge and the other occupants of the house. She was a tall, spare woman of uncertain age, with a rather agreeable smile and a pleasant voice. At nine o'clock each morning she made a private report to Andrew Gilman, whose only comment was a steady, almost imperceptible nodding of the head.

Toward the end of his third week, a most extraordinary thing happened. Had he not been in possession of certain facts, it would have been a commonplace, ordinary incident, unworthy of notice or comment.

Mrs. Compton came to call on Andrew Gilman!

Apparently her visit was not unexpected. Mr. Gilman was plainly disturbed and nervous during the mid-day meal, and there was a dark frown as of perplexity on his seamed brow. She came at three and remained in the house not longer than ten minutes. Her departure was as abrupt and unceremonious as her arrival.

The automobile waited for her at the bottom of the drive, and it was worthy of notice that the engine was not shut down during her brief absence. At the end of her interview with Andrew Gilman, which took place behind closed doors in the library, she strode briskly forth and made her way unattended down the walk. Mr. Gilman did not even accompany her to the front door of his home.

CHAPTER XV

REDPATH was curious but he was above spying. That this break in the rigid silence of thirty years was due to an overpowering necessity was perfectly clear to him. The redoubtable Mrs. Compton would not have withdrawn from the stand she had taken unless moved by something more imperative than mere sentimentality, or repentance, or even sisterly love. And, for that matter, Andrew Gilman would not have received her in the house she had disdained for so many years except under the most urgent and compelling circumstances.

The new secretary spent many an hour in speculation, but no light came to him. One feature stood out clear and well-defined, however, and it was worth all the thought he could put upon it: it was undoubtedly Andrew Gilman and not his visitor who went down to defeat in that unwitnessed conflict of two strong, resolute natures.

The change in him was immediate and noticeable. When Redpath reported to him soon after Mrs. Compton's departure, he found the old man pale and shaken; his effort to appear calm and natural was so obvious that Sherry was, for the moment, embarrassed. In time, however, the old man regained control of his nerves and then, strangely enough, he was more grim and remote than ever before. Not a word did he utter concerning his visitor or the object of her visit.

188

Redpath was shrewdly aware of an underlying motive back of the summons which brought him to the library. Something told him that Andrew Gilman was
deliberately testing his own powers of concentration.
Such was the forceful, arrogant nature of this sub-
lime egotist that he was willing to pit his shaken nerves
against the keen observation of a thoroughly stimulated
curiosity, for he had not the slightest doubt that Redpath's interest in the affairs of the household had long
since outgrown the passive stage.

"I have been thinking over that matter of Edgecomb's," said Andy Gee, stopping in front of his secretary, his hands clasped behind his back. "Perhaps
the man *is* telling the truth about his family in England. In that event —" and thus began a cool, matter-of-fact discussion of the dismal affairs of one
Henry Edgecomb, butcher, who was four months behind with his rent.

That night Redpath went to the theatre. It was,
as he drolly put it, his " night out." The manager of
the Grand Opera House, a gentleman of Hebraic ori-
gin and the possessor of considerable foresight, had
given him a " pass " a day or two earlier. The season
was just beginning. No harm, thought the long-
headed manager, in encouraging his one-time consist-
ently regular patron, especially as the " advance sale "
was meagre and the " attraction " one of the " seventy-
thirty " type,— which means that the local management takes but thirty per cent of the " gross " and re-
gards itself in the light of a victim of the high-handed
methods of greedy New York " syndicates," and so on
and so forth. (You should hear the small town man-

ager dilate upon the iniquities of the " system " if you
are at all pessimistic about your own miserable existence. He will make an optimist of you in five minutes.)

At half-past nine Redpath went out " front " and
poked his head through the door of the manager's
office. He was a privileged character,— or, at any
rate, he had been one,— and now presumed upon past
intimacy.

" Jake," he said solemnly, " am I right in thinking
that you told me this company was direct from New
York, or was it another hallucination? "

" I didn't say New York," replied the little manager speciously. " I said ' Broadway.' You needn't
tell me it's punk. Half a dozen people have already
come out here to tell me that, and they *paid* to get in.
I saw somewhere the other day that Broadway runs
clear from the Battery to Albany. It's a long, long
street, that Broadway, and it's got Yonkers on it, and
Peekskill, and Poughkeepsie. Do you get me? "

" I do. This one's from Yonkers. You got me
here tonight, Jake, under false pretences. I must ask
you to fork over what I paid for my ticket."

Jake appeared to be calculating. " You saw one
act of the show, didn't you? "

" Was it an act? "

" Sure it was. Didn't the curtain go up and down? "

" Now that you mention it, it did."

" Well, if you'll go back and see the other two acts
I'll let you sit in a box all by yourself. That will give
the rest of the audience something of interest to look at
and they won't be coming out here with blood in their

eye demanding their money back. You're the biggest
hit in town."

"Good *night!*" exclaimed Sherry, good-naturedly,
and departed. Bad as the performance was, he would
have remained to the bitter end if his search through
the audience had revealed the presence of Morna
O'Brien. She was not there, so he went home.

His return at ten o'clock was unexpected. There
was no one in the library. Mr. Gilman always sat
there reading until eleven or after. He never went
over his accounts at night. The days were long
enough, he claimed, for any honest man to do all that
he had to do; the nights were for relaxation.

In some uneasiness, Sherry mounted the stairs.
There was no light in the transom over his employer's
bed-room door, nor in his own. Just as he was on the
point of returning to the lower floor to search for Mr.
Gilman, the door to Mrs. Gilman's sitting-room was
opened. A stream of light flashed for an instant
against the wall opposite, and then was shut off by the
quick closing of the door. Mr. Gilman had emerged
from the room and was approaching. In all the days
and nights he had spent in and about the house, Redpath had never known the old man to approach his
wife's quarters.

"You are home early," said Mr. Gilman affably, as
they met at the top of the stairs. "Wasn't the play
any good?"

"It was awful." He ventured a bold inquiry.
"Isn't Mrs. Gilman so well tonight?" There was real
solicitude, real anxiety, in his voice.

"Quite as well as usual," replied the other. "There

is never much of a change, either way. I have just
been talking with Miss Corse,— and doing a little detective work, my lad. By the way, did *you* hear any
unusual sounds outside your windows last night,— or
any night, for that matter?"

"No, sir. I'm a very light sleeper, too."

"Ah, I am glad to hear that. Miss Corse says it is
pure imagination, and I am inclined to believe she is
right. Mrs. Gilman declares she heard some one on
the roof of the veranda this evening. Autumn leaves
blowing across the shingles, is what I make it out to be.
There is quite a strong wind tonight, isn't there?"

"A stiff breeze, and getting much colder. Frost in
the air. Would it relieve Mrs. Gilman's mind if I were
to take a turn around the lawn and garden?"

"I think she is convinced that everything is all
right," said the other. "I had a look myself, just to
satisfy her. Are you off to bed so early?"

"I have a little work to do in my room. I didn't
quite finish transferring the —"

"Never mind doing it tonight," broke in the old
man, quite genially. "Let it go over till tomorrow.
Only geniuses work at night,— geniuses and sewing
women,— there may be others, but —" He shook his
head dubiously.

"Such as under-graduates and safe-blowers," supplied Sherry, in a like mood. They were descending
the stairs together. Mr. Gilman had clasped the
young man's arm ostensibly in what was meant to be
a familiar manner. Sherry, however, was subtly aware
of a gentle force which urged him onward.

He smiled to himself. The story about the noise on

the veranda roof was a creation, pure and simple, inspired by sudden necessity.   There was not the slightest doubt in his mind that Mr. Gilman's visit to his
wife's room was for the purpose of laying before her,
even at the risk of grave consequences, the facts connected with the astounding visitation of the early afternoon.

He was now, more than ever, convinced that Mrs.
Compton, not through love or compunction, but because she was fair despite her antipathies, had come
with revelations which were of the utmost importance
to the Gilmans.   Back in his mind lurked always the
bit of news imparted by Morna O'Brien: there had
been a worthless brother to these two women, and he
had had an evil son.

For an hour the two men sat in the library.   Mr.
Gilman did most of the talking.   He appeared to be in
a jovially reminiscent mood.   As he related certain of
his experiences in dealing with the rich and poor of
Farragut, his sharp little eyes twinkled merrily, his
grim features relaxed into a quaint, almost shy smile
of amusement, in which there seemed also to be an appeal for the young man's sympathy.

The latter was vastly entertained.   He was soon
laughing heartily and unrestrainedly.   Andy Gee's
gift of narrative was incomparable.   He possessed a
dry, crisp wit and, true to form, was sparing of words.
He was terse almost to the point of abruptness, and yet
he was graphic.   An unsuspected phase of his employer's character was revealed to Sherry; he caught
himself wondering if this could be Andrew Gilman who
jested so marvellously well.   Former conversations of

an intimate nature had afforded him a glimpse of the man's intellectual attributes; there had been occasional flashes of the brightest sort of irony; but not until to-night had he appeared in the rôle of raconteur.

"By Jove, Mr. Gilman," cried he, after a particularly amusing account of old Judge Emmons' third marriage, " you ought to get out a book of these stories. They're marvellous. People would die laughing at some of the —"

"My dear boy, would you make a murderer of me?" cried the old man. "Would you have me, for the sake of a few paltry dollars and the pride of seeing my name on a title-page, kill thousands of innocent people? It is monstrous! I am shocked — Yes? What is it, Miss Corse?"

The nurse was standing in the open door. Both men had turned quickly as she tapped with her knuckles on the panel.

"Mrs. Gilman has changed her mind, sir. She will see you now, sir, if you will come at once."

Without a word, the master of the house sprang to his feet and hurried from the room. Redpath realized later that he had been holding his breath for a long time. He was dumbfounded. Mrs. Gilman had changed her mind and would see her husband *now!* He had not been with her earlier in the evening after all. Even as he began to smile over his own silly deductions, Miss Corse re-entered the library. She came straight to his side.

"I don't know what it's all about, Mr. Redpath," she said hurriedly, lowering her voice. "Maybe it means a reconciliation. I've been here nine years and

in all that time they've never spoken a word to each
other. In fact, so far as I know, they've not even seen
each other."

"Good Lord," cried Sherry, "I never dreamed there
was anything like that in the wind. I thought she was
so hopelessly — er — afflicted that she couldn't —"

"She's as well as you or I," said the nurse deliberately. "Except for her age, I mean, and the queer
fancies that sometimes come to old people. Nine years
of it, that's what it's been, and I don't know how
long it had been going on before I came. In all these
years this is the first time he has asked her to see him,
so it must be important. I guess it's pretty bad, whatever it is. Don't think I'm blabbing secrets. I just
had to let out to somebody. You look and act like a
sensible, trustworthy young fellow and I —"

"You say she isn't ill?" cried he, incredulously.

"She's the huskiest old woman I've ever seen," said
she tersely. "Has indigestion once in awhile and
touches of rheumatism, but that's all."

"And she stays in her room, day and night, with
nothing at all the matter with her?"

"That's exactly what she does. Like a groundhog.
By glory, I wonder if she'll be able to recognize him
after all these years. He has changed a lot. He used
to wear whiskers, they say. The funny part of it is,
she has queer dreams about him, and sees him as plain
as day walking about in her room, and without whiskers, mind you. That comes of me arguing with her a
few months ago about the way Mr. Gilman looks. She
never knew him when he didn't have whiskers. They
used to be the fashion a long time ago. According to

her, he must have had the niftiest set of whiskers in
Farragut on the day they were married. They used
to curl them, too. My Gawd, how she hates him!
He's had his orders, all right enough. Never a foot
can he put inside her room. He can't poke the tip of
his nose —"

"But he was in her room tonight," interrupted he.
"He came out of her sitting-room as I was going upstairs."

"You're mistaken about that. He may have been
down at that end of the hall, but *inside* her room? Not
much!"

"See here, Miss Corse, it's none of my business, and
I'm not here to pry into the private affairs of my employer, but I'd like to ask you one question. Did you
tell him that Mrs. Gilman thought she heard some one
on the veranda roof?"

"Yes. Wasn't anything, though. She's always
hearing queer noises. Maybe she *is* a little dotty, after
all. I told him not to bother looking outside, because
I was sure it was the wind blowing leaves against the
side of the house."

"What time was this?"

"About half-past eight. He went outside and in-
vestigated. Then he came up to my room and ordered
me — ordered, mind you,— to go in and tell Mrs. Gilman he had to see her about something vitally important. I told her. I wish you could have seen the way
she took on. I thought she was going to have a stroke
then and there. Well, he was fearfully upset. Pretty
soon he came back upstairs and rapped on her door. I
heard her ask who was there. He told her. Not a

word out of her. I opened my door and came out.
He had an envelope in his hand. He held it up for
me to see, and then stuck it under her door, speaking
loudly so's she couldn't help hearing. He said: ' If
you don't read this note you will be doing some one the
greatest wrong in the world, and that some one is not
me.' Then he went down-stairs. There is a bell in my
room that can be rung from hers. About ten minutes ago she rang it. I went in. She was perfectly
cool and calm. She sent me down to tell Mr. G. she'd
see him if he'd come up at once. It must be something
very important, or she wouldn't give in like this. I
wonder what it can be."

"The Lord only knows," said he, more to himself
than to her.

"First time in more than nine years, to my personal
knowledge," said she, glancing over her shoulder.
"I'm glad to have some one to talk to, Mr. Redpath.
Not that I'm dissatisfied with the job, mind you. It's
easy. She's no trouble at all, and he is perfectly
lovely to me. I don't believe half the mean things they
say about him. I guess I'd better be getting back upstairs. I wouldn't have him think I'd been talking
to you about — these things, and he'd be smart enough
to know it for sure if he saw us together. You can't
fool old Andy Gee. And say, Mr. Redpath, this hatred ain't one-sided, not by a long shot. When I said
she hated him worse than poison, I should have added
that the pleasure is not all hers. He despises her.
Sometimes I feel so sorry for old Andy Gee I could cry.
Whatever it was that happened to bring all this about,
I'll bet my soul he wasn't the one to blame. If you

could see the set, hard look about her mouth, you'd say
so, too."

"Don't you think you'd better be up-stairs, ready,
in case she — well, goes to pieces, as they say? You
may be needed in case —"

"No danger of that," said she firmly. "She's got
the whip hand of him now, and if anybody cracks under the strain it will be Mr. G. I sized things up when
I was in there a few minutes ago. Whatever it is,
she's got him where she wants him at last, and she's not
going to pieces about it, believe me. Still, I guess I'll
slip up and,— well, just *in case*, you know. Good
night. I hope you won't mention anything to Mr. G.
about what we've been saying to each other. As you
say, it *isn't* any business of ours."

"You may rest easy, Miss Corse."

At twelve o'clock Mr. Gilman emerged from his
wife's room and came slowly down the hall toward Redpath's door. He stopped at the top of the stairs and
listened for a moment. The house was dark, save for
a single light in the upper hall, a light that burned all
night. Then he tapped lightly on Sherry's door. In
response to a quiet "come," he entered the room.

Redpath was lying in bed reading. The old man
sat down wearily on the edge of the bed.

"What are you reading, my lad?" he inquired, passing his hand over his brow as if to wipe something
away.

"'The Murderers in the Rue Morgue,'" said his secretary.

CHAPTER XVI

THE household slipped back into its accustomed groove the next morning. There was no sign of uneasiness in the bearing of Andrew Gilman when he came down to breakfast. No matter how harshly his emotions may have been exercised on the preceding day, this new day at least bore no evidence that he had the slightest grudge against circumstance.

He was as bland and imperturbable as ever; the anxious, furtive expression no longer lurked in his eyes. He ate a hearty breakfast and relished it.

"The *Dispatch* gives you the lie," he said, putting down his coffee cup. "It says that the play last night was — wait a second, I have it here. It says,— now listen to this,— it says 'The performance last evening was the most admirable given in Farragut in many a season. Manager Cohen deserves the gratitude of all lovers of high art in the theatre. It is to be lamented that his effort to provide our city with the best that the theatrical world affords did not meet with a more generous response from the play-going public. There was a small audience, but it was made up of the most intelligent, discriminating, up-to-date people in Farragut. Manager Cohen laboured for months with the big theatrical interests in New York before he succeeded in getting them to book this splendid Metropolitan success for a single one night stand, and Farragut should have shown its appreciation of his efforts by packing the house.' There is a great deal more about the enterprising, self-sacrificing Mr. Cohen which you may read at your leisure. If my memory serves me correctly, you said last night that it was ' awful.' "

Sherry laughed. "Perhaps I am not smart enough to recognize a Metropolitan success when I meet it in a one night stand."

"I also read somewhere in the city news columns that your burglarizing friends are to be tried on the tenth of November."

"Is that so? Justice may be swifter than we suspect."

"I suppose you will have to appear as the principal witness?"

"Undoubtedly. I wonder if Mrs. Compton and Miss O'Brien will be subpœnaed. It seems entirely unnecessary to drag them into court."

If he intended these remarks as a "bait" he got nothing for his effort. Mr. Gilman merely said he thought so too, and a promising subject was dropped.

Miss Corse froze up over night. Her five minute reduction to simple nature in the security of the library was not likely to recur, judging by the manner in which she bowed to her late confidant when she met him in the lower hall.

"Everything all right this morning?" he had inquired, hoping to nourish the sprout of intimacy.

"Yes, it is a beautiful morning," she replied, and passed on up the stairs, carrying Mrs. Gilman's breakfast tray.

"Well," he said to himself, pensively, "it's none of my business anyway."

Later in the day he encountered her again. She was quite civil,— she was never anything else, for that matter,— but the Sphinx could have been no more silent than she on the one topic he was particularly eager to have revived.

He waited a week and then, hearing nothing from Mrs. Compton, decided that it was his duty as a friend to run out to her place in the automobile and talk over the coming trial with her.

She was more than pleased to see him. For as much as a quarter of an hour they discussed the case and the events of that historic night, and then for quite an hour and a half they talked of nearly everything under the sun. At last he arose to go. He may have sighed, but if so she was politely unobservant.

"By the way," he said, pausing on the porch steps, — and quite as if the thought had entered his mind for the first time, "how is Miss O'Brien?"

"She is always well. That is one of the reasons why she is my favourite grandchild. The others are for ever complaining about something. Morna is a tonic, not a depressant. It does me a world of good just to see her about."

"She is exceedingly bright and —" he began lamely, and then floundered: "I wish you would remember me to her."

"She will be sorry to have missed seeing you."

"Ahem! Yes, indeed,— exceedingly bright. Sorry to have missed seeing her. Kindly remember me to — Well, good day, Mrs. Compton. I really must be off.

I told Mr. Gilman I wouldn't be gone more than an hour. Why, it's five o'clock. That shows how entertaining you are, Mrs. Compton. Hours go like minutes when —"

"Stuff and nonsense," said she, smiling. "I am quite as disappointed as you, my friend. Next time telephone out beforehand and she'll be at home, and not in town at the dressmaker's. You must come again soon. By the way, you may meet her on the road coming home. When she is alone she invariably comes by way of the lower road and cuts through Compton's Woods. It appears that that is the long way home."

"I see," he said, and paused expectantly.

"The chauffeur is off for the day, fishing," she supplied, and he said good-bye from the gravel walk, halfway to the garden gate.

He thought it all out as he drove rapidly down the lane to the highway. Common-sense, with which he was amply supplied, directed him to take the shortest way to town, and that was over the turn-pike. Inclination ordered him into the less frequented dirt-roads of Compton's Woods. Common-sense, backed up by a certain regard for his own dignity, prevailed. He drove past the road leading down into the woods and, calling upon all the speed the car possessed, resolutely fled from temptation.

The first mile of his incontinent flight produced alternate moods of regret and satisfaction. He wished that he had gone by way of the woods and yet was glad that he hadn't. In the first place, it was quite possible that Miss O'Brien would not derive the same amount of pleasure from the meeting as he, and certainly there

was this to be considered: she would soon be by way of
knowing that he had deliberately planned the encounter, and he had no reason for assuming that she would
be gratified by the very marked attention.   Indeed, it
was not unlikely that she would be annoyed.   He was
nothing to her; he meant but little in her life.   Why,
therefore, should he take it for granted that she would
be agreeably affected by even a chance meeting with
him?   And, as for a premeditated meeting,— why, she
was just as likely as not to charge it to unmitigated
conceit and avoid him as adroitly as possible in future.

And so it came to pass that he, courageous and
strong of body, suddenly became extremely faint of
heart.   To be sure, he had not much of an argument
to put up for himself.   He certainly had nothing to
offer in the way of proof that he was worthy of a closer
acquaintance with Morna O'Brien, or any other carefully brought-up young lady, for that matter.   Six
weeks of good behaviour and clean living would not go
very far toward obliterating the record of as many
years perniciously spent in the effort to become as unworthy as possible.   Miss O'Brien was far too intelligent a person, far too sophisticated to accept so brief a
period of abstinence as proof that his regeneration was
complete.

His cheek burned as the result of an appalling suspicion that he had placed her in an embarrassing position by accosting her on the streets of Farragut!   He
had not thought of it in that light before.   Quite naturally she would prefer not to be seen talking with him
in public.   Other girls had made a practice of avoid-

ing him for years,— and properly, he was fair enough
to admit,— so why should he take it for granted that
Morna O'Brien felt any differently toward him than
they?

As he sailed along at top speed he attempted to justify the inclination to take the road through Compton's Woods by contending that it was no more than
right that he should let Morna know that her grandmother had paid a visit to Andrew Gilman's house, and
that there was something decidedly queer about it. He
was assuming that it would be news to Miss O'Brien,
and that while Mrs. Compton's visit in the broad daylight of a September afternoon could hardly be described as surreptitious, it was at least something to be
concerned about. In any case, Morna ought to know
about it, and would doubtless thank him for going out
of his way,— indeed for putting himself to considerable inconvenience — to —

But just at this stage of his cogitations something
happened that proved beyond all question that he was
right, if not inspired, when he resisted the impulse to
profit by Mrs. Compton's hint. A sharp turn brought
him in sight of two automobiles, stationary at the roadside a short distance ahead. He recognized one of the
cars instantly; the other a moment later. Two people
were examining the engine of a high-powered red road-
ster,— a man and a woman. There was no one else in
sight, unless you were to count the inevitable small boy
who always appears when anything happens to an automobile. This small boy was barefooted and carried
a fishing-pole and a string of sunfish, now sadly neglected and parched by the rays of the sun. He had

no bearing on the situation however. Neither of the investigators noticed him. He might just as well have been left out of the picture. A pair of heads were bent over the silent engine: one bare and curly and blond, the other crowned by a familiar panama.

They looked up as the Gilman car came rushing down upon them. It was then that Redpath recognized the blond curly-headed one. He sounded his horn in what was meant to be a courteous warning, but for some reason the miserable thing seemed to him to express disapproval, even irritation. He slowed down and was passing them at a snail's pace.

"Any help?" he called out.

"Oh, it's Mr. Redpath!" cried Morna O'Brien.

"Hello, Sherry," greeted the curly-headed one. "No, thanks. I think I can fix her. Thanks, just the same."

Without intending in the least to do so, Sherry brought his car to a standstill. He could have cursed himself the instant he did so,— and afterwards did say some very drastic things about his stupidity.

"What's the matter with her?" he inquired. (One always provides a steamship, a locomotive or an automobile with sex.)

"Don't know," responded young Mr. Burton, and there was an uneasy gleam in his sunny blue eyes. "Something's out of whack. I'll find it in a minute."

"I found him here quite a while ago," explained Miss O'Brien, "working like mad over —"

"I was in a terrible hurry to get home," broke in Burton uneasily. "Must have got too gay with the old pile of junk. Anyhow she died on me."

" And he refuses to let me take him home in my car and send some one back for his," said Morna. "It's silly, isn't it?"

Sherry suddenly grasped the situation. Young Burton was playing a very pretty game. The present condition of his engine was the result of some very clever tinkering on his part prior to the advent of Miss O'Brien.

" Let me have a look at it," he said, and hopped out' of his own car. There was no mistaking the wily Mr. Burton's chagrin. He was quite plainly embarrassed.

" I think she's slipped a —" he began, and a plead- ing expression came into his eyes. " Never mind, Redpath. Don't bother, old fellow. I'll let Miss O'Brien drop me at —"

" I'll take you all the way home, Mr. Burton," said she decisively. " It's really no distance at all, if we cut in through the woods just below here. Do you know anything about the mechanism of this car, Mr. Redpath?"

" I ought to know," said Sherry grimly. " I owned one just like it, same model and everything." He was inspecting the intricate wiring, and there was a sly grin on his lips. Young Burton looked on in dismay. " When did it happen, Jimmy?" he inquired, glancing up into the young man's eyes.

" About a half an hour ago," replied Jimmy, man- aging to give his head a significant shake unseen by Morna — and to add a very secret grimace expressing confidence in the fellowship of man. " Never acted like this before."

He was a likable chap, and abominably good-looking.

Sherry recalled Morna's lament that he was a Burton.
There was absolutely nothing the matter with the engine. A bit of tape and two minutes' time would re-
pair the damage that unquestionably had been inflicted
by the engaging and resourceful Mr. Burton. He had
trusted to Morna's ignorance. Any one who knew the
first thing about an engine would have detected the
trouble at once,— just as Redpath did, for example.

" Never had a thing like this happen when I owned
one of these cars," said Redpath, enjoying the other's
discomfiture. " Got a piece of tape? "

" Have you found it, Mr. Redpath? " cried Morna.
He may have been mistaken, but he thought he detected
a trace of disappointment in her voice.

" He knows more about a car than anybody in town,"
said Jimmy, giving up all hope and paying tribute.

He was so good-natured about it when he might have
been ill-tempered and cross that Redpath, won over
by the frank appeal in his eyes, withheld the exposure.
It was in his power to spoil this well-laid plan of the
enterprising and ardent Mr. Burton,— and he wondered afterward if he should not have done so if only
for the sake of preserving intact the feud between the
Burton and Compton families,— but he was too good
a sport to take advantage of the opportunity. Moreover it occurred to him that Morna was not quite as
ignorant as she professed to be. She probably knew
quite as well as either he or Jimmy Burton just what
it was that ailed the engine. So, frowning dubiously,
he stepped back from the car.

" Looks doubtful, Jimmy," and was rewarded by an
unmistakable sigh of relief. " If you say so, I'll stop

at Nolan's garage and have him send out a machine to pull her in."

"Thanks, old man,— if you'll be so kind. Mighty good of you, Sherry. I'll do as much for you some time."

"If I ever give you the chance," said Sherry, significantly, and turned to Miss O'Brien.

She was regarding him curiously. The instant his steady, mocking eyes met hers, she flushed and, after a second or two, turned away — guiltily, he was pleased to decide.

"I dropped in to see Mrs. Compton. She said you always came home through the woods."

"And so you took the high-road," she said sweetly, meeting his gaze once more. There was an ominous cloud in her eyes. "I suppose you are always in a hurry these days, so full of business and all that."

"I was late," he explained, suddenly feeling like a fool.

Jimmy was busily engaged with the magneto. A close observer might have noticed that his ears were very red.

She whirled abruptly and walked to her own car on the opposite side of the road. Redpath hesitated an instant and then followed.

"Let me help you up," he said, at her elbow.

"I am not decrepit," she exclaimed, and slid easily into the driver's seat. Then she leaned over and said to him in a low voice: "I don't want you to think that either one of you has fooled me. I know what's the matter with his bally old car,— and you know, and he knows. So good-bye, Mr. Redpath. Good-bye,

Mr. Burton. I'm so glad to have seen you again. Sorry you won't let me drive you home. Perhaps if you and Mr. Redpath get your heads together you may discover what the matter is,— and it will not be necessary to have Nolan tow you in."

In went the clutch, there was a vast roar from the exhaust, and then the car leaped forward with a bound.

"Well, I'll be —" began Jimmy blankly. For a full minute the two of them stood in the road watching the car. It took the turn at a dangerously high rate of speed, and then Jimmy sat down suddenly on the running board of the red deceiver. "Damned queer the way girls act sometimes, Redpath. She was as nice as pie to me until — er —" He paused, eyeing his companion critically.

"Until we all found each other out," said Redpath. "I'm sorry if I butted in and spoiled —"

"Lord, you didn't spoil anything. I couldn't have carried it so far as to let her take me home, you know. That would have been rotten. You think she knew what the matter was all the time?"

"Certainly."

"Well, by gosh, she fooled me all right. I never saw any one who could *act* as ignorant about a car as she did. You'd think she never had seen the inside of a hood before."

"That is a way they all have," said Redpath, sententiously.

Jimmy Burton drew a long breath. "Then, why the dickens did she string me along for half an hour, helping me with the tools, and suggesting all sorts of —"

"I must be on my way, Jimmy," broke in the other,

looking at his watch. "You've got a lot to learn about women. They've just got to act ignorant. They go on the principle that you can't possibly be interested in a thing after you once know all there is to know about it. For instance, she wouldn't have been half so happy this afternoon if she had let you see right off the bat that she was on to the fact that you had jerked that wire out of kilter on purpose. I'll admit it would have been the intelligent thing to do, but that's where they are so darned much smarter than we are. They know when and how to appear ignorant. So long, Jimmy. Better luck next time."

He climbed into the car. Jimmy came over and leaned on the spare tires.

"By the way, Sherry," he said soberly, "I suppose you know there is a devil of a feud between her family and mine. Been going on for God knows how many years. I don't see why she and I should respect that feud, though; do you? We didn't cook it up. A lot of crabbed old pirates back in the Dark Ages fussed about some land, that's all. There'd be an earthquake in our family burying ground if the news ever reached it that I'd been friendly with a Compton. They'd all turn over at once, and, Lord, there's a lot of 'em. Old Mrs. Compton thinks I'm a nice sort of chap, but she doesn't know my name is Burton. Would you mind not mentioning it to her, in case you see her,—"

"I'll certainly not betray you, Jimmy," said Redpath, laughing. "If Miss O'Brien doesn't think it advisable to mention it, it isn't my place to do it."

"She's a corker, isn't she?" beamed the infatuated Jimmy.

"She is," said Sherry.

He was half a mile nearer town when he looked back over his shoulder. Jimmy Burton was rounding the bend in the road, going at top speed. He sighed and set his face homeward. He was depressed. There was no use trying to convince himself that he was not depressed. Indeed, he rather encouraged the condition. It was a distinct pleasure to feel sorry for himself.

After all, as Burton had remarked, why should this fresh young generation be governed by the cantankerous old "pirates" whose bones were lying insecurely in two separate and distinct graveyards? Why should they be enemies? They had no quarrel with each other; they certainly were not old and cantankerous. They were young and they were interested in each other, not in a fifty year old dispute.

Yes, he was properly depressed. It was all very clear to him. Nothing could be more natural than that Morna should fall in love with Jimmy Burton,— if indeed she had not already done so. Jimmy's state of mind was not even doubtful. He was heels over head in love with her. And why not? Now that he thought of it soberly, why not? Falling in love with Morna O'Brien was the easiest thing in the world. He realized it perfectly now. Nothing could be simpler.

"Hang it all," he said to himself; "I wish I *had* taken the road through the woods. I would have slept better tonight, that's a cinch."

Sitting all alone on the porch after supper that evening he went over the situation calmly,— but argumentatively. He brought forward incontrovertible facts and then deliberately argued within himself against them. Jimmy Burton was a splendid fellow, but was he the right man for Morna to marry? He was rich, but would it not be better for her to marry a poor man? A poor and ambitious man? Jimmy was good-looking,— there was no getting away from that,— but good looks often lead men into entanglements. He had no bad habits, but was it safe to marry a fellow who had not sown at least a fair share of oats? When men start out to sow them late in life they don't get through with the reaping as expeditiously as they might have done in youth. He had gone to college, but it was a Middle Western college unrecognized by the board of governors of the University Club in New York. (Here Redpath struck a snag. He was not a snob. He was not so sure that it was an advantage to have come out of an Eastern college.) Somehow he had got it into his head that one cannot sow wild oats in a Western college.

But all of his arguments fell down before a single devastating equation: Morna's obvious liking for the much-to-be-despised Jimmy Burton. It was only too evident that she was not adverse to stealing fruit; the events of the afternoon established her guilt in that respect beyond a reasonable doubt. She was even more culpable than her ingenious admirer, for she took advantage of his ignorance. (That is to say, his ignorance touching upon her intelligence in the matter of automobile engines.) It was quite plain that she was enjoying herself immensely up to the moment of interruption.

And then, when all else was said and done, had not her own mother played hob with the family underpinning by marrying beneath it? Not only had she mar-

ried an Irish farm-hand, but she had done so in a
church that every member of her family abhorred.
The same blood flowed in Morna's veins. What the
mother did, so also would the daughter do if she set her
mind to it. Jimmy Burton was supposed to be a life-
long enemy; therefore a most conspicuous prize to
be taken single-handed. Family feelings be hanged!
That's what Morna would say,— and, if Redpath knew
his man as well as he thought he did, that also is pre-
cisely what Jimmy Burton would say.

He went to bed that night firmly convinced that some
morning he would wake up to find the newspapers running over with the news of a fresh complication in the
Compton-Burton controversy. Staring him in the face
would be the headlines telling of the elopement of Morna
O'Brien and James Burton!

CHAPTER XVII

"WELL, this is something like it," observed old Judge Emmons, inserting his venerable body between that of a paying patron from Chicago,— a man in the leather trade,— and the most productive steam radiator in the lobby of the Tremont. "Boy, push that chair in here for me, will you? Look out for your feet, Mister. These boys are mighty careless."

Taking his seat, with his knees well up against the coils, the old gentleman wiped the frost from his spectacles, all the while peering blindly in the direction of a vague collection of human forms,— (without his "specs" he couldn't say how many there were in the group),— uncertain whether he enjoyed the distinction of being the only one of the chronic habitués of the "corner" who had had the hardihood to venture down town in the face of the first snow storm of the year.

The leather salesman glared at the ruddy-faced old man for a moment, and was on the point of venting a sarcastic Chicago opinion on the habits of hayseeds when he encountered the genial, overpowering smile of the ancient who had summarily crowded him out of his position before the radiator. No one could resist the judge's smile,— not even a travelling salesman paying the full three dollar rate at the best hotel in town.

"Yes, sir," went on the judge, engagingly, "it's like it used to be when I was a youngster. We used to have

214

snow as early as October and, dang me, if we couldn't
sleigh from that day to the end of March. Snow two
feet deep over everything — and permanent. Some
say that the telephone and electric lights are the cause
of the change that's come over the weather in the last
twenty years. Electricity absorbs the climate, or something like that. Nineteen years ago this very day we
had a blizzard here that was a twister, gentlemen. I
take it you gentlemen are strangers in Farragut, so
you wouldn't be by way of knowing how the seasons
have changed in this section covering the last,— Has
anybody seen Amos P. Adams about this morning?
He keeps a record of the weather, day in, day out the
year 'round. I'd like to ask him to testify to the truth
of what I'm —"

" The seasons have changed everywhere, sir," said
the leather salesman agreeably,— much to his own surprise, for he hated being polite to any one living in the
" burgs " he had to " make " three times a year.
" Same in Chicago. Autumn lingers in the lap of winter —"

" As I was saying," interrupted the judge,— and
still the gentleman in the leather trade refrained,—
" we haven't had a blizzard this early in the year since
ninety-four. Lucky if we get any snow before Christmas, and as for sleighing,— well if there's more'n two
weeks of it all told everybody thinks we've had a devil
of a hard and cruel winter. I don't know what's come
over the universe. Everything goes by contraries in
these days. Just when you think we're going to have a
nice spell of spring weather it turns in and snows so
hard you can't remember when you've ever seen it snow

harder, and then just as you've got the danged stuff shovelled off the sidewalks it turns in and melts so quick you're likely to drown before you can get back into the house. A man don't know what to do these days. Middle of January you go down town with your ear-muffs on and a piece of newspaper over your chest and, by gosh, before you know it you've sweat so hard you have to peel the paper off and — No, sir, it's absolutely impossible to freeze your ears in January nowadays. You've got to wait till June. Why, last summer I wore my heaviest underwear right up to the Fourth of July, and I wouldn't have changed 'em then if I hadn't gone to bed with the grippe and it turned off boiling hot before I could get out again. You say you're from Chicago, my friend? "

" Yes, sir,— Chicago is my home. Ever get up there? "

" I don't like Chicago," said Judge Emmons bluntly. " Give me Indianapolis every time. Twenty years from now Indianapolis will be the greatest city west of the Alleghenies. Chicago ain't located just right. It's — but, I beg your pardon, sir. I oughtn't to run down your city —"

" Oh, I guess Chicago can stand it," said the leather salesman, smilingly. " Have you been up there lately? "

The judge reflected. " Last time I was there was in sixty-seven. As I said before, I don't like the town, so why should I go there — if I can help it? "

" Haven't been there since the great fire, then? "

" Nope. But we could see the smoke of that fire clear down here. Lasted several days and —"

"Perhaps you'd like Chicago better if you were to run up and see what we've been doing in the last forty-five years."

"Oh, I've heard how you've grown into the millions — that is, you *claim* you have, but I doubt it,— and I know all about your big sky-scrapers and the World's Fair. I got a portfolio of views of the Fair with a year's subscription to the *Dispatch*, by the way. But nothing can convince me that it's got the legitimate foundation that Indianapolis has. Take for instance the central location of the city I mention. It's almost in the center of the United States so far as population is concerned; it's almost in the middle of the State of Indiana, and — By the way, sir, have you any idea how many railroads run into Indianapolis?"

"I have not. I don't know how many railroads are obliged to cross Indiana in order to get to Chicago."

The sarcasm went over the judge's head. If he had noticed it he merely would have accepted it as another reason for despising Chicago.

"Well, sir, there are exactly — let me see, now, how many are there? I *did* know, but somehow — at any rate, there are so derned many they had to build a new Union Station a few years back. I guess you've seen the new station, travelling as you do. They tell me it's a whopper. I used to get over to Indianapolis every once in so often, but lately I haven't felt up to the trip. You might not suspect it, my friend,— let me see, what did you say your name was?"

"Carpenter," supplied the leather salesman, winking at the listeners.

"There's a Carpenter family here in Farragut.

Newcomers, however. Not by any chance related, I suppose? No, I thought not. As I was saying, you might not suspect it but I am eighty-six years and a few weeks old. Never had a sick day in my life. Smoked and chewed and — er — imbibed ever since I was sixteen. Bourbon is what I invariably take. What say?"

"I didn't say anything."

"Ahem! I thought you — er — somebody spoke. Yes, it started in snowing at four o'clock this morning," sighed the judge. "Thermometer went down twenty-eight degrees last night. I don't know when I've felt a colder wind than there is this morning. Cuts right through to the bone. Ordinarily we don't get any snappy weather here before Thanksgiving, and here it is only the ninth of November. I shouldn't be surprised if we had a long, hard winter. They tell me the climate in Chicago is the worst in the United States. Is that so?"

"It is the best in the United States, sir. We —"

"Feller in here from New York the other day was saying there wasn't any climate at all in the United States outside of his town. It's hard to know who to believe. I haven't much use for New Yorkers. They don't think there's anything west of the Hudson River. Why, there's a man right here in this town,— a feller named Letts, superintendent of the street-car line,— who never *will* get over the fact that he lived in New York up to the time he got this job. That was twelve years ago, and he still keeps his watch set eastern time. If you ask him what time it is he says ' it's four o'clock in New York,' and then he seems to calculate a second or two,— as if it was hard to remember where he is,— before he can decide that it's three o'clock here. As I was saying a minute ago, if a man will stick to Bourbon, — or rye, if he prefers it,— and never touch a mixed drink, he ought to live to be ninety. It's this thing of mixin'— How? Well, it's a leetle early in the day for me — but, seeing as it's you, a stranger in a strange land, sir, I *will* join you. Right this way, sir." And the judge led the way into the bar.

All of this preamble is merely intended to establish the fact that an unprecedented change in the weather had fallen upon Farragut. A balmy yesterday, a blighting today. The thick wet snow of the early morning hours was reduced soon after daybreak by an everfalling temperature to a fine sleet that whizzed through the air with biting force. Wires were down, street-cars blocked, time-tables disrupted. In every house in town there was a mad scramble for last winter's flannels; heavy overcoats were yanked out of dark closets and chests, smelling of moth balls; arctics and mufflers went to proper extremities; pale noses bloomed with the glow of health, broad shoulders and straight backs withered as with the plague, and fierce were the execrations of the unprepared.

Pneumonia weather, proclaimed every one in Farragut capable of expression. Doctors and druggists and undertakers brightened up perceptibly. They pulled long faces, of course, and looked grave, but they fooled no one. The ill-wind was blowing for them.

By two o'clock in the afternoon the snow ceased falling, but the wind still blew a gale. It was then that an amazing thing occurred,— or rather began to occur.

Men equipped with snowshovels appeared on the sidewalks abutting the various properties of Andrew Gilman, and before the incredulous observers fully appreciated what had happened they were swept and scraped and furbished into a state of cleanliness that suggested a trick on the part of Nature in that you would have sworn that snow fell everywhere in town except in front of buildings owned by the despised Andy Gee. Small segments of Main Street, Church Street, and Lincoln Street, in the business section of the city, were cleared as if by magic, while long stretches of sidewalk bounding vacant lots in obscure streets were treated in the same manner by briskly handled implements, directed by a tall young man who herded his labourers from place to place with all the push and authority of a Prussian general.

Andrew Gilman owned no fewer than fifty separate pieces of property within the city limits. Most of them were improved, and heretofore had depended on the moods and inclinations of tenants for the process that was now going on. Properties owned by the richest man in town always had been the last to respond to the thaw that is bound, soon or late, to do the work of man. Snow and ice caked on his sidewalks so compactly that an unusual spell of warm weather was necessary to restore them to their normal condition. Certain places,— such as the long stretch of unoccupied ground on Elm Street lined with an immense row of bill-boards which baffled the energies of the afternoon sun,— were so perilously slippery for weeks after the snow storms that pedestrians preferred to walk in the street rather than to risk their bones on the sidewalks.

No one in Farragut expected Andrew Gilman to clean the snow from his sidewalks. He always waited for the city, the tenant, or the sun to do it. That was understood. It had been going on for fifty years. And now here he was scraping the snow off before it had fairly settled on the ground! A great many people said that the world was coming to an end. Others took Sheridan Redpath aside and asked him what he meant by spending his own hard-earned money cleaning up Andrew Gilman's sidewalks.

A New York travelling salesman, impressed by the swift removal of snow from the sidewalks just east and west of the Tremont, said that it reminded him of the only city in the world, and was instantly involved in an altercation with the leather drummer from Chicago, who said that a snow-storm as big as this would paralyse traffic on Fifth Avenue for six weeks. Quite a crowd collected.

When Sherry Redpath crawled out of bed at half-past seven o'clock that morning the swirling snow-storm met his sleepy eyes. The trees were draped in white, the ground was covered, the street below was almost obscured from view by the veil of wind-swept snow. The gardener was trying to clear a path from the front steps to the gate below,— a futile and ill-considered undertaking, for his work was soon to be rendered void by the ceaseless fall and drift. As soon as he was dressed he sallied forth and stopped the man.

" Wait till it quits snowing, Joe. Save you a lot of elbow grease." And Joe was glad to stop.

Mr. Gilman was at the breakfast table when Redpath came in from the porch.

"I found Joe shovelling away for dear life, Mr. Gilman, and making no headway, so I told him to postpone the job for awhile. It's still snowing to beat the dickens. Nothing like this has happened since I can remember. A blizzard in —"

"You ordered him to stop?" said Andrew Gilman, his eyes narrowing.

"Yes, sir. He'd have it all to do over again before twelve o'clock if this keeps up."

An odd half-smile flickered in the old man's eyes. "I had just set him to work," said he drily. "You appear to have more sense than either Joe or I."

Sherry flushed. "I'm sorry if I have —"

"It is all right, my boy. Sit down. Breakfast should taste unusually good this morning. I find I enjoy my victuals better in cold weather than at any other time. There's a snap to the appetite, and there seems to be a real reason for eating. I'm glad you stopped the simpleton. He hasn't much intelligence."

Apparently in the best of humours now, the old man held forth on the astonishing turn the weather had taken, going back over a stretch of thirty years for a prototype. Suddenly the young man broke in upon his reminiscences with a proposition so bold that he faltered before the words were fully released.

"See here, Mr. Gilman, I've been thinking of something that we ought to do the minute this storm is over. We ought to get a gang of men together and clear the snow from the sidewalks in front of your property, all over town."

Mr. Gilman started. In fact, he gasped. "You don't know what that means, my young friend. I've never undertaken so stupendous a job as that in —"

"It isn't much of a job if we take it in time. I'll get the men and superintend the work. We can clear 'em all off in two or three hours. I've always maintained that if all property owners did that sort of thing we'd have a better town, a better citizenry and — better feeling all around."

"But I've never done it. I don't see any reason for spending money on such things as that. This snow will melt, just as it always does. Civic pride, that's what you mean, isn't it?"

"Yes, sir, that is what I mean," said Sherry bluntly.

Mr. Gilman leaned forward and eyed his secretary keenly. "What put this notion into your head?"

"I've always felt this way about it. People ought to clear their sidewalks."

"But they never do," said the other. "I am no worse than the rest of them. We're all alike."

"That's no reason why we should let the snow and ice pile up on the sidewalks, Mr. Gilman. It isn't safe, and heaven knows it stamps us as a jay town in the eyes of outsiders."

"So you suggest that I inaugurate the movement to stamp out this opinion of outsiders?"

"You are the biggest property owner in Farragut. If you begin it,— well, you'll see the others following suit in no time. They'll be shamed into it."

."I'm not so sure of that," said the old man grimly. "You don't know this town as well as I do."

"A great many property owners do clean their sidewalks, sir," said Sherry. "You have never done it. That's why I suggest that we —"

"Just a moment. Tell me what is really at the bottom of this idea of yours."

"Well, to be perfectly frank about it, ever since I can remember anything at all, I've heard people say that it was a disgrace the way you let the ice and snow lay in front of your unimproved properties. I may as well add that I have said it myself."

"And you want to begin at this late hour to reform the town's meanest man? A rather stupendous undertaking, my friend."

"Never too late to mend, sir," said Sherry coolly.

The result of this plain discussion was the appearance on the streets of a gang of able-bodied men, bossed by the town's one-time scapegrace, and a subsequent change of tactics by every charitable organization in Farragut. Andrew Gilman's spectacular change of heart filled his mail with requests for subscriptions to all sorts of benevolences, with some hope of success in the breasts of the senders who cheerfully believed that softening of the brain had set in at last,— and every one knows that a pronounced symptom of the affliction is an unbridled ambition to spend money. Such being the case, now was the proper time to engage Mr. Gilman's interest, for a little later on he would have a conservator.

No one was more surprised than Andy Gee himself. He wandered about the house all day like a lost soul. He never glanced at the big old clock in the library without experiencing a vague impulse to slip into his overcoat and sally forth into the streets and put a stop to the silly, quixotic enterprise now under way. Times there were when he stood stockstill and wondered if it

could really be true that he had permitted a young, pre-
sumptuous cub like Sherry Redpath to dictate a policy
that had been so rigidly opposed for more than two
score years. Then he would smile sadly, shake his
head and resume his objectless peregrinations. He
could not read. He could not concentrate on anything
except this amazing, unnatural event.

As the afternoon wore away he found himself engaged in frequent, and admittedly inane, efforts to de-
termine by calculation the exact location of his force of
snow-shovellers. Supposing they began operations at
Main and Seventh streets, on the sidewalk in front of
Blaine's dry goods store, and supposing they were
driven as hard as he would have driven them, they
would, at four o'clock, as near as he could figure it out,
be working on the southwest corner of Dorset and Polk
streets, cleaning snow off of the pavement in front of
three unimproved lots. At half-past four they undoubtedly would be in front of the residence of James
Forbes in California Avenue,— and so on throughout
the length and breadth of the city. He groaned faintly
as he thought of the tenement houses in the lower part
of town. Would the vigorous, inspired Redpath consider it his duty to look after the sidewalks down there?

The evening paper came at five o'clock. He watched
the boy plough his way up from the gate through the
banks of snow, and for the first time in his life pitied
the youngster who had been leaving papers on his door-
step, morning and night, in all kinds of weather, for the
past three or four years. This house of his was the
most outlying on the boy's long route: he traversed
four or five blocks of subcriber-less territory in order

to deliver his last remaining paper to a man he despised and feared.

Andrew Gilman met him at the door. "Come in and get warm, sonny," he said kindly. The boy stared, open-mouthed. "I mean it. Your feet are wet and your face looks half-frozen."

"I can't," said the boy, blinking. "I got to go home and shovel the snow off'n our sidewalk."

"Where do you live?"

"Banks Street. One of your houses, Mr. Gilman."

"Banks Street? Let me think. By this time they ought to be — I guess you'll find the snow all cleaned off by the time you get home, my lad," he said, not without a touch of pride in his voice. "My men are at work now, cleaning it away — everywhere. I — er — we are trying to set an example to all property owners. If every one in town would take hold of the snow problem —"

"Was them your men workin' fer Sherry Redpath?" inquired the boy, not politely, but with interest.

"Yes. Maybe you can tell me where you last saw them?" He spoke quickly.

"Down by the baseball grounds. You better not stand out here in the wind, Mr. Gilman, without yer hat. You'll ketch cold."

"Thank you," murmured Mr. Gilman stiffly. But after he had re-entered the house, and the boy was making his way down the hill, there came over him a warmth that was not produced by the heat of the rooms. A fine boy that, he said to himself.

He read the telegraphic news and the account of the

blizzard, and then fell once more to reflecting upon the persuasive influence of his secretary. He recalled an event now two weeks old. One of his business blocks had long been untenanted. The plate glass windows were plastered full of lithographs,— some of them a year old and most of them reminiscent of a circus that had come to town early in the spring. Free passes to the show had been the sole revenue from this property for five or six years. He could not understand why it never rented. And then young Redpath, to whom he expressed this wonder, told him point blank that if he would paint the exterior and remodel the interior he might stand a chance of renting the " old barracks."

It was sending good money after bad, according to his opinion as a landlord, and he swore he would not spend a nickel on the place. Somehow Redpath wheedled or argued him into it, however, and painters and carpenters had now been at work on the building for a week. And it was but yesterday that his agent in the Bank telephoned up to say that he had leased the building for a term of ten years to the Updyke Drug Company.

Staring over the edge of his newspaper he wondered whether the painting really had anything to do with the business. It was astonishing, he said to himself, the ideas these young fellows get into their heads,— and some of them, he was bound to admit, occasionally turned out to be of value.

Sherry came in at seven o'clock, rosy-faced and triumphant.

" Well," said Andy Gee, " did you make a good job. of it? "

"We certainly did. I had eighteen men and four wagons at it."

"Umph! I see by the paper that more snow is expected tonight. What have you to say to that?"

"If it comes we'll go right out after it again to-morrow," said Sherry cheerfully.

"I can't, for the life of me, decide whether you are an optimist or a young man who will make his mark in the world," observed Mr. Gilman cryptically.

Sherry laughed. "We hauled all of the snow up to your vacant lots in Banks Street and dumped it there."

"I see. A very good idea," said the old man, sardonically. "You remembered that the snow belonged to me, so you decided to save it."

"A little later on," said the young man, "we will have an absolute corner on snow-balls. I thought of that, you see."

Mr. Gilman slapped him on the back, and actually grinned.

"Foresightedness appears to be another of your virtues. Keep it up. You'll be a rich man some day. A corner in snow-balls! That's good!"

CHAPTER XVIII

R EDPATH went to bed early that night. He was tired, and by nine o'clock was overcome by the drowsiness due to a long day in the wind. His eyes refused to stay open; he came perilously near to dropping off to sleep several times during the evening while supposed to be intent upon the words of his employer as they sat before the fireplace in the library. Finally Mr. Gilman interrupted himself in the middle of a somewhat prolonged dissertation on the license enjoyed by newspapers in the United States, especially in the matter of ridicule as it is heaped upon the heads of government, and, squinting narrowly, inquired, raising his voice:

" Can't you keep awake? "

Sherry started, blinking his heavy lids. " I beg your pardon, sir. You were saying —"

" Better go to bed, my friend. You are half asleep now."

" If you don't mind, I think I will turn in. I'm dog-tired and dead sleepy. The wind, I guess."

" Run along. I will come up presently, and I'll try not to disturb you."

Sometime later on,— it must have been about ten o'clock,— Redpath was dimly conscious of the ringing of a bell,— an intermittent jingle that seemed to come from afar off and out of nowhere. He had fallen asleep the instant his head touched the pillow. The sound of the bell roused him for a moment; he tried to fix his mind on the disturbance, but his senses slipped away from him even as he struggled. The telephone downstairs,— the front door bell,— was it not his place to get up and answer the summons, whatever it was? He slept again, and in his dreams some one was hammering viciously on a great gong and people were trampling upon him in the rush to see what all the rumpus was about.

He was indistinctly aware of Mr. Gilman's passage through his bed-room carrying a candle which he shaded with one hand.

Long afterward,— it must have been, for the house was very still,— he found himself wide awake and listening. The sensation was uncanny. He could not remember awaking, and yet every faculty was alive and keen. The cold wind from the open casement blew across his face. Just as he was making up his mind that the icy draft had brought about this sudden return to consciousness,— and was on the point of crawling out from under the covers to lower the window,— a faint, almost inaudible sound came to his ear: the sound of some one breathing.

For many seconds he remained perfectly still, trying to locate the sound. He had his wits about him. If there was a burglar in the room, his safety depended upon his ability to feign sleep. The slightest movement on his part would undoubtedly bring about an attack from which he could have no defence.

Then came a soft shuffling of feet over the carpet, followed by the creaking of a door. He raised his head stealthily, and prepared to spring out of bed. The

door to Mrs. Gilman's sitting-room opened slowly.   A
thin stream of light filled the aperture, which did not
expand more than six inches.   The light revealed a
white, motionless figure, not on the opposite side of the
door, but standing in his own room.   His first thought
was that Mrs. Gilman had wandered away from her
room,— but even as he speculated the door was closed
softly and the room was in darkness once more.   He
acted at once.   There was no burglar in the room;
caution was unnecessary.

" Is that you, Mr. Gilman? " he demanded, rising to
his elbow.

There was absolute silence for a few seconds.   He
repeated the question sharply.   The answer was a long-
drawn breath which ended in a quick, deep exhalation,
as of sudden relief.

" Yes, it is I," came in subdued tones from the invisible figure.   A short, nervous chuckle followed, and
then the shuffling, halting footsteps approached Redpath's bed.

" Anything wrong with Mrs. Gilman, sir? "

" She is quite all right."   By this time he had
reached the foot of the bed and was feeling his way past
it to the partly open door.

" Better get into bed, sir.   It's as cold as Iceland
in this room, with that window wide open.   'Gad, sir,
your teeth are chattering."

The old man laughed quietly and, passing through
the door, closed it behind him.   Sherry did not fail to
observe that the room beyond was as dark as his own.

He lay awake for a long time.   The question uppermost in his mind was this: how long had Mr. Gilman

been in the room before he awoke? And out of that
grew another and even more significant question; had
he been in the room all of the time?

At the breakfast table Mr. Gilman failed to mention the incident, whether purposely or not he was unable to decide.

"You will not be obliged to go to court this morning to testify against your burglars," he said, looking
up as the young man took his seat. "They broke out
of jail last night and, according to the paper, hadn't
been apprehended up to the hour of going to press.
Here it is, on the front page."

It was true. On the eve of their trial for burglary,
the two men had gained their freedom by overpowering
a jailor. Secreting themselves in the prisoners' bath-
room in the corridor of the old-fashioned jail, they fell
upon the man who came in to lock the cells after throwing in the lever from the outside; before he could make
an outcry, they bound and gagged him with pieces of
bed-ticking. Taking his keys, they made their way
into the outer corridor and then, with a sudden dash,
bolted through the turnkey's office, where an aged
"trustie" was mopping the floor after a recent incur-
sion of snow and mud-covered policemen with an "in-
tox" in charge. The turnkey himself was down in the
furnace-room at the time, giving instructions to a new
fireman who had just come on the job. Before the
"trustie" could give the alarm, the prisoners were
out in the street and lost in the snow-storm.

Never had there been a more daring jail-break in the
history of the county. The *Dispatch*, the Republican
organ, came out flatly with the charge of gross care-

lessness and incompetency on the part of the sheriff's
men, and predicted the overwhelming defeat of that offi-
cial, a Democrat, when the next election came around.
He was responsible for the " appointment of ward loafers and political bums to positions of trust," and the
voters of the city and county " would hold him to account " for this and countless other instances of inef-
ficiency,— or, to use a stronger word, " corruption."

Two desperate criminals, wailed the *Dispatch*, had
escaped from the confines of the county jail, which had
just been overhauled and strengthened at considerable
expense to the tax payers by a Democratic board of
county commissioners, and was supposed to be burglar-
proof (from the inside, at least). They were now at
large, a menace to the life and property of every en-
franchised man in Farragut,— and why? The answer
was now only too plain, even to the most wilfully ob-
tuse: " The voters themselves had put into office a man
who . . . "— and so on at great length.

The whole affair looked to the *Dispatch* like a " put-
up job." There was but one defence for the jailors;
they may have been and probably were drunk. That,
and that alone, would absolve them from the more serious charge of having been " fixed " by an interested
" outside party." The ease with which the men made
their escape was bound to make Farragut the laughing-
stock of the country. Much better for the pride of the
city, said the *Dispatch*, that her keepers of the lawless
should be charged with bribe-taking than that another
and more sickening alternative should be allowed to
leak out: that stupidity of the rankest sort was responsible for the disaster !

Sherry found his own name mentioned in the account, — blazoned, in fact. His spectacular service to society was held up in contrast to the " puerile futility revealed by the individual who had been honoured by the electors . . . "

" It looks like a put-up job to me, Mr. Gilman," cried he, excitedly. " Some one has been fixed down there, sure as you are alive. 'Gad, the people of this county ought to go to the bottom of the thing, and if there has been crooked work in the sheriff's office —"

" It is easy to say that a jailer has been bought, but it will not be so easy to prove," interrupted Mr. Gilman. " Carelessness may be shown, of course, but that isn't complicity, you know. I know the sheriff of this county. He is an honest man. You must take with a grain of salt all that is said by the *Dispatch*. The printing from the sheriff's office amounts to a good deal in a year's time. All of it has been going to a Democratic newspaper and job office. The *Dispatch* wants a Republican in office. Politics is business, my boy. I am a Republican but I shall vote for Sheriff Jackson next election."

" But how easy it was," cried Sherry. " They practically walked out of jail. If the whole thing hadn't been arranged, they would have slugged that jailer into insensibility. They wouldn't have taken a chance on his putting up a fight. No, sir, Mr. Gilman, there is something ugly about this business. Desperate criminals don't handle men with kid gloves. They would have cracked that fellow over the head with something first, and then gagged him."

" You may be right," said the other, nodding his

head. " Anything is possible in these days. It is even
possible to buy up a jailer if you can pay his price.
Did these men have any money? "

" I don't know. They may have friends with
money, however, which would come to the same thing.
By George!" The exclamation was involuntary and
was preceded by a violent start. There suddenly had
shot into his brain the recollection of a bell ringing
sometime during the night, a hazy but definite incident
that had troubled him in a vague sort of way. An inquiry leaped to his lips but he choked it back.

" What's the matter?" demanded Mr. Gilman. For
the first time Sherry noticed a queer pallor in the old
man's face.

" Nothing. I just thought of something." He
took the opportunity to regain his composure while
slowly sipping his coffee. He thought quickly, however, and decided to take the plunge, not knowing where
it would lead him. " I may have been dreaming, but
I thought I heard the door-bell ringing last night, long
after I had gone to bed."

Mr. Gilman was staring at him oddly. He was slow
in responding to what appeared to be a question, and
when he did it was with something like relief in his
voice.

" The telephone rang about ten o'clock. I answered
it. Some one calling up to inquire how Mrs. Gilman
is. People who call up at that hour of the night when
there are twelve good hours of daylight ought to be
kicked."

Sherry bent his gaze upon the newspaper, and with
difficulty held it there. He was mortally afraid that

Mr. Gilman would catch the look of incredulity in his eyes. He did not question the statement that there had been a telephone call; it was not at all improbable. It was even probable that some one had inquired about Mrs. Gilman's health, but he was convinced in his own mind that a deeper motive than that lay behind the mysterious call.

His thoughts flew instantly to the one person who might have had reason for calling up Andrew Gilman at that hour of the night: his sister-in-law, Mrs. Compton. Her strange visit to the house was still unexplained. He had formed many conjectures, and all of them had to do with the man who had tried to rob her house. She knew the fellow, and perhaps Andrew Gilman knew him as well. Something like a shock came to him with the suspicion that she might have called up to tell her brother-in-law that George Smith, the burglar, was at large once more! This led to even more staggering possibilities. If a jailer had been bribed — but he would not believe that of her.

Finally he looked up from the paper. "They certainly made a clean getaway. Evidently they knew just what to do once they were outside the jail. The police have said all along that they were strangers here, — at least they were not known to any one on the force. That looks like help from the outside, doesn't it? Friends waiting in an automobile,— all that sort of stuff. Why, it's as sure as anything that —" His eyes went back to the first paragraph in the long account. The break had occurred at nine o'clock! "I say, Mr. Gilman, suppose I call up police headquarters and ask if they've been caught." He started up from the table, eagerly.

"Certainly," said the old man indifferently. "You are interested, of course." Which was as much as to say that interest was entirely one-sided. "Give me the paper, please. I haven't looked to see who is dead. When you get along to my time of life, you will be more interested in obituaries than in jail deliveries."

There was no news of the fugitives. A large posse was scouring the town and country, and all railroads were being watched. The condition of the telephone wires after the storm was handicapping the authorities terribly, but "they would land 'em before night, sure."

Hanging up the receiver, he turned to Mr. Gilman, a troubled expression in his eyes.

"They haven't got them, Mr. Gilman. It has just occurred to me that I ought to telephone out to Mrs. Compton's. She may not have heard of the jail-break, and she ought to be warned."

The old man regarded him in silence for a moment, a frown darkening his brow. "That seems to me to be quite unnecessary. Why a warning? Lightning never strikes twice in the same place. These rascals will not bother her again."

"That may be true, sir, but it is only fair that I should let her know. You see, sir, she depends on me to —"

"I have no objection," interrupted Mr. Gilman stonily. "But stay! I have a better plan. Take the car and run out to her place. If the roads are passable you can make it and back in an hour or so. Besides, she may have started to town and would thank you to intercept her on the way. I fancy she is expected to appear against the men in court this morning. Am I right? "

"Yes, sir. She has been subpœnaed."

"She has started in by this time, in that event. You may save her going the full journey. I have no objection to your using the car. No doubt her telephone is out of commission. Better start at once."

CHAPTER XIX

IT was not until Redpath was half-way to the Compton place that Mr. Gilman's real reason for sending him out in the car flashed through his brain. If there was any telephoning to be done, he preferred to do it himself. Assuming that it was Mrs. Compton who called up during the night, what could be more natural than that his employer should prepare her for certain questions that Redpath might reasonably, even innocently, ask? The thought took the form of a conviction. He had been very cleverly forestalled by the wise old fox.

Arriving at the house on the hill, after a laborious run over an almost unbroken road, he was greeted by Morna O'Brien. His first glance assured him that she was not contemplating the trip to town. That same glance also produced an extraordinary quickening of the blood. She was distractingly lovely in a filmy house gown of pale blue silk and chiffon, revealing her white, smooth throat. Her eyes were the colour of deep blue pansies, and liquid as with the shimmering dew.

A sort of ecstasy possessed him. He mumbled an innocuous greeting, smiling dizzily as he returned the warm, firm hand-clasp. The dimples in her soft cheek, the luscious redness of her lips, the adorable uplifted chin, the barely disclosed white teeth, the way her dark hair grew about her temples,—he was absolutely bereft of certain heretofore infallible resources: such as readiness of speech, for example.

He had not seen her in more than a week. He did not realize it, but his present ecstasy was due entirely to the fact that he had been so hungry for the sight of her that he fed his senses into a state of stupefaction. He was revelling in complete satisfaction. Unpalatable impressions had no place in this delectable feast of the senses. He even forgot that such a person as Jimmy Burton existed.

Presently he found himself sitting in front of the fireplace, talking to her in a most sensible, matter-of-fact manner. She was seated in the corner of a big, comfortable couch, snuggling back among the cushions. He remembered vaguely having arranged the cushions behind her, and the scent of her hair as he bent over to readjust them properly, but he hadn't much of a notion as to how he got into the chair he now occupied.

"— and if I had risked telephoning out to you I might have missed you altogether," he discovered himself to be saying, and for ever afterward wondered what he had said prior to that. There must have been something, of course, or she wouldn't be looking at him with such perfect understanding.

" As I said before, we were not even out of bed when the message came from grandmother's lawyer," she said. (So she had already mentioned it, had she? Doubtless everything would come back to him in time.) " He called up at seven o'clock, hoping to catch us before we started to town."

"And that was the first you knew of the escape?" he hazarded.

She raised her eyebrows slightly. "You wouldn't expect us to get the news ahead of people in the city, would you? How many in Farragut knew it before seven o'clock?"

"I thought perhaps some one might have called you up late last night," he explained hastily. "They escaped at nine o'clock. Plenty of time to —"

"We were in town last night, Mr. Redpath, and did not reach home until after twelve. We went in to see Sothern and Marlowe. I didn't see you there."

"I'm afraid you didn't look very hard," he ventured, leading her on.

"Indeed I did. You were not downstairs. Should I have looked higher up?"

He grinned happily. "I wasn't there at all. Thank you for the compliment, just the same."

"Mr. Burton looked too. The house was packed. He said it would be very easy to miss you in the crowd."

The grin died. "Was Jimmy there?" he asked fatuously.

"Obviously. He happened to have a seat directly behind us. Wasn't that odd?"

"You invariably sit in section C, don't you?"

"Yes. Granny will not sit anywhere else."

"Then I don't see anything odd about it," he said, almost gruffly.

She seemed momentarily perplexed; then a swift blush mounted to her cheeks. "If you think that he knew we were to be sitting there, Mr. Redpath, you are very much mistaken," she said stiffly. "I have never seen any one more surprised than he was."

"How was the play?" he inquired, resisting a mean desire to further embarrass her by putting the question that was uppermost in his mind. He might have asked, with propriety, whether Mrs. Compton was still in the dark as to the identity of Mr. James Burton.

"Gorgeous," she said succinctly, with the challenge still in her eyes.

He changed the subject. "I brought the *Dispatch* with me. It has a full account of the escape. Rather thrilling, and yet ridiculously simple. The whole thing looks fishy to me."

"Fishy?"

"It's a hard thing to say, but I believe some one was bribed by friends of one or both of the men."

She started. Her eyes widened quickly, and, before she could avert them, he detected an unmistakable gleam of apprehension in their depths. "Oh, goodness, do you really think so?" she cried breathlessly.

"The *Dispatch* practically makes the charge," he said. "On the way out here, I did a lot of speculating. Some one was determined that these men should not be brought to trial. That is my opinion, Miss O'Brien."

Her gaze rested upon him searchingly. He saw the colour fade from her cheeks.

"Do you mean —" A slight movement of the head completed the question.

"Certainly not," he said, glancing toward the door. "We both think that she knows the man, but I can't believe she would — No, she certainly was not in my mind." He hesitated for a moment before asking the

question: "Did any one besides her lawyer call up
this morning?"

"Yes. Some one telephoned about nine o'clock,—
just a little while before you came."

"Do you know who it was?"

"No. The cook answered the 'phone. She called
upstairs to Granny, and she hurried down. I asked her
afterwards if the men had been caught. At first I
thought it might have been you calling up, to give us
the news. It seems that it was something about a business appointment in town,— cancelling it, I think she
said."

He leaned forward. "Was it Mr. Gilman who
called?"

Her astonishment was genuine. "Who?" she cried.

"Andrew Gilman."

"Heaven above, Mr. Redpath," she whispered excitedly, "what put *that* thought into your head?"

"Why shouldn't he call up? He is her brother-in-
law, isn't he?"

"But I told you long ago that they hate each other
like poison. She would die before she would speak to
him,— and I dare say he'd pay her the same compliment."

"Nevertheless," he began slowly, "she came to his
house not long ago to see him."

"I don't believe it," she said promptly. "Whoever
told you that, Mr. Redpath?"

"No one. I saw her with my own eyes."

"You saw her at Andrew Gilman's house?" she murmured, incredulously.

"She came one afternoon and remained for fifteen

or twenty minutes. That is all I know about it, and that is one of the reasons why I felt justified in asking you if it was he who telephoned this morning."

"I — I never was so flabbergasted in my life," she said. "She did not tell me that she had been to see him. You cannot possibly mean to imply, Mr. Redpath, that she went to see him about that man in the county jail?" Her eyes were dark with trouble. She was sitting bolt upright now, rigid with interest.

"I don't know what to think," he said, after a moment. "I am not a Paul Pry, and I ought not to be coming to you with this tale. It is none of my business, and I am not paid to interfere in Mr. Gilman's. Mrs. Compton was good to me. I shall never forget it. If there is anything I can do now, I'll do it gladly. She may speak to you about all this later on. If she does, I want you to tell her just what I have said, and that she can trust me. Don't get it into your head, however, that I am working against Mr. Gilman. I am working for him, and I believe absolutely in his honesty. I am there to help him in every way possible. Circumstances over which neither of them has any control may have come to light suddenly, and they both regard them as serious enough to call for united action, no matter how distasteful it may be. I honestly believe, Miss O'Brien, that the big chap we caught out here that night is in some way mixed up in the lives of both of them. Some one called Mr. Gilman up on the telephone at ten o'clock last night. I will confess that I suspected Mrs. Compton. But, of course, as you were at the theatre, she couldn't have been the one."

"She is coming," whispered Morna, nervously.

"She has been in her room ever since that last telephone — Here is Mr. Redpath, Granny. He came
out to tell us about those men getting out of jail last
night."

Mrs. Compton, quite as serene and as self-composed
as ever, advanced into the room, her hand extended, a
cordial smile on her lips.

"Haven't they caught them yet, Mr. Redpath?"
she inquired, after shaking hands with him. She did
not attempt to conceal her anxiety.

"I am afraid not, Mrs. Compton. The police are
positive they will get them before night, however. I
thought I'd run out to tell you that you need not be
worried. They certainly will not come here again.
More than likely they are in Chicago by this time.
We've seen the last of them."

"I hope so," she said fervently. "It is good of you
to come all the way out here in this wretched weather.
Did you, by any chance, bring a newspaper with you?
Thank you. I should like to read the full account.
Our mail will be delayed this morning." She took the
paper and moved up to the fireplace. "The house is
cold, Morna. Tell Matson to poke up the furnace,
please." The girl scrambled up from the cushions and
hurried into the rear hall. Mrs. Compton drew close to
the young man's side. "Did you discuss this matter
with Andrew Gilman before leaving, Sheridan?" She
spoke hurriedly and in guarded tones.

"Somewhat casually," he replied. "Mr. Gilman did
not appear to be greatly interested. He does not agree
with my theory, however."

"And what is your theory?"

"That there was help from the outside, Mrs. Compton."

There was a brief silence. She was reading the headlines. He observed that her hands were very steady.

"You say Mr. Gilman was not interested?" she remarked, lowering the paper.

"Not especially. Why should he be? He was only interested in the matter because I had had a hand in the capture."

"You are a shrewd young man," she said, meeting his gaze frankly. "I have known all along that you suspect something. One of those men is known to me and to Andrew Gilman as well. I can tell you no more, and I tell you this much because I am sure I can trust to your discretion. Besides," and she smiled quizzically, "it partially relieves the mental strain you have endured for some time. I could see that it was beginning to tell on you."

"Discretion also includes forbearance, I imagine," he remarked. "I am not to ask any questions."

"Quite so. No questions asked."

"You will not regard it in the light of a question, I hope, if I surmise that you are glad the fellow escaped."

"I am not at all pleased," she said seriously. "On the contrary, I am extremely sorry."

"You were expected to appear in court as a witness against him."

"I should not have done so," she replied calmly. "That much, at least, was 'fixed,' as you would put it."

Morna was heard coming up the back stairs. He laid his hand on Mrs. Compton's arm.

"I would suggest that you tell Miss O'Brien what you have told me. She is quite as shrewd, Mrs. Compton, if not shrewder than I."

"Time enough for that," she said curtly.

Morna entered the room and, coming over to her grandmother's side, linked an arm through hers. "Won't you slip on that heavy sweater of mine, Granny, if I —"

"I am quite warm now. Besides, I don't fancy red and white stripes, my dear. Tell me, Mr. Redpath, are you not afraid that big brute will hunt you out and have his revenge for the injury you inflicted on him?"

"I don't think he'll bother me," he replied easily.

"He said he would 'get' you," cried Morna, and the anxious note in her voice pleased him. "I distinctly heard that policeman say —"

"They always say something like that, and then think better of it."

"Well, I'm not so sure," she insisted. "He didn't look like a person who could think better of anything. You must be on your guard. At least for awhile. Especially at night and in lonely places."

"I sha'n't sleep in Compton's Woods, if that will allay your fears, Miss O'Brien," he said, smiling.

"I shall never forget that man's face," she said, a slight quiver in her voice. "He was the vilest looking creature —"

"Now, now, my dear," broke in Mrs. Compton. "They'll catch him and that will be the end of him."

"I shall not sleep a wink until I know he is safe behind the bars again. What if he should take it into his head to come out here again, to get even with us?"

"Get even with us for what, my dear? For having an overabundance of loose silver in the house?"

"You never can tell what these criminals —"

"See here, Mrs. Compton," broke in Sherry, struck by a glorious idea, "suppose I ask Mr. Gilman to let me stay out here for the next two or three nights. He'll be glad to let me off if I put it up to him in the right way."

"I think it would be perfectly wonderful —"

. "Just a moment, Morna," interrupted Mrs. Compton sharply. "No, Mr. Redpath, it is not to be considered. No harm will come to us." She uttered the next few sentences slowly, somewhat portentously. "You must stay where you belong. Andrew Gilman is not romantic. He expects you to sit up and play dominoes or cribbage with him, and not to go bounding away in quest of fair ladies in distress. You are not to think of it, my friend."

The inference was plain. She meant that his place was in Andrew Gilman's home at this particular time.

"I merely suggested it, Mrs. Compton. Of course, if you are not afraid of being alone —"

"We are not alone. I have three able-bodied men on the place and two women with remarkably strong voices. Now, sit down and tell us all you know about the escape of these men. You must have a big cup of hot coffee before you start back."

He left for town in half an hour. Morna went out to the cold front hall with him.

"Telephone me if you hear anything, please," she said. "We are terribly interested. And do be on your guard. That man —"

"Bless your heart," he cried fervently. "*He* is not the man I'm afraid of," he went on, his heart thumping furiously.

She looked at him, astonished. Something that felt icy raced through his body.

"Good-bye!" he gasped, in utter confusion.

"Good-bye. It was awfully good of you to come."

CHAPTER XX

MR. GILMAN'S telephone rang persistently all that day. The speakers at the other end of the line invariably were exasperated tenants complaining about leaky roofs, and it was into Sherry's ears that these wails were poured by bold men and women who took instant advantage of the fact that they were speaking to a hireling and not to the formidable landlord himself.

Mr. Gilman was complacent. He heard each of Sherry's reports and commented briefly on the demands of the tenants.

"You see how it is, my boy," he said wearily, after the first few complaints. "This is the penalty of being an owner of habitable property. These people are yelling before they are hurt. How can their roofs be leaking when there hasn't been the slightest indication of a thaw? Roofs don't leak snow, you know. The instant a man rents a house he takes over the right to abuse the owner thereof. Tell all of them that I'll look into the matter as soon as the weather permits."

Redpath was occupied all afternoon checking up the rent accounts and preparing notices to delinquents. Andrew Gilman exacted payment on the first day of the month. On the tenth day he sent out imperative reminders to all who had neglected to pay, with the brief statement that the time would not be extended beyond the fifteenth. While he seldom carried out this veiled

threat to evict, he always sent the notices as a matter of
routine and principle. Heretofore they had been
signed in the cramped,— you might say miserly,— hand
of Andrew Gilman, who apparently economized in ink
and space as well as in other things,— but now his name
was appended in a dashing, unfamiliar scrawl, below
which appeared the initials S. W. R. On the morning
of the sixteenth the owner of these initials was expected
to follow them in person, with the polite request that the
occupant of the domicile " fork over." The occupant
of the house failed to take the visit as seriously as did
the flushed, embarrassed young man who stood on the
door-step and made the hateful demand. It was a detestable business, said S. W. R. after he had made the
rounds in the middle of his first month. Being an out-
spoken, honest sort of chap, he confessed his abhorrence
to Andrew Gilman when that gentleman softly inquired
how he liked being a " collector."

" The fact that I haven't brought home a cent as the
result of my experiment, ought to answer that question
for you, Mr. Gilman," he said, slapping the empty bill
folder on the library table. " I'm not cut out for this
sort of thing, sir. I simply cannot haggle with women
and it isn't in me to scowl at 'em as a rent collector
ought to do. I don't mind having the men growl at me,
but, by George, sir, I can't stand it when the women
look at me with tears in their eyes. I'm afraid you will
have to get some one else in my place."

Mr. Gilman's laugh interrupted this rueful attempt
to account for the empty pocket-book.

" My dear boy," he said, after a moment of real
amusement, " you may consider yourself lucky in hav-

ing drawn nothing worse than tears. The men are afraid to curse the rent collector, but that isn't true of the women. When they realize that tears are of no avail, they go to the other extreme. It would do the soul of a pirate no end of good to hear the things they can say on occasion. Possess your soul in peace, Sheridan; I do not intend you to become a rent collector. You would not be worth your salt in that capacity. I expect you to politely represent me once a month, and that is all. If they fail to pay, the matter is ended so far as you are concerned."

"Well, I'm mightily relieved to hear you say that," said Sherry, his face brightening. And so it was that when succeeding " sixteenths " came around he visited the poor, bedraggled wretches in the lower end of town with a countenance so pleasant that his ears must have burned later on because of the nice things the women said to each other across the alley fences.

The busy telephone transmitted no word concerning the all-important, though seldom mentioned, subject. Every time the bell rang, Redpath took down the receiver with the hope that something had developed in the hunt for the two jail-birds. At five o'clock Officer Barney Doyle came over from his home down the street.

"Good afternoon to you, Mr. Gilman," said the genial Barney, and was rewarded by a handshake as cordial as it was unexpected. (He afterwards informed his wife that Andy Gee was as fine a man in his own house as you'd ever want to see.) " I thought I'd run over before goin' down to headquarters to see if ye'd like to come along with a bunch of us this evenin', Sherry, me lad. (It's a wonderful house ye have here,

Mr. Gilman.)   The chief is sindin' some of the boys out
with Jackson's men to round up a couple of fellies reported by the station agent at Black Hill a while back.
(Ye're lookin' fine these days, Mr. Gilman.   The lad
must be agreein' with ye.)   It's twenty miles up the
line and we're to catch the six o'clock local.   They
were seen back in the woods by siveral reputable persons,— though what the divil reputable persons could
be doin' in the woods is a mystery to me,— and it is
the opinion of the station agent that they're layin' low
until dark when they'll sneak down to the siding and
board a freight.   There won't be a freight through
there till after eight o'clock, so we've plinty of time.
The chief ast me to run over an' see if ye'll join the
gang.   He says he's pickin' his men with great care,
and there's no wan he'd sooner have with him than
you.   Will ye come? "

Redpath turned to his employer, a wistful, eager expression in his eyes.   To his amazement, Mr. Gilman
was nodding his head briskly.

" If there is anything that we can do, Barney, to
assist in the recapture of these rascals, you may be
sure we will do it.   It rests entirely with Sheridan
whether he is to go with you or not.   What do you
say, my lad? "

" Good Lord, sir,— I'd like nothing better," cried
Sherry.   " But it may be an all night job.   Do you
feel sure you can spare me for —"

" I shall get along very nicely without you," said Mr.
Gilman.   Then he turned to Barney Doyle and added, a
twinkle in his eye: " I save the cost of a substantial
meal, you see, by letting him go before he has had

his supper, Barney.   That is worth considering in these
hard times, isn't it? "

"Bedad, sir, ye're right," said Barney, after an
instant's reflection.   His grin broadened.   "But have
ye considered what a divil of a breakfast he'll get away
with in the morning? "

"Sufficient unto the day, Barney, is the evil thereof.
It is the custom of a great many people to let tomorrow take care of today.   I shall try the experiment
for once in my life.   Go along, Sherry.   You'd better
take my fur coat and arctics.   By the way, Barney, in
the event that the sheriff has not offered a reward you
may say to him that I stand ready to give one thousand
dollars for the capture of one or both of these men."

"For the love of —" gasped Barney Doyle, his eyes
bulging.

"I consider it to be my duty as a citizen," added
Andy Gee, bowing ever so slightly as if in response to
shouts for a speech.   "You will not forget to tell
him? "

"I should say not!   But, bedad, sir, it's not up to
you to be offerin' a reward for —"

"The sheriff is a friend of mine," said the other
tersely.

"I'm not wishin' ye any bad luck, Mr. Gilman, but
I hope ye have to pay the thousand dollars, sir.
They're a couple of bad eggs.   They ought to be sint
up fer life."

"No doubt," said Mr. Gilman, without interest.   "I
know very little about the case.   My young friend here
is an unusually considerate chap.   He has not inflicted

me with repeated accounts of his exploit. Indeed, I
have had hard work to get him to talk about it at all.
Modesty is the rarest of virtues, my dear Barney, and
he appears to have more than his share of it."

"He's a great lad, sir," said Barney Doyle, beaming.
"I was sayin' to Patsy Burke only last night goin' over
the evints of the day,— (I came across him, sir, on his
way home after closin' hours at the Sunbeam, for fear
ye'd think I was frequentin' a saloon in uniform),— I
was sayin' to Patsy that —"

"Never mind what you said to Patsy, Barney,"
broke in Redpath, impatient to be off and not at all
fancying the encomiums of his friend, the barkeeper.
"We ought to be on our way. Sure you don't mind,
Mr. Gilman?"

"Quite sure. I shall wait up until you come in, just
to hear whether I am out the thousand dollars."

"Better not wait up, sir," protested Sherry.
"There is no telling when —"

"I have an old man's feeling that you are going on a
wild goose chase," said Andrew Gilman, pursing his
thin lips. "You will be home by twelve, and empty-
handed, I fear."

"And ye'll sleep better," said Barney Doyle affably,
"if ye know that your thousand dollars is safe for the
night at least, beggin' your pardon, sir."

"Perhaps," said the other, smiling. "It is a standing reward, however. Don't forget that, Barney."

Ten minutes later, Redpath and his friend the policeman were on their way to the street car line in Valley
Street, and Andrew Gilman was pacing the library, his

shoulders sagging a little more than usual, his thin
hands clasped tightly behind his back. In his eyes was
the look of one who has passed through a grave crisis
and still doubts his own senses. He wiped his brow; it
was wet with the sweat of relief. From time to time
he shook his bent head, and once he muttered: "God,
I never dreamed that I could tremble at the sight of a
policeman,— I never dreamed it could happen to me."

He had a bottle of burgundy brought up from the
cellar and drank two glasses of it with his supper. Not
in years had he done such a thing as this. The servant
was dumbfounded when she received the order. She
had been with the Gilmans for a decade and never before
had she served wine to the master except on rare occasions when moderately bibulous guests required some
sort of sacrifice on his part in the mistaken name of
hospitality.

The wine restored the brightness to his eyes; a sort
of fictitious confidence replaced the despairing look
that had been in them before. After supper he resumed his pacing of the floor, but now his head was
erect and his senses alert.

Not once but a hundred times in passing did he glance
at the face of the tall clock in the corner. At nine
o'clock he took down the telephone receiver, and in a
voice that shook slightly with nervousness, asked for
police headquarters. Before doing this he quietly
opened the back hall door and for a full minute stood
listening at the bottom of the servants' stairs. He
heard the two women chattering indistinctly in their
room at the head of the stairs. It was their habit to
go to bed at nine o'clock.

" This is Andrew Gilman. Have you had any word
from Black Hill? "

" No, sir. Nothing yet. There's a train down at
eleven o'clock."

" You don't know whether they got what they went
after? Wouldn't the chief have telephoned? You
must excuse me for calling up. I am interested, as
you may know."

" Yes, sir, I know. That's a good sized reward,
Mr. Gilman. Took my breath away, and everybody
else's. The chief said he'd let us know as soon as he
could get to a telephone. Shall I call you up later? "

" Don't bother. My secretary, Sheridan Redpath, is
with the posse. I daresay he will call me up. I should
have thought of that. You say there is no train until
eleven? "

" Eleven-thirty-five she's due here. They have arranged to stop her at Black Hill. It's the express, you
know, and never stops there unless ordered."

" Thank you. Good night."

Then he went slowly upstairs, his face set, his body
as rigid as a ramrod. He walked straight to his wife's
bedroom door and rapped.

Miss Corse opened the door. She was shivering.
For a moment she barred his entrance long enough to
whisper hoarsely:

" I don't want to get mixed up in this business,
Mr. Gilman. I'm an honest, law-abiding woman.
You've got to swear on your soul that my name will
never be mentioned if this thing gets out. It's my due.
I never dreamed —"

" You may rest easy, Miss Corse," he said persuasively. "You will not be mixed up in it." He pushed his way past her. She followed him into the room and closed the door quickly.

"You have no right to ask me to keep my mouth shut about this thing, Mr. Gilman," she was saying, rather excitedly. "I am not employed here to —"

He turned on her. His face was ashen now, and humility was in his voice.

"Miss Corse, I can only implore you to be generous. You have it in your power to ruin us. You are an honest woman, I am sure. If you were not, I would offer money to you for your silence. Instead of that, I humbly beg of you to remember that we are old and —"

"I sha'n't blab, if that's what you mean," she interrupted, a shamed look in her eyes. "You needn't think I'm mean enough for that. I only want to be sure you'll leave me out of it, if anything happens hereafter. That's all I want, sir. What I promised you this morning still goes. But you can see for yourself where I'd be if it got out that I was a party to this —"

"Oh, for heaven's sake, Miss Corse," whined a querulous, peevish voice from the opposite end of the room, "be quiet. Nothing can happen to you. Haven't I told you a thousand times today that everything will come out all right?"

Beyond the foot of the great four poster, in the depths of a chair that enveloped her fat little body quite completely, sat an old woman, her back to the door. She did not even so much as look around when the door was opened to admit her husband. She ignored him entirely.

"That's all right enough to say, Mrs. Gilman," began the nurse, " but —"

"Well, isn't my promise enough to satisfy you?" demanded the woman in the chair.

"You have nothing to fear, Miss Corse," repeated Mr. Gilman quietly, his gaze fixed on the formidable back of the big chair. There was a steely glitter in his eyes, and a strange tightening of skin about his lips.

"Young Redpath won't stand for this," persisted the nurse. " He won't be a party to —"

"Don't use that word again," snapped the old lady.

"Redpath will never know," said Mr. Gilman; " I can guarantee that much, Miss Corse. He has gone off into the country with a searching party. There! " he broke in on himself, smiling sardonically. " I made use of an objectionable word. My profound apologies! " The sound of a sniff came from the chair. " He will not return before midnight. It was really providential, his going off like this. I was racking my brain for an excuse to send him out for a few hours, and along came this bit of good luck."

He crossed over and opened the door to Mrs. Gilman's sitting-room, switching on the light as he did so. Miss Corse, her back against the hall-door, was going on feverishly.

"The papers say that outside influence was brought to bear on the jailers, and that there must have been bribery. What do you know about that, Mr. Gilman?"

Mr. Gilman was searching the other room with eyes in which perplexity soon gave way to alarm.

"There's no one here," he muttered, and again the moisture started out on his forehead. "What, in the name of God, have you done —"

"Bribery is a serious thing," went on Miss Corse. "If you had anything to do with paying those —"

He turned back into the room. The expression in his face was so terrible that the nurse's indictment trailed off into a mere whisper. His lips were working spasmodically, but no articulate sound issued. Suddenly his blazing eyes left the emotionless figure in the chair and fixed themselves upon a door in the upper corner of the room. It opened an inch, then two, then wide enough to disclose the figure on the opposite side.

Mr. Gilman leaned against the wall and put his hand over his heart.

"God, I thought you had ruined everything by letting him go out —"

"Come out!" said Mrs. Gilman, turning in her chair. "I told you it wasn't necessary to hide. No one —"

"I'm taking no chances," muttered the man who came forth from his hiding-place and shot a shifty, roving glance at all the doors and windows. "I'm too old a bird for that." He advanced a few steps into the room, his gaze resting on the shivering nurse. "Don't be scared. I've had a good supper. I'm not going to eat you, Miss Corse."

"Oh," gasped Miss Corse. "How can you joke about anything when we're all in such a stew over —"

"Stew!" he broke in gaily. "That's the word I've been wanting ever since I swallowed it. Stew, that's what it was, and it was all-fired good after the fare I've been having. I couldn't think of anything but hash, and I knew it couldn't be that."

He was wearing a long, quilted dressing-gown that fitted him much too snugly. His hands were shoved into the lower pockets and drawn around in front of him as far as the slack would allow. His strong, powerful neck was collarless. A glance lower down would have revealed feet encased in big carpet-slippers, and above them the legs of grey tweed trousers. His pale, heavy face had been recently scrubbed and shaved; the blue-black of the stubble formed an ugly shadow that extended high on his cheek bones. A livid red scar marked one of his cheeks, evidence of a wound recently healed. Devilish black eyes looked out from beneath thick eyebrows, and between them lay two deep furrows reaching well down to the bridge of a fine, broad nose. His lips were thin, his mouth wide, and there was always, no doubt, the suggestion of a smile at the corners. There were many grey hairs in the thick black mop that covered his head.

"It is not the time or place for jesting," said Mr. Gilman, straightening his bent figure and meeting the eyes of the other with some show of severity. "We have to decide upon some —"

"Just a minute," interrupted the other, stopping beside Mrs. Gilman's chair. She reached up and took his hand in hers. Andrew Gilman drew himself a little more erect. "Did I hear you say that a search party has gone out into the country? That means they must have had a tip of some kind."

"A couple of suspicious characters are reported as

being in the woods up at Black Hill," said the old man, his voice sinking.

"And this Redpath boy is out with the party?"

"Yes. I sent him."

"Well, that's comforting," said the big man, drawing a long breath and squaring his shoulders. "He's a naughty young thing! See what he did to me? I'll carry this for ever. I ought to make him pay for it."

"You are not to harm that boy, do you understand?" cried the older man sharply. "He did his duty as a man —"

"Oh, I'm not going to waste time on him. I haven't anything against him anyhow. Nobody likes a brave man more than I do. What's more, I guess I'm just as well off if I don't tackle him."

"Not face to face, at any rate," said Andrew Gilman.

"It is a shame the way your face has been disfigured by that —" began the old lady, a sob in her voice.

The intruder leaned over and stroked her grey head gently. "Now don't you go worrying about that. I was too pretty for my own good anyway. You wouldn't think, would you, Miss Corse, that I was a regular Adonis up to the time I got this crack?"

Miss Corse shrank back and muttered: "If you will excuse me, I think I'll go to my own room. I — I — if you need me, just call."

She vanished quickly. The man in the dressing gown was at the door an instant later, listening intently. He heard her close the door to the room across the hall.

"Do you trust that woman?" he inquired, scowling.

" We have to trust her," said Mr. Gilman. " She isn't blind," he added sardonically.

" I don't like her."

" It is quite evident that she doesn't like you, so it's all even. Was it necessary for you to hide in that closet just now? If there had been unwelcome visitors at the door, you would have stood a much better chance by remaining near a window. It isn't far to the ground. You —"

" I thought it might have been young Redpath."

" He never comes near this room. Have you found a decent suit of clothes, one that is anywhere near a fit? "

" Nothing but this one, and it looks new. Maybe you don't feel like giving it away. The coat and vest are a little tight, that's all."

" You are welcome to them. Shoes? "

" Yes. Pretty respectable. Pinch a little bit, but I guess I can stand 'em. It's a poor trade for you. The duds I'm leaving behind are awful. Stylish but awful! I got 'em in New York last year. They've seen some damn' hard use."

The old man passed his hand over his brow. " What a fool you were to come back to this town. What, in heaven's name, possessed you to come here after all these years? "

" Don't answer," cried Mrs. Gilman angrily. " You are a free man. You can go where you please. Least of all should you give an account of your movements to him. He has done nothing but ask that question since last night. After all these years, hey? I'd like to know what they've been to me. I'd like to —"

" Cut out the family rough-stuff, please," interrupted
the escaped burglar, not unkindly. "Let's stick to
cases. Just to satisfy your curiosity, I'll tell you why
I drifted down here. They were pretty close to me in
Chicago. I had to get out to Hammond on street cars.
It was no time for me to pick and choose my direction
or my destination. They would have had me in a
couple of hours, that's sure. This fellow Briscoe,— if
that's his right name,— has been trailing with me for
the last six months. I fished him out of the East River
one night and I couldn't shake him to save my soul.
He's all right. He'd die for me. Mean little rat, but
as square as they make 'em. It was he who tipped me
off in Chicago. Somehow he got wise to the bulls and
put *me* wise just in time. We beat it together. God
knows I hadn't the remotest intention of coming to this
gosh-awful burg. We got this far on a freight and
then received the kick. He boned a little grub up in
the north end of town and we hung around, waiting for
a chance to get out without walking. Then I remembered all that silver and stuff out there in the country.
I hadn't been on the place in more than twenty years,
but I knew it as well as I know my name. I always
hated the old rip anyway, so — we went to it, damn
the luck. That's how I happened to come to this burg,
and you know why I've stayed so long."

" You are not to be blamed for anything," cried the
old woman, twisting her fingers. "You were driven
into this awful life. God will surely punish some one
for all that has happened to you."

The fellow grinned. He had a sense of humour.
" God alone has a record of all the things that have

happened to me, so we'll have to leave it to Him. My
own memory is a little hazy, I fear."

" You must have been a fool to think that you could
get off with all that silver. You would have been —"

" You don't for a minute imagine that we were going
to advertise ourselves by carrying a sack of silver
around on our backs, do you? What was the matter
with burying it safely up there in the woods? It would
have been as safe as the Bank of England for just as
long as we cared to leave it there. We had the spot
picked out. Nothing to it! "

" My God," groaned the old man, suddenly covering
his eyes with his hands. " My God! "

The burglar stared at him unconcernedly. " You
hate the old girl as much as I do. You ought to be
disappointed because I didn't get away with the
stuff."

" She may be my sister, and all that," came from
Mrs. Gilman, her old voice hardening, " but I for one
wouldn't have cried much if she had lost the whole of
it."

Andrew Gilman, with an effort, regained control of
his shaken nerves. He faced the pair of them. The
younger man had seated himself on the arm of Mrs.
Gilman's chair.

" That is all behind us. We have to think of the immediate future. You cannot stay here a minute longer
than is absolutely necessary. I would to God you could
get away safely tonight, but I'm afraid, desperately
afraid. Tomorrow night, perhaps, but —"

" There he goes again," moaned his wife, " talking
about turning you out of the house, with danger every-

where, and zero weather — Oh, I wish God would pay him back for all the —"

"Never mind," soothed the younger man. "There's nothing else for him to do. I've got to get out of this town. I can't stay cooped up here in this room for ever. It would be almost as bad as jail."

"I don't care, it's inhuman, it's cruel —"

"And now about this partner of yours," said Mr. Gilman curtly. "Have you any idea where he is at this moment?"

"He's nowhere near Black Hill, if that's what you mean. They'll never get him. Unless I miss my guess badly, he's in St. Louis by this time."

"Does he know who you really are?"

"Nobody knows that."

"Where did you separate last night?"

"What's that got to do with the case?"

Mr. Gilman sighed. "You don't have to answer unless you care to, of course."

"Well," said the other grudgingly, "we said good-bye in the alley back of the jail. I gave him the proper steer, and that was enough. He's as slick as an eel. He thinks I'm in Chicago now, if that eases your mind."

"It does, tremendously," said Mr. Gilman. "You saw by the paper this morning that there is talk of bribery, and you heard what Miss Corse said. I want to say to you here and now that I would have let you rot in jail before I would have helped you by so much as the lifting of a finger."

"I can believe that," said the other, sneering. "I didn't ask for help, did I?"

" You knew it would be useless," said Mrs. Gilman.
Not once had she addressed a remark to her husband.
" Heaven knows that I could do nothing, tied down
as I am —"

" What do you want me to do? " demanded the
refugee. " Write a note exonerating the sheriff and
his men? That's the way it sounds."

" It looks bad for that jailer," said Mr. Gilman, in
some distress. " Of course, I know he was not tam-
pered with, but — Well, I'm sorry for him."

" Rats! He was an easy mark and he deserves a
panning. Well, have you doped anything out? How
am I to make my getaway? "

" You must remain here until tomorrow night, at
least. By that time I shall have arranged something.
Nothing can be done tonight. In the meantime, be extremely careful. Miss Corse will hold her tongue, but
the servants must not know that you are here. Don't
go near the windows, don't —"

" Good Lord, do you think I'm a damned fool? "
snarled the man.

Mr. Gilman hesitated. " I have thought so for
twenty-five years. Good night, William."

The fellow stretched himself lazily, and allowed his
arm to slip down over Mrs. Gilman's shoulder. There
was a hard glitter in his eyes as he looked over his
shoulder and said:

" Good night, Father."

CHAPTER XXI

WILLIAM, only son of the bitterly estranged Gilmans, was supposed to have died ten years prior to the events which culminated in his sensational return to the house in which he was born. The truth concerning his existence in the flesh was known only to the parents and to the sister-in-law who despised all of them. At the time of his banishment from his father's house many years before the report of his death was circulated in town, Mrs. Compton had given him shelter in her home, where he remained in seclusion for a fortnight and then went his way, cursing his father and his aunt, neither of whom he ever expected to see again.

At that time he was about twenty-six years of age; he had been looked upon as a model, more or less exemplary young man by all who knew him best, although none credited him with the stability that his father possessed. Only the father knew him for what he really was: a reprobate whose misdeeds had been screened from the public for at least a half dozen years.

A young girl's body recovered from the river into which she had thrown herself after pleading with her betrayer in the presence of that harassed father was the rock, figuratively speaking, on which Andrew Gilman's endurance split. For years he had endured constant and increasing acts of dishonour in which he alone was the sufferer at the hands of his unscrupulous son. Al-

ways he had carefully covered up the sins of the son,
and to this day not one of the men associated with him
in the conduct of his business had the slightest knowledge of the true situation.   He so altered his own books
and accounts that not even the book-keepers discovered
the frequent peculations of the junior member of the
firm of Andrew Gilman & Co.   The secret history of
the firm of Gilman & Co. abounded in transactions that
never saw the light of day.   From sly pilferings at the
outset of his career in business, William Gilman's depre-
dations developed into bold plunderings, the magnitude
of which staggered his father.

None save a man of iron could have faced the truth
as did Andrew Gilman.   The sickening wounds in his
heart were never exposed to the public eye.   The world
was not allowed to suspect for an instant that all was
not well with the integrity of the Gilmans.

William conducted himself with noteworthy decorum
in Farragut; for that much, at least, Andrew Gilman
was thankful.   So far as Farragut was concerned,
there was but one opinion concerning the younger Gilman, and that was never expressed in the hearing of his
forebear: behind his back it was said that William was
by no means a " chip of the old block."   On the contrary, he was a friendly, companionable young fellow
who spent money freely but sensibly.   Some instinct,—
perhaps that of self-preservation,— directed his conduct along the straight and narrow path while he was
under the observation of his fellow-townsmen.   He did
not deviate an inch from the course laid down by
provincial respectability; his dissipations were genteel,
his habits irreproachable, his morals unquestioned.

Certain analysts asseverated that he was a " light-weight " and would never be half the man that his father was, but this estimate was based largely on the fact that he wore a high collar and had been seen having his nails manicured.

Judge Emmons was of the opinion that he might outgrow these signs of ineptitude.

His good behaviour was confined to Farragut. Chicago, Louisville, St. Louis and occasionally New York saw the other side of him. He was bad to the core. Forgery, theft,— and on one occasion the pawning of his mother's jewels,— were charged up against him by a long-patient and bewildered father. He robbed his parent with impunity, confident that there could be no such thing as exposure or penalty.

Then came a day when, balked in his designs upon the family resources, he stole from an important customer, actually taking the man's purse from his coat pocket when that individual, suspecting no evil in the house of Gilman & Co., left the garment hanging over the back of a chair in the office while he went out into the shipping department with the head of the firm. A porter was suspected of the theft. Andrew Gilman, apologizing for his humiliated house, restored the money — six hundred dollars — to the victim and the matter was dropped.

This went on for three or four years. Not one word of it reached Mrs. Gilman's ears. She was serene in the belief that her son was immaculate. Andrew Gilman would have kept the truth from her for ever had it been possible. She worshipped her son; she bitterly resented what she called fault-finding in her husband

when he took the young man to task for mistakes
natural to the young and inexperienced, chiefly in connection with money matters.

Andrew Gilman bore it all in silence, and suffered
alone. He shielded the son, he shielded the mother.
He covered up the tracks of the thief so carefully that
they might as well never have existed, and he went on,
day by day, looking for fresh tracks to obliterate.
Thousands of dollars went for the preservation of the
family name and the protection of the woman who had
brought a thief into the world.

It was not until the unhappy girl came forward with
her story of an irreparable wrong that he arose in
revolt against iniquity. There was a frightful scene.
He cursed his son. The girl went to Mrs. Gilman, who
put a mother's curse upon her. The next day a dead
body was taken from the river. . . .

Andrew Gilman turned his son out of his house that
night. In the presence of the distracted mother, he
gave the young man a roll of bills and told him that
he was done with him for ever.

Hoping for results from the mitigating influence of
his mother, William sequestered himself at the home of
his aunt, who, loathing Andrew Gilman as she did at a
time when her own quarrel with him was flourishing,
was satisfied to believe that her nephew had been
cruelly mistreated by an unreasonable, narrow-minded
father. Whatever may have transpired in the Gilman
house during the two weeks that he remained with his
aunt and uncle,— Compton was alive at that time,—
William was brought finally to the realization that his
mother was powerless as an advocate. She had failed

to budge his father from the stand he had taken.

He sat down and wrote a letter to Andrew Gilman, and another to his mother. In both he declared that they would never see him again; in one of them he said it with diabolical fury, in the other so tenderly that its recipient never forgave the man who drove him out into the world. He forswore the name of Gilman. To his mother he wrote that he could no longer answer to a name that was hateful to him; to his father, with more nobility than he intended, he said that as long as his mother bore the name of Gilman he would not risk adding anything to her degradation by using it himself. He was " going to hell " and he " didn't want her to know it."

For ten years nothing was heard of him. They did not know whether he was alive or dead. The mother, adoring him in spite of all that she now knew to be the truth concerning him, grieved terribly. As time went on and no word came from William, she gave up all pretence of friendship for her husband. (Love had long since ceased to exist between them.) Her grief and despair and longing were made easier by the cultivation of a vast hatred for Andrew Gilman. Every day added something to the raging fire that consumed her.

More than once he was tempted to seek out his son and restore him to his mother's side, if only to escape the abuse she heaped upon him, but calm reflection offset this inclination with the certainty that conditions could not be improved by the return of the ne'er-do-well. Andrew Gilman had but one hope in his soul: that his son would work out his own regeneration and then — come home!

Farragut did not suspect, nor was it ever allowed to suspect. William Gilman was supposed to have gone to South America to engage in business for himself. In response to inquiries both of the Gilmans never failed to say that he was " doing well " and " might be home for a visit before long."

Mrs. Compton had a single but illuminating experience with the young man about eight years after his departure. He came to her hotel in New York and tried to borrow a no inconsiderable sum of money from her. She refused and he became so abusive that she threatened to have him ejected from the hotel. He was in no position to invite an encounter with the house detective or police, so he went away empty-handed, swearing that he would " get even " for the way his people had treated him. Mrs. Compton never spoke of this incident.

And then one day came an end to Andrew Gilman's secret hopes. His son was in jail in Philadelphia, charged with robbery. After ten years this was the first word they had had from him. He wrote from the prison, smuggling the letter out by a discharged inmate, and implored his father to come to his assistance. With a " wad of money " he could fix the guilt where it really belonged; they were trying to " railroad " him; it was a " frame-up " pure and simple. If they " got him " for this alleged crime, it would mean at least twelve or fourteen years in prison. Even the redoubtable William winced at that.

He was smart enough to direct the letter to his mother, in whom lay his only hope. Mr. Gilman wrote to his son, demanding full particulars. He addressed the letter to William Colby and signed himself A. Gill. He went to Chicago to post it. In due time a reply came from the prisoner. It was as his father had thought. Cold-bloodedly, William Gilman purposed to hire a couple of witnesses who would hang the guilt upon another man,—" a dirty crook who ought to be in the pen for life anyhow, so you needn't have any scruples."

It was then that the final crash came between Mr. and Mrs. Gilman. Despite her demand that he carry out the plan proposed by his son, he refused to have anything to do with him or his scheme to convict a man who was, in any event, innocent of the crime for which William was to be tried. Moreover, he put his foot down on her proposal to take the matter into her own hands and furnish the necessary cash. To clinch his argument he swore that he would go to Philadelphia himself and expose the " deal," if it were attempted.

From that day, Mrs. Gilman never spoke to her husband. She retired to rooms which she selected for herself, engaged a nurse to whom she confided nothing of her physical or mental sufferings, although she complained of both, and for ten years lived the life of a recluse. She had violent fits of weeping and tremendous depression, and so alarming were her symptoms at first that the physician, a good old-fashioned country doctor, " looked in " every day for six months, at three dollars a visit, and even at the end of that period seemed reluctant to trust her out of his sight for more than a day at a time.

Her one object in life was to make Andrew Gilman unhappy. With the short-sightedness of some of her sex, she believed that there is no surer way to make a man unhappy than to let him see that he is the supreme cause of misery.

She hated him with all her soul and revelled in it. The pleasure of hating him would not have been so keen, however, if she could have looked into his heart just once and seen what was there. It was not a part of her calculations that he should enjoy the privilege of hating her even more than she could possibly have hated him. His hatred of her terrified him at times.

William " Colby " was " sent up " for seven years. His father went east soon afterward and, with the aid of private detectives, learned much of the history of the notorious Bill Colby. He had served a short term in Sing Sing for larceny, and more than once had escaped punishment for other crimes through an almost uncanny ability to cover up his tracks. He was a thief, a card-sharp, a blackmailer and a bunco-steerer. The records also revealed a startling incongruity: he had never been known to take a drink of intoxicating liquor!

With these facts in his possession, Andrew Gilman buried the last, lingering hope. He returned to Far-ragut and the next morning the *Dispatch* printed the interesting news that William Gilman, only son of " our esteemed fellow-citizen, Andrew Gilman," had died in Buenos Aires.

Twenty years after leaving his home town, William Gilman reappeared in the flesh, but no man would have recognized in him the fastidious, natty figure of old. Time and experience had made another man of him. He had grown massive, burly, sinister. The evil in him had expanded its physical habitation to extraordinary proportions; it was as if nature had been compelled to meet a demand for more room.

Mrs. Compton broke the silence of years when she went to Andrew Gilman with the news that his son had come back to Farragut.

A few words only are necessary to explain the presence of William Gilman in the house he had dishonoured. It was his safest refuge. Fleeing from the jail in the driving snowstorm, he made his way direct to the big old house in which he was born. Peering through a window he discovered his father sitting alone in the library. With the assurance and confidence of a fatalist, he calmly rang the door-bell. . . . No one would think of looking for him there.

His mother provided him with money for the trip to the Pacific Coast on which his mind was set. Andrew Gilman, feeling like a rat in a trap, gave him suitable clothing and besought God's aid in the hazardous undertaking that was to follow.

During the long, trying day that he remained quietly in his mother's apartment, William was given the treatment of the prodigal son. Toward the end of the day the fond and excited old woman exhibited her last will and testament to him.

By this she meant to prove to him that she still loved and trusted him. At her death every penny that she possessed,— and she was a comparatively rich woman, — was to go to her " beloved son, William Gilman."

William put his arm around her and said that he hoped God would let her live to be a hundred!

CHAPTER XXII

THE posse rounded up the two men at Black Hill, and in disgust released them.

Sherry Redpath was in high spirits. His mind was at rest concerning Andrew Gilman. Obviously his employer was not involved in the escape of the two men. His offer of a reward for their apprehension was in itself reassuring. He chuckled delightedly to himself, however, as he thought of the bomb he could throw into the group of searchers if he were to announce that the big crook was known to both Mr. Gilman and Mrs. Compton.

The company of man-hunters, for strategic purposes, were scattered throughout the four day coaches in the local train. Sherry sat alone in one of the cane bottom seats. Looking out of the window into the swirling steam and smoke that blew low from the pounding, noisy locomotive, he allowed his thoughts to stray from the real business of the night.

Morna O'Brien came up out of the gliding abyss and took her seat beside him as he dreamed with wide-open eyes. He recalled her admonitions. They were pleasing. She had urged him to be careful. That signified something, at least,— indeed, the more he thought of it, the greater became the significance of her concern. He rehearsed their little scene at parting. His imagination placed her in the seat beside him, and as he repeated from memory every word that she had uttered, he revelled in the preposterous fancy that she snuggled close to him in the dreary day coach and whispered them into his enslaved ear.

All day long he had been thinking of her. That in itself was not an unusual occupation for him, but on this particular day he approached a state of confidence that made all previous days look black and chaotic. He had almost arrived at the conclusion that she liked him, and that was a great deal farther than he had ever permitted himself to go before. Her manner that morning,— well, he tingled a little as he recalled the look in her lovely, troubled eyes. She was really interested in him. She had been worried about him. And that brought the comforting thought that she might even now be sitting at home worrying herself ill over him! (He had called her up from Klein's drug-store just before the train pulled out, to let her know that he was off on a trifling expedition,— nothing to speak of, of course, as there probably wouldn't be a bit of fight left in 'em if they saw they were surrounded, even though they had been able to obtain firearms.)

His original resolution to turn over a new leaf now enjoyed the companionship of a thriving and even more attractive resolve: the determination to so order his life that Morna O'Brien would never have cause to be ashamed of him. In his kindly ruminations, he even went so far as to arrogate to himself the singular office of protector-in-chief to this wilful maid. Not saying that Jimmy Burton wasn't a most desirable, perhaps dependable chap, and all that,— but *some* one ought to take a hand there before it was too late. It would

never do for her to run away with and get married
to a Burton. No good could come of such an alliance.
As a matter of fact,— now that he thought of it,— it
would be quite as much of a calamity for Jimmy to
marry a Compton. Any way you looked at it, they
couldn't possibly live happily ever afterward. The
ghost of the feud would always be sitting beside them,
grinning, and the time would surely come when —

"Black Hill Junction!" barked a raucous voice behind him, and he got up with a sigh to go out into the
cold, unfeeling night.

There was not so much need of strategy coming down
on the eleven o'clock. The posse united in excoriating
the station agent at Black Hill. They crowded together in the forward end of the smoking car and raised
their voices in a withering chorus of scorn. They had
experienced an hour and a half of extreme discomfort
plodding through the snow toward a common centre;
the night was bitterly cold and the wind was high.
Nearly every man in the crowd had taken the precaution to provide against pneumonia and other ailments;
there were at least a dozen well-filled flasks in the posse
when it began the chase. It is safe to say that when
the station at Farragut was reached the flasks were
empty and the posse full.

Redpath was cold and tired. He sat with Barney
Doyle, his shoulders hunched, his chin buried in the fur
collar that was fastened close about his neck. From
time to time his teeth chattered. A dozen men tendered
their flasks.

"Take a good fat swig o' this, Sherry. It will tickle
you to the toes. Don't be a fool. It may head off a

cold." So spoke the lord high sheriff of the county, poking his " pint " at Redpath.

"No, thank you," said the other. "I'm on the wagon, you know."

"One drink won't hurt you a bit. Medicinal purposes. Just as you'd take quinine if it was prescribed by a doctor. Lord, how it warms a feller up! I was frozen stiff. Never felt warmer in my life than I do right now. Drink 'er down, you chump."

A lean deputy with a hollow voice waved the sheriff aside.

"Don't do that, Sheriff. He's our nice little Willie-boy. He's afraid of fire-water. You ought to know better'n —"

"Are you afraid to touch it? " broke in the sheriff, eyeing the young man curiously.

"Not at all," replied Sherry. "I simply don't intend to touch another drop of the stuff as long as I live, Mr. Sheriff, that's all."

"I never had much use fer a feller that couldn't take a drink or two and then say he'd had enough,—'specially when everybody else is doin' it sensibly and —"

Sherry interrupted the lean, sneering deputy. "How many have you had to-night, Swigert? "

"Two," said Swigert loudly. "On'y two. But, lemme tell you somethin', if I wanted any more I'd take 'em an' it woul'n' be any your damn' business. Do you get me? I'm no mollycoddle. I c'n take a drink with anybody. I —"

"I merely wanted to suggest that you've had enough," said Sherry pleasantly. "If you take another, you'll begin to show it, Swigert."

"Aw, you go to hell. I s'pose because you are old man Redpath's son, and went to college, you think you're —"

"Go and sit down, Swigert," said the sheriff roughly. "Go on, now. I don't want to have to tell you again. Now, Sherry, listen to me. You're shiverin' like a licked dog. Take a little pull at this. It can't —"

"Take it away," shouted Redpath angrily. The sheriff was gently waving the uncorked bottle under his nose. "God knows I want a drink,— and I need it, too. But I'm not going to take one! I know how good it would make me feel. You can't tell me anything about it. But you can't tempt me. Take it away, I say!"

"Well, if that's the way you treat a friend who's only trying to be courteous and —"

"I apologize, Mr. Sheriff. I'm sorry if I said anything to offend you. Forget it, please."

"And you still won't have a little nip?"

"No."

"Just as you say, just as you say." The sheriff took a long pull at the bottle and then, with grave precision, corked it. Slipping it into his coat pocket, he walked away.

"That's the stuff, Sherry, me boy," said Barney Doyle, his red face beaming with pride. "Whin I tell the old lady how ye turned all the booze down tonight, and you freezin' as solid as annybody and shakin' your teeth out, she'll raise the roof wid song. The sheriff has been hittin' it up all day. The things they're hintin' at in the newspapers, and all that, ye see. It's got on his nerves. I'll stake me soul ye've learned him a lesson this night. The way he put up that bottle tells me he's had his last drink for the present."

"He gave it a long farewell kiss, I'll say that for him," said Sherry, a twinkle in his eye.

Barney studied his young friend's face for a moment. "Did ye want a drink or did ye not? Ye don't have to answer unless ye want to."

"I never wanted one so much in my life," said the other frankly.

"Then all the more credit to ye," said Barney, vastly relieved. "I'm dom glad to hear it. It wouldn't have meant anything at all if ye hadn't wanted it. The best pleased man in town will be Patsy Burke when I tell him about it. Take my advice, lad; before ye turn in for the night soak your feet in hot water and mustard. Many's the time I've had Patsy Burke recommind the tratement to me. Bedad, I'm thinkin' it will be a tremenjous relafe to old man Gilman when he hears his thousand bucks is safe." He chuckled loudly.

.   .   .   .

It was Andrew Gilman who rummaged in the butlery for mustard, and it was he who prepared the hot foot bath for the shivering Redpath. The old man had waited up for him.

"Well?" he inquired as the young man entered the warm, cosy library. He looked up from the book he was reading, but did not arise.

"False alarm," said Sherry, answering the brief question.

"I thought so. Are you cold?"

"I guess I'm not as rugged as I thought," said the

young man sheepishly. "The fire feels good." He stood close to the blazing logs, his back to the fireplace. The fire had been lately replenished. "Mighty good of you, Mr. Gilman, to stay up and keep the fire going like this."

"Umph!" The speaker eyed the young man closely. "It must have been rather a strain on your courage to keep from it, my boy. There's nothing like it when you're chilled to the bone." That was his way of disposing of a subject that another might have gone into at length. "Be off to bed now. Anything you'd like?"

"If you'll tell me where I can find some mustard, I'll —"

"Stay where you are. I'll get it. It is as cold as Iceland in the pantry."

Half an hour later he piled some extra blankets on top of the grateful but mortified young athlete, and admonished him to be careful not to kick them off in the night.

"Sweat it out," he said, and passed into his own room.

And so it was that Sheridan Redpath slept soundly within whispering distance of the man for whom the whole country was being raked, on whose head a sardonic price had been put by a craftier man than any of them, and of whom he dreamed most unpleasantly under the weight of two extra blankets, each weighing a thousand pounds.

Much to his surprise he got up the next morning feeling as fit as a fiddle. There was no trace of a cold, nor was there any evidence of the dolefully anticipated stiff-

ness in his joints. He had to stretch himself prodigiously before he could believe his senses. He was
awake when Mr. Gilman came through the room at half-
past seven o'clock, and responded cheerily to the rather
anxious inquiry as to how he was feeling.

"Never finer," he cried. "I'll be down in two shakes
of a lamb's tail. Great stuff, that mustard."

Mr. Gilman stopped at the door, his hand on the
knob.

"I am very much relieved," he said slowly, almost
calculatingly. "If you had been under the weather this
morning, I should have felt obliged to go to Chicago
myself,— and it isn't a trip that I relish."

"Chicago? Something sudden, Mr. Gilman?"

"Not at all. If you are quite sure that you are
feeling up to it, I shall ask you to take the nine-thirty
train this morning in my place. You will have several
hours this afternoon in which to attend to the matter
I shall speak to you about later on."

"All right, sir. I'll be right down."

"You will catch the nine o'clock train home this
evening without the least trouble."

"I know. Due here at twelve-fifty-two. I've seen it
come in a hundred times, more's the shame. That
shows the kind of hours I kept."

"It also shows pretty clearly where you kept them,"
said Mr. Gilman drily.

"I had quite a range," said Sherry, in high good
humour. "I have said how-do-you-do to the two
o'clock on the Big Four, the two-forty on the Wabash,
— sometimes they were a couple of hours late, at that,—
and I've said good-bye to the milk train at six A. M. on

more than one occasion. It is no treat to me to see the trains go by."

Mr. Gilman was calmly reading the *Dispatch* at the breakfast table when he bounded downstairs at eight o'clock, after a hurried shave and bath.

" I say, Mr. Gilman, didn't Mrs. Gilman have a good night? " he inquired anxiously. " I saw Miss Corse dash out of the room just now and into her own. She seemed to be in a great hurry, so I —"

" Mrs. Gilman is sometimes very exacting and impatient," interrupted the other, controlling himself only with the greatest effort of the will. He even smiled, as much as to add in extenuation: " you understand, of course." If the line deepened between his eyes, and if his face went a shade whiter, Sherry, in his flurry, did not observe the changes. " Miss Corse has to fly about pretty lively at such times." He laid the paper down a moment later. A fine moisture appeared on his forehead. " Perhaps I'd better just step up and inquire. I sha'n't be gone a minute. Look over the paper. There is no news of your fly-by-night friends."

He was gone not more than five minutes. " It is just as I thought," he said, resuming his seat. " She had a sleepless night. Her nerves go to pieces at such times. Now about this trip to Chicago. You are to deliver a package to the Title and Trust Company to be placed in their vaults pending future action. I have written a letter of instructions to them, and they will give you a receipt for the package. That is all you will have to do."

" It sounds easy," said the other, smiling. " You don't overwork me, I must say."

"Umph! I suppose you are wondering why I do not send the package up by express or registered mail. It would seem more sensible, wouldn't it?"

"Not if you'd rather trust me than the express company or the U. S. Government."

"I am trusting you as I would myself. That explains everything."

After breakfast he placed a big sealed envelope in the young man's hand, and gave him the letter to the Title and Trust Company.

"You will need ten dollars for expenses. Five-fifty for railroad fare, seventy-five cents for your luncheon and the balance for a dinner at the Annex. You can get a very satisfactory meal there for three dollars if you are cautious,— including the tip."

"I'll return the change."

"You will have to spend something for street-car fare," the old man reminded him. "It will not be necessary, however, to tip the street car conductors," he added, and winked.

Redpath carried the sealed envelope to Chicago and delivered it safely. If he had known that it contained nothing but blank sheets of paper, he would not have heaved a sigh of relief when it passed from his possession into that of the Title and Trust Company, and it is quite certain that the gentleman who received it would not have been so careful about stowing it away in the vaults. Neither of them was by way of knowing what was in the mind of Andrew Gilman when he sent his secretary off on an errand that would keep him away from home for a well calculated length of time.

When the nine o'clock train on the Wabash railroad

pulled out of Farragut that night one of its passengers was a tall, prosperous looking man who had his suit-case carried into compartment C, and who shook hands cordially with Andrew Gilman on the station platform before following the porter into the car.

A reporter for the *Dispatch* accosted Mr. Gilman as he was returning to the automobile which had conveyed him and the stranger to the depot.

" Any news, Mr. Gilman? "

" Nothing that would interest the public," replied the old man pleasantly.

" You were seeing some one off. Would you mind giving me the name? We're awfully short on local stuff tonight. A two or three line ' personal ' would help."

" That was a Mr. Alfred Griffiths, of St. Louis. He stopped off on his way from the East to see me on a little matter of business. Nothing important."

The reporter was writing: " Mr. Alfred Griffiths, a prominent citizen of St. Louis, Missouri, was in the city yesterday for a few hours. He returned to his home last night. Mr. Griffiths, who has been in the East, says that the blizzard was particularly severe in west-ern Pennsylvania and Ohio. While here he was the guest of Mr. Andrew Gilman."

" What have you put down there? " demanded Mr. Gilman.

The young man read the " item," purposely omitting the gratuitous information concerning the blizzard.

" Scratch out what you said about Mr. Griffiths be-ing my guest. It was a business matter. No doubt he saw other people while here. I don't like to have my name in the paper, as a matter of fact."

"All right, Mr. Gilman.   Still pretty cold, isn't it?"

"Pretty sharp.   Want a ride down?   I go past your office."

"Thanks.   Drop me at the Tremont, please."

They got into the automobile, which lumbered off over the snow-piled street.

"Anything been heard of those fellows who broke out of jail?" inquired Mr. Gilman.

"Not a word.   They never will hear of them," vouchsafed the reporter scathingly.   "This gang we got in office now is the worst ever.   They couldn't catch a drop of water in a two-gallon bucket.   And see what a glorious street cleaning department we've got. Lordy, this is enough to tear an automobile to pieces. I wish we had a few more public-spirited citizens like you, Mr. Gilman.   You made a great hit the way you jumped in and cleaned off the sidewalks —"

"Ahem!"

"By the way, is it true that you intend to remodel the row of store-rooms between Cass and Logan streets next spring?"

Mr. Gilman gulped.   "Is there a rumour to that effect?"

"Somebody came into the office a day or two ago and said he saw Sherry Redpath sizin' the buildings up the other day.   That's enough to start a rumour these days."

"I am not ready to give out anything about it at present.   Come and see me later on."

"You won't mention it to any one else, will you? I'd like to get a 'scoop' on it."

"You may trust me not to mention it."

"Anything in Mr. Griffiths' visit that would be of interest to the readers of the *Dispatch?* I saw you talking pretty busily to him down at the far end of the platform. Sort of out of ear-range, you might say."

"The observation car, it seems, invariably stops at that end of the platform. He reserved a compartment from my house this afternoon. That is how we happened to be down there."

"I thought maybe he was a big doctor from somewhere, called in to see Mrs. Gilman," ventured the reporter. "He looked the part all right."

"Just because a man wears spectacles and a silk hat is no sign that he is a doctor, my boy."

"I guess that's right. The orneriest gambler in town wears a plug hat and a Prince Albert morning, noon and night. And he wears a fur coat, too,— phony, of course, not the real goods like the one Mr. Griffiths had on. You can always tell the real article, can't you?"

"Not always," said Mr. Gilman softly.

CHAPTER XXIII

FOR the next two or three days there was an atmosphere of restraint in and about the Gilman home. After that the air cleared perceptibly; not only was Mr. Gilman quite like himself once more, but the behaviour of Miss Corse also underwent a marked change. On the rare occasions when she was unable to avoid Redpath in the hall, her manner had been distant and unfriendly. There were times when he felt certain that she was afraid of him. And then, quite as inexplicably, her manner changed and she became even more friendly than before. She went out of her way to engage in somewhat protracted discussions with him, and there were frequent sly little confidences concerning the " crankiness " of the old woman " up there." " She is the limit," confided Miss Corse, and from that simple expression he derived what he considered to be an explanation for her recent conduct.

Coincident with the sudden rise in spirits on the part of Mr. Gilman and Miss Corse was the arrival of a telegram from Los Angeles, directed to Mrs. Gilman; a circumstance unknown to Redpath, however, and therefore of no value in the formation of his conclusions.

The affairs of all the persons connected with this narrative settled down for the winter, so to say. The weeks slipped rapidly by in a more or less desultory fashion; each day was a good deal like the other and they were all short. The nights were long, and for Sherry Redpath, tedious.

He was an active person, full of life and spirit, and the evenings spent with Andrew Gilman, while amazingly interesting after a certain fashion, were far from inspiring to one who had the call of youth in his blood. Moreover, Mr. Gilman had become more exacting in his demands. He begrudged the young man his occasional " night out." Sherry did not complain. He appreciated the other's dread of the long, lonely evenings, and quite as much through pity as through duty he allowed his privileges to lapse. As a matter of fact, the evenings were not unprofitable. Andrew Gilman was a never-ending source of help and inspiration. The young man realized that he was absorbing sound principles and acquiring a fund of knowledge that would one day be of great value to him.

And he gave to Andrew Gilman much that was of value in return. He had new ideas to exchange for old ones, and while his employer did not readily fall in with them, because habit was too strong to be overcome in a trice, he never failed to consider seriously, and not captiously, the suggestion of his wide-awake, occasionally visionary, companion in these nightly discursions. Not a few of Redpath's suggestions resulted in actual performances, and in such cases Mr. Gilman was more pleased than he cared to admit when they turned out to be advantageous, not only to himself but to a community he no longer despised so heartily as in the days gone by.

Redpath was becoming quite a novel figure in town. He was doing things,— and doing them with old Andy Gee's money. Men who had looked upon him with suspicion a few months before, now admitted that " maybe there's something in the darned scamp after all." He was not content to be merely a figure-head collecting agent; they couldn't understand any man working for Andrew Gilman and still possessing a mind of his own, or a shred of independence. How he managed to wheedle the hard-fisted old skinflint into such an astonishing state of progressiveness, was the question that every one asked and no one answered.

Old Judge Emmons meant every word of it when he remarked, while watching a gang of men tearing down the time-honoured and unsightly wooden awning in front of Bolger's meat-market, that he'd be "switched if he wouldn't vote for Andy Gilman for mayor if he'd only agree to run."

Socially, Sherry was being noticed, if not actually recognized. The women were more afraid of each other than they were of him. They were cautious. It was one thing to say that Sherry Redpath deserved a whole lot of credit and another to say "Oh, you must come, Mr. Redpath; we want you *so* much." Feminine Farragut was saying quite openly, however, that he was a terribly good-looking fellow,—" you wouldn't believe it, really, if you could have seen the way he looked last spring," and so on.

And when he finally took to skating on the ponds in the park above town,— a sport in which he excelled,— formidable matrons smiled benignly and said they hoped " to goodness it would last."

It came to pass, later on, that he was more severely criticized for an unbearable aloofness than for anything else he had done. He skated because he loved the exercise,— and needed it. It did not occur to him

that he should have offered his long, graceful body for
the support and education of awkward young ladies who
struggled with the rudiments; this wilful neglect was
not due to snobbishness.   Not by any manner of means.
He was acutely afraid of being snubbed if he ventured
farther than the simple, perfunctory smile of recognition with which he favoured one and all without distinction.

Six months ago these girls had drawn their skirts
aside when he passed them in the streets.   He was not
taking any chances with them now.   He knew most of
the older girls; he had grown up with them; he had
not the slightest feeling of resentment toward them.
They had been quite right in avoiding them.   If he had
had a sister he certainly would have counselled her to
steer clear of a fellow like Sherry Redpath.

Morna O'Brien came one afternoon to the ponds.
She was with a crowd of young men and women in a
huge bob-sled.   They were going on after the skating to
a house in the country for supper and a barn dance.

Redpath had removed his skates and, aglow from the
healthy exercise, lingered on the bank watching the
antics of a couple of beginners.   The ponds were
crowded.   He did not see Morna until she swept by him
on the ice, hand in hand with a man he knew.   She
flashed a smile over her shoulder and called out a merry
" Hello, stranger," to him.

His heart throbbed so violently for a moment or two
that he could feel it pounding against his ear-drums.
He followed her with fascinated, hungry eyes as she
glided through the maze of skaters.   Distance and the
throng that darted madly over the surface of the huge

pond failed to shut her out of his vision. She flashed by again, and again she smiled at him. Her cheeks were glowing, her dark eyes dancing. He felt suddenly sick and weak with longing.

She was wearing a check skirt that came down to her shoe tops, a dark green jacket trimmed with fur and a close velvet turban edged with the same brown material. (He credited her with nothing short of sable.) Something brightly scarlet was at her throat.

Drunk with the spell of her he watched and waited for that unfailing smile as she whizzed past — thrice, four times, five,— and then he lost count. There were a dozen girls on that pond who skated as well as Morna, and some of them better, but you could not have convinced him of that. He could hardly believe his own eyes. It seemed absolutely incredible that *any* girl could skate so marvellously well. (You must remember that to him, sport of any description was masculine. He gave it a sex.) What beastly luck, he was wailing inwardly. If he had waited but ten minutes before removing his skates! Or if fate had ordained that she should appear on the pond fifteen minutes earlier. It would be ridiculous for him to sit down now and strap on his skates. And even if he had been willing to make an ass of himself, what right had he to expect her to ignore the men in her own party for the sake of a few turns about the pond with him? Besides,— he remembered with a shock that plunged him further into gloom,— he was even now due at Mr. Gilman's to go over the afternoon's mail with him. He sighed profoundly and turned away from temptation.

"Hello, Sherry," called out a buoyant, sprightly

voice. A young fellow, with one knee on the ground, was feverishly adjusting his skates. It was Jimmy Burton. " How's the ice? "

" Great," replied the departing one, his spirits going clear to the bottom with a dizzy rush.

Jimmy picked his way awkwardly to the ice, and waited, his eager gaze sweeping the pond.

" Curse the luck! " muttered Sherry, and strode off, unwilling to witness the inevitable. He heard Jimmy shout a brisk, domineering " Next! " and to save his soul could not resist the impulse to look around.

Young Mr. Burton was coolly appropriating Morna, edging in between her and the monopolist who had had her from the beginning,— and Morna was smiling delightedly!

A few days later she appeared again on the pond, coming with her cousins. He was ashamed of the pretence that he did not see her, and yet he was doing his cause a world of good without knowing it. She was piqued. In his ignorance he referred to himself as a sulky, impolite idiot. A different sort of ignorance on her part caused her to wonder what on earth she could have done to offend him!

He could not understand himself. Here was he, a grown-up man, behaving like a silly school-boy, purposely avoiding her, acting as if she did not exist,— it was disgusting! What was there to be afraid of? She always had been nice to him, she never had snubbed him, she — Good heavens, it couldn't be that he was bashful?

For three days he had been trying to screw up the courage to telephone out and ask her to come in and

skate with him,— while the ice was good! Once he
went so far as to take down the receiver. For hours
afterwards he thought of himself as a spineless thing
unworthy the name of man. When the operator
droned " number," he stammered: " Can you give me
the correct time, please? "

He went home that day too without having had a
word with her. Mr. Gilman was a little crusty that
evening. His secretary was wool-gathering.

He studied the weather reports assiduously, dreading
a sudden rise in the temperature and the thaw that
would put an end to the skating at least temporarily.

February was half gone when he saw an " item " in
the society columns of the *Dispatch* that rendered the
whole day bleak for him. Mrs. Compton and Miss
O'Brien were leaving on the twenty-third for a six weeks'
stay in Florida. This was the sixteenth. It was his
day for making the perfunctory " reminder " visits to
delinquent tenants.

" Ain't ye feelin' well, sir? " inquired Mrs. Cassidy,
the first to be seen. She was now three months in
arrears.

" Never felt better," he assured her, and gave her
his customary though somewhat belated smile.

" Ah, thin, some one in yer family is sick," she speculated, having missed her first guess. " I hope it's nothing serious, sir. It's hard weather for —"

" You *will* try to pay a little this month, won't you,
Mrs. Cassidy? " he broke in, impatient for the first time
in her acquaintance with him. Whereupon she told
him what she thought of Andrew Gilman. She was still

telling him when he turned the corner into the next
street where Jacob Webber lived.

That afternoon Morna put her pride in her pocket
and, deserting the Bingham girl with whom she was
skating, swooped down upon him from an advantageous
angle.

"What is the matter with you?" she demanded, an
accusing light in her eyes. "Don't you ever intend to
speak to me again?"

He flushed to the roots of his hair. "Why,— er,—
there's nothing the matter. I'm awfully glad to see
you. I've been waiting for a chance to talk with you
for —"

"I don't believe you like me any more," she said.

"Don't say that. Of course, I do. But you always
seem to be so busy — er — don't you know. A poor,
out-of-the-running dub like me hasn't a chance to get
within a mile of you."

"We're going South next week," she said, a trifle irrelevantly.

"I saw it in the paper."

"You haven't been very friendly, Mr. Redpath.
Granny has spoken of it several times. Aren't you ever
coming out to see us again? Or does Mr. Gilman object? He —"

"I was thinking of running out to see you tomorrow," he said, which was quite true, for he was always
thinking of running out to see her "tomorrow."

"You might have asked me to skate with you," she
said, a little crossly. "Or perhaps you don't think I
skate well enough. Everybody says you are so high

and mighty you will not condescend to skate with ordinary mortals."

"Oh, my Lord," he gasped, genuinely amazed.

"You are becoming very unpopular. People are saying dreadful things about you."

"I don't doubt it," he said bitterly, misunderstanding her. "You can't expect me to live down a —"

"Oh, I didn't mean that," she cried, flushing painfully. "You mustn't think *that* any more. Nobody thinks of that nowadays. They just can't understand why you won't have anything to do with them. The girls, I mean."

"They don't seem keen about having anything to do with me."

"You are getting a reputation as a snob. I've heard a dozen girls say you are fearfully stuck-up."

"Well, I'm not," he exclaimed wrathfully. His mind leaped backward and released a thought. "Will you skate with me now?"

"It's about time," she said pointedly, and placed her hand in his.

They skated in silence. He was too happy to utter a word. The tight pressure of her strong little hands in his; the delicious nearness of her lithe, adorable person; the cool, refreshing perfume that filled his nostrils, — he was in paradise. Rapture was his at last. After all the weeks of longing, and doubt, and misery, he was happy again,— most unexpectedly so. Something was telling him that she had been hurt by his indifference; he was amazingly well satisfied with the impression that she had mistaken his thundering stupid-

ity for indifference! There was a whole lot of glory
to be got out of that.

"You ought to ask some of the girls to skate with
you," she said finally. "They think it's awfully queer
that you don't."

"I haven't the time to go in very strong for that sort
of thing," he said, assuming a loftiness he did not feel.
"I'm in business, you see," he added, with an apologetic
grin.

"Time is very precious, I suppose," she observed,
bitingly.

"More precious than girls," he replied. "I've never
been much of a hand for girls, you know."

"Your own experience ought to prove to you that
it's never too late to mend. Unless I am greatly mistaken you were not much of a hand for business up to a
very few months ago."

"Are you proselyting on the girl question?"

"I'm trying to teach you good manners. You
mustn't follow too closely in Mr. Gilman's footsteps.
You will be a dreadful person if you don't watch out."

"Thanks for the tip. I'll do better. Are you coming out tomorrow afternoon?"

"Yes, if it's decent weather. I'm coming with
Jimmy Burton."

"Oh," he said, and was silent for a long time afterward.

"He's terribly amusing, isn't he?" she said, as she
leaned lightly against him at the turn.

"Who?" he demanded.

"Jimmy Burton."

"Terribly," he agreed. "By the way, how is the feud getting along?"

"There isn't any feud to get along," she replied sweetly. "That is, so far as Jimmy and I are concerned. We've buried the hatchet."

"Was Mrs. Compton present at the ceremony?"

"Oh, dear me, no. The burial was quite private, Mr. Redpath. Granny wouldn't go within a mile of a Burton if she could help it."

"Still keeping her in the dark, I see," he said, inwardly raging.

"She is very fond of Jimmy," replied Morna, radiantly. "Will you be here tomorrow afternoon?"

"To see you skating around with Jimmy Burton? I should say not."

She squeezed his arm delightedly. "I really believe you're jealous," she cried, but in such a gay, sparkling manner that he could find no comfort in the thrust.

"I am," he confessed promptly.

She laughed as she looked up into his face. There was something in his grey eyes that held her fascinated for a moment. Then she suddenly looked away, confounded by the discovery she had made. He saw the blithe smile fade slowly from her half-averted face, and his heart sank. Poor fool! He had betrayed himself, and — now it was all over!

"Well," he said gently, after a long interval and as if he were completing a provisional statement of his case, "you might just as well know it now as later on. Much better for me too. Don't think anything more about it. I'm only one of a multitude and I guess I can stand it as well as the rest of them. I'd just like

you to feel, however, that the very best that's in me
goes out to you. You are wonderful, Morna. I shall
always be grateful to you. I — Well, you've given
me something that I wouldn't part with for all the
world. Now, don't be the least bit unhappy on my
account. I've never had a ray of hope, you know, so
there's really nothing to feel badly about. It's all a
part of the great game we have to play, and a good
loser never squeals." He drew a long, deep breath.
The familiar, quizzical smile crept into his face and he
fell into the pleasantly satirical way of drawling his
words: " I called you Morna a moment ago. I've said
it a thousand times to myself. It's like a caress.
Hope you didn't mind."

She smiled faintly. There was a slight quaver in her
voice, as of suppressed excitement, when she responded.

" I like you to call me Morna. As you say, it does
sound like a caress." She looked up at him out of the
corner of her eye, a swift, searching little glance that
he missed, being studiously intent on the landscape
straight ahead. Then suddenly: " Come on! Let's
sprint awhile. As fast as we can go ! "

There was a vibrant note in her voice. He went very
red in the face; a queer glaze came over his eyes. She
was laughing at him! But then he had made a silly
fool of himself,— so, why shouldn't she laugh at him?
Some one ought to kick him all the way home and
back for presuming to —

" Come on," she cried impatiently. " Top speed! "

They circled the pond three times at a furious pace.
Other skaters made way for them, some cheerfully, others grudgingly. When at last she gave the signal to

slow down, she was panting and out of breath, but her eyes were starry bright and smiling.

"Wasn't it great?" she gasped, leaning on his arm as they swerved in toward the crowded centre of the pond.

"I never knew it was in a girl to skate like that," he replied, wonderingly. "You are a wonder."

"I've skated at San Moritz with some of the best skaters in the world," she said simply, unaffectedly.

"I hope I didn't tire you," he apologized. "You see I've skated only with men. I'm not used to girls. Maybe I hit it up too —"

"I wouldn't have missed it for the world," cried Morna. "I loved every second of it." Her breast was heaving, her red lips were parted in an ecstasy of fatigue, her cheeks glowed warm and rich from the whipping of the chill February wind. Her voice was low and husky, and trembled slightly.

"And you will not let what I said a little while ago make any difference in our friendship?" he said, uneasily.

She laughed outright at that, a gay, excited little gurgle that consoled him strangely. He hadn't blundered irretrievably, and that was something to be thankful for.

"You might just as well ask me to be a sister to you," she said, still laughing.

"Good Lord! Do you mean that we can't go on as we were before I made that awful break about —"

"We can never be the same, I'm afraid."

He was aghast. "I — I can't tell you how sorry I

am, Miss O'Brien. Won't you forget that I said it? Your friendship means more to me than —"

" Didn't you mean it? " she demanded, severely. To herself she was saying that she was having the time of her life!

" Of course I meant it," he stammered.

" Then what kind of a girl would you take me to be if I even pretended to forget it? "

" Well, I didn't mean to put it in just that way. I should have asked you to overlook my impertinence. That's it," he cried; " my confounded impertinence."

" Since you put it in *that* way," she said demurely, " I suppose I'll have to give you another chance."

" You will? " he cried, relieved. " That's fine of you. Bully! "

" But, I warn you, don't ever do it again unless you are prepared to take the consequences."

He swallowed hard. She looked up into his face and her heart smote her. He was quite pale.

" I'll — I'll be as mum as an oyster," he said resolutely.

She appeared to reflect. " On second thoughts," she said slowly, " I don't believe I'd better risk giving you another chance."

" Oh, don't say that," he groaned miserably.

" I should hate to be disappointed, you know. You must promise not to disappoint me,— Sherry."

" I promise, Morna," he said humbly.

" You old dear," she whispered, squeezing his arm tightly. He looked down into her shining eyes and caught his breath sharply.

"God," he muttered huskily, "it's not going to be easy."

"I'll do my best to help you," she said quaintly. "So, do cheer up."

A hand was laid heavily on Sherry's shoulder and a hearty voice from behind cried out:

"Break away, old man. See who's here. Little old me. My turn, Morna. Clear out, Sherry."

Jimmy Burton thrust himself in between them and a second later skated blithely away with Morna. Things went red before Sherry's eyes. For a moment he skated blindly in their wake, hearing their gay laughter but seeing them only as a confused, mobile mass. Then he turned and darted back toward the benches. He missed the queer look of dismay that she shot over her shoulder, and the momentary gleam of pain and contrition that filled her dark eyes.

He was saying to himself as he trudged furiously down the hill, homeward bound: "But if I *had* punched his nose for him she would never have forgiven me, so what's the use thinking about it, you darned fool. She's in love with him and that's all there is to it."

CHAPTER XXIV

THE Prohibition Party invited him to go on its ticket in the spring elections. He was asked to " run " for councilman in the Sixth Ward. At the same time the Blue Ribbon Society formally requested him to address a big meeting in Alexander's Hall on the 25th of May. The committee,— which included, besides ladies, a number of bland gentlemen who had taken the pledge never to touch intoxicating liquor (some of them were proud of the fact that they had taken the pledge more than once, and would go on doing so indefinitely if necessary to overthrow the power of Demon Rum),— suggested a topic for the address they expected him to deliver: " The First Drink and the Last."

He declined both invitations. The Prohibitionists were shocked when he laconically reminded them that it was no good running for a local office unless you were prepared to buy drinks for half the voters in the ward, and, besides that, you couldn't expect them to vote for you if you considered yourself too good to drink with 'em. Moreover, being a Republican, he couldn't even vote for himself, and that ought to be reason enough why he shouldn't run on the Prohibition ticket.

" But you are the logical candidate," they insisted. " You've stopped drinking. You've made a man of yourself. You are a credit to the ward. You are a this moment one of the most popular, deserving young men in the city. Every one is talking of your manly —"

"But all of these can't make a politician of me," he said amiably.

"You don't have to be a politician to run on the Prohibition ticket."

"You have to be a politician if you want to be elected, however."

"Oh, we don't for a minute believe there is a chance of your being elected. That isn't the point."

"Just what is the point?"

"We are blazing the way. Some day —"

"Why don't one of you gentlemen run for the office? You don't drink, and you are quite respectable. Why wish it on me?"

"To be perfectly frank with you, we've been fighting the liquor interests so long that there isn't a chance of our getting a single vote out of the saloons, and that is important, you know. Now you are fresh from association with the very people we want to reach more than —"

"Set a thief to catch a thief, is that the idea?"

"Well, that's hardly the way to put it," very benignly, deprecatingly.

Sherry set his jaws suddenly and the amused smile went out of his eyes.

"Gentlemen, the saloon interests in this town,— or in any other, for that matter,— may not hesitate to make a drunkard of a man, but I've never heard of them trying to make him ridiculous. I will say that much for the liquor dealers, and that's more than I can say for you. You would make me the laughing-stock of the town. For five years I drank like a fish and you gentlemen held me up to public view as the horrible example by which all comparisons were to be made. I've been sober for a matter of six months, and you want me to run for councilman on the Prohibition ticket. How in hell, gentlemen, do you know that I'm going to stay sober for the *next* six months? How does anybody know? Six months on the water-wagon makes me the logical candidate, does it? Six months dry and five years wet, that's my record. If you think that I take your proposition as a compliment, you are very much mistaken. I take it as a joke,— and we'll let it go at that. Permit me to recommend a candidate far better supplied than I with all of the qualifications you mention. I refer to Patsy Burke, the bartender at the Sunbeam saloon. He hasn't touched a drop in ten years, he is absolutely honest and reliable, he provides for his family, he is popular with the element that frequents the saloons, and, gentlemen, he is a resident and tax-payer in this ward. He is your ideal candidate."

The Blue Ribboners came a little later on and told him that as a " reformed drunkard " he could set the town afire with his " experiences."

" We will bill you as the one big drawing card of the convention, Mr. Redpath, and you will fill the hall to its utmost capacity. We'll guarantee that. Every one will be crazy to hear you talk about the evil days you —"

" I remember, Mr. Edmonds, the last time I ever saw you spifflicated," broke in Sherry, with his most genial, friendly smile. "You certainly had me guessing. Patsy Burke said you were alive, but, by George, I didn't think so. Remember that time? In the alley back of the Sunbeam about a year and a half ago?"

Mr. Edmonds drew himself up. There were ladies present. He got quite red in the face.

"No, I do not remember any such occasion," he said, ponderously.

"Perhaps not. I'm not surprised. You were loaded to the ears. Maybe it wasn't the last time, either. Doubtless I saw you once or twice after —"

"What do you mean, bringing up such things, sir?" roared Mr. Edmonds. "I consider it extremely bad taste to —"

"Forgive me," said Sherry, humbly. "I didn't dream you would be offended. I thought you'd rather like to talk about those good old evil days. Believe me, sir, I hadn't the faintest idea that those jags of yours were private. Excuse me if I've betrayed a secret."

"I am not proud of them," snapped the red-faced Mr. Edmonds, "and I never speak of them. We came here in good faith to ask you to speak at our convention and you have the effrontery to refer to a part of my life that is a closed book, Mr. Redpath. If you think you are making a hit with me by parading my —"

"Don't lose your temper," admonished Sherry, shaking his finger at Mr. Edmonds playfully. "I didn't lose mine when you invited me to get up in front of a crowd and tell 'em about my sessions with old Mr. Booze. I am beginning to feel, Mr. Edmonds, that you are entirely too modest. You could get your name in large type on the bills if you'd only put your modesty

aside and volunteer to tell the multitudes how it feels to
be so drunk that you don't know it. I am an amateur
compared to you, sir. I've never been so full that the
police had to slap the soles of my shoes with a night-
stick in order to get a grunt out of me, and I've never
had the pleasure of sleeping all night in an alley. I'm
not the man you want, ladies and gentlemen. I am a
piker. Mr. Edmonds here is the logical head-liner for
your — Well, good-bye, Mr. Edmonds. I don't
blame you for feeling embarrassed. Fulsome praise always embarrasses me too. But I must say, before you
get entirely out of ear-shot, that Patsy Burke would
consider it a personal favour if you'd drop in at the
Sunbeam some day and pay him the ninety dollars
you've owed the bar for drinks since nineteen-four."

These profound indications of the new esteem in which
he was held by an astonished citizenry amused rather
than gratified him. He had many a laugh over the
incidents with Mr. Gilman and Barney Doyle, and once
when he met Patsy Burke on his way home from church
with the " old lady."

But there did come a proposition which interested and
pleased him more than mere words can describe. It was
on the day of the departure of Mrs. Compton and
Morna. He had gone to the station to see them off.
The through train which carried them away deposited
on the front door-step of the city (it isn't hyperbole to
call the platform of the Union depot a front door-step),
a distinguished and august visitor, to whom at least
two " sticks " were devoted in each of the evening papers
(involving the hurried and agitated unlocking of the
forms just as they were ready to go to press), and a

solid two column interview in the *Dispatch* of the morning after.

Double-leaded type informed the people of Farragut that the Hon. James W. Hazelton was in their midst for a day or two only, on business connected with the Interurban Traction Company, and that important extensions and improvements of the system were being contemplated by the Eastern syndicate controlling the property.

The Honourable James was not a stranger in Farragut. He had spent forty years of his life in the town, his wife was a first cousin of Sherry Redpath's mother, and his two daughters were graduates of the Farragut high-school. It was no good telling people in Farragut that Jim Hazelton was not a Farragut man, and always would be, notwithstanding the fact that he had been a resident of New York City for the past twenty-five years, or that his wife hadn't been " home " since the time of the World's Fair in Chicago, or that his daughters had been happily married to and happily divorced from men whose geographical information was limited to a conviction that there wasn't much of anything west of the Atlantic seaboard except congressmen — and ranches that supplied New York with food. Jim Hazelton was a Farragut man, and his wife and daughters were Farragut girls. (You or I would say women, but we don't count.)

He was the president of the Traction Company, chairman of the board of directors of a big National bank, a director in two railroads, receiver for a third, and was on speaking terms with J. Pierpont Morgan.

On the occasion of his rare visits to Farragut, he

created a profound sensation among his old acquaint-
ances by speaking of the various Astors and Vander-
bilts by their first names, and once (evidently letting it
slip out involuntarily) he spoke of Mr. Choate as Joe.
Mr. James Hazelton was that kind of a man, so now you
know him perfectly.   He talked of millions, abused the
administration at Washington, drank malted milk,
owned a Gainsborough and a Romney, consulted a
specialist every time he had an ache, insisted that the
country was going to the devil, knew an actress or two,
read the *Saturday Evening Post*, and was, as you may
readily see, and out-and-out capitalist.

But why go on?   He is with us for such a very short
time that it seems wicked to waste space on him.   His
stay is brief.   He got into this story at two-forty-five
on the afternoon of a certain day and goes out of it
for ever at eleven-ten on the sext.   And as he has nothing whatever to do with it except to shake hands with
Sherry Redpath and ask him how his mother was, we
leave him to the daily press and pass on to the next
day but one after his memorable visit to Farragut.

But while he was in town he found the time to express his amazement over the present appearance and
condition of his distant relative, Sherry Redpath.   The
last time he was West, that young man was a sight to
behold!   He remembered that very clearly.

Now he was perplexed.   He couldn't believe his eyes.
So he forgot his own affairs for a moment and inquired
who the deuce, or what, was responsible for the miracle.
Whereupon the general manager of the lines, and the
local superintendent, and the city engineer, and the
entire committee from the Common Council took up a

good deal more of his time telling him about the remarkable regeneration of Sheridan Redpath.

The next day but one the general manager of the
system hailed Redpath from his automobile as the young
man was walking briskly down Main Street.

"I say, Redpath! Look here a moment, will you?"
The chauffeur not only stopped the car but backed up
a few yards along the curb. "Any time you want to
cut loose from old Andy Gee and tackle a job that will
get you somewhere, let me know. I've had my eye on
you for some time. You've got the right stuff in you
and it's a pity to waste it as you're doing now. You'll
shrivel and dry up as every one else does in this burg
if you stick around here too long. Right now is the
time for a young fellow like you to get in on the ground
floor with one of our systems. Just say the word, and
I'll give you a job that's bound to lead up to better
things if you put your heart in it."

"That's fine, Mr. McGuire, but I'm under contract
with Mr. Gilman for a certain period. I can't consider
anything else at present. Thanks, just the same."

"When does your contract expire?"

"I have to give him a year's notice."

"A year? Good God, man, are you crazy? That's
the most idiotic —"

"Don't forget, please, that I wasn't in the position to
decline his good offices as I am yours, Mr. McGuire,"
said Sherry quietly.

Mr. McGuire stared for a moment. Then he smiled.
"I understand. Well, I just thought I'd put a bug
in your ear. I'm interested in you, Redpath, and I
want to see you get along. You've surprised the old

fogies around here, and I don't mind saying you've surprised me. But this isn't the place for you. You want
to get out before it's too late. We're at the back of a
new line from Chicago to — well, I guess I'd better not
say where. There's a good job for you with the syndicate if you want to grab it. You would go to Chicago
for awhile and later on to New York."

" I don't believe I'd like office work. I'm too strong
for that."

" It wouldn't be office work. We'd start you in as
assistant superintendent of construction. I guess that
would keep you out in the open a bit, wouldn't it? If
you make good, the next step would be into a five
thousand dollar job. What are you getting now, if
I may ask? About fifty a month? "

" Considerably more than that, Mr. McGuire."

" More than that out of old man Gilman? Well, you
are a wonder, that's all I've got to say. Nobody ever
did that to him before, believe me. Think the matter
over, anyhow, and if you put it up to the old man in the
right way, showing him the advantages you'll have, he
may release you from the contract."

" I am sure he would. He's a very fair man. On
the other hand, that's what I profess to be. I'll discuss it with him, however. I am sure he will be interested."

" We could start you off at twenty-five hundred a
year," offered McGuire, magnificently, and, waving his
hand in a friendly fashion, drove off.

This conversation set Sherry to thinking. He had
known for many weeks that he was not engaged in a
real man's work. The amazing agreement with Mr.

Gilman, while it provided inducements for a man with no fire or ambition in his make-up, offered little or no satisfaction to one whose aspirations carried him beyond the mere thought of earning easy money.

He decided to lay this new proposition before his employer, not with the thought of actually terminating his contract with him, but to ascertain, if possible, the exact nature of his present occupation. There was a deep and secret significance behind the far from business-like arrangement that the hard-fisted, sensible, old man had made with him in order to secure his services for a term of years that might reasonably include his dying day. He made up his mind that he would ask Mr. Gilman for a plain statement of the facts. His own good sense told him that no man could give an adequate return for the amazing wages that were provided for in their agreement. He was not worthy of his hire, and never could be. It was only fair to offer to release Mr. Gilman from his bargain.

Mr. Gilman listened to him without the slightest sign of annoyance or concern. When Redpath closed his crisp résumé of the situation with the flat statement that he did not believe it was fair and honest for him to accept the pay that was promised him as the years increased, and offered to tear up the contract at any time, the old gentleman said wearily:

" I know how you must feel, my boy. It is not an elevating occupation. Your pride revolts against taking money that cannot possibly be earned. I can see how attractive this proposition from Mr. McGuire appears to you. If it were left to me to decide for you, I should unhesitatingly advise you to accept. But you are under contract to me. I cannot see my way clear to release you at present. As for the rather direct and sensible question you put to me, I can only say that your actual duties here are plain. You are taking care of them admirably. If I have a secret motive for keeping you with me, and am willing to pay you the staggering wages you speak of so dubiously, it is solely my own affair. I cannot tell you now what your unknown duties here are and I pray God that they may never be disclosed to you. You are not, I perceive, disposed to get rich quickly and easily, and I am glad to see that spirit in you. Most men would jump at the chance you have had thrust upon you. It is not fair of me to hold you to your bargain. I have become very fond of you, and proud as well. You have better stuff in you than even I suspected, and I am a pretty good judge of men. Now, suppose we leave it this way: stay on with me for a year or two. If at the end of that time you feel inclined to cancel our contract, I shall not oppose you. But, I beg of you, do not leave me now."

There was a genuine appeal in Mr. Gilman's voice. There was no mistaking the earnestness of his manner. Sherry was filled with compunction.

" That settles it, sir. I see how you feel about it. I will stick to my part of the bargain as long as you are satisfied. You have been my best friend. I hope you may never be in a position to doubt my friendship for you. I'll stick as long as you like,— whether I'm worth it to you or not."

That night he was awakened by the sound of some one moving about in his room. He knew who it was. It was not the first time he had been aroused from a sound sleep to find Andrew Gilman shuffling across the floor, feeling his way in the darkness. Once a heavy sleeper, he now slept lightly, awaking at the slightest sound. He always called out:

"Anything I can do for you, Mr. Gilman?"

And Andrew Gilman, after a moment's hesitation, invariably answered: "Nothing,— nothing at all."

He observed a subtle change in Mr. Gilman's physical appearance as the winter progressed toward spring. A new and increasing haggardness deepened in his face; his eyes appeared to have sunk farther into their sockets and to burn with a strange brightness. There were times when they seemed to penetrate to the innermost recesses of his brain, pathetic in their intensity, searching always for something that eluded him. There was an odd expression, as of fear or apprehension, in them too. His shoulders sagged and he moved slowly, as if tired and dispirited. The sharp, incisive, direct tone was missing from his speech; his voice had dropped to a dull, sometimes droning monotone.

Redpath spoke to Miss Corse about it one day. He was really distressed by these signs of breaking health.

"He's old enough to crack," said Miss Corse, unfeelingly,— and, as she thought, professionally. "Can't expect him to go on being zippy for ever, Mr. Redpath. He's way over seventy."

"But why does he have that queer look in his eyes, as if he were horribly afraid of something?"

"Umph! He's afraid of death, that's what he is. They all hate to think of dying. You see, when they get to be seventy-four or five, they begin counting the years that are left. First they say five years, then

four, then three — and so on.   They usually give themselves eighty years at the outside.   Well, every little
month counts a lot when you're getting ready to shake
hands with Death.   He's afraid he'll die before that
old woman up there, that's what's eating him.   And
she's afraid she'll die before he does.   I never knew anything like it."

"I've got a notion in my head there's something going on that we don't know anything about," said he,
frowning.

She winced.   "What do you think it is?" she asked,
after a moment.

Struck by her tone, he shot a quick look at her face.
He was startled by what he saw.   The colour had
faded from her cheeks, leaving them a sickly white;
her eyes were half-closed and her lips twitched nervously.   Almost instantly she regained control of her
shaken nerves and smiled,— a forced, unnatural smile
that somehow horrified him.   It was just the stretching
of thin, pale lips, as if in agony.   He had heard lawyers
in a murder case refer to the "sardonic grin," or *risis
sardonicus*, that appears on the lips of one who has died
of strychnine poisoning.   Like a shot his own picture of
the "sardonic grin" flashed through his brain.

"It's something that you know a good deal about,
Miss Corse," he said quickly.

"I don't know anything," she said, and cleared her
throat of a certain huskiness.   "That's what scares
me.   It's getting on my nerves.   I don't sleep nights,
puzzling my brain over it.   It's awful the way they
live, those two.   I didn't mind much at first, but lately
I'm all on edge.   They hate each other so horribly."

"Do they see anything of each other nowadays? They seemed to be patching things up a little while ago."

"He has tried to see her a couple of times lately, but she won't have it. I wish to God she'd die."

"Great Scot, Miss Corse! Don't say a thing like that."

"Well, I know it's terrible, but I can't help it. She's the whole trouble here, Mr. Redpath. I oughtn't to talk like this, being paid to take care of her and all, but it just has to come out. She wishes everybody else was dead, so why shouldn't I wish the same for her?"

"Do you mean that she wishes *you* were dead?"

"She sure does. She's said it a hundred times."

"She doesn't mean it, Miss Corse. It's only a —"

"Oh, yes, she does. She says I'm paid to spy on her and that I'm nothing more than a dog in the manger. She keeps telling me that Mr. Gilman hires me as a sort of jailer. She hates me worse than poison,— and she hates you too. I —"

"Why should she hate me? She's never even seen me."

"Yes, she has. She looks at you through the window blinds every day. She hates you because he likes you. Yes, sir," she went on, drawing a long breath through her teeth, "it would be a godsend if she'd shuffle off and be done with it."

"Why do you stay?"

She answered very deliberately. "Well, you see, I've been here so long that I'm sort of used to being miserable. I don't believe I'd be content to leave be-

fore she died. It would seem as though I'd wasted the
last ten years if I wasn't here to see her die."

" By Jove, Miss Corse, you're a queer one," he exclaimed, impressed by the singular candour of the
woman.

" Maybe I am," she said curtly, and left him.

His peace of mind was further disturbed by an
" item " in the *Dispatch* a day or two later. It was in
the " Personal and Society " column and read:

" Mr. James Burton left today for a three weeks'
sojourn in the Sunny South. He will visit Palm Beach,
Jacksonville and other resorts in Florida, returning via
Old Point Comfort and New York."

That settled it. It had all been arranged beforehand. She was expecting Jimmy Burton to join her in
Florida. He put his fond and secret hopes aside, but
refused to languish. If it was in the cards that Morna
was to lose her heart to Jimmy Burton there wasn't
anything he could do to prevent it. Obviously he had
no chance himself, and he was learning to be a philos-
opher. So he buckled down to work and tried to put
her out of his mind.

And then, two weeks later, he received a long letter
from her, written at Ormond. She began it: " Dear
Sherry," and signed herself " Your good friend,
Morna." The first two pages were devoted to a glowing account of the rare good time she was having, and
then, abruptly: " Jimmy Burton is here. We were
staying in the same hotel at first, but, would you believe
it, Granny suddenly decided to move to another. She
had found out who he really is. She said she never

dreamed that he could be one of *those* Burtons. Somehow she had gone on all the while believing him to be one of the town Burtons,— no connection of the Burtons out our way, you know. Or do you know? There is a Burton family in Farragut, one of the oldest there, so I suppose you must know of them. The funny part of it is that I let her go on believing it, and I am afraid Jimmy did the same. But the other day, she asked him point-blank if he was related to *our* Burtons, and what could he say but yes? He couldn't lie to her, could he? You'd think his honesty would have appealed to her, wouldn't you? Well, it didn't. She flew into a perfectly dreadful rage, and so did I. Of course in the end, I begged her pardon. She cried a little, and so did I. But when I went on to say that she ought to be ashamed of herself for picking on poor Jimmy for something he couldn't possibly help,— (he cannot help being a Burton, can he?) — she calmly informed me that I was not to have anything more to do with him. I was not even to speak to him. I was furious. It was too absurd. I told her so and that afternoon we moved over to this hotel. I had to telephone Jimmy and he was terribly cut up over it. He can't understand why he and I should be punished because our silly ancestors rowed with each other. Neither can I. Being a Burton doesn't make a Bill Sykes of him, does it? Granny and I had another flare-up last night. She said I had gone out to sit with him on the porch,— (I don't know how it was possible for her to see us, it was so dark),— and I didn't deny it. I will not put up with such treatment, Sherry. You would think she knew me well enough by this time to see that she cannot bully me any longer. I am quite able to think and act for myself, and I told her as much. I started to run away and leave her once before and if I ever start out to do it again, there will be no turning back. I told Jimmy that I wouldn't stand it, and he said he wouldn't either if he was in my place. The way I feel tonight it wouldn't surprise me in the least if I packed up my duds and walked off for good. But I don't want to bore you with my troubles, so I'll close before I say anything foolish."

He was profoundly distressed. All day long he thought of the impending calamity. She was likely to *do* something foolish, and it might be that she would regret it all the rest of her life. If she ran away with and married Jimmy Burton —

He rushed down town to the telegraph office and sent a night letter to her. It was the result of an hour's effort in composition.

" My earnest advice in the matter you have consulted me about is to go slow. Don't do anything without long and careful deliberation. There are a great many things to consider. There is a lot of good sense in the old saying, ' Think twice before you leap.' "

The reply came that afternoon.

" Thanks. I have thought twice. Morna."

CHAPTER XXV

ON the morning of the sixteenth of March, Mrs. Gilman was found dead in her bed. She had been murdered some time during the night, strangled to death by hands that left cruel black marks on her white neck!

A wild shriek of terror aroused Sheridan Redpath from the first sound, heavy sleep he had enjoyed in many a night. He sprang out of bed to find that it was broad daylight. Some one was running frantically down the hall, screaming inarticulate calls for help. He felt his hair rise on end as he leaped toward the door. A chill ran through his body, leaving it as cold as ice. As he threw open the door, Miss Corse, her hair down, a loose dressing-gown clutched tightly across her breast, almost fell into his arms.

"She's dead! She's dead! Oh, God save us all!" burst from her writhing lips.

"Sh! For heaven's sake, be quiet," he cried, pushing past her into the hall and closing the door. "The shock will kill him. Calm yourself —"

"She's dead as a door nail! My God, don't you understand? She's dead!"

He caught her as she slipped toward the floor. The light from a window at the end of the hall fell upon her face. It was livid with terror. He shook her with more violence than he intended.

"Brace up, can't you? What kind of a nurse are

322

you anyhow? Haven't you seen a dead person before?
Don't act like this. You've said yourself that she
might go off at any — Keep quiet, I say! We've got
to break it gently to him. He is —"

" She didn't die, she didn't die," moaned the quiver-
ing nurse, clutching at his arms.

" Then why in thunder are you making all this row
over —"

" She was murdered,— killed in her bed,— choked to
death. Oh, God, it is horrible! The bed is all torn
to —"

" Murdered!" he gasped.

"— pieces. She fought for her life. Bed clothes
scattered everywhere. Pillows on the floor. Black in
the face, and — oh, what a looking face! I —"

He dashed off down the hall. The house-maid was
standing near the head of the stairs, where she had
halted, frightened almost out of her wits.

One glance at the occupant of the bed was convincing.
There had been a violent struggle; there could be no
doubt that Mrs. Gilman came to her end in a most horrible manner.

For a full minute he stared wide-eyed and fascinated
at the gruesome figure of the woman he had never seen
before. Then he came out and closed the door behind
him.

" We've got to tell him at once," he said, hoarsely,
as he came up to the two shivering women. The house-
maid was supporting the tragic figure of the nurse.

" Who done it?" she whispered, almost dumb with
awe.

" Telephone for the doctor at once," commanded Red-

path. " And you, Miss Corse, go in and see if by any
chance she may still be alive. You never can be
sure —"

" I wouldn't go in there again for a million dollars,"
chattered the nurse. " She's dead all right. Been
dead for hours. I felt of her. I did that much."

" I guess you're right. Go and telephone, Maggie.
I'm going in to Mr. Gilman."

Andrew Gilman was standing in the middle of the
room, clad only in his night-shirt. He had just left his
bed and was unmistakably puzzled by the disturbance in
the hall outside.

" What's the matter? " he demanded irritably.
" What is all this noise about? Did I hear a scream
or was I dreaming? Speak up! Don't stand there like
a post."

" Something shocking has happened, Mr. Gilman,"
began Sherry, going quickly to his side. " Mrs. Gilman,— you'd better sit down, sir. It's really quite terrible. I — I don't know just how to —"

The old man caught his arm in a grip of iron.

" Go on! Don't be afraid to tell me. I can stand it.
Is — is she —"

" She is dead, sir."

Andrew Gilman's face went deathly white.

" In — in the night? "

" Yes, sir."

" Was she alone? Why wasn't I called? "

" Miss Corse didn't know until a few minutes ago.
I've had them telephone for the doctor. He ought to
be here in a few minutes."

" Are you sure she —   Have — have you seen her? "

"Yes, sir. Just for a second. You'd better not go in yet, Mr. Gilman. It's — it's horrible."

"Horrible? What do you mean?" He sat down on the edge of the bed suddenly. His face was ghastly.

"I can't tell you, sir,— I don't see how I can possibly tell you what has happened."

The old man was staring at him, glassy-eyed. His lips began to work spasmodically, his bony hands clutched the bedclothes and trembled so violently that the whole bed shook.

"Don't — for God's sake don't tell me — she has killed herself!" he groaned.

"Not that, sir. It couldn't have been that. She couldn't have done it. Some one else — Oh, the most horrible thing has —"

Mr. Gilman's chin sank to his breast. He uttered a hoarse, gasping cry, and his body stiffened. Sherry threw himself down beside him and put a strong arm around his shoulders.

"I'm sorry, sir, if I've broken it to you too —"

"Go away," muttered the old man hoarsely. "I'll — I'll dress at once. Wait for me in the hall."

"Better let me assist you —"

"Put on your own clothes," said Andrew Gilman, lifting his head. "Leave the door open. You can tell me everything you know while we're dressing."

"We've got to get busy at once, Mr. Gilman. Don't you understand? A dreadful crime has been committed. This is no time to think of —"

"You think she was murdered? Why do you think that? Why, I ask?" cried the old man, struggling to his feet. He was panting thickly.

" There is every indication of a struggle. She was strangled to death. The marks —"

" Strangled? " fell from the lips of Andrew Gilman. He sat down again heavily. " Choked to death? My God, boy, do you know what you are saying? "

" There has been a murder, Mr. Gilman," interrupted the younger man firmly. " Some one in this house may have done it. Pull yourself together, sir. Leave everything to me. I'll send for the police at once. There isn't a moment to waste."

" The police? Oh! not the police! "

" Why not? There's got to be a search, an investigation while the trail is warm. Good Lord, sir, can't you see the position the rest of us are in here? Suspicion may fall upon any one of us —"

" No, no! " cried the other. " That must be headed off at once. No one here shall be suspected. You are right. Go at once and telephone."

The doctor arrived a few minutes later, coming in haste from his home down the street, and soon afterwards three or four police officers.

There could be no question as to the cause of Mrs. Gilman's death. The doctor announced at once that she had been throttled by a powerful pair of hands, and that she had been dead for four or five hours.

Andrew Gilman waited in the hall while the examination was going on. He refused to enter the room. Dr. Andrews seemed to understand. He knew more of the unhappy history of the two Gilmans than any one else.

The police, after inspecting the room, began to question the occupants of the house. Inquiry drew from

Miss Corse the facts which follow. She had put Mrs. Gilman to bed at ten o'clock, after which she opened all of the windows as usual. The old lady was half asleep when she left her and retired to her own room across the hall, where she was soon sleeping soundly. It was after seven o'clock when she awoke and tapped on her patient's door. She always went, the first thing in the morning, to see if Mrs. Gilman was in urgent need of anything. Failing to receive the usual response, she opened the door and went in, expecting to find her asleep. She described the scene that met her gaze. Not suspecting that Mrs. Gilman had come to her death by foul means, she rushed over to the bed and began to work with the stiff, cold body, hoping that life was not extinct. . . . She ran out of the room, hardly knowing what she did, and screamed for help. Mr. Redpath came into the hall in his pajamas.

" Were the windows open when you went in there this morning? " inquired the " plain-clothes man," who, up to a year or so before had been patrolman No. 17, but was now a detective.

" I didn't look. I guess they were," said Miss Corse, twisting her fingers nervously. " That's all I know about it, so help me God. You don't think I know anything more about it, do you? I swear to God I —"

" Nobody's accusin' you," said the detective, eyeing her steadily. " Was Mrs. Gilman feelin' all right when you put her to bed last night? "

" What's that got to do with it, Ed? " demanded the chief of police roughly. " It don't make any difference how she was feeling. See here, Miss, did you hear any sounds during the night? Anybody in the hall? "

"No, sir. I never woke up. I'm a light sleeper too."

"Do you know whether Mrs. Gilman kept any valuables in her room?"

"She kept her jewels in the bureau drawer, that's all I know."

"This bunch of rings and bracelets and dewdads I've got here in my hand?"

"Yes, sir. I think that's all of them."

"Any money?"

"I don't think so. I never saw any, except occasionally five or ten dollars when I had a check cashed for her."

They got no more than this out of Redpath, and nothing at all from the distracted servants. Mr. Gilman was so crushed that they forbore questioning him.

The densest mystery surrounded the murder. The strangler, whoever he may have been, was not actuated by thoughts of robbery, for nothing had been taken from the house. A search for footprints on the ground outside the windows, an easy drop of ten feet, was without result. One of the windows opening onto the side porch was unfastened, but if it had been used as a means of entrance to the house the invader was careful to close it on his departure. The house-maid was prepared to swear that it had been fastened. Mr. Gilman, she said, was very particular about having the porch windows locked; he had been especially strict about it during the past few months, frequently testing them himself.

The coroner, as usual, was late in arriving. Nothing could be done until he had " viewed the body." He got there at ten o'clock. Being of an opposition political

party, he did all that he could to retard the activities
of the police department. Everything stood still until
he was (as he put it himself) "good and ready." He
set the inquest for the next day and summoned the witnesses on the spot. Then he went down town and told
every one he knew that the police force of Farragut was
the rottenest, stupidest gang of blockheads the Lord
ever let live. (This is no place to repeat what the
police force was saying about him.)

Mr. Gilman established himself in the library, and
there he remained all day, seeing no one except Redpath and his lawyer. He seldom left the chair in which
he had dropped, wearily, after listening to the profoundly sympathetic remarks of the coroner and the
statement of the chief of police that he would " get the
perpetrator of this dastardly crime if he had to rake
the United States from one end to the other."

The shades and curtains in the library were drawn.
He complained of the cold, unfeeling light that poured
in through them when he first came downstairs. A
sombre dusk pervaded the room, which was as still as
death itself. Only Andrew Gilman spoke in ordinary
tones; every one else in hushed half-whispers.

Men came and went all day long: the undertaker and
his assistant, the pastor, the reporters, the detectives.
Scores of curious people stood on the sidewalks below
the lawn and stared by the hour. Some of them boldly
encroached upon the lawn itself, and a few got as far as
the porch. Officer Barney Doyle, routed out of bed
at noon, stood guard over the lawn and had no easy
time of it keeping it clear of trespassers.

It was not until the gloomy day was far advanced

that Redpath's thoughts reverted suddenly to the conversation he had had with Miss Corse a few days earlier in the week. For a moment he felt that his heart was standing still; his blood seemed to turn to ice. Miss Corse! Could it be that she — But it was too monstrous! Nevertheless he experienced strange, ugly sensations, when, on several occasions thereafter, he found her gaze bent upon him with curious intensity. He became convinced at last that she had a very definite purpose in following him about the house,— never closely but always somewhere within earshot.

He confessed to an actual shiver when she finally beckoned to him to follow her into the kitchen, at the moment unoccupied.

" Say, Mr. Redpath, you mustn't pay any attention to what I said to you a day or so ago," she began, in a low, agitated voice. "About her, I mean. If the police ever heard what I said about wishing she was dead they'd — well, they'd suspect me sure, and, so help me God, I am as innocent as an unborn child. I was terribly foolish to say the things I did. As a matter of fact, I loved Mrs. Gilman. I didn't have a thing against her. So just forget that I —"

" My dear Miss Corse," he broke in, " I don't mind confessing to you that I have just recalled your remarks, and I've been thinking it would be foolish for you to repeat them. I don't believe you had anything to do with this ugly business, of course, but my advice to you is to keep your mouth closed from now on."

" And you won't blab on me? " she cried eagerly.

" Certainly not. But let me go a little farther with my advice. If you know of a single thing that may

have any bearing on the case, tell the authorities, no
matter who it may hit the hardest. The chances are a
hundred to one you will be put through the third degree
before they're done with you. They may even go so
far as to try to fasten the guilt upon you."

"The third degree?" she murmured. "I've heard
of that. It must be frightful." She began twisting
her fingers again. "They can't accuse me," she went
on, holding her voice down with an effort. "I don't
know any more about it than —" She broke off
abruptly and clutched his arm in a frenzy of desperation. "See here, Mr. Redpath, I want you to tell
me just what to do. I am not supposed to breathe a
word of this, but I'm not going to keep mum if they
begin to pump me too hard. I'm not going to have
them suspect me, and I don't care a hang who is hurt
by what I can tell. Will you be absolutely square with
me and tell me what to do?"

"If there is anything to tell, Miss Corse, you'd better
go straight to the police with it," he said, a thrill in his
veins. "You see, I am more or less in the same boat
with you. Why shouldn't they suspect me as well
as —"

"They won't suspect any of us if I tell all I know,"
she said doggedly. "Listen: there were great goings-
on in this house last November, things that not a soul
knows about except me and Mr. Gilman. She knew, but
she's out of it now. You were the worst fooled person
on the place. Lord, how he *did* pull the wool over your
eyes."

"What are you talking about?"

"That jail-break,— you remember that, all right, all

right. Well, all the time you and the police were
scouring the country for those fellows, one of them was
hiding right here in this house. Not only that, but he
was hiding in her room, and all three of us knew it."

"Good Lord! The — the big one?"

"Yes. Talk about nerve! He came straight to this
house and — Say, and why shouldn't he? Do you
know who he is? He's their son!"

The whole story came out, hurriedly, jerkily, cautiously. Sherry listened like one in a daze. As she
went on, he began to piece things together and, when
she had finished, the whole situation, from beginning to
end, was as clear as day to him. First of all, Mrs.
Compton's interest in the man was explained, and lastly
Mr. Gilman's extraordinary agreement with him. Now
he knew who it was that Andrew Gilman feared and
against whose malevolence he was preparing when he
engaged a " body-guard." And he had failed to perform the one important duty! The blow had fallen
while he slept!

"And she made a will leaving everything she had to
this son of hers," Miss Corse was saying. "Mr. Gilman tried to stop her, but she laughed in his face. That
was just a little while after I came here. They didn't
speak to each other again until last fall. When this
crook was here in the house, she showed him the will,
just to prove her undying love for him. She always
kept it in her room, locked up. Now, I'll tell you what
I think, Mr. Redpath. That fellow was just mean
enough to sneak back here and kill his own mother.
They'll never be able to prove it on him though. He
is too slick for that. All day long I've been thinking

it out. If he did come back, you can bet your life he
has covered up his tracks so well that they'll never
prove he was here. He went to California last fall. If
he didn't do it, he hired some one else, and will pay him
after he gets the money. It amounts to more than a
hundred thousand."

"But he cannot claim the estate without giving himself up. He is a fugitive from justice."

"I never thought of that," she muttered.

"On the other hand, no one knows that George Smith,
the jail-bird, and William Gilman are one and the same.
Unless his father is willing to admit that his son is
alive, when supposed to be dead, and that he aided him
in escaping, he is quite safe so long as he remains far
away from Farragut. The settlement of the estate can
be accomplished through lawyers. He will not even
have to appear. Even though his father may suspect
him, he is probably clever enough to have prepared an
alibi. By Jove, it may be the solution!"

"I'll bet my head that Mr. Gilman gets a letter from
Los Angeles inside of the next ten days," said she, significantly. "The news of this murder will go all over
the country. You see if I'm not right. And Mr. Gilman won't be able to do a thing. He'll have to sit
still and see this scoundrel get away with it."

Redpath was silent for a long time, thinking hard.
Miss Corse watched him anxiously.

"See here, Miss Corse," he said finally, "it's up to
you to go to Mr. Gilman and talk this matter over with
him. Don't breathe a word of this to the police at present. If the son committed this murder, it will be a
simple matter to land him. He will put in a claim for

the estate under his own name, and a word from you will
reveal his dual identity to the authorities."

"I can't talk to Mr. Gilman about it," she said,
nervously.

"Why not? You are in on the secret. It's only
fair that you should give him a chance. He may decide
to tell everything to the police."

"He'll never do that. I'll be leaving here I suppose.
My job is finished. I can't get away quick enough."
Her voice sank to a low, husky whisper and her eyes
were filled with terror. "That fellow knows that I can
do him a lot of dirt. He'll try to put me out of the
way. I'll be the next to go. I know too much. He'll
get me sure as —"

"Nonsense! He'll not bother about you. You're
as culpable as the rest of them. All he'll have to do
to you is to threaten to include you in the conspiracy,—
and that would mean disgrace, if not jail. He is willing
to gamble on your silence. The thing for you to do is
to go to Mr. Gilman at once and state your position.
You have nothing to fear from the law, and you have
nothing to fear from him. I want to see that scoundrel
sent to the gallows."

"You promised you wouldn't betray me," she whined,
"so you can't repeat what I've told you and be honourable."

"I shall not breathe a word without your consent.
But here is the situation so far as you and I and the
servants are concerned: detectives from Chicago will be
put on this case and they will suspect every one of us.
They will work on the theory that the crime was committed by some one in this house."

"I've always liked Mr. Gilman. He is a fine man and he's had enough misery. I don't want to hurt him now. I'd rather keep still and take the consequences, than to turn against him," she said, with a strange dignity that he did not believe she possessed. "He trusts me."

"'Gad, what a position he is in," said Sherry, feelingly. "A word from him would send his own son to the gallows. It's horrible."

"He doesn't love his son, and he didn't love his wife. I'll bet my head he's glad she's dead. Maybe he gets some satisfaction thinking how she must have felt last night if she recognized her precious darling as the fellow who was choking her to death. Maybe —"

"Oh, for God's sake, Miss Corse!" he cried, revolted.

"You say they'll have Chicago detectives on the case?" she inquired suddenly.

"Probably."

"Who'll hire them? Not Mr. Gilman, you can bet," she said, eyeing him sharply.

"Mrs. Gilman's relatives,— there are nephews, I believe,— and a sister, you know. She isn't going to let this thing —"

"Old Mrs. Compton? They hated each other like poison."

The cook came into the kitchen at that juncture. She started violently on beholding the two in close communion, and in that instant suspicion began to shape itself in her bewildered brain.

Much to Sherry's surprise, Mr. Gilman instructed him to telegraph to Mrs. Compton. Not only that, but he sat at the table with the young man and assisted in shaping the message to his sister-in-law. It was so worded that the shock would be lessened when she read the full details of the crime in the news-dispatches.

The old man's face was like marble. Every vestige of colour had left it, and it seemed incredibly old and worn out. There were other messages to go by wire. Redpath took them to the telegraph office at three o'clock. He found himself wondering, as he walked down town, what Sherlock Holmes would have said to this freedom of action on the part of one of the inmates of the house of murder!

Late that evening a reply came from Mrs. Compton: " I am leaving tonight for Farragut, arriving day after tomorrow. Morna is not with me."

CHAPTER XXVI

ANOTHER telegram came up with the one from Mrs. Compton. Andrew Gilman opened both of the envelopes and read their contents. He passed one of them to Redpath, and, calmly arising from his chair, crossed over and threw the other into the fire that blazed in the grate. For a long time he stood with his back to the room, clutching the mantelpiece with one bony hand, his head bent, his body as rigid as steel.

Sherry was staring bleakly at the message from Florida. " Morna is not with me." Five words that told a vast and complete story to him!

It was impossible to sleep that night. The horror in the room at the end of the hall, the awful stillness of the house, the knowledge that a police officer sat in the library downstairs, and, as may be suspected, the dismal certainty that Morna had quarrelled irrevocably with her grandmother and was even now fleeing happily with a triumphant lover,— all these conspired to baffle the slumber that might have assuaged the united pangs of dread and despair.

Mr. Gilman was sleeping soundly, heavily, for the first time in many weeks. His deep, stertorous breathing could be heard in the next room.

It must have been long past midnight when he heard the creaking of the bed in Mr. Gilman's room, and a moment later sounds which indicated that the sleeper had waked and was moving about. He watched the crack in the partly opened door between their rooms for the light that must soon come streaming through. Instead of that, however, the door was opened slowly, cautiously, and, by the dim light from the star-lit window, he saw the shadowy form of his employer.

Only for a second or two did he remain motionless in the doorway, apparently listening. Satisfied that Redpath was asleep, he advanced, stealing softly past the bed and making his way toward the door of Mrs. Gilman's sitting-room. Sherry did not move. He lay perfectly still, watching the dim figure with fascinated eyes. As the old man disappeared into the room beyond, after turning the knob with extreme stealthiness, Sherry slipped out of bed and followed with equal caution.

He knew, even though Mr. Gilman may have been ignorant of the fact, that the door to Mrs. Gilman's bed-room was sealed by order of the coroner.

It was quite clear to him that Mr. Gilman was actually on his way to the room from which he had been persistently barred for so many years, urged, no doubt, by the resurrection of a long-dead love for the woman who lay there dead after the bitter storms of half a life-time. He was going to her now to make peace with her, to kneel at her side, and to kiss the still, cold brow.

But if such was his object he was going about it in a most extraordinary manner. The light from an arc lamp in the street below revealed his white figure, bent low at the intervening door, his ear to the keyhole! From his position Sherry heard, rather than saw, his hand turning the knob. Then, after a moment,

the bent figure straightened slightly; it was evident
that he was straining to open the bolted door.

A sudden impulse, created by pity for the unhappy
old man, moved Redpath to switch on the electricity,
flooding the room with light.   He expected Mr. Gilman
to whirl upon him in consternation.   To his utter
astonishment, the old man did not change his position.
He continued to strain at the locked door, to all intent
utterly oblivious to the light or the presence of a witness.   For a moment the watcher stared in wonder.
Then the truth burst upon him suddenly.   Mr. Gilman
was asleep!

He felt his flesh creep.   Dazed for an instant by his
discovery, he started to withdraw, overcome by a feeling
of awe.   The spectacle of that unconscious old man
pulling vainly at the immovable door was one that he
would never forget.

He was back in his own room, his eyes still glued upon
the pitiful object, before the great question flashed into
his brain.   Was this the first time that Andrew Gilman
had passed through his room while asleep?   For a
moment it seemed to him that he was in utter darkness;
everything went black before his eyes.   A monstrous
fear possessed him. . . . He crossed the room swiftly
and laid a heavy hand upon the old man's shoulder.

"Mr. Gilman!" he shouted.   The old man had
abandoned his efforts to open the door and was in the
act of crawling through the window to the roof of the
veranda.

A quavering cry rose in Gilman's throat.   His body
stiffened convulsively and a second later he began beating the air with his clenched hands.

"Help! Help! Keep off of —"

"It's all right — it's Sherry Redpath," cried the young man. "Steady, sir,— steady!"

Mr. Gilman clutched him frantically, gasping with fear; his bony fingers sank into the young man's arms with the power of a vise. His eyes were tightly closed, as if he dreaded to look upon his assailant; for an instant, however, they had been wide-open and charged with utter bewilderment.

"What is it? Where am I? What are you trying to do with me?" he whimpered, querulously, his voice high and thin.

"Don't be afraid, sir. Come back to bed. You —"

"Why am I here in this — Oh, my God!" He crumpled up suddenly and would have fallen to the floor but for Redpath's strong arms. Moaning and mumbling meaningless words, he suffered himself to be half-carried, half-dragged from the room. It was with difficulty that Sherry got him into bed, and there he lay speechless for many minutes, his eyes closed, his lips working spasmodically, his fingers bent like great, gaunt claws.

The young man turned on the lights and stood beside the bed, helpless and bewildered, watching the heaving breast and surging throat of the old man. He did not know what to do. The horrid truth was fastening itself upon him, and he was appalled. A great pity began to take possession of him; his throat was tight; there was a sob of anguish in it that he could not release.

Finally Andrew Gilman turned his haggard face toward him, and, bleak-eyed with consciousness, raised

himself upon his elbow. His voice was low and hoarse
and something seemed to rattle in his throat as he
spoke. His mind was clear; he had succeeded after a
mighty effort in regaining command of himself.

"Tell me everything," he said.

"You were walking in your sleep, sir. I was awake
when you passed through my room, and I got up to
follow you. You — you were trying to enter the room
where — where Mrs. Gilman is."

Mr. Gilman's eyes began to burn with a strange intensity. "You were awake, eh? How does it happen
that you were awake tonight and not last night?"

Sherry felt the cold chill creeping over him again.
Sweat stood on his brow.

"Do you mean, Mr. Gilman, that if I had been awake
last night that —" He did not complete the sentence,
but hung expectantly upon the words that were to fall
from the old man's lips.

"Sit down," said Andrew Gilman wearily.
"Through no actual fault of yours the thing has happened that I have dreaded for years. Tell me first,
have you ever known me to walk in my sleep before?"

"I do not know, sir. If you were asleep I did not
know it. I cannot tell you, however, the number of
times I have been awakened by your presence in my
room. When I spoke to you, you always answered,
and then went back to your own room. You must have
been awake. Don't you recall those —"

"I have no recollection of ever having been in your
room. If what you say is true, I was sound asleep on
all of those occasions. God help me! God help me!"
He covered his face with his hands and fell back upon

the pillow. Instantly he withdrew them and, holding
them off at some distance, surveyed them with infinite
loathing. After a moment, he turned fiercely upon the
young man. "Damn you, damn you! You fail me
when I —" Gasping for breath, he clutched at his
own throat and glared in speechless hatred at his companion. Again the claw-like hands were pressed to his
eyes; his body stiffened in the renewed struggle for self-
control. Redpath was silent, overwhelmed by the recoil
of his emotions. At length the tense figure relaxed and,
with sorrowful, appealing eyes, Andrew Gilman sought
to meet the other's gaze.

"Sheridan," he began weakly, "I ask you to forgive
me. You have done your best. I can ask no more. It
so happens that on one night God let you sleep more
soundly than the rest. It is fate,— fate. I thought
you would be my safe-guard. I —" He broke off,
shudderingly. "You found me tonight. Why could
not God have let you stop me last night?"

"Good heaven, sir," groaned Sherry, "you do not
know what you are saying. You are assuming that —"

"Ah, but I do know what I am saying. Assuming,
you say? You are right. I am assuming something
of which I am absolutely ignorant and yet I speak of
a moral certainty. The thing I prepared so fully
against has come to pass. Now you know what your
true position here has been through all these months.
You know why I hired you, why I made it worth your
while to stay on, year after year,— each year more
productive than the year before, the final years bringing
recompense out of all proportion. You were to keep
me from becoming the unconscious slayer of one whom

God permitted me to hate with such venom that I lived in constant dread of myself. You —"

" Stop, sir! You are saying things to me that you may have cause to regret."

" What matters now? " He sighed. " It is all over. The thing is done. I needed but this night's experience to convince me that my worst fears are realized. I do not know what happened last night. I shall never know. No one can ever know. It will remain for ever an unrecited story, horrible in its every detail."

Sherry sat down on the edge of the bed. He was trembling in every fibre of his body; his teeth chattered.

" For God's sake, Mr. Gilman, don't say anything more. It is too horrible."

" There is nothing more to say," droned the old man. " Nothing. If I were to be dragged into the presence of my Maker and called upon to tell what happened last night I would be dumb, and yet I can draw a ghastly picture of that black, unholy deed. There was utter darkness in that room, and yet I saw as if it were broad daylight. I saw her there and yet my eyes were sightless. I — But do not shrink away from me, boy! I am not a murderer in God's eyes,— nor in man's. Only in mine own eyes am I a destroyer. You slept. So did I, but oh, how vastly our slumbers differed. You dreamed of pleasant things and in sweet repose. I also dreamed, but stalked through the darkness with murder in my heart, a restless soul that had no peace. There is nothing more to say. They say she was throttled by a pair of strong hands. That is true. Strong hands did it, but not one of God's living creatures saw those hands at work. Draw closer, boy. No one but you must hear what I am about to relate. No! I must and will speak. You shall be my judge."

Redpath closed the door to his own room and resumed his seat on the edge of the bed.

"I saw you and Miss Corse go into the kitchen this afternoon. She is in a very peculiar and unpleasant position. I do not ask you to betray what she said to you in confidence. At the time I was convinced, however, that she told you the story of all that happened last November. You have had it all from her, I daresay. I have no apology to make. I did what any man would have done. Miss Corse will connect that incident with the occurrence of last night. In her mind she will doubtless argue that my son is responsible for — for all this. I had a telegram from him this afternoon. The message you sent to Wallace Grant in Los Angeles, was for him. He is conducting a gambling place out there. You saw me throw his message into the fireplace. He merely said,— I could not forget the words if I lived to be a thousand,—'I can only say I hope they hang the murderer!' That was all. He guessed the truth. He was prepared for it by the admissions of his mother. She has always said that I would kill her in my own good time. She expressed this fear to William. He believes, however, that I committed the act deliberately and with premeditation. He would never believe that I did it while asleep.

"My sleep-walking habits were known to Mrs. Gilman. I have always been a somnambulist. In my waking hours I had no thought of taking her life, but in my sleeping hours I have had a hundred dreams in which that act took place. A hundred times have I paused outside her door in the morning waiting for sounds from within to convince me that it was a dream and nothing more. I need not describe my dreams. They were singularly alike, and always with the same ending. I was always stealing upon her while she slept, and —" His gaze dropped slowly to his hands, and a mighty shudder ran through his frame.

"I began to live in a state of mortal terror. The night would come when it would not be a dream. You will ask why the doors were not locked. She had the locks removed a year ago. It was perversity on her part. Whatever I did was wrong in her eyes. If I had insisted on keeping the doors unlocked she would have had them barred and bolted.

"Obsessed by the dread that followed me to bed every night, I soon fell into a condition of health that alarmed me. Can you not understand what it would mean to be afraid to go to sleep? And the havoc of a hundred sleepless nights? I was wearing myself out, fighting against the thing I feared. Twice in the month before you came to this house, I tested myself. On one occasion I shifted that heavy bureau in front of my door. The next morning I found that it had been pushed aside! Can you appreciate what that meant to me? For two weeks I moved that bureau over to block the door, and for two weeks it remained as I had placed it. I began to take hope. Then one morning it was shoved aside again. My second experiment came the following night. I tied both of my feet to the rods in the footboard of this bed, using stout strips cut from a

soft woolen blanket. I made the loops and knots as
secure as I knew how, and went to sleep, sure that if I
struggled against these bonds I would awaken myself.
The next morning I found that I had untied those hard
knots and freed myself! I had done these things in
my sleep. The proof was before me. I could no longer
doubt. It was then that I thought of putting a living
barrier between me and those rooms beyond. That is
how and why you came to this house. You served my
purpose well for months. I have no recollection of
being in your room, and yet you say I was there a number of times. I never dared to ask you if you had
found me walking in my sleep. I was afraid of your
answer.

"No man will ever know whether I took the life of
that unhappy, helpless creature who lies in there now.
I do not know it myself. I believe that I did. You
believe that I did, and the world would agree with both
of us if we asked for an opinion. You see I am quite
calm now. That is because I am convinced in my own
mind that all doubt has been removed. I am not guilty
of murder. God knows that in my waking hours I
would not have harmed a hair of her head for all the
wealth of the world, even though I had come to despise
her as no one was ever despised before. She is dead and
cannot defend herself, but I am forced to declare to you
that there was a time when my life was not safe. That
was ten years ago. I shall utter no more than the one
word 'poison' and leave the rest to your intelligence.

"You have heard me to the end. I rest my case with
you. If you deem it best to tell the police all that you
have discovered and all that I have confessed, I shall

abide by your decision. I shall deny nothing. Indeed, I shall repeat all that I have said to you."

He sank back exhausted. For many minutes Redpath, torn and harassed by his emotions, sat staring at the floor. What was he to do?

Mr. Gilman spoke again. " They will never believe that I was asleep when I did it," he said, pulling the bedclothes close about his thin neck.

" You mean that they will hold that you were awake and conscious of your act? "

" They will assume it. I am a well-hated man in this community. People have said that I kept her locked up here, a prisoner. A man who would do that, would not have much to stand on if it came to a —"

" My testimony would offset all such prejudice as that, sir. I can swear that you were asleep tonight —"

" But you cannot swear that I was asleep last night."

" Circumstantial evidence would certainly have its effect —"

" Am I to understand, then, it is in your mind to go to the authorities with this story, Sheridan? " His voice was thick and he spoke haltingly, with a perceptible effort.

" I shall not tell the authorities a word of this, sir, unless the time comes when some one else is unjustly accused."

" I would have you tell them in that event," said the other. " Miss Corse may accuse my son. The police may even try to fasten the crime upon Miss Corse. In either case, I give you full permission to speak. Your real work here is ended. I release you from your con-

tract. I would be very happy to have you stay on with
me for awhile longer. Some one will have to look after
my affairs. I shall not be able —"

"You will be all right in a day or two, sir," said
Sherry lamely. "I will stay as long as you need me,
however. Try to go to sleep now."

"Will you sit here in the room with me?" pleaded
Andrew Gilman. "Wrap some blankets about you and
sit in that big chair. I — I don't want to be left alone
tonight." His voice sounded tired and far-away, but
little more than a whisper.

Redpath got the blankets off of his own bed and prepared to make himself as comfortable as possible.

"Shall I turn off the lights?" he asked gently.

"No," replied Mr. Gilman, after a long wait.

Before settling down in the Morris chair, the young
man leaned over the bed and tucked the covers in about
the old man. Andrew Gilman did not speak. He kept
his eyes fixed on Redpath's face, and they were begging,
frightened eyes that the young man found hard to encounter. There was colour in his cheeks too,— a dark
and growing red that encouraged the observer in the
belief that he was warm and comfortable and would soon
fall into a restful sleep, confident that all was well with
him for the night at least, let the morrow bring what
it would.

It was a never-to-be-forgotten night in the life of
Sheridan Redpath. For hours he sat huddled in the
chair, watching the gaunt, still face on the pillow. The
old man slept. His breathing became harsh and loud,
his restless movements ceased.

Daylight came, slowly, pallidly,— sneaking out of

the darkness as if it too were afraid to venture incau-
tiously. The watcher, confessing to relief from an
unholy fear such as he had never known before, wel-
comed the grey dawn that streaked in through the window shutters.

He arose stiffly and turned off the electric light. The
room was still so dark that he caught his breath sharply,
and was on the point of pushing the button again when
his pride intervened. What was there to be afraid of
now? Why should he fear this limp, frail old man?
And yet he felt his flesh crawl as he turned his back for
a moment to throw open the window-shutters. He tried
to laugh at his fears, and the fears that had kept the
vigil with him since one o'clock. Now he knew what
it was that he had dreaded through all those intermin-
able hours. Not the man himself, but the possibility
of his rising from the bed to prowl forth on another of
his sinister nocturnal missions.

Commanding his shaken nerves, he deliberately drew
his chair over to the window and sat down with his
back to the bed to watch the breaking day.

Sitting there, hunched up and bleak with misery, he
went back over the months and summed up his experiences; out of his calculations came the final responsibil-
ities that now confronted him. There was not the
slightest question in his mind as to the course he should
pursue. For the present at least he would shield this
broken, wretched old man who had depended on him for
so much, and who, despite their singular agreement, had
more than a passing interest in him. He believed that
Andrew Gilman, cold and hard and unfriendly as his
nature may have been, had developed a sincere and last-

ing affection for him. He would not deliver Andrew Gilman up to the Philistines.

Sparrows were chirping noisily in the trees, and the gongs of early-hour trolley cars were clanging in the distant, invisible streets when he turned from the window and trod softly across the thick carpet toward his own room. It was six o'clock. He would dress and — but he stopped short as he came to the foot of the bed, struck by the extraordinary change in the sleeper's face. It was horribly contorted; the mouth was open, one corner being drawn down so that the teeth and gums were exposed. The eyes were open and followed him as he moved slowly toward the head of the bed.

A moment later he was running down the hall toward Miss Corse's door. She came back with him.

"Lord, if I haven't had enough for *one* day," she grumbled in the hall. One glance, a single grip on the limp wrist, and she looked helplessly up into Redpath's face.

"Stroke," she whispered.

CHAPTER XXVII

REDPATH met Mrs. Compton at the railway station. His eager eyes searched in vain for another figure among the few travellers who descended from the through train at Farragut. Mrs. Compton was quite alone.

As briefly as possible he described the distressing events of the past forty-eight hours. The coroner's inquest had been held that morning, and the verdict, after the examination of the inmates of the house, was that Mrs. Gilman had come to her death at the hands of " a person unknown to this jury." He was taking her to Andrew Gilman's house, where services were to be held at four o'clock.

A nephew of Mrs. Gilman had consented to enter the house after a lapse of thirty years,— first making sure that Andrew Gilman was flat on his back and helpless,— and had assumed charge of the arrangements. He was a pompous, middle-aged person who insisted on everything being done " nicely." As he recalled his poor, departed aunt (through the haze of years), he was sure that it would be like her to want everything done as nicely as possible. Indeed, he was positive she would want a nice, quiet funeral ; no fuss and feathers about it.

Insisting that the services and interment, which were to be strictly private, should be nice and quiet, he commanded the police to disperse the morbid crowd that had been hanging about the premises since early morn, and the police in carrying out his wishes explained to the voters that Eliphalet Blair was responsible for the orders, with the result that a perfectly inoffensive and hitherto highly-esteemed citizen of Farragut took the place of Andrew Gilman as the meanest man in town.

All the way up from the station in the limousine Mrs. Compton eyed her young companion closely, speculatively. As they turned into the street below the Gilman gates, she laid her hand on his arm and said:

" And the doctor is convinced that Andrew Gilman will never speak again? "

" He is hopelessly paralysed, Mrs. Compton."

" Then I am afraid the mystery will never be cleared up," she said slowly. He started. Had she divined the truth? Her next remark was even more cryptic. " The walls have ears, but, like dead men, they tell no tales."

Andrew Gilman lay inert and helpless in his room upstairs. There was intelligence in his dreary, hopeless eyes,— and that was all that was left of the vital Andy Gee. His last word had been spoken to Sherry Redpath. He would never utter another.

.   .   .   .

There were " third degree " proceedings, conducted by the local police and the prosecuting attorney. Contrary to Redpath's expectations, Mrs. Compton did not engage private detectives to unravel the mystery. She went upstairs to see Andrew Gilman after the services, and for a few minutes was alone with him. She looked into his eyes and spoke to him, and he understood, for he lowered his lids and tears stole out between them. And when the chief of police asked her a day or two later if she could authorize the offer of a substantial reward for the arrest of her sister's slayer, she flatly refused to have anything to do with the case.

Miss Corse had a hard time of it at the hands of the examiners. They had her " on the mat " for hours ; she came out of the ordeal triumphant but with her nerves so shattered that she took to her bed for several days.

" I never told them a word about that man being here in the house last November," she said to Redpath, eager for his approval. " Not a word. I took your advice and kept my trap closed about that business. I can see where it would lead to, and God knows I've had hell enough here without adding anything more to it by mixing myself up in — Why, they might clap me in the cooler, just as you say, as an accomplice. Besides, I've got a heart. I couldn't stand it if they got to brow-beating and questioning that helpless old man up there. I wouldn't bring anything like that on him, not for the world. Now, I want you to swear on your soul never to repeat what I told you. We've got to stand together on this. I can see that you don't believe William Gilman had anything to do with this killing, so let's drop it. I'm beginning to think he didn't myself. Have I your promise? "

" You have, Miss Corse,— my sacred word of honour."

" All right. They can't get it out of me now, no matter what happens."

It should go without saying that the authorities were completely baffled. At first there was talk among them of demanding a true bill against Miss Corse, but that plan was abandoned when it became clear to them that they could not produce the slightest bit of evidence against her.

Finally an advanced criminologist appeared on the scene, coming from Chicago of his own volition and at his own expense (being an amateur of means), and upset all of the calculations by calmly asserting that Mrs. Gilman had not been murdered at all! She had committed suicide! He went on to prove that she had strangled herself in a fit of insanity,— and the police, failing to see how any one else could have done it, came to the conclusion that he was right. This, of course, was after weeks of fruitless investigation, covering the detention and examination of every loafer and crook in Farragut.

Meanwhile, Andrew Gilman's lawyer had gone into court and had himself appointed temporary custodian, pending the restoration of his client's faculties. The first thing he did was to dispense with the services of Sheridan Redpath.

He summoned the young man to his office. Redpath, anticipating what was to follow, rummaged among the papers in Andrew Gilman's desk and finding the duplicate of the contract he held in his possession, coolly destroyed both papers. He was no longer of any use to Andrew Gilman, except as a collecting agent; he could not explain his position without exposing the secret motives behind that amazing contract. The housemaid and chauffeur who witnessed the signatures to the instrument, as a matter of form, did so without acquainting themselves with the contents, being satisfied with Mr. Gilman's statement that they were signing a simple agreement between himself and his new secretary.

Now that he knew all that was in Mr. Gilman's mind at the time the agreement was made, his own sense of fairness rebelled against the premise that he could hold the old man to his bond and go on accepting a salary that was even now out of all proportion to the return he gave for it, to say nothing of the future with its preposterous emoluments.

Nothing was farther from his thoughts, however, than the desertion of his employer at this critical time. He smiled as he threw the papers into the fire, and then went blithely down to the lawyer's office, ignorant of the fact that he had no right to terminate an agreement with so little regard for the law, even though his intentions were of the best.

"I see by these vouchers that Mr. Gilman has been paying you two hundred dollars a month," said Mr. Blanding sourly.

"Yes, sir. Two hundred," said Sherry.

"Do you think you were worth it? "

"No. But Mr. Gilman thought I was."

"Ahem! My office will take charge of his affairs from now on. Your services will not be required after the first of the month. Eighteen dollars a week is ample pay for a collector, Mr. Redpath."

"Do you mean that I am discharged? "

"You are merely discontinued," said Mr. Blanding politely.

Redpath arose. He sighed, but it was unmistakably a sigh of relief. "All right, sir. I wish there was some way of letting Mr. Gilman know that I am not leaving of my own accord. He counted on me to stay by him, and I am sorry to go for that reason. Perhaps it would not be wise for me to say anything to him about it. He is so helpless and — well, I'd be afraid of the effect it might have on him. You need not smile, Mr. Blanding. I am quite serious. I meant more to him than you can understand."

"I admit all that, my boy. He has often spoken of you to me. But he no longer needs a fireside companion, and an eighteen dollar a week man can take care of the rest of your duties. I have engaged a trained attendant to look after him from now on. It is a man's work, not a woman's."

"Miss Corse is also to go?"

"Obviously."

"Mr. Gilman does not like strangers," said the other, flatly. "He hasn't much longer to live. Pardon me for suggesting that you can make his last days happier and easier if you permit him to retain his old and familiar —"

"I think I can manage without your advice, Redpath," said Mr. Blanding curtly. "As you say, Mr. Gilman is helpless. That is why I have been appointed to safeguard his interests. It is high time some one took charge of them. Even you, sir, will admit that fifty dollars a week is rather stiff pay for a collector of rents." There was something significantly accusative in his manner.

Redpath flushed. "If you mean to imply that I am —"

"I am not accusing you of anything wrong, Redpath," broke in the lawyer. "I merely make mention of the fact to support my claim that Andrew Gilman has not been capable of looking after his affairs for some time past."

"Good Lord!" Fierce, bitter words were on his tongue, but he held them back. He glared at the smug lawyer for a moment or two and then allowed his whimsical, humorous smile to come into play. "I'd hate to be in your shoes, Mr. Blanding, if Andrew Gilman should happen to recover from this attack."

"Good morning, Mr. Redpath," snapped the lawyer.

"Good morning, Mr. Blanding," replied Sherry, and sauntered out of the office.

On his return to the Gilman house, he found Miss Corse in a high state of excitement. The male attendant had arrived from Chicago, and was now upstairs with Dr. Andrews and the sick man.

"I've got my walking papers," she said. "I'm glad of it, in a way, too. It lets me out of having to give notice to Mr. Gilman. It's a rotten shame. He'll die, sure as shooting, with that fellow yanking him around as if he was a bag of meal. Poor old man!"

"I'm in the same boat. I'm sacked too."

"Good gracious! Why, you were his main stand-by and — Say, Mr. Redpath, there is something important I've got to tell you." She lowered her voice. "You remember the will I spoke to you about? Well, it's gone. Her lawyer was here a while ago and I was in the room with him and his assistant when they went through her desk. I never mentioned that will, you may be sure, but I had my eyes and ears open all the time they were going through things. She kept it locked up in a little drawer of her desk, and the key was always on a string around her neck,— in a sort of little bag. Well, sir, they found a lot of receipts and things, but not hide or hair of the will. It's gone. And like a flash I remembered that the key wasn't around her neck when I found her that morning. Now what do you think of that?"

He had very definite thoughts about " that," but he was careful not to express them to Miss Corse. The solution was perfectly clear to him. He allowed her to ramble on for a few minutes, excitedly, and then inquired:

" How did the lawyer open the drawer if there was no key?"

" Just simply opened it. It wasn't locked. What do you suppose became of the key and the string and bag?"

" Ask me an easier one, Miss Corse. If we knew who took that key from her neck we'd know everything. Was the lawyer looking for a will?"

" Yes. He says there ought to be one. He says if they can't find one there will have to be an administrator appointed."

" She probably destroyed the will herself, Miss Corse."

" I thought of that, but you bet I kept my mouth shut in front of those lawyers. I'm not saying *anything*."

" A very sensible idea," said he.

Redpath spent portions of the next two days in a surreptitious search for the missing key and bag. He was convinced that Mr. Gilman had destroyed the will, but the doing away with such material objects as a key and a chamois-skin bag was a precaution that would not have entered into his somnambulistic calculations. His efforts were unavailing. He had his theory as to the manner in which the sleep-walker had disposed of the will, and it was not inconceivable that the other articles had followed the scrap of paper into the drain pipe.

A week later he walked out of the house with his few belongings and, depositing his suit-cases and bundles on the curb at the corner below, surveyed his late home with troubled and regretful eyes. His heart was sore over the plight in which he was leaving his friend and bene-factor. Before leaving he had gone to the old man's room. Sitting down on the edge of the bed he took the limp hand of Andrew Gilman in his own. Intelligence was in the haunting, piteous eyes of the helpless man. He could neither move nor speak and yet he could hear and understand. In as few words as possible Redpath made it clear to him that he was not leaving of his own free will. His only reference to the secret they shared was a tactful one and considerate.

" I shall always think of you as the finest man I've ever known, Mr. Gilman. My heart aches for you. You have been my friend. If I live to be a hundred years old I shall never do anything to cause you to feel that I am not your true and loyal friend. You will like to know, perhaps, that I have destroyed our written con-tract. I owe you a very great deal; you owe me noth-ing from this day forth. God grant that you may soon be on your feet again, sir,— and if you should ever need me I will come from the end of the earth to be of service to you."

There were tears on his cheeks as he turned away

from the bed. Andrew Gilman had closed his eyes in mute acknowledgment.

For eight months he had lived in that grey, quiet old house. He had gone there with a single dollar in his pocket; he was leaving it with a substantial balance to his credit in the bank. Out of his wages he had put aside over one thousand dollars. It was his pleasure to regard the proverbial rainy day and prospective matrimony in the same genial light. One ought to lay up something for both emergencies. He had enough already for the rainy day, but for the other? Well, the rainy day was at hand; the other was at present the most remote and intangible thing imaginable.

CHAPTER XXVIII

A YEAR ago he would have called a taxi-cab and moved in such splendour as that ample conveyance could provide. But now he was content to be thrifty. He picked up his bags and his bundles and, with no consideration for pride, strutted down the hill toward the street-car line in Valley Street, five blocks away. Spring was in the air. His heart was not light, however, and there was no song on his lips. He was not as pleased with the future, nor as buoyantly optimistic as he was in the early days of his regeneration.

The flavour was gone; there was nothing left but dull, tasteless, matter-of-fact reality. Romance had lodged with him for a brief spell and had fled incontinently, leaving a sear and barren spot on which he was now morally certain nothing could ever flourish.

That spot was sacred to the memory of Morna O'Brien. Indeed, he was pensively, even dolefully, convinced that it was a place where love was buried.

Down the hill he trudged, laden with all his goods and chattels, objective the boarding-house of the Misses Pinkus in Cedar Street, where the day before he had arranged for room and board.

The Misses Pinkus conducted a " select " boarding-house. You could not get room or board there unless the middle-aged sisters happened to know you personally, or your parents, uncles or aunts, or, in a pinch,

some one who belonged to the Presbyterian Church.
They had known Sherry's mother.   They spoke of her
as "the salt of the earth."   So he took the room for
two weeks.   He would have to wait some time before he
could see the General Manager of the Traction Company.   Mr. McGuire was in New York on a "combined
business and pleasure trip," according to the *Dispatch*.

He was half-way down the hill when a voice, almost at
his elbow, brought him to an abrupt standstill.   He had
been so busy with his thoughts that he had not heard the
approach of a smooth-running automobile from behind.

"Hello, tramp!" was what the voice said, and,
strange to say, it was the very voice he had been thinking about for weeks.   "Don't you want some one to
give you a lift with your ill-gotten gains?"

"For the love of —" he began, and then breath failed
him.   He stood stock-still and stared.

"Taxi, sir?"

He found his tongue and a few of his wits.   "Would
you believe it, I was thinking of you at that very moment.   Where did you spring from?"

She did not answer.   Her interest was centred in the
bags and bundles.

"Don't tell me you've been bounced," she said.

"Absolutely.   I'm on the town again."   He should
have said it lugubriously, but did not.   Instead, there
was a decided trace of hilarity in his voice.

"What have you been doing, sir, to get discharged?"
'she demanded.   She searched his face intently.   What
she saw there brought a faint sigh of relief to her lips.
There were no ugly, disturbing traces to warrant the
sudden apprehension that had gripped her heart.

"It's a long story," he replied.

"Jump in," she said. "Put your things in behind and get up here with me. I'll take you wherever you want to go."

"You will?" he cried. "Then take me to the moon."

"Begorry," she said, flushing slightly, but meeting his gaze fairly, "I may take you to heaven, which is almost the same thing, if a front shoe blows out. I feel very reckless today."

"Good! I'm glad to hear it." He tossed his belongings into the empty tonneau and climbed into the seat beside the wheel. "You didn't answer me a moment ago. Where did you spring from? When did you return?"

"Three weeks ago," she replied, taking her foot from the brake. "Say where?"

"Just drive slowly to the end of State Street, and then turn around and drive slowly to the other end, and then turn around and —"

"Don't be silly! You can't afford it. I charge five dollars an hour. Turn about is fair play. You charged me an outrageous price for carrying my tiny little bags last —"

"You say you've been home for three weeks?" he interrupted. "Where have you been keeping yourself?"

"I've been keeping myself in my room most of the time, Mr. Redpath."

"Aha! Under lock and key, I suppose. Been trying to run away again?"

"Not at all. I had the measles."

"Good Lord!" He laughed heartily.

"It's great to hear you laugh like that," she said. "You haven't really laughed in your nice old way for four or five months."

"I haven't had anything to make me laugh," he said, sober at once. "A fellow's got to be happy to laugh like that, you know."

"Were you happy just now?"

"For a second or two," he admitted.

"Because I had the measles?"

"Certainly not. I was just happy to see you. Don't be alarmed, Morna," he went on, his voice softening. "I sha'n't say anything I shouldn't. That's all past and gone."

There was something like alarm in the swift glance with which she favoured him, but it gave way instantly before a confident, fulgent glow of relief. Then she looked straight ahead. A faint smile played about the corners of her adorable mouth.

"Why haven't you called us up on the telephone?" she asked. "Don't you know that Granny adores you? She's really quite a snob in her way. She's always telling me that you come of a terribly good family. Family counts with her. That's what I mean when I say she's a — a kind of a snob. You really ought to call her up once in awhile."

"I've been very much occupied with all this awful business at Mr. Gilman's. Besides, I — to be perfectly honest with you,— I couldn't call her up without making some sort of inquiry about you, and that I *couldn't* do."

"What!"

He turned on her suddenly, his jaw set. " See here,
Morna, I've got to have the truth. How is it with you
and Jimmy Burton? What happened down there in
Florida? Why did you run away and leave Mrs. Compton? Where —"

" For the love of heaven, man, ask one at a time,"
she cried, her eyes sparkling. Now she had him where
she wanted him! There was fire in his eye. She liked
that. " How is it with Jimmy Burton and me?
That's number one. Well, I can answer that by saying
I'm sure it's all right with us. Number two. Granny
and I quarrelled horribly about Jimmy. Number three.
What do you mean by saying that I ran away from
Granny? What do you mean? "

" Why,— why, she telegraphed that you were not
with her. She came home alone. What the deuce was
I to think, tell me that? Only one thing, of course."

" And what was that? "

" That you'd made a goose of yourself and run away
with Jimmy, that's all. You can get mad if you want
to. I had to get it out of my system. I had —"

" Oh, you old stupid! " she shrieked, and laughed so
gaily that pedestrians smiled in compliment. " Lord
love you, I'm not angry. Now, tell me, why would I
be running away with Jimmy Burton? "

" Because your grandmother objects to —"

" Answer the question."

" Well, there's only one answer to that. Because
you were in love with him."

" And why would I be running away with him when
I'm in love with somebody else? " she asked, looking
straight into his eyes.

"Oh, Lord! Then — then, it isn't even Jimmy," he groaned.

"He's not the man," said Morna flatly.

"I'm sorry. If it has to be anybody, I'd like Jimmy to be the one. He's a fine fellow, and I — I like him. Confound him, I like him." He sighed. "By George, I like him better than ever, now that we're shipmates."

Morna was suddenly silent. Her heart was beating like a trip hammer, and she could not trust her voice. An amazing shyness took possession of her. As an outlet for her emotions she deliberately sent the car headlong at a telephone pole, and as he cried out in alarm, as quickly swerved back into the roadway, very much as the clown bicyclist behaves in the circus act.

"I'm glad Mrs. Compton likes me," he said, after a moment.

"Oh, she liked Jimmy before she found out who he was," said she, maliciously.

"Does she approve of this other chap?"

"What other chap?"

"The one you're going to marry."

"I didn't say I was going to marry him, did I?"

"I thought you —"

"I said I was in love with him. Now, tell me, just where do you want me to take you? I promised Granny I'd be home before six."

He gave her the number in Cedar Street. "I'm going to board there till something turns up. The chances are I'll be shaking the dust of Farragut from my feet before long."

She started. "You mean you are — going away?"

"Nothing for me in this town," said he, and did not know how the caustic rejoinder hurt her. "Mr. McGuire wants me to take a place with the Traction Company. It's a great chance. I couldn't accept it as long as I was —"

"He wants you to go to Chicago?"

"Construction work, wherever it takes me."

"How perfectly splendid," she said, but half-heartedly. "Granny will be so pleased. She has always said you would go straight to the top of the ladder. I've never known such unbounded faith as she has —"

"She's an old dear," cried he, genuinely pleased. "Here we are. My new lodgings. Sorry I can't ask you in. Thank you for —"

"Just a moment. Five dollars, please."

He laughed. "I haven't that much in my pocket. One precious silver dollar, two quarters, a dime —"

"I'll have to seize your baggage," she threatened.

"Over my dead body. You'll have to seize me with it, I can tell you that."

"All right. I'll seize you too. Get back into the car at once. I promised Granny I'd bring you home for dinner."

"You did *what?*"

"Here! Take your old bags into the house. I'll wait for you. You are going home with me for dinner. Granny's orders."

"But how does she know that —"

"She knows everything. I've told her. She said I *must* bring you out this very evening."

"She knows I've lost my place? You told her? But you didn't know it yourself until —"

"Move on, now! That's the Irish in me. I am a born policeman. Hurry back!"

He was back in five minutes.

"Shall we take the road through Compton's Woods?" she asked. "It is longer — and prettier, even at this time of the year."

And as they skirted the lower end of Compton's Woods he pointed out to her the distant ridge on which he had spent several memorable nights; he told her of his lunch-box and the pugnacious tramp; of the crawfish and silver-sides in Burton's Creek; of the resolutions he had made while lying in the cool, green wood; of his determination to make a real position for himself in the world.

"But listen to the way I go on talking about myself. Terribly bad form, I call it."

"As a rule," said she, most engagingly, "I like a man who talks about himself all the time. He never says anything disagreeable."

Shadows were falling as they wended their way through the narrow, tree-lined road into the depths of the wood. She was listening as one entranced. The blue in her eyes seemed to have deepened; she was strangely self-conscious and filled with alarms, and yet the smile on her lips was soft and sweet and tremulous.

"Of course, I realize that my position with Mr. Gilman would never have got me anywhere. I jumped at it, to be sure, but I couldn't have stayed on with him for more than a year or two. It wouldn't have been fair to him. I wasn't anywhere near worth my hire. Then came this horrible —"

"Wait! Don't tell that part of the story now.

Please! It gives me the shivers. I'll be seeing spooks if you go on. And now what kind of a position is it that Mr. McGuire wants you to take?"

"I don't know. He says if I make good in it, I'll have a mighty fine chance to go to the top,— whatever that may be."

"Granny is sure you will be a great man one of these fine days," said she, so softly he barely heard the words.

He laughed. "She thinks pretty well of me, I must say."

Morna's eyes twinkled. "She was saying only last night that you ought to be getting married so that you'd have some one to really work for — besides yourself. Isn't it queer that old people are always harping on —"

"Morna, there's only one girl in all this world that I'd marry, and I've promised her never to mention the subject to her again."

"Meaning me?"

"Yes."

"Will you be kind enough to inform me just when such a promise was exacted of you?"

"Why,— why — Morna, what do you mean? You — God, how lovely your eyes are in this light. How lovely you — Oh, Lord, stop me! I swear I couldn't help it — I couldn't —"

"Answer me this wan question," she said, in her most delicious brogue. "Are you in love with me? Yes or no!"

He was utterly unconscious of the fact that the car had come to a complete stop. His eyes, his thoughts, his whole being were intent upon the smiling, starry-eyed creature who made this heartless, selfish demand upon him.

"Yes," he almost sobbed.

Her lip trembled, something sweet and shy swam in her dark eyes.

"Haven't ye a grain of sense, Sherry Redpath?" she murmured, striving hard to control her voice. "Haven't ye an eye in that silly old head of yours?"

"Morna!"

"I'll not move an inch from this spot till you've asked me to marry you!"

CHAPTER XXIX

THE burly figure of Officer Barney Doyle moved slowly, tortuously up the hill toward the crest of his long and lonesome beat. Far below him in the still heart of the sleeping city the clock in the court-house dome had boomed out the hour of one.

A pedestrian approached, walking swiftly, coming from the top of Hooper Street and the sombre stretches that lay beyond. Officer Doyle came to a halt under the suspended arc light. True to training, custom and the wariness of experience, he chose the spot deliberately. Experience had taught him many things. One of these was that if you have to meet a man, friend or foe, contrive to do it in the light and not in the dark. Moreover, it is best to have as much of him in the light as possible and as little of yourself. Hence, Barney managed to halt a considerable portion of himself in the shadow of the pole that carried the light.

The pedestrian's chin was high and his head was bare. He was whistling merrily.

" Hello, bedad ! " said Barney Doyle, and advanced a couple of steps. " Is it you? "

" It is," said the night-farer, stopping short.

" And what the divil are ye doing out this time o' the night? "

" I'm the happiest man in the world, Barney."

" Is it true that ye've lost your job? "

" I'm as free as the air we breathe," said the other, waving his hand expressively.

" Begorry, is that anything to be happy about? Jobs don't grow on lilac bushes. Ye'll be a divil av a while finding another —"

" Yes, sir, I am the happiest man in the world," interrupted the pedestrian irrelevantly. " When a fellow's as happy as I am he just has to walk it off, Barney. I've walked three miles and a half since eleven o'clock."

" And it's one o'clock now. Have ye been walkin' backwards? I do *that* much in an hour."

" They wanted to send me home in the automobile. Not much, said I. I just had to walk, and be alone with myself to think it all over and —"

" Say, what's the matter wid ye? Are ye daffy? Bedad, I don't wonder they wanted to send ye home, whoever they be."

" How long have you been married, Barney? "

" Going on twinty-five years. What the divil has that to do with it? "

" It's great, isn't it? "

" Begorry, I believe ye've been drinkin' ag'in. For the love av Mike, don't tell me —"

" I've been drinking ambrosial nectars, and I'm drunk as a lord. Have you ever been tight on ambrosial nectars, Barney? "

" I have not! I'm dommed particular what I drink. That's more than I can say for you, you —"

The night-farer laughed loudly, and slapped Barney on the back.

"You don't know what you're talking about. I'm going to stay drunk all the rest of my life, just as I am right now. I'm never going to be sober again. The nectar of the Gods!" He raised his shining face and wafted a kiss from his finger tips to the gods in the starless sky.

Barney groaned. "It will be the hardest job av me life when I tell the old lady that ye've gone back to the booze, me lad. And poor Patsy Burke! He'll die av grief. I was tellin' him this very hour, down beyant the ball park, that ye'd lost your job and I was afeared ye'd take to the stuff again if we didn't get hold av ye in time. But, how could I —"

"Ho! Ho!" laughed the other, and linked his arm in that of the perplexed policeman. "Which way do you fare, my hearty? Up hill or down, I am with you. I sha'n't go to bed at all. I'm not going to spoil this glorious night by sleeping in it. No, sirree! This is one of those rare Arabian nights. Have you ever read the Arabian Nights, Mr. Doyle?"

"I have not," declared Mr. Doyle, holding back.

"Well, they're full of magic. First the prince or the princess is turned into a toad or something and then along comes a cobbler and smites —"

"For the love of heaven, lad, come home with me, do. Ye're not fit to be wandering about the streets in this condition. Ye've a fever. Ye're delirious, so ye are. Come along, now, there's a fine lad, and I'll have me old woman —"

"Do you know, Barney, I never realized until tonight what a beautiful brogue you've got. I could stand here till morning listening to you talk."

"Well, begob, ye'll do nothing av the kind, me bucko."

"What is it about the Irish brogue that touches the heartstrings of —"

"Are ye trying to make fun av the Irish?" demanded Officer Doyle, bridling.

"By the way," cried his companion abruptly, "I want to ask a special favour of you, Barney."

"It's best to humour them," muttered Barney, helplessly. Then aloud, in a wheedling, conciliatory manner. "Anything you like, me lad."

"Well, I wish you wouldn't say a word to anybody about what I've just told you. We don't want it known at present. You won't mention it, will you? That's a good fellow."

"Not a word," said Barney Doyle, vastly plagued and bewildered.

THE END